The Meadowlark

by B.C. Walker

The Meadowlark is inspired by true stories. As a work of fiction, all incidents and dialogue are products of the author's imagination and are not to be construed as real. Where real-life figures appear, the situations, incidents, and dialogues concerning those persons are entirely fictional and are not intended to change the entirely fictional nature of the work. In all other respects, any resemblance to persons living or dead is entirely coincidental.

Excerpts from *A Tale of Two Cities* (Charles Dickens, 1859) used herein are from the public domain.

Copyright © 2022 B.C. Walker. All Rights Reserved.

ISBN: 9798364322296

To my mother, Alice, an angel above me.

More than any other, she pointed me to my roots.

One of our sweetest, loudest songsters is the [Western] meadowlark; this I could hardly get used to at first, for it looks exactly like the Eastern meadowlark, which utters nothing but a harsh disagreeable chatter.

But the…air seems to give it a voice, and it will perch on top of a bush or tree and sing for hours in rich, bubbling tones.

Theodore Roosevelt

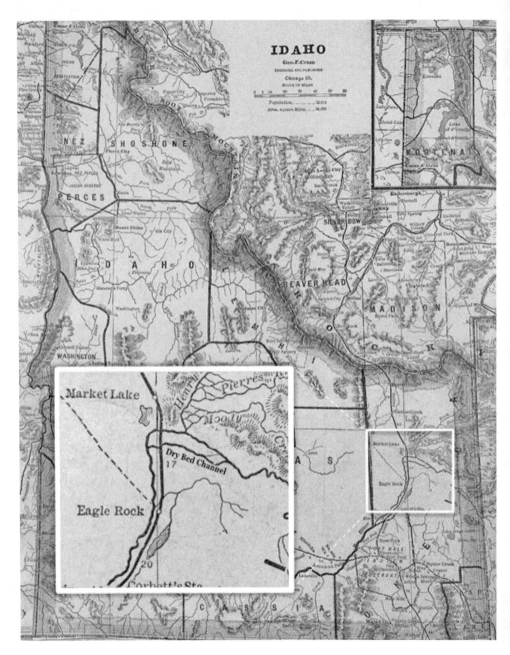

Idaho (circa 1885) with area of focus highlighted and enlarged.

Part I

Chapter 1

Idaho Territory, 1885

Cassie heard rushing water ahead and shifted uneasily atop the blue enamel stove strapped to the middle of their wagon. Her father had loaded the wagon ten days earlier, packing boxes and bags around the stove. Now, hundreds of miles from the only home she had ever known, Cassie shivered from the cool air as they entered a shady grove.

"We're not far now," her father exclaimed. "Next stop, Willow Creek! Homesteaders we are! Farmers we will be! One crossing ahead, and then welcome to our new home!"

Drawn by four wet and weary horses, the wagon jostled along the dusty, well-tracked trail. Wheels scraped against rocks. The load groaned constantly. Cassie crawled to one side and stripped a handful of the greenest leaves from tall wispy river willows that lined the trail, releasing them one by one to the path below. Willow branches scraped along the wagon's sides until released with whapping sounds as they pushed along. The creek sound diminished as they turned away and into an open meadow surrounded by tall trees.

Cassie looked up at a large bumblebee buzzing slowly past and then dropped her leaves, grabbing for puffs of fuzz floating lazily through the air. "Ma, summer snow!"

A "Yip" from her father in front made the horses snort and heave the wagon forward, shifting the girl back against the stove. The horses whinnied at the smell of water and picked up speed across the meadow.

Cassie's mother moaned slightly on the bench ahead.

"You okay, Esther?" the girl's father said softly.

Young and clearly expecting a baby, her mother pulled her long blonde hair back and shifted uneasily in her seat. "I'm fine," she said. "Just fine." With one hand on her midsection, she scooted nearer her husband to rest her head on his shoulder. She brushed at his bushy black beard and added softly, "All fine except your beard is tickling my cheek."

Cassie giggled at her parents.

Her father glanced over his shoulder with a smile, only his tan nose and teeth glowing past the shadow of his hat. "And what's got you laughing?"

"That beard…could use a trimming," Cassie laughed, parroting something she'd heard her mother say the night before.

Her father scoffed a bit and turned back toward the horses, shaking the reins encouragingly against their backs. "Ha," he said.

Cassie smiled. She was sure he was talking to the horses. Looking ahead, glinting light and a growing rumble hinted they were closing on a creek. She climbed to her knees to see and held onto the back of the stove as the wagon lurched over some obstacle. She watched her father pull masterfully at the reins, navigating the heavy wagon left and right along the dusty path. The load shifted downward just as a bright patch of water came into view ahead.

"Hold on…Cassie," her mother urged, reaching for the iron handle at the edge of the bench, her speech punctuated by gasps as she steadied herself as the wagon lurched. "Looks like…another crossing ahead."

"Twenty-one," Cassie exclaimed, righting herself. "This will make twenty-one crossings!"

Smiling back at her, her mother remarked, "You've been counting all this way?" Turning to her husband, she said proudly, "And only seven—Simeon, we do have a bright child."

"Uh huh…" Simeon said, his voice trailing off as he navigated the road's abrupt descent toward the creek. "Look at that run-off," he exclaimed, bringing the wagon to a stop at the edge of a wide, muddy, roaring creek. The two duns in front bent down to sip at the water, with the chestnut gelding and roan mare shifting uneasily in their traces behind.

Pointing at the rolling water ahead of them, Cassie said, "It's looks like chocolate ice cream."

Esther smiled back at her and added, "Wouldn't that taste good right now. It does remind me of when Granddad Rapp brought his last ice from the cellar last summer and churned that batch of ice cream. Rock salt and all."

Cassie licked her lips just as a large section of dirt fell from the opposite bank and splashed into the creek. "Oh, my," Esther said, reaching for her husband.

Simeon shook his head and squinted as though it would help him better understand the situation. "Something's not quite right." He craned his neck up and downstream before reaching for the map under his seat. Unfolding it across his lap, he pointed. "This here should be our final crossing—of Willow Creek itself. And here," he said, tracing with his finger, "*here* is our destination—the Willow Creek settlement. Seems sensible to…" Looking up, his voice trailed off as a lazy column of smoke rose in the near distance. "I believe there's a house over that way!"

"And there's more smoke," Esther said, still seated but noticing a few other faint columns rising across the way. "Oh, we must be close! This must be it!"

"Still, something's off…confound it!" Simeon muttered to himself as he tied the reins to the wagon's handbrake. He climbed down from the wagon and inspected the ground around him. "Dry ruts—I figure it hasn't been used in the past few days." Talking to himself, he said, "See how high the water is up on the roots of these bushes—likely deeper from the warmer weather these past few days." He touched the water and then licked his finger. "And muddy, to boot. More melt-off coming down than the past week or so." Wading out to the top of his boots, Simeon leaned forward to make out what he could of the creek in front of him. He splashed back ashore, arms held wide and declaring loudly, "It doesn't seem all that deep here, but I can't really make out much. For my life, something tells me this can't be the best place to cross."

Looking up at his wife's concerned face, he said, "I'm going for a walk."

…

CASSIE WATCHED HER MOTHER lean back and stretch uneasily. "Ma, are you okay?"

"I hope to be," Esther said. "This baby is going to be born sooner than later." Addressing Cassie's concern, she said, "Which better be in a more comfortable spot than this wagon box or beneath a sage brush! Your father has assured me of that."

Cassie giggled. "Does it hurt?"

"Oh, no. But the baby is mighty tight in there and kicking up a storm," she said, holding her belly. "Must be a boy—with all that energy."

Cassie retrieved her rag doll from under one of the straps and rocked it back and forth. A little baby! Her mother had seemed just as large and as uncomfortable when they had left home. Of course, babies were eventually born. She'd seen kittens, calves, and colts born. But *when* was a mystery to her.

It was the winter before when her father had come into the house, kicked off his boots, and announced they would be homesteading in Idaho. Her mother had wiped her hands on her apron and looked up unsurprised. She had said matter-of-factly, "Any pioneering I do won't be without baked goods." Cassie had watched her father smile at the reminder.

Earlier that spring, when her mother had announced she was expecting a baby, Cassie had seen the same smile as he beamed brightly at the news and gave his wife a big bear hug. Later that day, he had taken Cassie to the barn and pulled a tarp off a heap in the corner to reveal the stove he was planning as a surprise for her mother. "And see here—a full-sized oven. For all those baked goods," he had added, opening and closing the oven door. He had seemed so very pleased.

Even their packing seemed to revolve around the stove. Her father had explained why the stove sat in the middle of the large freight wagon. "It will keep the load balanced and not over-stress the axles," he had said. Lifting Cassie up to the wagon, he had added, "And you might find it a suitable resting place on our journey."

Now, waiting for her father to return, Cassie felt hot and so clambered off the stove and over wooden boxes filled with her mother's porcelain dinnerware. She patted one bag she knew contained alfalfa seed and rubbed the bulges of a potato sack before reaching the side of the wagon. Using the spokes on the rear wheel, she climbed down and then crawled under the wagon into its shade, her preferred resting place whenever they stopped. Sitting cross-legged on a patch of grass, she unexpectedly bumped her head against the long iron rail her father had acquired late the day before at the railyard in Eagle Rock—the last town they had passed through. She rubbed the contusion away and then smiled as she recalled hearing the old man who had sold them the rail saying, "No better way to clear the sage. Drag it behind good, strong horses like these here. You might have to dig out a few roots, but there's no faster way to pile up as much kindling for the winter." Patting one of the horses, the man had added, "And if I was a young whippersnapper like yourself, you know, with an outfit like this, I might try homesteading myself."

"Best horses a man ever had," her father had replied before adding that he was becoming a farmer.

"How's that?" the man had asked.

Her father had explained how he'd worked these past five years as a teamster, paid by the trip for hauling goods with no real upside—"it's hard to accumulate assets to make freighting anything but a solo enterprise. Cash crops," he had said, "promise a boon that could motivate a man willing to work hard with his own hands and ingenuity ahead." He had added, "My hurry has been to save up for an opportunity like this. Hadn't expected what folks are calling the Snake River Valley to open as soon as it did, but the door seems open now."

The man had nodded knowingly. "Well, you're standing smack in the better part of that valley," he had said. "But it's all claimed. Much farther north, it's becoming a fight with nature for water. That government money will help some—to build ditches and the like. Some folks will suffer. Those who endure may win—eventually."

Shifting his stance, Cassie's father changed the subject. "Had to purchase this here stove for my sweetheart—which was the only way she would come along." The old mad had rubbed his hands together and said, "As the good book says, it's not good that man should be alone. Well done, young man!" They had both chuckled.

The two men had set about figuring how to load the heavy iron rail on the wagon, struggling until they spotted Cassie playing under the wagon, running a long stick between the bed and axles. Her father had called her "brilliant." He would pull the wagon around and drive it directly over the rail, at which point they could tie end of the heavy bar up to the axles, front and back.

Now relaxing on the grass under the wagon, Cassie still wasn't sure how she had contributed to the plan. Watching horse legs ahead shift, the rear ones pawing back at the dry dirt and the front splashing at the creek's edge, she began to smile, recalling how the night before the same feet had stepped gingerly and almost frightfully at her father's urging, nearly prancing alongside the unfamiliar rail, heads bobbing up and down to better sense the size and distance of the rail. "Horses don't see well," he had said. "It can be good when running through a field but darned difficult when crossing a puddle or walking past a rail." The horses balked. "Confound them!" her father had uttered before the horses finally came around.

As the rig pulled away that night, the old man had removed his hat. "You've got ballast with the rail tied underneath like that. It'll want to hold you going straight on turns at speed."

Seated in the wagon, her father had laughed. "We have close to two tons on board, so this extra weight won't do much." Looking back at Cassie, he added, "Further, that little one there is my ballast—keeps me steadier than otherwise." Cassie's puzzled look had made the two men laugh.

Pulling away from the railyard that night, Cassie thought how the old man had made it sound so undesirable then tapped her father on the shoulder and asked, "What is 'ballast'?"

...

CASSIE'S MOTHER CLIMBED DOWN from the wagon and sat beside her in the shade. "What else have you learned?"

Cassie looked up, puzzled.

"You counted twenty-one crossings. What else?"

Cassie reflected on a few of her favorite things from the trip so far—the yellow wildflowers her mother called Butter and Eggs, Cassiopeia's Chair in the night sky because it sounded like her own name, her own coyote howl that her father had said was spooky, resetting the roadometer on the wagon each day after noting in her journal how far they had traveled, the large bone in so many animal skeletons seen along the way called 'the femur,' and evening time reading the family bible with her parents by lamplight.

"Ballast," she whispered, trying out the word. Then louder, she said, "Pa says I'm ballast."

Her mother looked up. "Ballast?"

"Yes, like the iron rail we tied on last night. He said that we both hold things steady."

Esther smiled. "How nice."

Simeon startled them both as he emerged from a stand of willows brushing leaves off his shirt and then pointing. "There are newer wagon tracks back that way in the grass—but could be they go anywhere. I'm uneasy about this, but I can't see how this isn't the crossing." He tugged at his beard.

Esther looked up at him, waiting for him to say more.

Simeon reached for his wife's hand. "Well, we only have one crossing to go—number twenty-one, right?" He winked at his daughter before adding, "Fifty more feet until we can stop for good. I figure we go forward as is, and then we can call it a day!" He helped Esther back on board and waited for Cassie before climbing up to his own seat. Taking up the reins, he said, "Let's clear this crossing, ladies, and tomorrow we will be scraping land," Simeon shouted, releasing the handbrake, and clicking his tongue. With a "Giddyap!", he urged the two pairs of horses forward, horses he had intentionally paired to produce the right amount of hold and go. His greatest confidence, however, was in the chestnut gelding nearest the wagon, a horse he knew to keep the other horses pulling at the right speed and in the right direction. The roan mare next to him did what he did, and together they intuitively dug in and could hold any load on a downward slope.

At Simeon's urging, the chestnut shook his head and snorted, flinging froth from his mouth and neck. He was stalling, which caused the roan to lean back into her harness as well, moaning as the full weight of the wagon bore down from behind. Simeon reached for the chestnut with his foot and pushed. The horse lifted its head, its side view shielded by the blinders that focused it on the trail ahead.

"Ho!" A snap of the reins convinced the chestnut to pull in its traces. With that, the duns out front began to pull. Simeon alternately yanked and eased off the handbrake as the lead team stepped past where he had waded earlier—and a foot or two later dropped suddenly as they stepped off an underwater shelf that had them instantly up to their withers. Jolted by the drop, Simeon sucked in his breath, recognizing instantly the eroded creek bed as one possible reason this crossing was out of use. Too late to go back, the chestnut and roan still pulled back but were dragged forward as the duns kept pulling while working to keep their footing.

"Easy, easy, EASY," Simeon repeated. The wagon creaked forward into the stream. Simeon glanced back to confirm he was following the angle of the tracks entering the water, but he no longer trusted what he could see and instead began to navigate more by feel. Through clenched teeth, he guided the wagon slowly forward, and said, "And now we know the trouble with crossings like this!" In more hopeful tones, he added, "Our weight should hold us steady."

"Ballast," Cassie barely got out before being thrown to one side as the front wheels bumped over another submerged object. Looking over the side, she could see the water had surged within inches of the wagon box.

"Yup, yup," Simeon yelled, urging the lead pair forward, the deep water now pushing against their chests. "Let's go! Don't stop now," he shouted above the creek's roar, snapping the reins and pushing again at the chestnut with his foot.

Pulling hard, the right lead horse went down on its front knees, nearly going under and dragging its partner hard right. Each pulled frantically in opposite directions. The one regained its footing by lunging forward—confusing the second team by the increased pace, which they resisted until being pulled forward as well.

Nearing the opposite shore, Simeon's sigh of relief was interrupted as the right rear wagon wheel caught up at the deepest part of the stream. Water began pillowing against the sidewall and then under it, lifting it with force and tipping the entire wagon downstream. Esther shrieked as she was thrown against Simeon, nearly knocking him out of the wagon. Simeon instinctively reached across her belly for the iron grip and braced her with his arm, his feet locked against the front of the wagon box and his free hand rapidly winding to draw in the leather reins to direct the horses ahead. He yelled back, "Hold tight, Cassie! Hold tight!"

"Yaw," he shouted. "Yaw!" The chestnut smartly pulled hard left, miraculously directing the other horses to pull together. The wagon teetered back to flat with a splash, and the teams pulled together, recovering the original path up and out of the creek.

Water poured from the edges of the wagon box as it topped out on the high bank. Breathing hard from a ruckus that had taken less than a minute, Simeon pulled the horses to a stop and said, "Good work. Good work." He looked up and caught sight of a dark-haired man leaving a house they could now plainly see over near a stand of trees and running toward them, waving his hat overhead and pointing toward the stream below. He was shouting, "…flood water…warning…quarter mile that way…" until he seemed to realize his warning was of no use now.

Simeon grimaced at what he now fully understood—this hadn't been the best place to cross after all. "Live and learn," he whispered with a tired wave back. Glancing back, he could see the oven's door flung open with a cask of molasses stored there oozing syrup from a broken seam. Helpless to the situation, his shoulders rolled with as he chuckled. "Those baked goods…may taste like molasses…for a while, Esther."
Then a stark realization forced him to look back again. "Where's Cassie?"

Chapter 2

Willow Creek, 1885

Cassie's plunge into the ice-cold current of Willow Creek took her breath away. To her immediate wonder, she found herself floating at first and tried imitating the swimming motions she had seen the boys use in the neighborhood pond back home. Her naïve optimism retreated as she quickly sank below the surface. Panic set in.

Pushing against the bottom, she resurfaced briefly and shouted, "Help!" Her panic turned to horror as her words were washed away by the water coming over her head. The creek picked up speed. Cassie wondered if she would ever see her parents again. Pushing off the bottom once more, she caught a brief glimpse of her father scrambling down the bank and corrected herself—she had seen him but now knew that was the final time. She felt herself being swept around a bend as pokey branches yanked at her clothes and angry rocks bruised her knees. Last of all, she heard a cracking sound against her head, and the creek's sounds and her own sense of motion went dark.

"Cassie! Cassie!" Simeon yelled as he jumped into the waist-deep waters. "My daughter," he shouted, ambling frantically downstream and beckoning toward the man standing above on the creek bank. Without further thought, the man tossed his hat aside and slid down the bank into the creek.

Simeon splashed downstream toward the abrupt left turn where he thought he last saw Cassie. The other man intuitively went right alongside a willow-covered island with slower waters going that way.

Esther climbed down from the wagon and screamed, "My little girl!" before dropping to her knees.

Eyes scanning the creek, Simeon turned back upstream, bucking against the current to keep his footing. "There she is!" he shouted hopefully, only to realize what he was seeing was the tip of a bleached log. Only ankle deep one moment and then above his hips the next, the uneven waters and rocky creek bed made steady movement nearly impossible. Simeon automatically clenched his fists at the deepening chill of the snowmelt to ward off the cold. Pushing hard right against the current, he grabbed handfuls of willow branches and climbed to the island.

"Cassie! Cassie!" he shouted and then heard the man whistle loudly from the other side. Simeon thought he heard, "Found her!" above the noise and pushed his way through a dozen or so feet of dense willows to the other side. He saw the man lifting Cassie's limp and lifeless body from the water and immediately felt pangs of despair and cried out, "Oh, God, please!"

The man turned his face upward to meet Simeon's face with a smile that immediately resolved Simeon's despair. "Found her pushed up here against these branches," the man said pointing, breathless and handing her to Simeon. "I think she's okay," the man said reassuringly. "Look!"

As Simeon took his daughter in his arms, he watched her blue lips twitch and then open slightly. It was only then that he noticed a bright red streak near his chest building slowly and then running through Cassie's blonde hair. He checked himself first and then quickly brushed back her hair with his fingers to see a long gash above her right ear. "This can't be good," he said, pressing her head to his chest. Without speaking, the two men turned and began walking to the head of the island and then back up the easier part of the creek. With one hand on Simeon's back and the other on his elbow, the man steadied father and daughter as he pushed them back upstream. When they came up the bank to the green grass above, Simeon turned and said, "Thank you, thank you," his eyes alternating between the man and the sky.

Esther gathered her skirt and rushed forward. "Is she okay?"

Simeon nodding, laying Cassie down. He hurried to the wagon and retrieved a blanket. Handing it to Esther, he said, "Warm her, will you?" before turning his attention to the bleeding near her ear.

Dreading the worst, Esther drew her daughter close and cried, "I can't lose her. I've already lost…" She began to sob.

The man pulled a faded yellow bandana from his back pocket, squeezed water from it, and handed it to Simeon. "That's a good-sized cut…right there along her hairline," he said, pointing. "My guess is she'll heal right up."

As if on cue, Cassie stirred.

Simeon reached for Esther's hand and gave it a squeeze. Just then, Cassie's eyes fluttered. "She's going to be all right, Ma." Pausing, he added with a relieved smile, "I believe we made it."

Cassie looked up peacefully. "Oh, Momma!" Her voice was hoarse. Esther reached to hug her. Cassie smiled faintly and said, "I'm learning to swim!"

…

SIMEON CARRIED CASSIE toward the family's homesite, insisting this was better for her than walking. "Are we in Willow Creek?"

"Well, the beginnings of it," the man answered. "If you're planning on staying, perhaps introductions might be in order," the man said.

The group laughed.

"I'll shake a good brother's hand later," the man said. "I'm Will Walker. And you?"

"Simeon Rapp, sir, and grateful to you," said Simeon. "And my wife Esther, sir." Esther nodded alongside.

Will smiled. "I took you two for three children with no parents. Why you hardly look old enough to be out here on your own," he added with a chuckle.

"You're too kind," Simeon said. "Despite my lousy judgment when it comes to crossings, I'm nearly 30, sir." Esther drew close. "We two have been at this a while," Simeon added.

"Well, I have you by nearly a decade. And some decade it's been. We can discuss that—and the crossing just now—later," Will said with a wink. "And no reason to call me 'sir.' 'Will' is just fine."

As the group drew near the house, Cassie spotted a young girl playing alongside the house and raised herself up.

"That's my daughter, Sarah. About your age, I guess. She just turned eight. Third of four young'uns."

Sarah came toward them and said, "Hello."

Shivering in the blanket, Cassie clenched her teeth and said, "I'm Cassie, and I'm almost eight."

Will looked at his daughter and said, "Sarah, be so kind as to run and get another blanket—at least a dry one. We need to warm this little one up…and ask your mother to come." Sarah returned with a blanket, and the men wandered toward the garden while Esther helped Cassie out of her wet clothes and wrapped her in the dry blanket. Sarah came over to assist. "That's a pretty dress," she said. Still shivering, Cassie smiled from all the attention. Sarah carried the wet dress toward a line that drooped in front of the house and hung it to dry.

Putting the events of the day behind them, the Rapp family now heard a variety of new sounds—mooing from behind the house, a small boy scooping at hay with a pitchfork and tossing it over a nearby fence, and the noise of a chicken cut off mid-cackle making it clear that supper was being prepared. Even the smoke from the house whispered a quiet welcome to the weary party.

A woman emerged from the log house, wiping her hands on her apron. "Sorry for the delay. Dumplings," she said, as though the word conveyed an explanation. "I'm Mary Walker," she said with bright tones, smiling. "Wife to this here handsome man." She took Will's arm in hers.

Another taller boy came around the house carrying a headless chicken. Will said, "Come here, boys," beckoning them both to come near. The older boy laid the chicken on the front step and walked over. "This here is my family—you've met Mary," he said, acknowledging his wife. "And Erastus here is ten or so," tussling the hair of the boy responsible for the chicken. "And this is Samuel—he's eight going on nine. Our youngest, Thomas, is probably in the house," he said, looking to Mary to confirm. "He's four—born on Thanksgiving. Good stock," Will said proudly.

The two boys looked at each other, and Erastus whispered snidely, "Girl…" They both laughed.

Standing wrapped in a blanket, Cassie looked confidently at him and said, "Why, thank you," unsure that her reply fit the moment but a little bothered by the laughter.

Will turned and sternly said, "Boys!"

"Sorry," the boys replied quickly in unison.

Simeon drew Esther close and said, "Nice to meet you all. And thanks again for your help just now. We're eternally grateful."

Will nodded expectantly. "Of course, you're very welcome. We feel like we know you already. So, you said you're staying around these here parts?"

"Sir...I mean Will, you asked, but I don't recall answering." Simeon laughed at his wisecrack.

Will looked toward Simeon sternly. "Well, I figured you at least owe us to spend the night."

Simeon raised both hands. "And likely more." The group laughed.

To the side, Cassie and Sarah exchanged smiles. Cassie drew the blanket tighter and asked, "Would you like to be friends?" Sarah clasped her hands and rocked. "I sure would."

Esther explained how they had plenty in their larder, but Mary Walker insisted the Rapps join them for dinner. After retrieving a dry dress from the wagon for Cassie, Esther followed Mary into the log home, which was two large rooms divided by a fireplace. Hand-tied rugs covered the rough wood floors. For a frontier home, it was immaculate. Esther immediately admired this woman, imagining that she herself would soon enough be welcoming another pioneering family into her own such cabin—perhaps even before winter.

Esther noticed a retouched photograph hung in its frame to one side of the fireplace. "My parents," Mary said warmly. "Left Vermont in 1832 for Kirtland and then Nauvoo. Came west in '47 with the Big Company—second group into the Salt Lake Valley. I was born there the year gold was discovered in California—I'm glad I was too young to go rushing off," Mary explained with a smile. Esther laughed warmly. A stout woman, Mary straightened her apron made from flour sacks sewn together and said, "Well, can you help me with these potatoes?"

Esther said, "Gladly. I have an apron in the wagon..."

"Oh, no bother." Mary reached into a basket and produced another apron. "You're welcome to borrow this one," she said with a smile. "It's always good to have another woman around, especially one who already suits me so well."

Will pressed Simeon to camp on their land for at least one night—and Simeon delighted both his wife and daughter by agreeing. While dinner was prepared, Sarah noticed Cassie's rag doll and retrieved her own pair of rag dolls from the house. After playing for a bit, Sarah asked if Cassie would show her their wagon. Cassie walked her over and began explaining how she had ridden each day on top of the stove. "It's for baked goods," she said proudly. "Ever seen a roadometer?" she asked as she walked Sarah to the rear. "That's what my pa calls it. This here cog turns once each time the wagon wheel turns—because of this," she said, pointing to a small wooden peg on the wagon axle. "And every hundred times this cog turns, this one here turns once." Changing the subject, Cassie asked, "How long have you lived here?"

"Since the snow melted," Sarah said. "Last year, we lived in Eagle Rock, over that way," she said pointing back the way Cassie's family had come. "We moved here after Pa built this house. Before that I was born in Utah. But I don't remember that." Sarah shrugged her shoulders as if unsure how all of this had happened. "Can I see your cut?"

"All right," Cassie said, "If you'll help me put it back on." The girls carefully untied the bandana.

Cassie asked, "Do you like the creek? I do."

Sarah looked surprised after what Cassie had gone through. "I'm scared of it now, but when we first got here it was only a tiny stream. But then it got bigger and colder. Papa says it will get small again in a few weeks after the snow finishes melting." Sarah looked around with concern. "I can't see any snow in the hills, so it must be all melted, but the water is still deep."

Cassie smiled and explained, "My momma says the snow melts in the mountains far away. And it comes down in small streams that flow into bigger creeks like this. And then into rivers like the Snake. And then *it* flows all the way to the ocean." Cassie raised her eyebrows, satisfied with her explanation. "She taught me a song about it. Would you like to sing it with me?" Cassie began to sing:

"Give," said the little stream,"

"Oh, I know that song too," Sarah said, joining in. The two girls sang brightly together as Sarah retied the bandana under Cassie's blonde braid to hold it in place.

"Give, oh! give, give, oh! give."
"Give," said the little stream,
As it hurried down the hill;
"I'm small, I know, but wherever I go
The fields grow greener still."

As the song finished, Sarah cocked her head to one side and softly said, "You're smart…and pretty."

Cassie smiled and said, "You have a nice voice. You're pretty, too."

…

FEW THINGS REARRANGE LIFE'S STAGE so quickly or profoundly as new experiences. When shared with others, the result is nearly always immediate, deep, and lasting friendship.

That first night eating cornbread and chicken quickly forged a solid connection between the parties sitting around a table made from repurposed wagon boards. The room filled with laughter at Simeon's overly humble description of his mindset that led him to cross the creek. Then tears took over as Esther shared the heart of a mother watching her daughter swept away in the currents. Will wiped tears from his eyes at both, and the three boys weren't sure what to do. Cassie and Sarah just looked at each other as though the best life for each of them had just begun.

When Mary and Esther shooed the children from the table for some play before bedtime, Simeon turned to Will and asked, "What are my best options for homesteading here? I'm ready to be a farmer." He thumbed his suspenders and announced sounding more ambitious than experienced.

"In my estimation…," Will leaned forward, his arms on the table, and began to answer. He paused, collecting his thoughts for a moment. "With the creek flowing through here and the south fork of Snake less than five miles that way, as it were, you're right where you need to be. There's a parcel available downstream that connects to my land here I highly recommend you consider." Will leaned in closer. "But you've got to pick land and get it cleared, of course."

Simeon nodded, his only downstream experience being the few minutes that afternoon he had spent in the creek searching for Cassie. Nothing of what he had already seen or previously heard suggested he needed to act as hastily as Will made it sound.

Sitting back, Will said, "I noticed you've got a steel rail swinging under your wagon. Should you stay nearby, might you be willing to loan that out once you're finished? I've been saving for one but haven't made it to that point yet."

"Of course." Simeon smiled contritely, assuming he would be asking for many future favors himself.

Will swallowed a last bite of corn bread. "Just as important as clearing land, you've got to find water and put in ditches right away. Some are attempting to 'dry farm'—to let nature takes its course and rely on summer rains. In my experience in this area, it's a foolish notion. There's no hope of farming success in this part of the country without a steady source of water for irrigation. Make water your highest priority, my friend."

"Say more." Simeon leaned forward and asked, "So, why here and how has it been for you?"

The two women had returned, listening in on the conversation. Mary interrupted, looking toward Esther. "If the talk has turned to farming, I think I'm nowhere near ready to sit but would rather clear these dishes and consider another topic. Sweet Esther, can I count on you to help me?"

Esther carried a few dishes toward the sideboard and said, "Finally. I think I can only stand or lay—these past three weeks have filled my bucket for sitting to overflowing." She patted her stomach. "And with a baby this close, I'm not sure I can get comfortable in any position." The women laughed, placing the dishes in a tub near the stove.

As they walked, Mary asked, "Is this your second?"

"Actually, it's my fourth pregnancy," Esther answered. "My first produced that beautiful little girl," she said, watching Cassie through the kitchen window playing tag with the Walker children. "I thought it would be easier from there. The next two pregnancies weren't hard, but neither baby even took a breath."

"Oh, I'm so sorry."

Esther sighed and shrugged. "I am generally at peace with the matter. I guess it's just what it is. But I am looking forward to this little one," she added, patting her stomach.

The two men moved from the table and took seats by the fire. Will looked over at the women working and smiled. "I'm a blessed man. And a fortunate farmer, too. We're all giddy with our luck. The last two years have been good for us—I farmed cash crops here for two good seasons before we decided to move here permanently. The homesteading act made expanding the five acres I had purchased from old man Johnson an easy decision. I now have a hundred and sixty-five altogether."

Simeon's eyes grew wide. "How much of that are you farming today?"

"Only ten acres so far." Sensing Simeon's willingness to learn, Will said, "We call that 'under plow.' I only have ten acres under plow today. Not quite a tithe," he added. "Clearing the brush has been one of the hardest jobs I've known—perhaps known to man. It takes at least a week to clear an acre—if the brush is low. And granted, that's with a horse and plow. Now, with that rail of yours…"

Simeon interrupted. "I'm told it will make a difference."

"And how, my friend! Otherwise, at the rate I'm clearing it, this here land that for eons has grown only sagebrush and cedar will never produce anything else. A rail can speed up clearing efforts—as though five men were working by hand, maybe ten. I'm no prophet, but with a friend like you…," Will said winking, "…and your rail, I can see all of my land cleared and covered within two years by the greenest alfalfa, wheat, corn, and potatoes you've ever seen. It's no requirement, but I know several others who would willingly return the favor of using your rail by helping at your place, whenever and wherever you pick. Around here, one hand really does wash the other."

Behind him, Simeon could hear the women discussing family matters. The sounds of children laughing and yelling came in through the open door. "It's a deal," he said, extending his hand. The two men shook hands and smiled warmly.

Will said, "There, we finally shook hands. I guess our acquaintance is now official."

Simeon smiled, pleased by Will's vision, a description that had sounded almost too good to be true back when he first began hearing about Idaho. Will made it all sound possible.

Cassie burst through the opening with Sarah trailing behind and exclaimed, "Pa, I love it here! Can we stay forever?"

…

THE DARKENING SKY TURNED a bright pink before the sun dropped almost instantly behind the hills to the west. The two young girls begged their mothers to let them sleep together under the tarp staked alongside the wagon, and both agreed. When the women returned to the cabin after putting the children to bed, the men were still at the fire talking about farming.

"…and the Smithies over that way," Will said pointing, "along with a few others have even taken to grazing cattle on new grass—a hundred or so, as it were." Will took a deep breath, extending his hands toward the fire, and continued. "This land is teeming with new life. We're seeing rabbits so thick I've had to set traps. And earlier this year than last—and maybe because we're living here now. We have mice and ground squirrels that spring to life out of nowhere.

The Robinsons over yonder have a cat expecting a litter any time, and I'm hoping to pick up a good mouser from them to keep the rodent population under control."

Simeon looked up, marveling. "How do you fit it all in? I mean, between clearing and ditch building, who has time to plant?"

"Most of the men," Will sighed, "split their time between work-in-trade building ditches and the labor of farming—and we all need more water for crops, animals, and—don't forget—households. A good ditch can supply it all." He tugged at his beard. "Once we each get some land cleared—and we can pull a group together to help with that—well, that's when the real work begins, as it were." Will winked. "That's why I suggest you scout the parcel downstream from us. It might be the place for you, my friend."

His eyes glowing in the firelight, Simeon glanced up at Esther who was resting in the corner. Relieved at the promise of help and a potentially perfect parcel nearby, he looked up at Will and said, "That sounds mighty fine."

The rumbling voices of the two men could be heard well into the night. Simeon said he planned to ride the adjacent property the next day.

"It won't look like much more than desert for now," Will said. "Willow Creek here has been reliable for as long as anyone around here can remember. It flows constantly out of the hills southeast of here from springs fifty-sixty miles that way. You can count on that."

Failing to understand Will's attention to Willow Creek, Simeon asked, "Is anyone taking water from the Snake River?"

Will shook his head vigorously. "Not so successfully just yet. Well, there is the Eagle Rock canal that cuts way east of here. I hear a man, last name Gunfer, has devised a canal that should draw river water over and merge with Willow Creek soon. Shares will cost, but it all costs, right? We should be entitled to the first wave of shares since we're living on active claims—at least you will be after tomorrow." Will rubbed head. "Willow Creek promises an even brighter future, but don't take my word for it. Take it all in before you commit—no reason to have an ounce of doubt."

Simeon said he planned to ride out first thing and asked if he could park the wagon and leave his two girls here for the better part of the morning.

"Of course," Will said. "While you're out, look for what locals call 'the Dry Bed'"—and went on to describe what was more scientifically referred to as a dry channel or swale that during spring run-off captured the Snake River's overflow to the northeast and carried water like a fork of the river for a few months. In good years, he said, it carried a fair supply of water until August or maybe September. "It's probably the most unusual geology of the area besides the lava flows out west and volcanic buttes to the north. When it comes to water, it makes the land north and west of here very tempting but more complicated and nearly impossible to farm—that is, unless you get your crops harvested by August—or we get regular rain in August and September, which hasn't happened yet in my time here."

"North and west?" Simeon pulled out his map, and Will pointed out how the Snake River flowed from right side of the map before making an abrupt turn north for a few miles before arching due west for fifteen miles or so before gradually turning south again. Will said. "Right here," he went on, pointing to a spot on the map, "the Snake turns north. And see this line?" He traced a line that ran directly across the map from the river on the right side straight back into the river on the left side. Will cleared his voice before solemnly adding, "This is the dry channel—well the Dry Bed that never doesn't live up to its name in my experience. During the spring and summer, you might get a cutting of alfalfa over this way," he said, pointing to the western half of the valley, "but you'd likely spend most of your time praying for rain. And replanting the following year." Will chuckled. "It's been tried, but no one has succeeded with later harvests—potatoes in October and wheat a bit earlier. As such, most who strike out that way find soon enough they're on a fool's errand. Those who have settled over this way consider the west side of the valley a no-man's land—impossible to farm."

Simeon finally understood this strange river course on the map he had stared at almost religiously for months. While he had initially intended to ride that way, he quickly revised his plan and would take Will's advice to heart. His thoughts began to race.

"Out here near the middle, well a bit to the right," Will said, tracing over the middle-right of the valley, "we have Willow Creek and a few other natural water sources. Someday, we will figure how to get water from the Snake, but that river has defied our efforts so far." Then, ominously, he added, "Remember, water brings life. Without it, there is no life. Don't be seduced by waterless land. You will either leave there or die there. But you won't live there."

Simeon took it all in.

Will looked up, satisfied. "Now that's a geology lesson!"

Simeon patted him on the back and said, "Well done. I finally know something that was only a puzzle to me before."

...

COME MORNING, SIMEON SET OUT ON HORSEBACK to scout along Willow Creek and beyond. He was especially curious about the river to the north where this dry channel brought spring runoff toward the land to the west, teasing the idea that farming there could work. Why he had to see it defied his own logic, but he had to.

As he rode downstream along Willow Creek, he saw vast miles of undulating sage brush, which confirmed that the land was flatter than it felt and found himself agreeing with Will's description that this could be an ideal parcel. The land was covered with sagebrush as tall as a man, so he figured it had to be capable of growing something. He had hoped for more naturally open land—so Simeon urged the chestnut horse along. As he rode, he came across a newly cleared field—still strewn with twisted limbs of sage and with a ditch in the process of being cut across one end and out along a new trail. Rising in his saddle, Simeon could see the ditch snaking east along the contours of the land toward Willow Creek. He imagined many days of labor ahead for this farmer before anything could be planted here.

Roosting along the sagebrush at the edges of the field, a plain bird bobbed as it released a watery, flute-like song—a meadowlark with its long familiar phrase. These birds lived along the boundaries of farms on fence posts, sagebrush, and abandoned farm equipment. They seemed to always arrive with new settlement but never fully move in, preferring the edges instead. Contrariwise, as Simeon crossed the field, he flushed a pair of mourning doves already nesting in a loose accumulation of dry grass and sage bark.

A few miles to the north, he came across what he determined must be the Dry Bed—a wide river course with abundant cottonwood groves and a very shallow, slow-moving creek. He could see from the high bank along the south side that the land sloped away to the south. He followed a parallel ditch carrying a trickle of water for two or three miles until he encountered the dam diverting water out of the stream and felt shocked by how much work had been required for such a weak result. Riding a few miles due east, he saw how the channel widened and collected its limited water from a swampy overflow of the Snake River. There, the river was wide and deep, hinting at mountain tributaries not too far upstream, and turning quickly north and away along its well-defined channel. Its eroded near bank teased his mind with the idea of a deep canal, but river's force made him wonder how anything manmade could hold up. Looking at his map, he could see a solid line representing where the Dry Bed began, but what he was now witnessing was hardly as precise as his map declared.

Upriver a bit, he came across a wooden structure on the right bank of the river. No one was there, but he saw a recently constructed headgate taking water from the river. Scrawled into a wooden placard nailed to the structure were the words "Willow Creek Canal." The gate was closed, but behind him, a newly dug canal diverging east from the Dry Bed promised to carry water to that side of the valley. Looking west, he could see how the two routes were separated by a low valley that ran south and east. The Dry Bed was the only source of water for the west, sporadic as it was.

Everything Will had described to him was now clear.

Near noon, Simeon returned toward the Walker's homesite and felt immediate peace when he saw the parcel Will had recommended. Compared to what he had seen that day, why this land had not yet been claimed was beyond him! There was good access to water from a creek familiarly lined by willows. And with a small clearing already featuring a lone cottonwood tree, this really was the perfect homesite!

"We will be neighbors," he told Esther and Cassie while loading their wagon. They pulled less than a mile downstream and spent the afternoon setting up. Dinner that night was under a makeshift shelter from a tarp tied to their wagon box and what Esther had called "my new tree."

After dinner, Simeon invited Cassie to join him on a walk. "Let's explore around a bit," he walked out into the sagebrush that in most cases was taller than she was, with some even taller than Simeon.

"This here is good land, Cassie." Walking downslope toward Willow Creek, he said, "I imagine we can pull good water this way for at least a few acres, maybe more."

Cassie asked, "'Pull' water?"

Seeing the complexity of the word, he said, "It's a funny term. We will have to turn some water out of Willow Creek upstream a ways, with a small diversion dam, one I hope to make permanent. We will add what's called a 'head gate' so we can turn the water down a feeder ditch whenever we want." Tracing the land with his outstretched arm, he added, "And bring the water from over that way to the top of our field. Whatever water makes it all the way down our new field will flow back into Willow Creek about right here where we're standing is my guess."

Cassie asked, "Will we water the sagebrush?"

"No, no, no," Simeon chuckled, putting his arm around his daughter. "There's no market for sagebrush. Remember the rail under the wagon? We'll use it to clear this entire area before we can plant—and before we cut in our ditches," he added, smiling. "Come this way," he said, beckoning her to follow. They walked down a faint trail that had been formed by their wagon and horses passing over. The crushed sagebrush gave off a strong scent. Simeon and Cassie climbed to the top of a natural mound a few hundred yards from their campsite.

"This is your new world, Cassie—our new world," Simeon said, sweeping his arm and turning in a complete circle. "There are already farms upstream, that way." Pointing ahead a short distance, he added, "See the trees over there? That's where Sarah lives. Just get on a high spot like this and you can spot the Walker's trees to find your way there—and our tree when you're coming back," he said, pointing toward the lone cottonwood behind them.

Happy at the thought, Cassie said, "I hope we can be friends forever."

Simeon smiled absently. His eyes were focused on the area past the Walker's land. He mumbled, "I figure here we will have water for ten or twenty acres, and the new canal carrying river water into Willow Creek promises more. Lots to learn here…"

Bending down, Simeon drew in the dirt. "Well, Willow Creek edges toward the Snake over that way before turning this way…strange that it flows south to north." Simeon reflected for a minute, convinced they would be okay. "I suppose…," he said aloud and pointing, "…we can always expand the canal." He stood and raised his arms. "Widen the stream as needed…surely enough water for our land and probably others as well."

Within two days, Simeon had used his teams of horses alternately to pull the iron rail and clear about an acre. With enough tugging, every piece of sagebrush had yielded its centuries-old footing to the hard work of homesteading.

"Here's where we will build our home," he told Esther and Cassie.

"Oh, and we'll have shade," Esther said, smiling and pointing to their one tree. "And a garden?" she asked as Simeon began to turn the dirt with a shovel.

"Yes. I'm hoping to get seed in today," Simeon said. "We will have to hand water this from the creek until I get the ditches in."

Later that afternoon, he rode out with Will to meet several other men and returned happy. "Most agreed—what with that new canal, we should have plenty of water. All are new to the area, just like we are. Only one fellow named Hutchins came last year. With more of us here now, the work won't be quite as overwhelming. Still overwhelming, mind you." He laughed. "We'll get to work and get our crops in," Simeon reported back to Esther.

Esther raised her eyebrows and asked, "And when do you expect that to be?"

Simeon cleared his throat. "I worked out a plan with Will. First, the Smithies and then the Walkers. Then the Hutchins and Lundquists. And then our property. One day each. We will get as many acres cleared in one day as we can for each man and then move on. Might be as many as three to five acres. We'll probably make a second round once we get crops planted and ditches in."

"So, you'll be gone?" Esther rubbed her belly. "It's getting close. I might—" Her words revealed worry.

"I'll be nearby," Simeon said, drawing his wife close. "Not like before—this won't take me away like freighting did. Home at nights. And home to help you when the baby comes…as much as I can."

Esther looked up at him and said, "I know this is all new to you. You're a good man. Just don't forget that."

Simeon put on a forgetful look before smiling. "Forget what?"

They laughed together.

Cassie interrupted. "Can I go see Sarah?"

Esther asked, "Can you find your way there?"

"Pa taught me how to look for the trees. And I figure they're upstream from us a bit, so Willow Creek can show me the way," Cassie replied with a nervous confidence.

"Just stay back away from the creek," Esther warned.

Cassie touched the bandana around her head knowingly. "I will, Ma."

That evening, by the light of a lamp, Esther handed Cassie her journal, one she had started when the family left their Utah home. "It's been a busy few days, but I'd like you to write a bit."

Cassie asked, "What do I write about? I can't think of a thing!"

Esther said, "Remember the ideas we've discussed before. Think about what's happened recently—our arrival at Willow Creek? The crossing? Sarah? The cut on your head?" Sitting under their makeshift shelter, Esther drew her daughter close. "Or you could draw a picture of our homesite and imagine how you think our first home might look. You'll come up with something."

Cassie began to write.

We made it to Willow Creek. Well, after we almost didn't make it. I fell into the creek and about drowned. I cut my head. A nice man named Mr. Walker found me and helped the cut on my head. We all made friends.

And I met his girl, Sarah. I love her so much. She has dark hair and some rag dolls. I went all alone to see her today. I was scared I might see a ki-yoty…

Cassie looked up. "Momma, how do you spell coyote?"

Chapter 3

A Sleepless Night

The last-minute invitation to keynote Pilot Consulting's annual client conference caught Emma by surprise. "Who cancelled?" was her first insecure thought until Pilot's CEO Sean McKilroy announced, "And, you've been selected to receive our Breakthrough of the Year award."

Emma was speechless. *She* would be receiving the coveted crystal obelisk, the same one she had seen on Sean's bookshelf at Pilot headquarters when she worked there. She wondered at first if Sean wasn't teasing before awkwardly stuttering, "Yes, I think…let me check…" Sean's words slowly sunk in—mind-blowing, dream-come-true, pinch-yourself kind of stuff. In her wildest dreams, this wouldn't have happened for another decade—if ever—but not at thirty-four. Hard to believe, it was all living proof of the fact that Emma's new venture was succeeding, affirmation she desperately craved but had a hard time accepting. That Sean himself had called with the news made it that much clearer.

"Emma?"

Emma put him on speaker and waved her business partner Lacy over to hear the details. Struggling to compose herself, she put Sean on mute and whispered to Lacy, "We won…please say something."

Lacy looked at Emma curiously and said, "Hi Mr. McKilroy!" She sounded appropriately enthusiastic.

"Hi Lacy! Good to hear your voice again. And it's still 'Sean,' okay?" Sean repeated his invitation before adding, "Your 'Staring Down Culture' platform is so *it* right now. You're speaking all over the country and training people everywhere. You're who we want to honor." Sean gushed. "And in front of a couple hundred of the world's top business leaders!"

Emma muted the phone again and hugged Lacy. They each squealed. "This is huge!"

"Hello, are you still there?"

Unmuting the phone, Emma said, "Yes, we're still here. Did you say day after tomorrow?" Emma gave Lacy a questioningly look since Lacy handled all operational details. Lacy nodded and then mouthed "I guess…" feigning inconvenience.

"You two know how we do this, right? Less notice means more excitement—makes the celebration in the room more real, less drab." Pausing, Sean added, "And Lacy, put Emma in first class, on us."

"Okay, wow!" Emma said, looking again at Lacy and mouthing "first class!" before pinching herself so Lacy could see.

They could hear Sean say something muffled before he came back on the phone. "Hey, I need to go. See you in Paris day after tomorrow!"

Paris? Did he say Paris? Emma dropped to the couch. Her mind raced. Not Paris, please! Her ex-boyfriend Jake had ruined it for her. Ruined it! Why did he have to do *that*—propose marriage! *We were not…that!* She winced at the memories of her last trip to Paris three years earlier—a vacation with Jake that had gone too far.

Emma's hands began to tremble. "I don't know if I can go back."

Lacy sat beside her and knowingly took her hand. "This is a big honor, Emma. It's above and beyond what we've been working for. For this, wouldn't you want to go back? Emma?"

Emma looked up with concern in her eyes. She forced a smile and said tentatively, "Yes…"

Lacy said patiently, "Whatever happened *happened*. Can we at least talk this through? Remember, we live in the present, not yesterday?"

Emma drew in a deep breath. "Okay, I accept that it happened and *this* is happening. I just didn't see this collision coming at all!" She added circumspectly, "But this isn't that…I can't believe…!" Pausing to think, she then asked, "Do you think we can at least avoid anything too Paris? Just get me in and out? No quaint, corner hotel rooms? Maybe on a floor high enough so I won't be able to hear the *wee-ooh wee-ooh* of local police cars?"

Lacy nodded. "I'm sure we can."

"And no buttery morning croissants?"

Emma clenched her hands tightly as she remembered flying home from Paris, sitting awkwardly next to Jake without as much as a word between them. She had totally shut down, unable to say anything. Jake had tried a few times to hold her hand and even slipped her a note of apology. Toward the end of the flight, she thanked him for being such a nice guy.

Emma had spent the following three days nearly catatonic—sleeping, staring out the window, sipping from her insulated cup of ice water, and eating next to nothing. She had ignored everyone's calls and texts—some from work and quite a few from Jake. When someone had knocked at her door for thirty minutes, she had peeked through the peephole and saw Jake standing there in a nicely tailored jacket holding flowers before deciding to ignore him then too.

On the third day, after finally eating a container of yogurt and delighted at how good a bagel from her freezer tasted—in a place like Manhattan with bagel stores on every corner—Emma had felt herself coming back around. Sean was her boss at the time, and when he called that morning, she had decided to answer. After a brief discussion, he had said, "Take whatever time you need—we've got your back. But just know we really need you." An hour later, the haze of the past several days had lifted and Emma had showered, making it to the office by noon. Her work had been invigorating enough for a few days until she had started reliving the entire experience again, this time knowing none of it would have happened if she had just spoken up and not let things with Jake go as far as they had. How could she have known! The whole thing had been so embarrassing—and he had totally put her on the spot in front of all of Paris!

Overwhelmed then by her meltdown, Emma had called her mother, who suggested she come home for a few days. "Come see us in Carlsbad. The ocean air will get you back in top form before you know it."

So, with Sean's backing again, Emma had flown to California—for a very long weekend. She had been happy to see her parents, but it was her visit with a therapist that had made the biggest difference. Her name was Serena, someone her mother had recommended. Emma had high expectations that Serena would live up to her name and give her some peace.

"You couldn't have called at a better time this morning—literally one minute after a cancellation. I'm glad I could fit you in," Serena had said that Monday morning. "I leave tomorrow for Greece—and a much-needed vacation."

Emma had shared about Jake, how she still couldn't put her finger on why she had reacted the way she did—still frustrated that Jake had misread her so horribly. Why had she shut down? And for several days? Hearing herself describe the event made her seem so erratic, yet another part of her felt her reaction was entirely logical.

"You probably won't like this term, but I'd call what you experienced a panic attack. Watching your body language now, I think you're still in it."

Emma had felt watched before realizing she was quickly clamping and releasing her hands, wondering how something like this could be happening. To her. The queen of keeping it together. She had talked with Serena for much longer than an hour and begun to understand better what was going on. "I clearly felt ambushed," she had admitted. "That doesn't mean Jake was trying to ambush me, but the disconnect was a bigger shock than I guess I could handle. I thought we were just good friends—perhaps with long-term potential but just not then."

"Good observation," Serena had said. "Clearly, Jake was seeing something else in your relationship. I'm sure he was shocked as well. Have you thought about how he felt?"

At first, Emma had resented the question but then realized she hadn't really spent much time thinking about how Jake must have felt. She had immediately begun to sob.

"Ahh, there's your humanity," Serena had said.

Emma had wiped at her face and looked up dismayed. "My what?" She had expected an arrogant or haughty look from Serena.

Rather, Serena lived up to her name with a bright and loving look. "Your humanity. Panic and anxiety turn us inward. I've found that the best way out can come from connecting with someone else. Even simply connecting with the thought of someone else."

To Emma, it had been an utterly novel idea at the time.

Serena had looked at the time and said, "And knowing just that much can lead to healthier responses."

"Are you saying I might have said 'yes' to Jake under other circumstances?"

"Not at all, but you might have been able to answer honestly without feeling so assaulted or spent the next several days avoiding everyone and everything." Serena had said, "I can tell you're not a self-absorbed person, but anxiety can force us deeply inward. Choosing to connect with others in that moment rather than retreat can work." Serena paused again. "Now, I really need to wrap up—oh, one last thing, don't get hung up on the label, but you may want to read about this and even talk to someone else about it. I'd be happy to—once I get back from Greece." She had laughed. "You're fortunate to know something new about yourself. You had a huge experience that taught you something you can use to your benefit in the future."

"How so?"

"Again, I don't want you to hear me tell you to read books and books about anxiety, but maybe a few articles. For some people—and I think this is true for you—it's more of an adrenaline disorder. Recognizing that something like this happened to you, watching for the early signs of it, and then getting outside yourself—calling on your humanity—can really help address it."

Emma had felt worried. "Is this a disease?"

Serena had smiled and said, "Well, it is about *dis*-ease. I really don't expect this will be a regular thing but given how long this last episode lasted, I recommend you talk with your doctor about something that can help if this happens in the future. Something to slow down the effects of adrenaline. He or she will have you take it *when* you feel your heart starting to race—or your thoughts for that matter. I've seen it do wonders for many of my clients." Pausing, Serena added, "Just don't set yourself up for an unexpected marriage proposal again anytime soon."

Looking back on things, Emma realized it had taken her almost three weeks to sort through the aftershocks of turning Jake down. When her thoughts began racing on her way to her next scheduled speech, something that was beginning to happen almost weekly now, she had opened the prescription bottle, glad she had met with her doctor. She had taken one pill for the first time. Swallowing, she had worried for a moment that the muscles in her neck would choke her and prevent the pill from going down. But she had swallowed successfully, and within twenty minutes her heart had calmed down and her sweaty palms had dried. On top of that, she had followed Serena's counsel to think about her humanity, going so far as asking the backstage crew questions about themselves, their families, and dreams—to their puzzled looks—until it was time to walk out on stage. Altogether, the speech had gone quite well.

Emma looked up to find Lacy watching her. She pushed the memories aside.

Lacy squeezed both of Emma's hands and said calmly, "I get it. Paris, but *not* Paris. I'm on it." Sighing, she added, "Let's make sure to pack your meds."

Emma forced a smile as her mind began to race. It wasn't just Paris. What about the speech? She felt her platform was a work in progress at best—would people think she was a poser? Would all the CEOs and leaders there find her content convincing or play Tetris on their phones or worse still fall asleep? She caught herself spiraling and deliberately formed a question. "Lacy, do we really deserve this?"

"I don't think that's up to us to decide," Lacy answered wisely. "You've poured your heart and soul into this venture—we both have! And you can be sure that I deserve this," Lacy said, laughing. "Not sure about you, though."

Emma smiled at the thought. "New territory," she whispered. Raising her eyes, she squeezed Lacy's hands back and said, "Let's find a great way to thank Sean."

"New territory," Lacy repeated. "I like the sound of that. And, yes, let's do thank Sean in a big way. And, you can rest assured that I'll do everything I can to make the travel part as easy on you as possible because, no pressure, but you are still what we sell—you're the product." Emma *was* in fact responsible for much of their revenue.

Lacy held both of Emma's hands. "You do the hardest part of the job—being on stage. You light yourself on fire and people come to watch you burn," a well-worn phrase Lacy had lifted from John Wesley.

When Emma squeezed back and said, "And you're the glue that keeps all of this together," Lacy knew she was relaxing. Emma had only recently begun calling her "the glue." They really were perfect equal opposites—both so capable, committed, and accountable but different in so many ways. Emma was the creative force and great on stage, and Lacy flawlessly managed every operational detail and every dollar their firm received.

Emma took a deep breath and smiled at her good fortune.

...

AFTER COORDINATING TRAVEL PLANS for forty-five minutes, Lacy reported that Emma's only option was the red-eye flight departing from JFK at 11:05 the next evening. "That's unless we cancel tomorrow's webinar—but we have almost five hundred registered. Don't think we want to do that."

Emma nodded, her mind wandering. Their monthly webinars were a highlight—an hour overview of their key concepts. Hundreds of people came to each one. Many clients were asking for follow-on details about how to bring Emma's training into their organizations. Emma pushed thoughts of Paris to the background with mounting concern that she would be able to sleep on the plane and arrive in Paris somewhat rested.

Lacy waved her hand to get Emma's attention. "The best seat I can get right now is two rows back from the bulkhead in what they call 'preferred.' They say it's slightly better than the main cabin. Oh, and a window seat, so you at least have the option of leaning against something. I have you wait-listed for an upgrade, but there are twenty-one people ahead of you for business class and sixteen for first class."

Emma took a deep breath and worried some more.

Their afternoon webinar the next day was a success—well attended by people from all over the country, their best to date. Lacy coordinated the controls and feigned *oohs* and *ahhs* and fake applause throughout, lifting Emma's spirits and keeping her smiling. As usual, Emma's delivery was impeccable.

"Flawless as usual," Lacy said as Emma prepared to leave to pack for her trip.

"Yes, you are." Emma deflected the compliment. She pulled a pill bottle from her handbag, feeling bolstered by the fact that she filled the prescription. "And I did it without my meds!" They discussed their follow-up plans for the webinar and other details before Emma realized she really needed to head home and pack. On her way out the door, she asked, "Any news on the flight?"

"None. I've turned over every stone I can find. I'll keep checking the stand-by lists."

Riding to the airport that evening, Emma called the airline one last time to make her case and was told the flight was now in control of the gate. At the gate, she asked again. "No one from the waiting list is getting upgraded—if that makes you feel any better," the Delta agent said.

Emma's last hope was dashed as she boarded the flight, hoping some of the seats in front would be empty. As she pulled her roller bag down the aisle, the first class and business class sections were already mostly full. She stowed her suitcase and then tried reclining her seat, relieved that it went back farther than she had expected. It was then she noticed a flight attendant hurrying down the aisle, toward her, she hoped. Emma leaned forward, expecting good news.

"Please raise your seat back for takeoff," the man said.

"I'm checking my seat..." Emma stammered, working at her seat controls and realizing the attendant knew nothing of her situation. Resigning herself to her assigned seat, Emma smiled at how not so long ago she would have been willing to travel by mule train for an opportunity to give a speech. How things had changed! "All for a once-in-a-lifetime honor. First class, shmirst class."

Her head filling with new doubts about whether she deserved Sean's award, Emma watched people taking seats around her and imagined using this moment in some future speech. She imagined describing how someone had offered to buy her a first-class ticket—had a seat been available—but how she had been stuck in coach, exhausted and hoping to sleep. She wouldn't add the part about how she had been on her way to receiving a prestigious award or that she was only thirty-four at the time. Chuckling to herself, she concluded this was a problem most people don't have and abandoned the story line altogether, worrying again that Sean really had called as a joke.

An hour over the Atlantic, Emma tried reading to get sleepy. After an hour, she watched an in-flight movie, shifting frequently in her seat, all the while jealously eyeing those around who were sound asleep.

After landing, Emma quickly cleared customs and then spotted a man holding a digital tablet that read "Ms. Rose," obviously her ride to the hotel. As they walked to the curb, the man directed her to a limo with darkly tinted windows. Emma felt it was way over the top but still committed to thank Lacy for the pampering. When the driver held the door open, he asked with a strong accent, "Mademoiselle, you prefer hearing the Bon Jovi music?"

Emma nodded and slid into the seat, further delighted that Lacy had even informed the driver to play her favorite music. Soon enough, "Livin' on a Prayer" came over the speakers as they drove the Paris beltway toward the hotel, fully dimming any Paris vibe. Within minutes, Emma fell sound asleep across the seat.

"We're here, Ms. Rose." Emma awoke, noticing the car was completely stopped with the driver leaning through the open door and her bag already on the curb. After a dozy but quick check-in, she entered her suite and immediately fell back onto the bed, eager to get back to sleep. Until she remembered she hadn't updated Lacy. She quickly texted her status.

I'm here. Good job on the limo and the music! Sensory deprivation was exactly what I needed! Finally fell asleep! Doesn't feel like P at all!

A few moments later, Emma's phone buzzed.

Bonjour, Miss Rose! Sofia Bement, here. I am coordinating your speaking. Have you landed?

Emma composed a text to send back. *Yes, I'm in Paris. Very tired…*

Before finishing her text, her handler texted again.

You must be so tired. Please do get some sleep. I will contact you before your big speech.

Emma put the phone down on the bedside table and began to relax before it buzzed again. It was Lacy.

Go to sleep. It's the middle of the night.

…

EMMA FOUND HERSELF staring at the ceiling. The short nap on the way to the hotel had taken the edge off. With only four hours until her speech, Emma was feeling the full effects of a long flight and a sleepless night—on top of a not-so-great sleep the night before.

And now not sleepy at all.

On the verge of receiving an amazing award, Emma's thoughts wandered down memory lane. For the decade prior, Emma had been a rising star at Pilot Consulting. She had hired Lacy a year or so earlier, and, of the three executive assistants she had worked with while there, Lacy was by far the best at what she did. And beautiful. Emma teased that she'd hired Lacy straight off the runway, which was almost true—Lacy had in fact funded the first year of her MBA by modeling. "Coming to work here," Lacy had said, "was a serious upgrade—more predictable pay, regular hours, very challenging work, and loads of opportunity." Lacy's slim build, long dark hair, olive skin, and her composure regularly caught people's attention. That combined with her no-nonsense approach to work had most team leaders at one point or another recruiting Lacy for their own teams.

"It's a battle for resources around here," Emma had routinely said. "I fight to keep the wolves away almost every day. Not only are people trying to poach you now, but you know the minute you graduate, someone who needs a solid second-in-command will take you, don't you?"

"Whatever," Lacy always answered. "I won't cross that bridge until it's built. Just one more semester!" she added with a smile.

Well before her time at Pilot, Emma had dreamed of striking out on her own someday. Eventually, she had begun developing a business framework—key concepts, offerings, and so on—but always stopped at just how she would be able to afford a team, people who would push back or bring fresh thinking, a dynamic she felt was essential to growth. One day after working together for a while and over a long lunch with Lacy, Emma had decided to be vulnerable and confide her dream with Lacy, sharing how she felt very confident in her key concepts, comparing her thinking to Pilot's foundations—at least in its early days. At the time, she had felt more exposed than she expected.

But Lacy had seemed more than interested than Emma expected.

Emma had put her fingers to her lips. "This stays between us for now," and then took another chance. "I'm telling you because I want you to join me. I can't imagine ever working with anyone else. Ever." With that, her notion of team felt complete.

Within days, Pilot co-founder Sean McKilroy had asked Lacy to his office. Puzzled, Emma had watched through the glass wall of her office, preparing herself for a conversation she expected would go something like "Lacy is awesome, and I want her as my own assistant," unable to imagine what she would say in response. Of course, he deserved whatever team member he wanted—he owned the place! Emma could almost see the writing on the wall—he takes Lacy and whatever good Emma had pulled together would come unraveled. She'd be through. Caput.

Plus, their plan was now in motion. *Ish*. She and Lacy had begun meeting outside of work on the details for their new enterprise—timing for which neither of them felt was quite right. Emma was in the middle of a large project with one client. And Lacy was in the final semester of her MBA at NYU.

Still, Emma's hand shook as she had half-wondered what Lacy would say to Sean's offer. She had watched for fifteen long minutes until Lacy emerged from Sean's office laughing and a bit too happy. Lacy had walked perfectly poised to her cubicle and flipped her dark hair as she sat, turning to look through the glass wall of Emma's office.

Raising her eyebrows and nodding in Sean's direction, Lacy had said, "You're next."

Emma had worried, daring a look toward Sean's office and seeing him standing in the doorway, beckoning with his finger. "Me?" she had innocently whispered. She had walked past Lacy, asking quietly, "What's going on?" Lacy had shrugged coyly.

The walk had taken what seemed like hours, and Emma's head had swum with more than enough negative self-talk.

In Sean's office, he had begun with, "Have a seat. I found your TEDx speech on the corner of your desk one evening when I was looking for the Parson's report—you remember that family trust we once worked on together…before you got the TED invite, right?"

Emma had expected bad news about Parson Holdings, Emma's largest client since Sean had asked her to lead the account a few months back. And why bring up the TEDx speech since it was Sean who had encouraged her to submit a proposal? And he had been so delighted when she was invited to speak at the Chicago TEDx. "There's no better forum for breakout thinkers and movers," he had said at the time. "What a great career move!"

Emma had laughed awkwardly, feeling she was being set up. While she considered her ideas to be fresh and motivating, plus the TEDx invitation, she still felt a bit like a poser. Even though her ideas were individually backed by real behavioral science, bringing them all together was her own thinking. There was still the matter of real-world testing ahead.

At the heart of her speech was her big point that "the cultural forces around us will eat personal character for breakfast, lunch, and dinner." Culture, Emma insisted, will always overwhelm, undermine, and defeat how we "show up" if we let it. But if we get conscious about what makes us who we are, we have a chance. We can stare it down—our upbringing, the media we consume, thought patterns and thinking errors, the habits we've formed over our lifetimes, even an awareness about why we dress the way we do, and more. She would urge listeners to get intentional about how much culture they keep, reject, or remodel. Only with an awareness of that foundation could anyone hope to build a version of themselves that isn't merely a by-product of culture, she asserted.

And not all culture is bad or wrong, she urged, but modern cultural forces can play out in insidious ways, perhaps more than ever in the past. For instance, we used to refer to "peer pressure," a phrase she argued was on its way out or already out. In its day, peer pressure came from those closest to us—as few as three to four close friends or as many as one's entire high school class. "But nothing like the magnitude of today's 'social pressure,'" she contended, "Where vast online hordes fight for our attention, creating constant pressure that can lead to false conclusions—that everyone everywhere has snappy and authoritative opinions or is always doing something more fun or is happier because of new clothes, new cars, or newly decorated houses, cooler tchotchkes, nicer cars, or swankier gender reveal parties." Over-listening to those pressures—then and now—can make us smaller versions of ourselves, she suggested, not bigger.

After years of working with therapists and life coaches, and following abundant self-examination and no lack of self-doubt, Emma believed she had become aware enough of her own cultural upbringing. She had carefully reviewed the effects of being raised by parents older than most of her friends' parents and in a religiously conservative city. She had looked at the downward pressure from competing in a male-dominated workplace, unpacked a few defining teenage experiences, and even reverse-engineered her exposure to new critical thinking methods in college—all until she felt like she knew what made her who she was. "The horse that brung me here," she often joked. Until recently, she had intentionally turned off her social media accounts to avoid too much input—until she and Lacy realized how vital social media was in reaching out to audiences gathered there that could accelerate the growth of their new enterprise.

"I'm a hypocrite on that account," she included in her speech. "And strictly self-interested," she would chuckle, "since we only use these tools to promote what we do—and free people from their own traps along the way." Half the time, audiences laughed with her. The rest of the time, people looked puzzled at the irony. She knew she was making a weak case there, recognizing that her own thinking was being shaped by social pressure. Culture.

"I've been staring my own culture down for a long time," she claimed. "And I do a little more work every day, most days." The rest of her speech provided a framework to address one question: So, how can you stare down culture?

Called into Sean's office that day, Emma had watched him wave a printed copy of her TEDx speech draft at her. "Well…," he had started to say.

"—In case you're wondering, I didn't print it here," Emma had said a bit defensively, worried she would be fired for misusing office resources.

Sean had laughed for longer than usual. "It's the best thing I've ever read, Emma Rose!" Sean had glanced down at the packet.

"Really?" Emma had blushed.

Dropping the packet on his desk, Sean had said, "I made a copy…and, yes, with the office copier." He had looked around, his smile disarming. "Don't tell anyone." Then, after a long pause, he had said, "Emma, you have to run with this *staring down culture* thing. There's nothing like it out there, and in a world where flavor-of-the-month wins, go while it tastes great!"

"Go?"

"Yes. You have incubated this long enough—here, within Pilot. Stay here any longer and it will go through too many iterations—you'll either draft it to death or we will keep you too busy. Your ideas need fresh air—independence, focus, freedom to fly." Taking a breath, he had added with finality, "It pains me to say this, but I think it's time for you to leave. With a platform like this, you could easily make it to the moon and beyond!"

Emma had felt like she was free falling. She hadn't really heard anything he had said. "Are you firing me?"

"Not exactly," Sean had said. "But, in a way, I guess I am. You're immensely valuable to Pilot, but what you have here…," he had trailed off.

Emma knew her ideas were becoming better defined and had been remarkably well-received by the TEDx audience. Still, she need to learn how better to engage an audience and finish her business plan. Not to mention office space, whether or not to have a refrigerator in the breakroom, and arranging for high-speed internet. Emma's thoughts had raced.

"And take Lacy with you. You two make a powerful, dynamic team, one that blazes through obstacles and gets amazing amounts of work done."

Shocked, Emma had looked up to see him smiling back at her as though he had just seen the best movie ever and couldn't recommend it enough. Had he just said to take Lacy? In a flash, Emma recalled Sean's reputation for fostering talent. She had heard about at least three other *New York Times* bestselling authors he had launched, multiple successful internet ventures, and a superanalytical hedge fund led by twin PhDs, a brother-sister duo who frequented the Pilot offices. All had at one point worked for him at Pilot.

"Oh, and I want to be your first—and perhaps only—investor."

Emma had fallen back in her chair. "So, I'm not fired…" Then, what Sean had just said finally hit her. *Investor?*

In what had felt like a dream, they had discussed terms and some key milestones Sean thought Emma could reach in six months and then twelve, each of which meant he was prepared to invest additional dollars "if you still need my money by then," he had said, again laughing long and hard.

Walking back to her office, Emma had avoided looking at Lacy for fear they would both squeal, laugh, or cry—or all of the above. Lacy had waited a bit before finally walking into Emma's office and closing the door. They quickly gave each other big hugs and arranged to leave work early that day to celebrate more publicly somewhere else.

Within days, Emma and Lacy had resigned their posts at Pilot Consulting. Emma's TEDx talk entitled, "Staring Down Culture," had become the basis for a longer sixty-minute speech. Now two years later, her talk was still trending among TEDx speeches. Because of its popularity, she had now given to thousands. People loved her simple framework—testimonials of its power showed up daily online, via email, and even in cards and letters. Based on this thinking, Emma and Lacy had developed and recently launched a professional development curriculum that was gaining traction across corporate America. Calls had begun coming in from other parts of the world as well.

Emma regularly dreamed someone in one of her live audiences would raise their hand and challenge the scientific basis of her ideas. In this recurring dream, she would pause, then stammer, saying something self-deprecating like, "it just came to me…over a few years…and I wrote it down," even though that wasn't true. In her waking moments, she regularly reminded herself of her deep studies and the dozens of expert interviews she had conducted after leaving Pilot—all to validate what people in her field referred to as a "platform," her packaging of important ideas aimed at producing better results for the people who applied them.

"The most successful versions of who we are or who we can become," Emma asserted in her presentations and speeches, "must, must, must be defined internally, and not externally." The four tenets of her platform were to do the deep work, listen to your inner advisor, connect authentically—something she had learned from her therapist in Carlsbad— and stay awake to the hard-to-detect-but-potentially-erosive forces of culture.

Emma used powerful visuals in her speeches—beginning with a projected image of a larger-than-life goldfish in clear, blue water. "An older fish swims by two younger goldfish," she would say. "The older fish asks, 'How's the water?' Both smile and nod. Once the older goldfish swims on, the youngest goldfish turns to the other and asks, 'What's water?'" She would wait for the laughter to subside before adding, "We're each like a goldfish—and perhaps the last to know we're in water. That's culture. Even though it's all around us, how aware are we of it? How aware can you be? Even though we each experience culture differently, it's easy to be a lot like these goldfish—unaware, unconscious, and unintentional." Letting the point sink in, she would wait until the audience began stirring uneasily before adding, "Let's talk about how you can become aware of the forces that make you who you are—some good and some potentially bad—and get intentional about what you do from here."

Since leaving Pilot, Emma had hired speech coaches to hone her delivery and tighten her stories. The laugh-lines in her speeches were now dialed in. Even the gestures to enhance her points had been choreographed. She continued to add stories about the mini cultures in organizations of all sizes, where employees swim in quite different water at work than they do when they go home at nights. "The confluence of cultural forces washes over us daily, unexpectantly, and erosively. Watch out—owning just that much is the beginning of change," were words she had recently added to her speeches.

Emma's platform had been heralded in a recent *Wall Street Journal* article as a prescription for greater personal and professional success. "What kind of goldfish are you?" the article's title asked. After briefly explaining the title, the writer quoted Emma saying, "Open your eyes to the fact that you live in water—the cultural forces around you. Some are turbulent and some lulling. The key is not to drift along but to become aware of the water. It takes effort. Put in the work, and then you can deliberately choose how you let it all affect you. Swim, goldfish, swim!"

Speaking engagements were paying well. And revenues from their training program were growing! Lacy had recently detailed how they likely no longer needed cash infusions from Sean, perhaps their most significant growth milestone yet.

...

"Relax, Emma Rose. Relax." Emma pushed deeper into the pillows and pulled the down duvet over her head. She began picking up a faint sound that grew louder until she recognized the up-and-down siren of an approaching Paris police car. With head fog building and once again fully awake, Emma rolled over, desperate for sleep.

She counted down from one thousand, got bored at eight-hundred fifty-five so switched to thinking up three-letter words for each letter in the alphabetic, committing to look up more words than "key" and "kit" that start with "k." *And what about "x?"* she wondered when she reached that point in the alphabet.

Finally, she covered her head with a pillow and fell asleep.

Chapter 4

Goldfish

The Eiffel Tower seemed so tall. "Only one-thousand seven-hundred and ten steps to the top," Emma found herself insisting to someone nearby. A disagreeable, high-pitched voice said it was exactly ten stairs taller than that. "No, twenty," the voice said shrilly.

This time, it wasn't Jake's idea, and he was nowhere to be seen. Still, she felt prodded along, so climbed. In the distance off to her right, she could see the Arc de Triomphe and then just past it was surprised to see her home in Salt Lake City, the one where she grew up, with her mother and father standing out front in snow to their knees, waving. It all seemed so normal. She wanted to reach out and hug them but smiled and waved back, compelled to keep climbing.

Until she felt hungry and lifted her hand, glad to see a croissant. She chewed on it but couldn't get a piece to tear away. Noticing she was nearing the top, she checked both armpits to see if she was sweaty. She didn't want to be sweaty for whatever was about to happen. She put on some lipstick, unsure how that had replaced the croissant in her hand, and then worried immediately that she had applied it too liberally, far beyond the outline of her lips. She searched briefly for a mirror before sucking heartily on a water bottle that turned out to be empty.

Clearing the last few stairs, she met a crowd at the top that looked expectant but said nothing. Her parents were there, of course, still standing in a small pile of snow. Emma looked around for Jake but couldn't see him. "No questions of any kind," she desperately wanted to say.

She panicked, remembering she had a speech to give so raced down the stairs, slipping on one and falling off the Eiffel Tower. While she fell, she could see an audience below her *seated in row after row of seats, all pointing at a video playing on a large screen—one of a goldfish shaking its head. She tried to shout "no," but couldn't form a sound.*

Emma woke suddenly, startled by the dream and thinking she had barely slept. Delighted that it was already eleven o'clock, she rubbed her eyes and knew it was go time. She climbed out of bed and threw open the curtains to the bustling traffic fifteen stories below. In the distance, the Eiffel Tower peeked above the morning haze.

Her heart began to race. "Don't do this," she told herself. Looking again at the Eiffel Tower, she rehearsed her third point—connect authentically. "Reach out to someone real," she whispered. Her next thought was a name that produced a landslide of emotion and memories.

Jake?

Despite efforts to suppress or even erase her memories of Paris with Jake, Emma knew calling Jake in that moment would not be her best idea. "I'm in Paris, just thinking of you," would sound heartless, even cruel. Still, something about the thought made sense. Even though they had spent a lot of time with each other in the two years they were together, Emma had never considered them an item, insisting that she was focused on launching a new business and had no time for a boyfriend.

For a while, Jake had been okay with her busyness and would hang around the office in the evenings playing video games or reading while Emma worked. They would run along the Hudson together on weekends when Emma wasn't working and occasionally meet for dinner. He'd pay most of the time, but once she started drawing a salary, she would often treat him. Best to keep things equal, she had thought at the time.

At the office one evening, he had slipped up behind her and kissed her on the cheek. "You look so cute sitting there reading whatever it is you're reading," he had said, but then one kiss had turned into quite a few more—which continued nearly every night after that. When Lacy had asked what was happening, Emma had said, "Oh, he's a great kisser and so warm!" Catching Lacy's look, Emma had said, "What? We're just having fun."

"Is that the conclusion you think he's forming?"

"For sure, he knows we just having fun."

"Don't be heartless, Emma Rose. I don't know a red-blooded person besides you that would ever think that!"

"Oh, Lacy, I can't tell you how many times I've talked with Jake about this—even while we're kissing. He knows I can't let him distract me right now." In her heart, Emma knew Jake really liked her. And she liked him, she told herself, but just needed six more months to get ahead of her business concerns. He had to know how she felt.

Even to Lacy, Jake had seemed to be going along, until about when he and Emma began planning their Paris trip. Neither had taken a vacation in a while, and Emma had finally agreed to take five days off, with two being Saturday and Sunday. And one was a holiday.

Around that time, Jake had begun asking for Lacy's advice on how to get Emma to take their relationship more seriously.

"Be careful, Jake," Lacy had warned. "She feels way too much pressure to take her foot off the gas right now. I'd read less, not more, into whatever signals she's sending."

Once tickets for Paris were purchased, he had asked Emma to dinner at Sarabeth's. When he met her dressed nicer than usual, she had begun to dread that something was up. That he had only wanted to ask about "us" and "what's next" and "would you ever want a family?" was a modest relief. She had been all business—"us" being friends, "next" being at least six more months of long days and lots of travel, and the answer to the "family" question being "of course, but not now." Even to her, Emma's answers had felt flat and insincere. What she wanted was not to have anyone ask her questions like those!

That night, it struck Emma that she was in a relationship whether she wanted to be or now. Was he someone she could be with? Perhaps, was the best answer she could give herself. She had wanted to say, "Can we park this discussion for six months?" but hadn't. *He has to know*, she had continued to tell herself.

Two weeks before Paris, Jake had stepped things up a bit—flowers a few times, bringing dinner each evening to the office, hanging around longer than usual. Emma could feel the momentum building and had really wished she'd said something before. Instead, she had found herself saying things like, "Oh, Jake. Thanks for *this* or *that*. You really didn't need to," or "That's such a sweet question. Not now" or "This article isn't going to write itself—I really need to focus here."

Before leaving for Paris, Lacy had pulled Emma aside and said, "Emma, I wouldn't be surprised if he proposed while you're there."

Emma had scoffed. "What! No way, Lacy. He has to know. I'm nowhere nearly ready for that." But she had thought about things and began to see Lacy's point—and immediately dreaded the possibility. For the entire flight, Emma had retraced her steps and most interactions with Jake, convincing herself and then doubting that he really knew where she stood. She had worried herself at the time, wondering what if he planned to pop the question.

Emma had been careful to guard herself for the first few days of their trip. They had already jogged Paris streets the first two mornings, so when he suggested that rather than use the elevator they take the 1,710 stairs to the top as part of their morning run, Emma had said, "Even better cardio! We'll really get our heart rates up," convinced that it was only a run and nothing more.

Emma remembered seeing Jake reach the bottom first, waiting there leaning against the rail and smiling as though he knew something. She had run past him, beating him up the first two flights, until Jake had raced ahead, beating her by several flights to the top. Walking the last several flights to catch her breath, Emma had finally reached the top. As she cleared the final steps, Jake had already taken a knee. At first, he seemed out of breath but hadn't been sweaty at all. She had watched him pull a small black box from the pocket of his running shorts and begin to open it.

And things had gone foggy from there. Shocked and surprised, Emma had heard the crowd of tourists immediately begin oohing, cheering, and clapping. Her senses had shut down except that she could still hear Jake asking, "Emma Rose, will you marry…?"

Technically, Emma knew she hadn't heard the full question because panic had set in. She had turned abruptly and raced back down the stairs, her shock replaced by hysterical crying as she ran. Jake hadn't caught up with her until halfway across the plaza.

Emma now wondered how things would have gone if she had simply heard him out. Or what if she had more honestly said, "That's so sweet. Not now. I'm not ready for this. Maybe later." Or something to that extent. At the time, the whole thing had been so shocking, so out of place. She insisted in her own heart that she *had* never been unclear with Jake. *He* had overstepped—well, at least misread her signals.

Only months after talking with Serena the therapist had Emma acknowledged how much courage Jake had mustered and how devastated he must have felt. Emma knew she had only protected herself at the time—not that she owed him, but that she had recently added, "connect authentically with others," to her platform brought this whole encounter resoundingly to mind. Finding the opportunity to make things right with Jake was the human thing to do. She hadn't been sure what to do or if she could even handle it, so she had waited.

...

PACING AROUND HER HOTEL ROOM and scrolling through emails in the morning light, Emma returned to the window and watched as the haze completely cleared, giving her a full view of the Eiffel Tower. She folded her arms tightly across her chest and turned away from the window, trying to put away all thoughts about her last experience there with Jake.

Checking the time, she saw she had an hour—enough time for a quick visit to the hotel gym. As she changed clothes, she contemplated how everyone had their own way of reading the world around them—"including Jake and you, Emma Rose." What had happened last time she was in Paris was no one's fault. She shook her head. "Jake, Jake, Jake." And then under her breath whispered, "Emma, Emma, Emma."

Little had been said that day or since, but Emma knew there was no way to put that relationship back together. Over a year later and after no lack of contemplation on the matter—whether to call him or not—Emma had run into him a few weeks earlier at a bagel joint and caught up briefly, finally seeing that he wasn't really her type after all. It was the first time she had apologized to him directly, sad that she had hurt him. He had hugged her awkwardly and said, "Thanks, Emma. Means a lot." He had gone on to tell her about his fiancé. Clearly, Emma hadn't been his type either. She had walked away with a sesame bagel with extra cream cheese feeling genuinely happy for him.

Walking to the bathroom, Emma caught her reflection in the full-length mirror in her room and wondered, "Just what is your type, Emma Rose?" Jake clearly hadn't been, even though their first year together had been fun. She had always wanted to marry, but the word "eventually" was always her answer whenever the question came up. Jake had only been the most recent suitor in a string of what Lacy often referred to as Emma's "far misses"—meaning, even though proposals had been made in a few cases, no one really knew the Emma she knew. Lacy had told her a "near miss" would be more like someone Emma really loved but just couldn't get past squabbles over which of them would be paying the bills or how many children they would have. A far miss was being surprised by a proposal from someone Emma thought was only a good friend.

Looking up as she brushed her teeth, she whispered, "You clearly haven't found your type," adding a sinister laugh, toothpaste foaming at the edges of her mouth. "Ha, ha, ha."

On her way to the hotel gym, Emma listened to her favorite playlist and further reflected on her dating life.

Before Jake, there was Peter, the chef. With broad shoulders, great hair, and olive complexion. Peter was an incredible foodie and always knew exactly what to order, and not order, anywhere. But he had this thing for oysters that Emma had not been able to get over. She had tried them on several occasions with a little of this or that, as he had suggested. She hadn't ever really told him how she felt about the matter and would eat no more than one, trying to keep from gagging as she swallowed. His insistence on oysters had been over the top. Out of the blue, he had given her a very hard-to-open oyster—at his place of work of all places—with a pearl ring that he had somehow slipped inside with a note that read, "Want to be exclusive?" Inside, Emma had wanted to throw it at him but instead placed aside and sat quietly while Pete waited. Her thoughts had raced—was this relationship really going anywhere? And what was next—marriage? She was traveling nearly every week at the time and particularly loved not being attached. Would this pin her down? Finally, she had excused herself with, "Probably not." Later, she had felt so clever when she told Lacy, "there was clearly no pearl in that relationship." Once again, Serena's coaching had helped Emma see how overly self-focused she had been in the relationship—that simply speaking her mind along the way in her relationship with Peter could have shaped it in oh, so many ways.

Her therapist at the time helped her see that she had room to grow. "As do we all," he had said, reassuringly. "You don't get do-overs, Emma. But you do get do-betters."

Then there was Evan, the artist. He was handsome and considerate, always letting her on the subway first, sliding a chair out for her, and doing other gentlemanly things. They had even talked about marriage—"someday, after my art is picked up by a gallery or two," he had said. She had loved everything about Evan—about her height but fit like a gymnast, and bookish in his tortoise shell glasses, fun and smart—until one day when she had asked him if he would be willing to take commissions for paintings. He had said, "As long as I can still paint whatever I want." They had argued over how he would ever make a living with that kind of attitude. She had teased that if he looked "capitalist" up in the dictionary, his name and picture would be listed there among the antonyms. When Emma had invited him to a nice restaurant one evening, he questioned how she would be able to pay for it. After quite the discussion, she had felt so frustrated and whispered loudly, "I work for money!" They had stopped seeing each other after that. He was still a starving artist as far as Emma knew.

Not exactly a do-better, Emma chalked that relationship up to worlds-apart paradigms. From her therapist at the time, she learned that she could "sweep her side of the street. But most people don't take it kindly when you try to sweep their side of the street." Emma walked away from Evan craving a relationship where there just wasn't so much sweeping to do.

After a year or so of random dates, Emma met Maxwell, the attorney. He had a strong jaw, perfect posture, and thick dark hair. He had already made partner at a small Manhattan firm focused on entertainment law. He was so fun to be with—ski trips to Vermont, sailing down the Hudson, and deep insight into every piece of art they ever saw together. After six months of dating and despite her hunches, Emma had felt herself falling in love. One day she had come across an article on prenuptial agreements and teased about why anyone would really want one. Max had said he would "never do that" but then emailed her a draft of one the next morning, "something to look over," his email had said. The thought had rocked her, causing her to stare at her computer, fidgeting and agitated. Forty-five minutes later, she had quickly composed a response, one she only later realized contained far too many capitalized words. Max had replied with "okay."

Emma's therapist had asked a profound question: "Was Max proposing a prenup agreement or simply sending an example of what they contain. Perhaps sharing, not asserting?" Emma had cried herself to sleep for several nights, drafting too many versions of an apology to Max and always deleting them since she couldn't really be sure what his intentions were. Recounting this experience to Lacy after they first met, Lacy asked another profound question: "Did you ever ask what his intentions were?" Emma had cried herself to sleep again for the next several nights.

Most recently, there had been Jake. She had met him early the day before leaving Pilot Consulting. She was the only one in the office at the time, and he had knocked on the office's main door. Carrying a package, he looked nothing like the regular couriers she saw but wore a tailored sportscoat with slim jeans and boots. His blonde hair was short and perfectly parted. She had noticed all of this immediately upon letting him in and said, "You're not really a courier, are you?" He had introduced himself as Jake, not actually a courier but a guy covering for his friend who had been in a terrible accident the day before. Jake had said he was trying to get in ten deliveries before hurrying to his agency job by nine. As he hurried out, Emma had asked him to lunch the next day. He had said yes.

Along the way with Jake, she had tried to apply all of what she had learned in previous relationships, hoping beyond all hope that things might finally feel easy—natural. Until the final two stairs on the Eiffel Tower that day, she would have sworn they were.

Why not settle down? Why all the drama? Was it them or her after all? Just mismatches or was she somehow off, wounded, or even broken?

In time, she knew—or hoped. She craved an easy relationship, one where things like timing and topics would come naturally, where opening her heart would just happen. Nodding toward an imaginary audience of former suitors in the mirror, she bowed and said, "It's clearly all me, and not you."

After thirty minutes of spinning in the hotel gym, Emma grabbed a banana and headed back to her room. After showering, she pulled a sky-blue skirt and darker blue blouse from the closet, a carefully coordinated ensemble that contrasted remarkably with her blonde hair that mirrored the color tone of the goldfish backdrop where she would be standing shortly.

Straightening her outfit and grabbing her clutch, Emma drew a deep breath and said, "Time to focus, Emma Rose. Only present thoughts from here. The time for prep is over. It's time to light this place up!"

...

HUMMING BON JOVI as she walked toward the hotel's grand ballroom, Emma felt her phone vibrate.

Bonjour, Miss Rose! Are you nearby?

It was her handler for the speech, the one who had texted her earlier that morning. With Bon Jovi on her mind, Emma texted: *Yes. We're halfway there!*

Smiling, she had barely slipped the phone into her clutch when it vibrated again. She dug the phone out and saw it was her mother.

At the ER with Dad. Can you talk? So sorry to bother you.

Emma stopped in her tracks and quickly found a chair off to one side. She sat staring at the words before looking around, thinking about the speech she had to give. With precious little time, she knew she needed to respond to her mother.

For the past several months, her father's health had grown worse. Emma worried about him. Being so far away pushed her concern to new levels. Looking at the text again, Emma calculated the time difference and concluded it had to be the middle of the night in Carlsbad. Long since retired, her parents had moved to Southern California several years earlier to escape the cold Utah winters and live where her mother had always wanted to live. Her parents had started a family late—her mother was forty and her father almost fifty when Emma was born. Single until his late forties, her father had traveled extensively before quitting that job with the specific aim of finding a wife and settling down—finally, at nearly fifty. Nine years younger, her mother "just happened to be available." That, at least, was the way they described things, always followed by an affectionate smile and kiss.

Over the past few years, Emma's father had grown progressively sicker. He would get pneumonia and then recover. The next scare would involve not being able to swallow well, which led to pneumonia, a brief hospitalization, and then home again. All roads seemed to find their way to pneumonia. The frequency of bouts had increased. His doctors would say this type of long, slow decline was really a natural part of the aging process—a general failure to thrive with nothing more specific that they could diagnose. Now in his eighties, her father wasn't getting any younger or better, and trip after trip to the emergency room and visits with specialists were generally frustrating for her mom who was still spry and in her seventies.

Since Emma had moved to Manhattan, her consulting job and now her own company had kept her so busy, making trips to Carlsbad difficult to fit in. She made it there for Thanksgiving two months earlier. "But you missed Christmas," her father had since reminded her several times, acknowledging how busy he knew she was. To compensate, they had traveled quite often to see her—three or four times over the past year. Emma made it a priority to call weekly if not more often. Despite their visits and regular calls with her parents, Emma knew she was their only child and always wanted to do better.

Talk or text? Emma fumbled with her phone, worried that calling her mother at this moment would take longer than she probably had but desperate to talk with her. She was torn between needing to know more and meeting her handler. Finally, she typed a quick response as she stood and began to walk.

I'm walking onto a stage in just a few. Stable enough that I can call in about an hour?

After hitting send, Emma worried she had sounded rude, insensitive, or at least cold. A bit jaded by so many of her father's trips to the ER, Emma worried she was forming the wrong conclusions from what little information her mother had provided. She knew her mother very likely needed Emma's support. Her mother was the type who frequently apologized for barging into Emma's busy life, so after thinking for a moment, Emma typed another line.

I'll cancel everything and get on the next plane if you need me.

Her mother responded quickly.

No need. Just more of the same. I'm sure docs will say Dad will be ok.

Her mother was the self-aware type, careful to capitalize the D in "dad" because he was Emma's father and not just any. Dots indicated her mother was still typing.

You stay focused. Do what you need to. Call when you have the award in hand!!!

Then more dots.

Proud of you!!!!

Followed by six emojis, all with some form of heart.

Emma stood to walk again, slowing a bit to type, "Kiss Dad for me," and adding a smiley face with hearts over the eyes before hitting send. She looked up with a silent plea for her parents and for a few positive vibes for herself, now worried that she would fall apart when she took the stage. Her father had to be okay. He always had been. He had been her biggest supporter throughout her life. He had coached her soccer teams when she was younger until she qualified for a more competitive team. He had encouraged her MBA and embarrassingly cheered far too long when she had received her diploma.

And on that trip to Carlsbad, her father had held her hand every morning as they walked on the beach. In her mind's eye, she could still recall how those cool mornings turned instantly hot when the sun came out with a brightness that blinded their eyes as they watched the dawn patrol surfers paddle in to make it to work on time.

On their walks, Emma had rehearsed her disappointing love life.

"You will be ready when you're ready," he had said repeatedly. "Which might involve actually finding a man who can handle you, my dear. You have a big personality."

"What does that mean? Overbearing? Crushing?"

On their walk that morning, her father had chuckled. "More like a focused ball of energy that moves a little too quickly for some people. But don't stop being you. Someday, someone will read you correctly, and it will feel entirely natural to you. Heaven knows it took me a while to find the right woman—even though I'm a more 'chill' personality," he had said, looking proudly around the southern California beach like saying 'chill' made him fit in better.

They had talked at length about how we're shaped by our upbringing—the way we think, the signals we give off, and even the way we form relationships. "Sooner than later, you'll find a reason to open your heart up to someone," he had said at the time.

At the time, she had reminded herself to listen better to her inner advisor going forward, especially in the early stages of relationships.

Picking up her pace, Emma sighed to regain her focus. Glancing at her watch, she saw she had ten minutes before her anticipated speech and quickly rehearsed her speech framework. Taking a deep breath, she turned down a hallway and was greeted by posters declaring "Breakthrough of the Year" in lights. The background design was her trademarked goldfish in water, a stunning idea Lacy had proposed and then made happen. This was the real thing. Simultaneously delighted and nervous, Emma looked around to confirm she was alone and shook her shoulders and arms like an athlete entering a big game. Her phone buzzed.

Miss Rose, are you nearby?

Emma looked up to see a woman coming out a side door holding a phone and smiling with relief.

"…hold on ready or not. You live for the fight when it's all that you've got…," Emma hummed Bon Jovi again as she nervously walked through the doorway.

Chapter 5

Homestead Claim, 1885

Before sunrise, Esther sensed her baby would come that day. She also knew Simeon planned to leave at first light, so she had him help set up a cradle of sorts—emptying the wooden box carrying her porcelain dinnerware and stacking it to one side. "Getting ready," she said without sharing her full concern. The day before, he had placed the stove near the back corner of their makeshift shelter, and Esther's preference was for the cradle to be over that way as well.

"That area over there will be shaded most of the day," Esther said, draping a shawl across her shoulders to ward off the morning chill. "And there will be warmth there for the child if the night is cool."

She gathered and rinsed her available dishcloths and towels in water from the creek, hanging them to dry on a line that stretched from their lone cottonwood to a nearby juniper.

As Esther walked with Simeon over to prepare the horses, he took her hand and asked, "Everything okay? We have a full day ahead at the—"

"—I'll be fine." Esther interrupted, trying to sound calm. Simeon had been working from sunup to sundown each day, making the most of the long summer days—leaving early each day and coming home toward dark each evening covered in dust and smelling like the sage brush he and others had been clearing from acreage up and down Willow Creek. "At least we have a comfortable spot," she said, indicating the covered area with the stove at the back. "I can boil water. I can lay in the shade. Should the baby come, I can…" She began to cry.

Not noticing, Simeon began pulling at the makeshift fence of sagebrush he had arranged as a corral for the horses. The chestnut gelding came toward him through the opening first, ready for work. Then seeing his wife wiping her tears, Simeon asked, "What's wrong? Think the baby is coming today? If so, I can be…"

Esther wiped at her tears and rubbed her enlarged midsection. "Oh, nothing. And yes, probably any day now. I just sense…" She caught herself, not wanting to worry him.

Holding reins in one hand, Simeon bent to kiss her belly, and smiled saying, "And I can ride out and tell the crew I won't be helping today if that would ease your mind. I'd be back within the hour. You know I'd do that, right? Give the word."

Esther looked up. "I just don't know when. Nothing but my sense says it's coming any day now. I'd hate to have you stay here and then have nothing come of it."

Simeon drew her close and said, "Give the word, and I'll be here."

Esther kissed his scruffy cheek and said, "You better get going. Don't want to keep those men waiting."

Simeon kissed her back and turned to gather the other horses. "Oh, and tomorrow will be our turn! We'll be at Lundquist's today, and the crew will be here tomorrow to clear our land—first thing in the morning." He grabbed the lead ropes for each. "Tack is already at Lundquist's place. And the rail," he said, tying the horses off in single file. "I better get moving."

Esther watched him leading the team of horses down the trail that led away from their place. From all the back and forth of people and horses, what had started as matted grass and broken sagebrush was beginning to look worn in.

Esther walked slowing back to the shelter, stopping at one point as a new sensation in her midsection caught her attention. She took a deep breath, and as quickly it was gone. She briefly considered yelling for Simeon but brushed the idea aside.

As the sound of the horses and her father's "Giddyaps" faded, Cassie asked, "What did Pa mean by 'our turn'?"

"The five men are working together to clear each other's land, one farm at a time," Esther said, counting them with her fingers. "They started with the Smithies, then Walkers and Hutchins, and today they will be at Lundquist's." Sticking her thumb out, she went on. "Tomorrow is our turn—the Rapps' sagebrush will become farmland. We've got to get at least a few crops planted as soon as we can."

As the predawn sky grew lighter, Esther said, "Darling, we need to talk about something important. I'm going to need your help when this baby is born." Then, with emphasis, she added, "Today."

Cassie rubbed her hands together against the cool, imagining this would mean swaddling and holding a new baby while her mother continued her chores.

Right then, the sun broke above the horizon and instantly warmed the air. Esther and Cassie busied themselves with breakfast and straightening their sleeping quarters. After cleaning up, Esther handed a pail to Cassie. "Will you get some water for the garden?"

"Can you come with me, Ma?"

"I think this is the day for you to venture back there alone. I believe it's slowed quite a bit now," she reassured Cassie.

"But Momma," Cassie protested. "I'm just…"

"Let's check it together. Take my hand," Esther said and began to hum, "'Give,' said the little stream," and Cassie joined in with the words. Walking to its bank, Cassie was relieved to see the stream was no longer raging at all.

…

CARRYING HER SECOND PAIL OF WATER FROM THE STREAM, Cassie looked over to see a yellow-breasted bird on a branch near their garden. Its long melodious call was unfamiliar. "Momma," she called. "Can you hear that bird?" Listening, she said, "There it goes again!"

"What a beautiful song!" As she waited for Cassie to fill her pail, Esther said, "I believe it's a Meadowlark. I wonder where it came from. Maybe, like us, it's scouting for a new place to call home." Walking toward the garden, Esther held her tummy as it tightened. Wincing, she said, "Maybe we've found our new home here together."

Cassie shouted, "There it goes! Oh, come back and sing your pretty song!"

Watching her daughter empty her bucket where seeds had been newly planted, Esther reached for a second pail and walked again with Cassie to the creek. On their third trip, Esther's water broke. She looked around with worry with weak hope that help was waiting behind a sagebrush or down along the willows that lined the creek. Labor pains weren't unfamiliar, but they seemed to come more frequently and stronger than previously. Her instincts told her she had precious little time to finish preparations. She dropped the bucket and dragged Cassie's cot to the back corner of the makeshift shelter near the cradle. The tarp overhead whipped up and down with the breeze, held down by ropes tied here and there.

Esther stood and stretched herself. Could this be happening? And now with only the two of them? Reaching Simeon would be impossible. The pains came more steadily and forced her to Esther. She turned calmly to Cassie. "I have a feeling this isn't going to be a regular day in any way," she said, wincing at the next contraction. "I'm especially going to need you. Will you get those towels…uh…from the line" Esther gasped as another contraction came. "It's okay if…they're a little damp…from the dew."

Cassie pulled the towels down one at a time and returned with an armful of white. The baby was coming!

Midmorning, Cassie rang water from a wet towel for her mother as she spotted Sarah coming down the trail carrying a basket. From her cot, Esther looked up, relieved to see another person, even if Sarah was barely older than Cassie.

"Momma sent these," Sarah said, puzzled at first to see Esther in bed before realizing what was happening. "Oh, you're having…how can I help? Should I run for Momma?"

Cassie smiled at Sarah, raising her eyebrows at her mother seeking direction. Esther gasped from her bed and reached urgently for the towel Cassie was holding, her fingers grabbing at the air.

With the pain retreating, Esther said, "Thank you. You can see that I'm having a baby. If you would like…to help Cassie…stoke the stove. Fill the black pot…half full and get the water heating." Relieved that another contraction was passing, Esther fell back onto the cot before gasping, "And thanks for whatever you brought."

"Only some potatoes and carrots from our root cellar—"

"Well, thanks," Esther said, looking toward the stove, unable to do much more as another contraction welled.

Cassie turned to the stove and opened the door, slipping in more twisted pieces of sagebrush. Right away, Sarah found the black pot poured in water from a nearby pail. The chimney pipe extended well above the temporary roof at the back and began belching smoke that swirled high into the morning sky.

"All right, now what?" Sarah stood there, rubbing her hands together.

Esther propped herself up on one elbow and pointed away from the camp with her free hand. Her eyes wore an anxious look. The girls stood waiting.

"Sarah…?"

Sarah looked up at Esther's worried eyes.

"Sarah…dear, will you be a good girl…and run get your mother?"

Sarah hesitated.

"I'm going to need…her real soon. Real soon." Esther could no longer hide the concern building inside her even though the Walkers were less than a mile away.

Without a word, Sarah turned and ran, her long dress swishing as she raced up the trail.

As the next contraction came, Esther said, "This baby may not wait—"

Cassie stood nervously, watching her mother, wringing her hands.

Breathing as the pain passed, Esther relaxed and said, "This is a far cry from home—our old home—with a midwife only four houses away." Reflecting for a moment, she added, "You came slowly but it wasn't hard. The last two came too quickly. Too quickly." Looking around, she bit her lip as the next contraction came.

…

ESTHER FELL BACK ON THE COT TO REST. She glanced down their narrow trail leading out through the sage to where the Walkers lived, hoping for a sign of Mary or Sarah returning.

"A miracle would be nice about now," she said, laughing as she wiped sweat from her upper lip and forehead.

Cassie busied herself breaking wood and checking the pot. "It's boiling," she announced. "But there's not much left."

"Pour more in from the bucket." Esther waited for Cassie to finish before asking, "Cassie, can you come help me get that…board…up behind me?"

Cassie lifted the board her mother had pointed to, looking expectantly as Esther helped position the board against a pole at the back of the bed. Esther pulled herself up and leaned back against it.

"Now, help me with…these bed clothes." Esther fidgeted with her gown, and Cassie moved to quickly rearrange her mother's gown and the blankets around her.

"Does it hurt?"

"In a good way, dearest. In a good way," Esther said, breathing in and out through pursed lips. Esther's breathing was growing shallower. She felt the urge to push but panicked at what Cassie would do with a baby and all that followed.

Yet, this was the frontier, after all. She could hear Simeon saying, "When you live on the frontier, you make do." Of course, they faced challenges, but she always considered his words to apply to injured cattle or finding wood for fences. They had already made do in so many ways—a shelter with a functioning stove. A planted garden with seeds already sprouting. A pen for the horses made from a wall of broken sagebrush.

Until now, she couldn't see how it applied at all to bringing children into this world. But with neither Sarah or her mother in sight, Esther gathered her wits and took stock. "Cassie, when this baby comes, you'll need to…take good hold of the baby…first by the head…and then carefully by one leg….and carry it carefully there," she said, pointing to a flat surface made with boxes near the stove." Worried she might pass out or be unable to direct, Esther continued, "Then wet the towels…and clean the baby…" The pain was becoming unbearable. Esther's head was spinning. "Actually, first, see the scissors…over there. Before you clean the baby…there will be…a cord coming from the baby's…belly. You will need to…"

She was interrupted by a shout from the trail.

"Hello the camp!" Mary Walker drove a small wagon toward the shelter and climbed out with Sarah at her side. She carried a small black bag. "We're here, Esther! And so is my frontier medicine bag," she pronounced as she took charge of the situation. "You never know what to expect out here."

Esther fell back momentarily into her cot, relieved that another woman was present, and glad it was Mary. Mary seemed to know exactly what to do. Both Sarah and Cassie watched closely and followed instructions exactly. "You two make a great team for two eight-year-olds," Mary exclaimed.

"I won't be eight for two weeks," Cassie corrected.

Mary smiled. "Well, all right, but you're both very young and smart in all the right ways!"

Esther groaned from her cot. "I want to…push!" as another contraction took her breath away.

"Go ahead, my dear," Mary said, busying herself. "Let's get this baby here."

Esther smiled, then began to cry as she bore down. Within minutes, a baby boy was born. Moments later, Mary handed a cleaned up, swaddled, and crying baby boy to his mother.

Exhausted, Esther cuddled her new son. She stroked his full head of dark hair, saying, "Sweet Eugene, just like your papa."

Sarah and Cassie whispered off to the side about how amazed they were at what they had just witnessed. When Esther invited them to hold Eugene, they sat together and gently gazed at him.

"His face is so tiny and perfect," Cassie whispered.

Sarah responded, "He smells so sweet!"

Late that afternoon, Simeon raced down the trail bareback on his chestnut horse, clouds of dust rising behind them. He dropped the reins as he jumped off and ran straight to Esther. "I have a boy!" he said, kneeling before his wife. "I so wanted to be here. The duns ran off—Mary came by with the news, but I didn't hear about it till we got the horses up back to where we were working. I came right away."

Esther looked up with an understanding but tired smile. "I want to call him Eugene."

Simeon reached for his baby boy, beaming. "Eugene it is."

...

AFTER DARK, CASSIE RETRIEVED HER JOURNAL from the wagon box and sat to write by the soft firelight coming from the oven's open door. The graphite tip of her pencil had worn down, so she took a paring knife and whittled it to a point.

> *Today was a really long day. Willow Creek has calmed down—it's hard to imagine anyone drowning in it now. And Momma had a baby boy today. I was so scared to help and thought I would be on my own. But Sarah ran for her momma and came back with her bag with all the right things. Sarah's momma knew what to do. Momma cried a lot, and I said a prayer that she would be okay. I thought she might die. I didn't know.*
>
> *I now have a little brother. Eugene. I want to show him all around our new home. Well, it's not a home yet. Just a tarp and Momma's stove. But I have a baby brother now, and I plan to give thanks for him when I go to bed.*

Cassie chewed at the end of the pencil and felt the warmth coming from the stove's crackling fire push away the cool at her back. Crickets chirping and the gurgle of Willow Creek out in the dark made her smile. She wrote a final line before adding a period with a bit of a flair.

I love this place.

Chapter 6

Rapp Homestead, 1885

Early the next morning, Cassie watched a group of men, boys, and animals coming briskly up the rough trail toward their property, silhouetted by the morning sun at their backs. The dust they stirred up created a dramatic halo and turned the whole scene yellow and brown. When they were closer, she could make out six men in hats, three teams of horses, with four boys off to one side. The boys stumbled a bit as they ran alongside, stopping to kick now and then and swinging sticks they must have picked up along the way.

Her father left the horses he was harnessing and hurried out to meet the group with a loud, "Yahoo!" Cassie could see them eagerly shaking hands and hear backslaps as they greeted each other.

This was the day for clearing sagebrush from their land. Their turn. Cassie walked out toward the group and immediately recognized Sarah's brothers Erastus and Samuel among the group of boys, all standing nervously with their hands in their pockets and each kicking at the ground as though an assignment had been given to do so. She didn't recognize two of the boys.

Will Walker hugged Cassie and looked over toward the Rapps' makeshift shelter. "How's your mother and your new little brother?"

"Just fine, I believe." Cassie said politely, straightening her apron. She looked around expectantly, hoping Sarah would emerge from the group.

Shading his eyes, Will looked toward the dark area under the tarp and could barely make out Esther sitting there holding the new baby. Waving, he said, "Morning, Esther! Well done on that new son! How are you feeling today?"

"Just fine, Will. The baby is healthy, and so I'll be just fine," she said sounding relieved. "Thank goodness for Mary. I couldn't have done this without her…well…"

The horses snorted and stamped, reminding Will they were ready for work. "I better get back over there."

From near his own horses, Simeon yelled, "Let's get going!"

Will shouted back as he walked, "I brought the rail back—over this way."

Cassie came back into the shelter, smoothing the baby's hair with her hand. "Momma, what's it going to look like without sagebrush?"

"Wide open is my guess," Esther said. "One big wide-open space."

Throughout the morning, Cassie followed her mother's directions in preparing dinner for the men. Feeding the workers was an unspoken expectation when it came to helping another landowner for a half day or more, and a courtesy any other time. While giving instructions, Esther held Eugene when he wasn't sleeping or nursing and otherwise rested. Cassie knew to keep the stove stoked and worried about the smoke wafting down into the shelter occasionally and making her mother cough. She found herself worrying about the baby. And then worrying about dinner.

Esther talked Cassie through rolling out the dough and then lining the pans for meat pies. Her father had purchased a large beef roast from a neighbor the evening before, and she had already helped cut it into chunks and had it boiling in a pot on the front corner of the stove. At the appropriate time, Cassie scooped out chunks and spread them in the lined pans. She then poured in a sauce from another pan before topping each dish with more dough and putting it in the oven. As a final step, she cut up vegetables from the basket Sarah had brought over the day before and placed them in a large pot.

Simeon checked in toward noon. He pulled back the cloth covering his new son's tiny head to give him a kiss, followed by a kiss on his wife's forehead. "And how are you feeling now? How's Eugene?"

"We're doing fine," Esther smiled up at him. "But you're so dusty. Get back out there! No one wants a loafer."

Before leaving, Simeon asked Cassie, "How's dinner coming?"

Cassie looked up with pride. "Dinner is going to be tasty!"

Simeon gave a casual wave with his hat before putting it back on and trotting back toward the dusty work area, kicking up his own trail of dust as he moved.

Now that everything was baking, Cassie walked out of the shelter and watched as the open space in front of their homesite grew. The men periodically pulled their hats down low over their eyes and repositioned some red and some blue wet bandanas worn over their mouths and noses to fight the dust. Occasionally, one would walk over to the stream, shaking out his bandana before dipping it in water, squeezing the water out and then tying it again over his face. She watched as one-horse team was traded for another to work the long railroad rail. The horses sweated profusely as they dragged the rail across the land, while the resting teams happily munched oats, oblivious to the work ahead for them.

Throughout the morning, Cassie could hear the "Come alongs" and "Whoas" of the men as the horse teams grunted and dragged the rail, tearing at the sagebrush. The breeze whirled the dust, shifting it at times to give momentary views of progress. The four boys were put to work, laughing and coughing at the dust as they dragged the broken pieces of sage and threw them onto quickly growing piles.

The breeze shifted and blew dust her way, and Cassie could smell pungent sage mixed with the dust stirred by the men at work. When the dust settled or blew away from her, she could see the men had already cleared a full acre or possibly two. She was surprised to see the horizon expanding with a few more trees now visible off in the distance, possibly marking where other neighbors had settled.

Shortly after midday, the men tied the horses off near the creek, where they drank deeply and began munching the tall grass that grew along its banks. Covered with dust, the men walked toward the shelter for dinner. Each in turn removed his hat and washed his face and hands from the pail she had filled. Mostly free of dust, their tan faces and dripping gray, brown, black, and red beards were striking against the white of their foreheads or any area that had been covered by their hats. Hats off, the men looked very different. She wondered why some like her father sported a full head of hair while others were bald or extra white on top with a fringe of red or brown around the sides. She noticed Will Walker's thick hair was graying evenly along with his beard.

As the men approached the table, Cassie heard them say, "Thank you, Mrs. Rapp" and "Looks delicious" with a nod toward Esther before taking a plate.

Esther said, "It's all been Cassie's hard work."

The group turned and simultaneously said, "Thank you, Miss Rapp."

The boys waited awkwardly to the side until urged by their fathers to come eat. Sarah's brothers Erastus and Samuel came forward first, and Cassie heard "Timothy" and "Philip" as the other boys were beckoned.

The group served themselves from the large bowl of potatoes mixed with carrots and took portions from the piping hot meat pies. Esther had Cassie pour cups of water for the men from another bucket.

Some of the men sat on the ground, leaning back against the wagon box, while there was room for four or so on a log Simeon had found one day along the creek and pulled over with his horses. They seemed to focus on eating at first and then almost at once began talking about their work, how one horse pulled better than the rest, how the boys were playing more than working, and how delicious the food was.

Cassie joined her mother at the back of the shelter.

"You did so very well." Esther handed Cassie the baby and said in a whisper, "I don't know how this would have happened without you!"

The group quieted as Esther stood up slowly and began to offer seconds to the men.

"Thank you, Mrs. Rapp."

"Don't mind if I do."

"Congratulations on having a son!"

"My pleasure, and thank you," Esther said. Simeon smiled as she walked stiffly among the men. He raised up from his seat to catch Cassie's attention and winked her way as she rocked the baby.

One of the men spoke up. "A couple days ago, I got that line running out of the creek on the north end of my property. Well, the cleared section, that is. The line was clean and delivered water straight to the head of the rows we'd planted." Chuckling, he paused momentarily and then added, "Next morning, sure enough, the banks had washed out in one spot and flooded the whole darn place. Took the corn *and* the wheat. All gone." He began chuckling.

Another asked, "Why are you laughing, Hutchins?"

The one named Hutchins began to laugh heartily, almost unable to contain himself. "Well, Frank, I can see it now—a pile of corn and wheat all growing down in one small corner along the south end of the field where it all collected..." His face began turning red from laughing as he tried to finish his story. "...but not at all where you wanted it to grow." Hutchins wiped at his eyes.

The men laughed along, half-heartedly as though they'd experienced the same thing or knew they might soon.

Hutchins recovered a bit and scratched his head as he continued. "About half my potatoes were staring straight up at the morning sun the day after we planted last week. For the same reason—washed over, but not quite washed away. Louisa and the girls covered them back over with dirt while I got the banks patched back up." He wiped his mouth with the back of his hand and wiped his eyes again before taking another bite. "Happens to the best of us," he added.

A chorus of "sure does" and "I'll be" could be heard from the other men.

Simeon asked with a big smile, "So Bert, are you saying you're the best of us?"

Hutchins looked surprised before realizing what he had said. His cheeks turned red as he searched for something to say in response. The group erupted in laughter.

Hutchins held up a hand as he tried to contain himself and now said more seriously, "That's right. We had a couple of acres of mud day before yesterday, but once the mud dried out a bit, it was far superior to the dusty dirt I'd started with. Once it takes water, it's almost clay-like and holds water well. Doesn't dry too quickly but does dry in time."

One of the men reached down and dug at the dirt with his knife. He said, "This dirt is like flour—like it's never even seen rain. It downright defies water at first. Dusty and fluffy. But give it a good soak and it sets up real nice."

Cassie looked down at the soft dirt forming the floor of their shelter. Experimenting, she tipped some water from her cup, and it sat on top of the dust for a moment before suddenly disappearing into the soil. She stirred at it with a stick to make a small ball of mud. As she stirred, the ball took on more dust before breaking into pieces. With a few more stirs, it blended back into the dust around it.

Hutchins said, "I'll tell you what I'll do next time. And this goes for you, young Simeon." He looked directly at Simeon. "I'll run water first for a few days. Make sure the ditch banks hold. Then let it dry for a day or two. And then plant." Shaking his head, he added, "Consider that free advice."

The other men nodded.

"We replanted the corn day before yesterday," the man named Frank said. "Hope it still takes. I still didn't sleep a wink last night but turned the water out about dusk. I walked the ditch all night. I'd hear that trickle and get spooked, thinking the banks were breaking all over again. Right about when I could hear birdsong this morning, I turned the water downstream and crawled under a blanket for an hour before coming here."

...

CASSIE WALKED OVER TO THE CREEK where the four boys were playing. "What are you doing?"

Erastus shrugged his shoulders and spoke for the group. "Throwing sticks. Hey, this is my sister's friend Cassie." The two named Timothy and Philip looked up, but Samuel only poked at something with a stick.

Philip said, "We don't want to play with no girls."

"She's fine," Erastus said, giving him a look. "Want a stick?"

Wondering why his approach from a few days earlier had changed, Cassie said, "Yes, please. Thanks."

They all tossed sticks in the creek and watched them float away. Not much was said. After a bit, Timothy said, "Let's have a race." The boys seemed to know what was meant and each got another small stick.

"Mine's the one with loose bark," Erastus said.

Cassie picked up a twig with a green leaf on one end.

One boy yelled, "Go!" and they each tossed their sticks into the stream then looked at Cassie, expecting her to do the same. She tossed her stick, and the boys ran downstream, following their floating sticks.

"Whoever's reaches the rock first wins," Timothy shouted.

Philip declared his stick the victor until Cassie retrieved hers with the leaf from a bit further downstream. "I think the leaf made a difference," she said, and the boys got busy looking for new sticks with leaves.

Erastus looked over at Cassie with a smile. "Sarah said you were smart," he said.

Cassie felt her cheeks redden.

A few minutes later, one of the men whistled the boys back to work. After helping clean up dinner, Cassie asked if she could help with the clearing and then joined the group. She worked alongside Erastus and Samuel picking up pieces of sagebrush and tossing them onto one of several large piles.

With something on his mind, Samuel turned to Cassie and asked, "Why don't you have a house?"

Erastus elbowed him. "They just got here, silly. Don't you remember?"

Samuel nodded but still asked, "Why do you only have a tent?"

"That's the same question!" Erastus said.

Cassie smiled. Not much else was said.

Before the crew left late that afternoon, the land almost resembled a workable field except for several large piles of sagebrush. Simeon remained hard at work along the far edge of the field with the team of duns and a scraper borrowing dirt from the flat ground to make banks for a ditch until nearly sunset.

...

AFTER PUTTING THE HORSES AWAY in the sage-enclosed corral, Simeon repositioned a few of the straighter pieces of sage for the gate, beat at his shirt and pants to shake some of the dust loose, and walked out to one of the loose piles of brush.

Esther lifted baby Eugene into her arms and walked slowly with Cassie out to meet him.

Cassie asked, "Are you all right, Momma?"

Esther held her free hand to her back and said, "I'm fine. Just another day on the frontier!"

Simeon greeted the two, kissing each on the forehead. "What an incredible day," he said exultingly. "Look what we have accomplished!" He swept his hand across the cleared area, now spotted by several large piles of sagebrush. "We couldn't have done this without you two women," he said, catching Cassie's attention. "That's right, Cassie. After what you did today with the dinner and yesterday helping with little Eugene, you're growing up something fine."

As if on signal, other folks began coming up the trail to gather—men, women, and children. Cassie recognized Timothy and Philip from their work that day returning with their families. Then the Walkers came with Sarah waving eagerly from her perch in front of Erastus, both bareback on a horse, their faces lit by the setting sun off to the west. Samuel walked alongside his father.

Cassie waved in return, wondering why so many visitors.

"Oh, how wonderful!" Esther said. Turning to Cassie, she said, "We haven't been able to go out and help the others like this because I was so close with Eugene. I guess it's a local tradition on days like this." Changing the subject, she said enthusiastically, "And ours on such an auspicious day."

Cassie looked up, curious.

Esther studied her family expectantly. "It's June 21st! That makes it...?"

Simeon smiled and shrugged. "Wednesday...?"

Esther bumped him with her elbow, careful not to disturb the sleeping baby in her arms. "It's summer solstice! Remember?"

Remembering a lesson on the days getting longer and the nights shorter, Cassie exclaimed, "Oh, that's right—it's the longest day of the year, right?"

"Correct. You are the prize pupil!" Esther smiled sideways at Erastus before giving Cassie a kiss on top of her head. "Now go gather sticks."

Their new neighbors set about gathering the remaining loose brush and chopping at roots with axes and shovels to free any pieces still attached, occasionally stumbling over unseen clumps. All chatted as the piles grew bigger, taking advantage of the opportunity to be with each other, arms shielding their eyes as gusts of wind whipped the recently liberated dust into the air around them.

The sky above stayed blue until very late that night. Finally, after a very long day, the sun set in the hills far to the west, turning a light pink and then a deep orange.

Simeon invited the group to gather near the largest of the piles and began to speak. "Let me express my gratitude to you all," he said with a little emotion. "And to my very strong wife who delivered a son in the middle of it all—just yesterday!"

The group looked Esther's way and cheered loudly.

Cassie watched as her father took a match to the first pile. The sage began burning quickly, sending great puffs of sparks into the darkening sky overhead. Within moments, it was the biggest fire she had ever seen.

The sudden heat forced everyone to take a few steps back, the glow on their faces the hue of the thick line of orange sky to the west.

"We call this 'a bonfire,'" Esther told Cassie in a teaching tone.

"Bonfire," Cassie mused. She watched others light the remaining piles and could hear the laughter of neighbors as other bonfires burned.

Several women gathered around Esther, introducing themselves and welcoming her to the area, and oohing over baby Eugene before returning to their families.

Simeon walked over and reached for the baby.

Esther teased, "Aren't you a little too dirty?"

He smiled and gave her a quick kiss. "I would like to hold my new son."

Esther passed him the baby and drew her shawl tighter. Simeon pulled her close with his free arm. Cassie joined them in a hug. Simeon's eyes scanned the wide space in front of them. "Centuries of sagebrush now replaced with a couple acres of progress! And our first child born in this country!" He smiled down at baby Eugene.

The neighbors stayed until only embers remained before walking back down the dusty trail away from the Rapps' property toward a maze of trails that took them to their homes.

Chapter 7

Another Side of the World

With a standing ovation still thundering in her ears and the weight of a crystal award in her hands, Emma hurried to find a quiet place where she could collapse before calling her parents. The audience had clearly approved of her speech even though Emma had forgotten a key story and been off with her jokes. She couldn't remember feeling this off in quite a while. At one point, she had even paused, looking around for a drink while people in the audience whispered, wondering if she was okay.

Glad it was all over, she now had twenty minutes before a private afternoon reception with Sean McKilroy and his team. And then a flight to catch. Finding a small meeting room, Emma closed the door behind her. The signal seemed strong enough, and once a video connection was made, Emma's focus quickly shifted to her parents. She felt a load of anxiety as she said, "Hi, Mom. So please catch me up."

Emma's mother appeared calm as usual, but Emma sensed something was different. Her mother moved over to sit at her father's hospital bedside, and her father tried to muster more than a nod but looked exhausted. "Oh, hi, Dad," Emma said, tears welling instantly in her eyes. She had never seen her father like this.

Her mother said, "He's not doing well. It's probably pneumonia again. They're running some tests," the strain in her eyes saying more than her words.

Her father gathered his strength and leaned toward the camera. With a weak smile, he muttered, "It's just old age, Emma."

She smiled but could see her mother scowling as her father rested into his pillow. Emma had lived her entire life with parents older than those of her friends—their late start getting married and having a child was mostly obvious with an occasional, "Are these your grandparents?" "The best of both worlds," Emma always said. They had always felt just the right age to her.

In answering her mother, Emma wanted to be encouraging. "Oh, you two are still so vibrant—you're spring chickens!"

Emma's mother smiled uncomfortably before inserting, "Well, anyway, they will do some tests today, but say they can't do a few until tomorrow for some reason. I'm sure we will hear the same thing we've been hearing. Nothing new or any clearer. It's a mystery with no answer." She sounded defeated.

Emma could see how much this was taxing them both, the feeling welling within her that she needed to get to San Diego sooner than later. She made an immediate decision. "Mom and Dad, I head back to Manhattan in a few hours and will catch the first flight to San Diego in the morning," she committed. Both parents brightened at the news.

After talking logistics for a minute, her mother changed the subject and said, "Now, let's talk about you." Emma could see her father once more trying to lean forward but was unable to lift himself from the pillow. Emma answered several questions, urged on by occasional raised eyebrows and smiles from her father. He looked especially encouraged by how well things were going for Emma. He motioned for his reading glasses and the phone to be held closer so he could better see the two-foot award when Emma showed it, blushing as she waved her hand over it like she was introducing it on *The Price is Right*.

"You won't be able to fit that in your carry-on bag," her mother commented, sounding worried and amused at the same time. They all laughed. Her father's soft chuckle was followed by a coughing fit. "No more laughing, honey," Emma's mother urged as she helped resettle him in his pillow and wiped the corner of his mouth with a tissue. Despite all this movement, her mother held the phone reasonably stable with one hand, doing all of what she did with her free hand.

"I'll get it home somehow," Emma said, wondering momentarily just how she would get it across the ocean without it getting banged up. "Don't you worry," she added, immediately worrying. She had a quick vision of chipped crystal on her bookshelf at home and resolved to find some way to protect the award on her flight.

Her father struggled to clear his throat. He looked at the phone and then up toward his wife like he was preparing to say something, and for her to get ready with tissues since it might not go so well. In barely more than a whisper, he began, "When you get here…I want you to drive me…somewhere…" He coughed weakly once and looked off to the side, waiting for a few seconds for the urge to diminish. "…road trip north," he added, gesturing toward the window of his hospital room.

Emma said, "That would be nice, Dad. Let's do that. I'll have Lacy block out a few days as soon as possible." She had a sinking feeling about the whole idea.

Her father wanted to say more and tried to sit up, speaking louder and more urgently this time. "We need to do this. I have…a place I want to show you" before falling back into his pillow, coughing and exhausted.

…

EMMA'S FATHER HAD ALWAYS BEEN VAGUE about their trip plans—trips the two of them had taken together throughout her teenage years but not since she had moved to Manhattan. They had taken numerous drives to see little towns, historical plaques, ancient rock art, and off-the-beaten path waterfalls. Most held special meaning for him. She remembered those trips with fondness even though she always complained that the cell service was mostly spotty. And she had often felt sensory deprived in other ways—no shopping except for funny t-shirts and all-things camo at gas station convenience stores, craft stores, pawn shops, and dollar-only stores that popped up in the oddest places. They had stayed at roadside hotels—seeking out those with a hot tub whenever they could find one.

As she had grown older, Emma had become more resistant to trips with her father, protesting that she already had plans with friends or a football game to attend or "haven't we already been there?" Eventually, her string of "social commitments," as her father had called them, really got in the way. But even then, her father generally won out, and she recalled missing not just a few school and church activities to join him on one more drive.

Whenever she had probed and pried about their intended destination, his generally tight-lipped "out there" was often the best she got, tracking his arm pointing randomly east or west. Living in the Salt Lake City area, "out there" in any direction was either mountains or desert.

But school, church, and friends all came and went, while her memories of time with her father were cherished. And in time, she had become acquainted with parts of the state that most of her peers had never heard of let alone been to—Nine-Mile Canyon, the Pony Express trail and stations, Dead Horse Point, Butterfly Lake, the geode beds, Fifth Water, Horseshoe Bend, the Rochester Panel, the Nebo loop, and his favorite little towns of Tabiona, Mount Pleasant, and Helper, to name a few.

Emma had generally enjoyed the trips—likely because of the bad cell service, she only later realized. She now recalled with fondness the licorice of any color, vintage sodas, and long talks while they drove. She had hundreds of photos from the most obscure places. They had truly enjoyed adventure and made memories around every bend.

When she had visited the past Thanksgiving, her father had confessed that he had always prepared a big list of questions for her in anticipation of these drives, and how he had found driving together to be the best way to get her talking. "My kind of 'social lubricant,'" he had said. "I never wanted you to feel like I was interviewing you. I mainly wanted to hear how you thought." His list hadn't been all that long but had been thorough. He had said, "I wanted to know how you put your thoughts together about school, boys, friends, makeup, fashions, what you believed, religion. Or topics like bullying, evolution, God, and your college plans. Basically, everything in your life."

"I knew," Emma had said, even though she had been mostly grateful her father had wanted to get to know her.

At the time, her mother had sent a knowing smile Emma's way, indicating she had been in on these plans all along. His signature wink affirmed the fact that he was truly interested in her. And because of all their time together and his authentic questions and listening ear, she had grown to trust that she could talk to him about anything.

It was on one of these drives that she had acquired the first two of her four tenets. She could now only recall ever hearing her father talk about "doing the deep work," which for him meant working out whatever issues you have so you could live life as authentically as possible. He had also regularly used another line—"listen to your inner advisor"—when Emma had asked questions about boys, school, fashion, or whatever. The other two—connecting authentically and staying awake to the cultural forces in your life—had come much later from, one from her therapist Serena and the other a class at Columbia. After validating all of this with extensive research, she still regularly gave him credit for starting it all, for providing what she considered her guiding lights.

...

THE COUGHING FIT OVER, her father beckoned for her mother to bring the phone closer. He said with a weak smile, "Let's take that trip…and this time…no agenda." His eyes searched as though he could find Emma in the camera somehow.

Emma wiped at her eyes. "Just hang in there, Dad. I'll be there on the first flight tomorrow, and then we will make this trip happen."

He smiled and seemed to rest his head. "I love you, sweetie. See you in the morning!"

After hanging up, Emma stared blankly at the wall for a few minutes before breaking down. Shudders at first turned to a steady stream of tears. For the first time ever, she felt she might lose him. He had never looked so fragile, so frail. And here she was, literally on the other side of the world, over-gripping a crystal award that suddenly meant so little in the grand scheme of things.

Emma's handler peeked into the room. Surprised, Emma hurriedly wiped away the tears.

"So sorry. Is everything all right, Miss Rose?"

Her makeup smeared, Emma collected herself and said, "Yes. Just a family matter. A situation that just is." She stood and smoothed her skirt over. She could hear her father saying, "It just *is*," over and over—his well-worn phrase she had tried to adopt in all aspects of her life. "Accept what *is*, love what *is*, work with what *is*, and don't let what *is* keep you from growing." His words, not hers. Her heart protested.

Emma looked up at the woman and asked, "What do you do when you don't like what *is*?"

The woman returned a puzzled look.

Emma quickly apologized and wiped her eyes once more and asked for directions to the restroom so she could fix her makeup. As she walked, she could almost hear her father's answer. He would repeat the first part. "You can't change the past and you can only hope to influence the future, so accept what *is*. String a hammock between the words *over* and *next* and sit in it. That's what *is*. Begin working from there."

The notion, however wise, did not make situations like this any easier. Despite wanting to be somewhere else, Emma knew she had one more obligation before catching her flight home. That was what *is*. Both the obligation and the flight across the Atlantic were inconvenient facts. Not to mention the flight the next day across the country. Only then could she see her father again. Emma silently prayed, trying to get comfortable in the moment but aching to make it in time for whatever came next.

...

AT THE AFTERNOON RECEPTION, Sean suggested Emma really consider writing a book called, "Staring Down Culture," and offered to introduce her to his agent. "You really have to do this," he said.

While Emma knew that writing a book sort of came with the territory of running a business like hers, she had imagined up to this point that she would write one someday—just not so soon. Nothing over the past few weeks except this new award would have pointed to now as the time to start. Regardless, she hadn't really given what it would take much thought, which became clear when she asked, "Agent?"

Characteristically, Sean didn't let up. "It's easy! You probably have at least fifty thousand words in you on the subject, right? Write it all down—or simply transcribe your speech from today as your starting point—and you'll have a book! From there, it's your agent who will take you into orbit!"

While Emma felt encouraged by Sean, she had the odd sensation that she was now standing on the edge of a cliff and being told to jump—but in a tone that suggested, "Don't worry. It's not that hard."

She zoned out a bit as Sean began explaining how a book agent could negotiate with multiple publishers at a time—something she couldn't do on her own—and get Emma the best deal, a possible advance of fifty to a hundred thousand dollars and ensure her book would get the best marketing possible. She recalled from past discussions with other authors how an agent makes the deal while the publisher prints the money, meaning the book.

Sean's enthusiasm was irrepressible, which motivated a few questions from Emma—questions she quickly realized sounded more premeditated than they really were. "Will your agent find me a publisher who is more of a promoter than printer? If I were to write a book, will it show up on airport bookstore shelves? How do they get the word out? Or will my book just sit in boxes in a warehouse somewhere waiting for a miracle?"

"Hold on, Rose," he said, holding up a hand and chuckling. "Good questions, but you'll have to ask your agent. I'm just the middleman here." His trademark deep laugh warmed Emma's heart. "Mine has been good to me, but then we really have the Pilot clientele to thank for making us a *New York Times* bestseller."

The word "clientele" caught her attention. Emma asked, "Your clients made you a bestseller?"

Sean spent the next ten minutes talking about what it took for his book to become a bestseller, whether you could "wire" or manipulate that, and how others played the game so well. "It's like anything else," he said. "Relevance doesn't always mean instant popularity. Having something to say is a good start. Whoever you work with will want to know what you bring to the table. Not merely fifty thousand words. They will ask you a bunch of questions that have little to do with what you have written. Questions like, What's your platform? How many social media followers do you have? Who else do you have in place—like clients or associations—that will buy your book? How many email addresses do you have in your database? As someone explained it to me, it takes ten to fifteen thousand books in the first week to make the *New York Times* bestseller list, so start thinking about how you can sell that many!"

Independent of the effort writing a book would take, selling even a thousand books that first week seemed hard. Emma smiled at the vision that instantly formed in her mind of inviting her New York friends and their friends to her tiny apartment for cheese and crackers with her awkwardly pushing her book at them. Could she even sell ten to twenty books? She smiled at the thought.

"Getting on the *New York Times* bestseller list can be life changing. It was for me," he added. "It's like an instant PhD from the court of public opinion. The credibility you gain is enormous. Not that I was lacking," he joked.

First things first. She began running some numbers in her mind. Sean had suggested she transcribe her speech. Quickly doing the math, she calculated that her "Staring Down Culture" speech was thirty to sixty minutes long, but even if she spoke three hundred words a minute, that would leave her with eighteen to twenty thousand words at best. Sure, she had written a few articles, but the online magazines she had recently written for had limited her articles to three thousand words—less and not more.

Write fifty thousand words? She knew she could talk a lot but wondered how she would ever come up with that much to say.

The thought simultaneously intrigued her and scared her.

...

ON THE FLIGHT HOME, Emma began thinking about her parents—especially her father—and felt helpless at thirty-thousand feet. Needing a diversion, she opened her laptop and began framing up an article, testing her ability to come up with new material. She had been contemplating the idea that there are layers of culture and how each layer can keep us from really knowing ourselves—sort of the gateway to her four tenets. She began jotting down her thoughts.

If you don't know where you came from, your family background and even the effects of birth order or your parents' parenting style, how can you begin to do the deep work? The first layer of culture is addressed by answering the question, "What brought me to this point in my life?" A few supporting questions include,

- *What makes me who I am?*
- *What's my family background, religious upbringing, and educational background?*
- *What kind of people are in my social circles? Who are my friends? Who influences me the most?*
- *What are my ambitions in life? How have those changed over time? What have I achieved?*

Then, courageously write down how you feel about each of your answers. With this as the baseline, ask yourself, What is it that I really want? What would it take to get there?

Culturally speaking, you're beginning to do the deep work.

Closing her laptop, Emma reflected on how she would answer these questions now, imagining her answers hadn't changed all that much from when she had first written about this topic a few years earlier. Raised by older parents with strong Utah roots. From pioneer stock that had come west and settled in the Salt Lake area. Religion had been a big part of life, but more of a social "go to church" thing than deep conviction. She had met most of her extended family on both sides—all very likable people. She knew her father's side better than her mother's, since her mother's siblings lived mostly in Southern California. Her own friends were typical—mostly from upper middle-class households with similar habits, clothing, likes and dislikes, and all taking similar vacations. She liked 80's music. She came alive in college as she discovered deeper learning and had now completed two college degrees. She had always wanted a big city experience and moved to Manhattan after college when she took the job with Pilot. She had never been great with boys or men—perhaps her tight relationship with her own father stood in the way of that, something she wondered about from time to time. She had become very entrepreneurial, a recent shift. She was now exploring the idea of writing a book. All things she felt she clearly understood about herself.

She had an insecure side, where she over-worried she was just posing as someone successful. That had been a constant for her. One of her recent therapists had suggested she develop "healthy ego." "List what you're good at," he had suggested. "What can you own that makes you who you are?"

At first, she had struggled with the assignment but eventually come up with a few things—writing well, speaking well, attracting clients, growing a business, perhaps not pretty but put together. "I guess I kind of know the water I swim in," she had thought at the time before worrying she was still a poser. She had wadded the paper up and tossed it away.

Reclining her seat, Emma took a deep breath and repeated something her parents had frequently said to her. "You're a Rose with very few thorns." She whispered that to herself, knowing her life had been very straightforward to this point, confident she could at least own this point before beginning to wonder about the thorns.

She shook her head and felt a wave of exhaustion. She reclined her seat and drifted off to sleep, surprised when she woke up two hours had passed. Her immediate thought was that she hadn't yet booked a flight to California for the next morning. Grateful for the in-flight internet connection, she booked the first flight out of JFK the next morning.

With the mounting stress seeing her father as soon as possible, her time in Paris already felt like a distant memory. She desperately wanted to call him, to simply connect. He had always been there for her, something she now felt slipping away.

"What can I get you?"

Emma looked up to see a flight attendant in a bright red jacket. She wanted to say, "Get me to southern California…" but instead felt parched and whispered, "Water…please?"

She drank the small bottle of water without taking a breath and reclined once more, pulling the provided blanket around her shoulders, and tucking it along her sides. The snug feeling took her back in time to her sophomore year in high school.

...

THE PARTY HAD BEEN AT KYLE'S HOUSE, a friend from school. Rachel, Emma's friend from church, along with ten or so other kids her age all had gathered in Kyle's basement. They had enjoyed chips and salsa, Italian sodas, foosball and pool, and a movie in the home theater.

Just before eleven, Rachel proclaimed, "Why do you have so much plastic wrap?" pointing to a large roll of plastic wrap on the counter of the kitchenette.

"We're moving some furniture," Kyle began to explain. A tall boy named Nate then chimed in with, "I have the coolest idea. My brothers did it to me once—they wrapped me to our banister. The stuff was so strong, it held me there with my feet off the ground."

One thing led to another, before everyone looked at Emma. "Emma!" one of the girls had said.

Why her, Emma hadn't been able to figure out at the time. Not exactly wanting to be part of *that* kind of fun, she had felt herself shrugging but said nothing despite something inside screaming at her to say something rather than go along. It wasn't until in therapy years later that she owned feeling very cornered at the time and that, at the time, she had defined going along as the only way to get along. "I wanted to be liked," she had told her therapist.

That night, Emma's experience had turned awful from there. The group had looked around, but Kyle's house didn't have a banister or any other pole that would work. Until Kyle perked up with an idea and said, "There's a streetlight in our cul-de-sac."

Outside, Rachel and two other girls helped hold Emma up while the boys began wrapping her waist then torso and arms and finally her feet. At first, Emma laughed along with the rest, humoring them more than feeling any amusement herself. She had felt a sort of weightlessness at first, and then felt a vibration along her back as the wrap compressed her against the pole—which was buzzing from the light overhead. It gave her chills. She had looked up, where she could see the light overhead flickering a bit. The breeze blew a strand of her hair into her mouth that she tried to blow away.

A moment later, the group stood back and one of the boys said, "Ta da!" They all laughed. With everyone looking at her, Emma felt more obvious than ever. "Okay, get me down—" Emma tried to say—holding back tears, unable to move her arms and legs.

About to beg, Emma heard someone shout, "Cop car!" and then watched helplessly from her suspended position as everyone darted behind bushes. The police car had driven past without slowing at all.

She heard whispering from the bushes and turned her head to see shadows running toward the house. She called out, "Rachel? Kyle?" Nothing. Then the night grew eerily quiet with the ratcheting sound of crickets all around in the darkness and the light buzzing overhead.

A sense of panic had settled in. Already past eleven by that point, questions raced through her mind: What about her parents? Why had she agreed to a party? Why was no one coming for her? She felt so embarrassed and called out repeatedly. "Rachel...?" Her arms were trembling by that point. Her right cheek itched but the pole prevented her from rubbing it. Already fall, the temperature was quickly growing cooler as the breeze from a nearby canyon whipped even more hair into her mouth. She remembered feeling glad she had worn her new sweatshirt.

One of her hands had been bound flat against the pole, but Emma had worked the other loose and tear what felt like a small hole between seams in the plastic. She pried at it until she could fit two fingers through and then her hand. The air had instantly chilled her hand.

She had hung there suspended from the light pole for twenty minutes or so before hearing a car come up the driveway, her view blocked by a tall evergreen. A door opened, then closed, and the car backed into the cul-de-sac before pulling away. She had recognized it as Kyle's car. The party had to be over.

"Rachel! Kyle!" she had yelled to no avail. She had felt angry, abandoned, and embarrassed. She began to worry that she might die, that perhaps her parents or someone else wouldn't find her body until morning.

Then, the neighbor's house lights turned off, leaving the flickering light overhead as her only source of light. She began to feel nauseous, waiting and waiting. Then panicking again, she clawed in every direction with her free hand at the thick plastic.

After what had seemed like forever, car lights appeared and pointed back into the cul-de-sac. Emma had felt a ray of hope. Had Kyle finally returned, and would he help her down? As the car slowly pulled around the cul-de-sac, its lights had disappeared behind the bushes. Emma recalled concluding it too must have pulled away, sobbing futilely, her head hung down.

Moments later, a car door had slammed—and she heard someone hurrying toward her.

"Emma? Oh, my sweetheart. Who did this to you?"

She had looked up with red eyes at her father, feeling absolutely helpless but so relieved. He had carefully pulled away the plastic wrap and lifted her down.

Emma hadn't gone back to school the next Monday. She knew her parents were giving her space to work things over.

A few days into the next week, her father had said, "By the way, I finally heard back from that boy's father, and no one from the party is admitting to anything. I'm thinking of going to the police."

Emma remembered bracing herself and saying, "It's not worth it, Dad."

"I don't disagree—I only want you to know I would." He had hugged her, pausing for a moment before adding, "It just *is*. We don't always get to choose what happens to us or why, but we do get to choose what we do with it."

Lifting herself, Emma had felt warmed by the thought. "That…'that' happened," referring to the incident at the party. "I get it. It just *is*." Looking up into his eyes, she said, "I'm going back to school. I can do this."

Her mother had looked concerned, distressed by the thought.

"That's my girl," her father had said.

…

EMMA WAS STARTLED WHEN THE OVERHEAD SPEAKER squawked. She suddenly felt confined by the blanket she had so carefully tucked around her and quickly pulled it loose.

The pilot begin saying, "Folks, we expect some turbulence up ahead. Shouldn't be for more than ten or fifteen minutes. Please return to your seats and fasten your seatbelts." Moments later, the airplane began to shake.

Emma's thoughts turned to the call with her parents. Had she said the right things? Would she see him again and have time to hug him? She had to do something to take her mind off things. The moment the turbulence stopped, she made a quick trip to the restroom.

On her way back to her seat, Emma's worried that she had been critical of Lacy's travel plans for her and that she had seemed resistant to Sean's encouragement to write a book. Checking the screen in the seatback in front of her, she saw she had hours of flying to go and squirmed restlessly in her seat to get comfortable. She couldn't put her finger on why she had reacted the way she had. Lacy had done her best given the circumstances, and Sean had offered to introduce her to his agent—exactly the type of thing Sean did—and for that she was truly grateful.

Determined to make sure they both felt her appreciation, Emma reached for her laptop to compose a few emails.

Hi Lacy—you did well on the travel plans—especially the hotel AND the return flight! Thanks for always having my back. I couldn't do this without you.

Something is going on with my father again. They don't know what is going on. I'm heading to Carlsbad first thing tomorrow. I can tell my mom needs me there.

Will you cover for me (as usual). Text me about anything urgent. I will keep you posted.

XOXO, Emma

Reflecting for a moment, she wrote a second email to Sean.

Hi Sean,

I literally wouldn't be here without you—I'm flying home from Paris after receiving an award that I coveted whenever I saw it in your office. And it's much more than crystal that has me reaching out.

Thanks for believing in me, for encouraging me, and for acknowledging that with this award. I too often move on from each success like I often do from failures—like it's in the past, will never happen again, and doesn't matter. But recognizing those who made the good moments of my life happen is something I'm trying to be better at.

You're one of my moment-makers. Because of you, I am a better person, business owner, and maybe someday an author. You always seem to see more in me than I see in myself. I owe you at least part of my world—the rest goes to my parents.

Please let me know how I can show up in the future for you like you do so consistently in mine.

All the best!

Emma

Feeling better about things, Emma closed her laptop and leaned back in her seat.

Chapter 8

Dark Manhattan Night

After midnight, Emma walked through customs carrying her crystal obelisk over her arm in a large brown bag, dragging her roller bag behind her with her free hand. Before leaving Paris, her handler had found the big shopping bag, "a way to discretely get this back home" as Emma had instructed. At the curb, Emma hailed a taxi, thinking it would be safer and faster than taking the train. The driver asked if she was carrying a "very tall bottle of hooch." She only smiled, busying herself with her phone, not feeling much like talking. Emma's thoughts were jumbled with new worries for her father and another short night ahead.

Scanning her calendar, Emma remembered the speaking commitment she had agreed to the very next week. Not knowing how long she would be needed in California, she started to text Lacy but saw the time and decided instead to email her. "I hope our contract has a clause on medical emergencies," she wrote. "If not, we probably should add that to the next one." Before hitting send, she thought things over. Perhaps she could fly out for an afternoon if her father was stable by then. "Fingers crossed on all fronts. But do connect authentically—let them know what's happening. Do what you can to make them happy."

She hit send and looked up. "I'm up ahead, there by that white truck on the right," Emma said as they neared her Upper East Side apartment. Stepping out into the cold night, she watched the driver pull away and wondered if the weatherman would get it right this time. The forecast said there would be snow by morning. Despite the streetlights, the nearly empty roads and darker buildings drew Emma's eyes up. She strained and could almost see stars—not a cloud in the sky. She could see the blinking light of a helicopter and a crescent moon over Central Park. It felt good to be home.

With no doorman at this hour, Emma punched the buttons and pulled her roller bag into the building, clutching the large brown bag under her left arm. Reflecting on her last forty-eight hours, Emma slipped into the elevator and pushed the number for her floor. A few questions nagged at her—did she really have a book in her? Was Sean blowing smoke? Could she cough up even fifty thousand words? Those collided with more urgent questions about her father. What was really going on with her father? Just where did he want to take her?

As the elevator door began to slide closed, a hand slipped in followed by an arm to force the door open. Worried at first, Emma was only slightly relieved when she recognized the tall, well-dressed man hurried in, as a guy who also lived in the building. Now, planning to repack her bag first thing in the morning, Emma felt a wave of impatience as she waited for the elevator door to close. She sighed loudly to push the thoughts away.

"Sorry," the guy said, looking perplexed by her expression. "Saw this as an opportunity." He reached over and pushed the button for the top floor.

"No problem. It's been a very long day."

"What's in the bag?" He chuckled and said, "That's either a very tall bottle of alcohol or a toilet plunger. I'm going with plunger. Clogged toilet?"

Emma forced a smile. She knew describing the award would mean nothing to a stranger and might sound arrogant. Rather, she said nothing. She was grateful when the elevator dinged for her floor.

The guy paused for a moment and then nodding toward her brown bag, adding with a smirk, "You know the building superintendent will take care of stuff like that."

He was a little too awake and alert for this hour, Emma thought. As the doors opened, Emma mustered a tired laugh—being exhausted was not her best way of showing up. "Good night," she said, stepping out onto the fourth floor. Ten minutes later with her white noise speaker playing, she was sound asleep.

Part II

Chapter 9

Willow Creek Townsite, 1890

Cassie hadn't written in her journal since the day she woke to huge snow drifts piled against the house and blocking the barn doors—all from strong winds during the night. Now summer and approaching her thirteenth birthday, a new event stood out even more prominently and had become the source of recent nightmares. She finally decided to write with the hope that the night terrors would go away.

"Last week, I was walking along Willow Creek, as I often do, when the water came down our creek with monsters in it," Cassie wrote late one warm evening. Sitting comfortably in front of the fireplace of their new two-story home, she rested her elbows on the hearth and stared into crackling embers, reflecting on the scene before continuing.

> *Momma told Eugene to stay away from the creek. The water was deeper than I ever saw. I remember falling in when I was little, but this spring is more awful and scary. Big logs and branches came all at once. Papa said it was because another canal broke, that all of its water flooded over into our creek. It looked like monster arms reaching to the sky. The sound they made from crashing into each other was terrifying. It kept getting bigger. Water flooded out into the barnyard and on our front grass. I thought we were goners. And then it passed. Except for big puddles in the barnyard.*
>
> *Momma called it a flash flood. I never want to see one of those again.*

The creek monsters were all cleared out by later that day. The water in our creek stopped being muddy a few days ago. Downstream a bit there are logs and branches everywhere. And a few dead critters that are now starting to smell.

I think I have dreamed about this every night. I hope those nightmares end.

Just this week, Momma took sick with winter fever, we think. Why do they call it a winter sickness if you can get it in the summer? Sarah has it too. A few people have died. I'm scared of that. It seems I'm scared of everything about now. I can't imagine losing Sarah. Or Momma.

Cassie folded her arms for a pillow on the hearth and rested her head. The heat from the fire was comforting. She woke with a start when her father nudged her.

"It's time for bed."

...

LATE THE NEXT MORNING, Simeon stood in the doorway of the home he had built with his own hands the previous winter—with the help of Will Walker and several other men. There was a porch along the front, and he had wrapped the entire structure with wood siding.

Not all was well. He could hear Esther in the bedroom coughing. He stretched upward toward the sun as he tried to shake off a sleepless night. Eugene, now five, was across the yard tossing feed from a small pail to chickens cackling and pecking at the ground around him.

A solo rider came down the dirt road toward their home, kicking up a trail of dust. From the man's flat-brimmed hat, Simeon guessed it was Will Walker.

"Good morning!" Will said enthusiastically.

Simeon replied somewhat flatly. "Morning."

From astride his horse, Will gave him a puzzled look before putting one knee over the horn of his saddle. "Well, it looks like statehood is coming," he said. "Not sure what the difference is between a state and territory anyhow—especially when Willow Creek runs crazy like that."

"Confounded ditch banks," Simeon moaned. "I certainly hope the Hillside canal owners get theirs fixed and prevent this whole mess. I've got enough repairs of my own because of that flood." He could see Eugene dipping the

The Meadowlark

bucket into the burlap feedbag a second time and yelled over, "Son, that's enough food for those chickens!" Eugene looked up disappointed and left the bucket in the bag. Simeone shouted again, "And be sure to fold that bag shut and put that rock there on it! Don't need any critters getting into it."

Eugene did as he was told before walking slowly back toward the house.

Still confused by Simeon's mood, Will took off his hat and looked at Simeon wryly. "Hillside owners are meeting today. I'm riding to the meeting now. Want to ride along?"

Simeon nodded knowingly as he tussled Eugene's thick dark hair and said, "Darn the need to be in two places at once!" He rubbed the heel of his boot at a wooden porch plank. "Esther's not well, Will—winter fever. Up all night, and when I came back after chores this morning, she was coughing even worse than yesterday." He looked around. "I think it's best I stay here."

"I'm sorry to hear that, Simeon. She's a strong woman—and a good one. I'm sure she will be well."

About then, Cassie came out of the house behind her father.

Will put his hat back on his head and touched the bill. "A good morning to you, miss Cassie. How's your momma?"

Cassie looked up, squinting from the sunlight. "She's fighting something that has her down like I've never seen her before." Cassie drew a towel from her shoulder and wiped her hands before adding, "But she's asleep now. First time since yesterday." Cassie paused for a moment and then asked, "And Sarah? Still sick?"

"She's on the mend. I give it another day or two and she'll be back to her regular old self. It's good her momma can care for her. That woman seems to know a lot about many things."

Cassie straightened her apron. "Tell Sarah I miss her, okay? And that we're praying for her."

"Sure will. She asks about you every day. I guess it's best to stay away when people are down like this."

Cassie looked resigned to that fact. "Guess so," she said.

Will looked expectantly at Simeon, brightening with an idea. He turned to Cassie and asked, "With your mother finally sleeping, mind if your pa rides to that water meeting with me? The Willow Creek company is meeting with the directors from the Hillside company on how canal repairs are coming along. Looks to me like he could benefit from a change of scenery."

"Go ahead, Papa. I can tend mother."

"And Eugene?" Her father looked worried.

"I'll watch after Eugene," Cassie said.

...

As the sun climbed toward midday, the two men rode into the fledgling town of Willow Creek and tied their horses in front of a barn that was also serving as the town hall. They heard men's voices coming through the open door as they approached.

"...will not make a difference!"

"It has to," another man said adamantly.

As Will and Simeon entered, all heads turned.

James Heath, water master over the Willow Creek system, addressed the newcomers. "Simeon. Will. Thanks for coming. We're discussing the Hillside break."

The two men joined the group around a long table. Another man said, "We know you two probably got the worst of it. Tell us about what happened at your places."

Simeon looked at Will, who nodded. "Well...at first I didn't know if our own head gate failed or what. The volume was so high that I guessed the Snake had broken through the new Willow Creek headgate. The sheer volume of debris that came down was astounding, something I couldn't figure since we have so little up along Willow Creek. I figured it had to be some other breakthrough. I'm still clearing logs. It wreaked havoc on every improvement made in the past five years!"

About half the group nodded knowingly and looked across at the other men at the table.

"We're sorry for the mess," Sam Lundquist said. "We have a high spot where the Hillside canal rises above the grade of the land by about three feet. Retained with rock, mind you, but something gave—it could have been rodents or just plain bad luck. It's been repaired, and we will have men ride the banks daily to be sure it holds."

The Willow Creek men looked around expectantly. Heath asked expectantly, "And...?"

Lundquist hesitated before saying, "And we'll cover any repairs...within reason."

The group across the table erupted. "What about my crops..."

"My pasture is a swamp…"

"I've lost at least three weeks of the growing season!"

When the comments died down, Simeon raised a finger and said, "Friends, I'm fine to consider this whole episode a thing of the past. As my dear wife always says to me, 'Comfort and ease don't bring you to your knees.' This disaster has produced anything but ease—we've been humbled by our circumstances. I say that since we've only got ourselves and our ingenuity to work with, let's find a way to prevent anything like this in the future—and remain on speaking terms with one another. Once we get some downtime around winter or so, we'll need to clear the tree limbs, logs, and brush from our banks as well." Looking at the men on his side of the table, Simeon added, "And possibly work with the Hillside owners to do the same for theirs. That work is ahead of us, and that will prevent a future catastrophe like the one we're still cleaning up."

The men around the room nodded. Heath added, "Agreed. We will plan on that. And all will do their part to cover your losses."

Simeon and Will both waved off the need to cover any losses. "Look," Will chuckled. "If we went looking for handouts at every inconvenience that comes to pass, you would all be broke." The other men laughed and nodded. Will added, "Best to just go to work."

Still, the rest of the meeting was spent discussing what the Hillside canal owners could do to help rebuild headgates and other canal fixtures. All shook hands as the meeting concluded.

"Right in time for statehood," Will said. The men around the circle chuckled. "A forty-third star on the U.S. flag!"

Simeon patted his friend on the shoulder and added, "Remember, men, another star will not put food on our tables. But working together like this, and the good Lord smiling down upon us, we have shown we can accomplish that job quite well!"

On their ride home, Will asked, "So, what do you make of this statehood effort?"

"I really haven't given it much attention," Simeon replied. "I've got bigger problems to solve—well, meaning I'm not the governor. I'm but a lowly farmer merely searching for enough water—AND not the way the Hillside canal brought it, as it were."

Will smiled. "And your new spread? How's that coming along? I still can't believe you purchased that—no matter how good a deal it was!"

"You remember we extended the ditches last year, right?" Simeon said, "The Lewisville and Parks canal men—all good men, mind you—were happy to run that extension to my land since it involved two other owners. I got a few acres of alfalfa in this spring before the Dry Bed ran dry, up to its no good name earlier this year than anyone could remember. Dryer than a bone!" Simeon chuckled as he added, "Back when old man McDonald signed the contract, I should have seen that wink in his eye when he said I was getting the land for cheap but that getting it under ditch might break me." Simeon's laugh rose as he looked around at the landscape. "I'm bent, I'll tell you, but not yet broken. I figured if it never produced anything, I was still ahead a bit by just owning the acreage. I can at least graze a few head of cattle there should nothing else work out. And that's about where things sit. I'm sure old man McDonald is rolling in his grave—not at all sure that's where he is, mind you."

The two men laughed heartily as their horses trotted along.

Will said, "It's good to see you've still got a sense of humor, Simeon."

"I figure my only other choice is on my knees, weeping," Simeon said, smiling. "I choose to be up and about." Clearing his throat and leaning in his saddle, he added with a smile, "Most mornings, I do spend a long moment on my knees. Generally not weeping, mind you."

Will chuckled. "So what about your alfalfa?"

"We only planted five acres. It'll come back once we can get real water to it or with a few days of good rain—as though that happens. Maybe one cutting a year, just not this year."

The two men rode in silence, the horses clipping at the dirt and whinnying at the sight of two horses pastured across the way.

Reaching the lane that turned toward the Rapp's, Simeon slowed his horse and then tapped his head with his finger before saying, "I am thinking about it, though. Been working on a plan to keep the Dry Bed full year-round." He looked around circumspectly, before adding, "It's unfortunate Willow Creek doesn't flow far enough north." Looking east and then west, he added, "If I were God…well, never mind." He smiled and pointed in the direction of the Snake River and went on. "With all the water flowing north, west, and south around us, there's got to be a way to solve this problem once and for all."

"It's all been tried," Will said. "Not to discourage you, but I hear that rock diversion dam they put in last year out past the flood plain didn't make it past spring—washed out with the first runoff. Even after a light winter." His gesturing told the story very clearly.

"We'll see. God built it, and don't you think the same God could give us an idea or two that would help us revise it slightly for the betterment of his children?"

Will smiled. "Meaning, for your personal gain on some miserable land you should have never purchased?"

Simeon laughed, looking up more seriously. "Yes…and not just mine. You've seen that last group of homesteaders out that way struggling and suffering? It's what was left, I'll say, but they came with as much hope as we did—only five years too late." Musing, Simeon added, "I believe in a God who'd want them to be less miserable, at least."

"That's a kind thought, my friend."

Looking down the lane toward the back of his house, Simeon said, "Well, I best be getting home." He turned his horse and nudged it with his heels.

Will shouted after him heartily, "I don't think I have a relationship with the Almighty like the one it sounds like you do. Put in a good word for me!" Will made a clicking sound to hurry his horse along.

…

COMING AROUND THE FRONT OF THE HOUSE, and riding toward the barn, Simeon spotted Mary Walker's black runabout parked in the front yard and looked behind him wondering if Will knew his wife was here. He was glad to have her stop by again, the second day in a row. Whistling, Simeon began opening the large barn door to put his horse away when Cassie ran toward him from the house crying. The towel she carried had red spots on it.

"Papa, it's not good. Come quickly."

Simeon looked down at the reins he was holding, dropping them instantly, knowing the horse would stand for hours right where he left it, believing it was tied to something. "What's wrong?"

"Momma…" Cassie couldn't finish, sobbing as she hurried back toward the house.

Simeon caught up with her and held her as they walked quickly toward the house. Eugene was sitting on the edge of the porch, whittling a block of wood and swinging his legs, oblivious to the commotion. Simeon came through the front door and spotted Mary's black medical bag on the front table. Through the bedroom door, he could see Mary daubing at Esther's forehead, a cloth in one hand and spoon in the other that she was putting down on the nightstand. She beckoned them both in and handed Cassie the cloth before taking Simeon by the elbow and guiding him back into the front room.

With tears welling in her eyes, Mary said, "Things have…how do I say this? Things have turned for the worse. She's coughing up blood. I don't think we have long."

Simeon grew instantly weak and looked for somewhere to sit.

Mary gripped his arm to hold him up. "She needs you."

Gathering his strength, Simeon could hear Esther's attempt to cough from the other room and pushed past Mary. He saw Esther there in her white bed clothes, laying on top of the sheets and damp with fever. She stared blankly toward the ceiling.

Simeon knelt at the edge of the bed and whispered, "Esther." He took up her hand gently. "Sweet Esther." He felt a faint squeeze in response.

Esther moved her lips as if to say something but was interrupted by a coughing fit that produced no sound and left behind only a bit of bright red phlegm at the corner of her mouth. She slowly relaxed back into the pillow.

Cassie took the cloth from her shoulder and wiped her mother's lips. "There, Momma."

Simeon could hear Esther's strained and gurgled breathing. He asked, "What can we do?"

With pursed lips and raised eyebrows, Mary measured what she was about to say carefully. Turning to Esther, she spoke a few words reassuringly. "Esther, dear, you're a strong pioneer. Draw deep on that strength now."

Simeon bent forward, kissing his wife on the forehead and whispering, "Please pull through." He released her hand and walked quickly from the room. Hurrying past his son and toward the small orchard of apricot trees he had planted a year earlier, he found the lone cottonwood that had welcomed them that first day in Willow Creek.

Falling to his knees at its base, he prayed, "Dear Lord, my wife is my strength and my salvation in this life. I need her…more than you do. Please don't take her now but return her to strength." He choked up, unable to speak for a moment. Wiping at his eyes, he finally whispered, "If you really do…need her more…or if you have something important for me to learn…" He paused, unable to finish. Moments later, he looked up at the sky and uttered, "Thy will be done."

...

"Momma is gone," Cassie wrote in her journal that evening.

I won't ever sleep again. I can barely breath. I don't know what to do. She up and stopped breathing. I can't even think clearly. This can't be happening. She was all right and then she wasn't. Sarah's mother came to help and even said she thought Momma would pull through. But Momma suddenly stopped breathing. I wanted to shake her and yell for her to breath.

She's covered by a blanket in the other room. I don't know what to do. I peeked under the blanket just now. It can't be. She is still there…but then she's not there. Not moving. Not breathing. Not anything.

Oh, Momma! Please come back. Please never leave. I can't live without you. I don't want to live without you. I don't know what to do.

I don't know what to do.

...

That Thursday afternoon, Simeon walked past the barn and down along the creek. He needed to turn the water away from a field of dark green corn and back downstream. Across the empty landscape to the west, he could imagine the new cemetery, a recently established four-acre section of land that he and others had donated from the corners of their own parcels. It had all happened earlier that year, and some had debated it was too big for a cemetery while he and others had urged that four acres wasn't nearly big enough—at least for the years ahead. It sat off in the fields a half mile or so away from what was emerging as the town center. In his mind's eye, he could see the border of evergreens he and others had planted around the cemetery, imagining how someday they would tower over those buried there. He knew that even he, in time, would one day benefit from such a hallowed place—only a distant time, he hoped.

A light wind pushed at his hat as he shook away the events of the past two days. Esther was over that way now, he knew, buried in a service earlier that day.

Her brief struggle had ended the afternoon before, moments after she had fought utter exhaustion to whisper, "Take care…" The simple graveside service had been attended by a few friends and neighbors who dared leave their homes. It nearly broke him.

Now it was just him, Cassie, and Eugene.

Simeon wanted nothing more than to rush into his home and meet Esther there—to take her in his arms and hold her. Or walk to her grave and muster divine power to raise her up—now and not in the eventual hereafter. Movement off in the distance caught his attention, and for a moment, he thought he spotted her walking among the few markers already in place. But shaking his head, he knew it couldn't be her. Still, he felt Esther might be away somewhere, still alive and well, just not at home—that she would return home soon, perhaps by the time he came in from the fields, and greet him on the front porch when he came in. He shook his head again.

Walking back up the creek past the towering cottonwood toward the small dam that diverted water into his fields, he muttered, "The Lord giveth," as he opened the head gate to turn the water back downstream and watched as it cascaded over a small shelf that made it gurgle. The sound was usually uplifting, but that day he despondently watched the water turn downstream again and added, "…and the Lord taketh away."

Moments later, Simeon heard a trotting horse approaching. He hurried over and recognized James Heath, the water master, approaching.

Even though they had seen each other earlier that day at the cemetery, when he arrived Heath, said, "So sorry about Esther. So sorry!" Removing his hat, he added, "We just received word. I had to come and share the news, Simeon. We're a state—Idaho is the newest star on the flag! Parade tomorrow at noon!" He waved his hat and yipped loudly as he turned back down the road.

Simeon waved him away with his hand and said under his breath, "Statehood won't bring…my wife back!" He knew there was more at stake here with a new state and all—more federal aid for canals and other land improvements. It was hard to muster enthusiasm for anything at a time of such great loss. A parade? It dawned on him that the next day was the Fourth of July. He knew it might be nice for Cassie to take Eugene into town.

Simeon walked into the house and toward the bedroom, passing Eugene playing with blocks on the front room floor. There would be no sleep or even work that day or the next. He would feed the livestock, of course. And finish his turn at the water. Beyond that, he couldn't sort his thoughts at all.

Sitting back on his side of the bed, he looked across to where Esther had lain and immediately turned toward the window. The sky had bright yellow tones, suggesting the day was nearing its close. As Simeon rested there, he began to hear Cassie from the other side of the house humming at first before singing a song, heavy with her own emotion, her beautiful voice resonating throughout the house.

"Give," said the little stream,
"Give, oh! Give, give, oh! Give."

Simeon rose and found her in the kitchen preparing dinner. Cassie stopped when she saw her father. "It was Momma's song."

Simeon nodded and asked, "How can I help?"

"Bring Ma back," Cassie said, wiping at her tears and leaning against the kitchen counter.

Reaching for his daughter and pulling her to his chest, Simeon held his own tears back and said, "Your ma was everything to me too. And gone now—only for a time. It's all on our shoulders now."

Cassie looked up into her father's eyes. "Why?"

"I'd like to have answers myself." He paused, squeezing his daughter before letting her turn back to the job at hand. "But I don't." Attempting to brighten things a bit, he tried to change the subject. "I hear Sarah's on the mend. Folks are starting to come out again. Apparently, most were spared this tragedy."

Chapter 10

South Fork of the Snake River, 1894

A little over a month after her seventeenth birthday, Cassie found herself wanting to ride out to the river. The talk all around her was that the Snake River was shallower than ever and might even run dry, something she had to see for herself.

One Sunday afternoon in late August, Cassie saddled her father's roan mare and followed the course of Willow Creek north to the bridge near their property where the main road crossed the creek. Willow Creek itself was no longer the babbling brook it had once been but had gradually been worked by man and horse into a wider, straighter canal. From its headwaters fifty miles away in the hills to the southeast, Willow Creek was now augmented by one of the few successful diversion canals coming off the Snake upstream a ways and had been split multiple times downstream into branches called Harrison, Union, and Anderson.

She urged her horse across the bridge and into the growing town now officially named Willow Creek. The horse kicked up clouds of dust along the way. Everything was coated with a fine layer of dust.

The expanding town now featured a new rock building for a school, a blacksmith's shop, a barbershop, and a bank—all on sixteen acres, four of which Simeon had combined with the corners from his three adjoining neighbors to form a sixteen-acre town. The land had been purchased by pooled funds to form the community. A newly formed town council was already in discussions to acquire another connected fifty acres from Harry James on the north side of town in anticipation of future growth. The big barn used as a town hall had recently been expanded with a second big room for church meetings.

Cassie turned her horse toward the only mercantile for fifteen miles in any direction—a small store she and her father had opened ten months earlier. It was generally closed on Sundays, except for emergencies, but the thought that she may have forgotten to lock it the night before nagged at her. She tied her horse off at the hitching post in front and caught her reflection in the dusty plate glass window where "Rapp Mercantile" was painted in gold letters. She would wash that first thing Monday morning. Jostling the doorknob, she was satisfied to find she had locked it after all.

The mercantile had arisen out of necessity and opportunity. After too many ten-mile trips to get supplies—either downstream to Eagle Rock or a similar distance west to the railroad town of Market Lake—and tired of the high prices there, her father had drawn on his earlier days of freighting and started up a local mercantile. He once again hauled goods—this time from as far as Salt Lake City and closer sources in Pocatello—all to bring costs down. Already a land clearer, ditch builder, farmer, and cattle rancher, he was now a merchant as well.

Cassie was now the store manager and did a fine job of keeping matters tidy—the store was clean and organized and she always collected payments once someone's tab was due. She was pleased at this new challenge—of keeping the store well supplied, anticipating what people wanted, discounting items that weren't in as high demand to move them out, and fastidiously tracking every transaction—both the financial aspect and the volume purchased, usually down to the ounce, cup, or button. Only the day before, she had sold the remaining yard of black and white checked gingham to Jane Starkey at twenty-five percent of what was originally being asked—and was pleased to have broken even.

Cassie recalled Mrs. Hutchins coming into the store that spring saying, "My husband says the Snake River up and created a new channel, living up to its name. It by-passed the Dry Bed altogether, which," she had said, "is apparently living up to its name now too."

Folks had been coming into the store all summer talking about how dry the year was looking because of the light winter just experienced that many said was the coldest they could remember and the only one with so little snow. Since May, they had been calling it a drought year. By July, most were saying it was only going to get worse, not better. Now, several claimed the river itself was drying up. "For the first time since the Creation," Mrs. Hutchins had said.

There was little else to discuss. The talk ranged from how nature takes its course to how cash crops were wilting. A week earlier, the talk had turned to how the crops were now dying under the scorching sun.

...

Even Cassie's father had grown desperate. Despite the canal extensions Simeon had invested in a few years earlier, the head gates of both the Lewisville and Parks canals were high and dry—the slow trickle that barely flowed along the bottom of the Dry Bed wasn't enough to supply water for much more than a few acres. One of the tenants leasing his land had moved, leaving livestock behind, telling Simeon, "Those cattle are yours. I hope you can feed them."

Based on a steady supplement of Snake River water from earlier improvements, those along Willow Creek were a little better off. But the majority of the valley, from the middle to the west side—including those renting Simeon's new land holdings—were struggling. Simeon knew he wouldn't evict his tenants but thought he might have to forgive a debt.

A few weeks earlier, living too close to the edge had turned tragic. Willard Townsend, the town's part-time sheriff, had been called out to the Johnson property, according to Townsend's wife Lavon who had come into the store that afternoon all shaken up.

"Sally plum went insane," Lavon had reported. "She had apparently been out chopping at sagebrush when she suddenly grabbed a hen and chopped its head off. Then another, and another, and another."

The three other women shopping in the store at that time had gathered around to hear her out.

Lavon had continued. "Everyone knows chickens aren't hard to catch. But when her James returned empty-handed from his effort to roust up supplies, he found her there with bloody chickens flapping all around—and her children huddled and scared standing off to the side."

The women had recoiled at the thought.

Lavon had continued. "Farmer Johnson yelled and cussed, frightening the children more." Then, with a dramatic flair, Lavon leaned forward and said in whispered tones, "They said Sally looked at her children and then pointed at her husband. 'Go get the old man,' she said, 'and hold him while I chop his head off!'"

Those listening had looked shocked and uncomfortable. A few days after that, it was said that Sally Johnson was committed to the newly opened sanitorium in Blackfoot.

As the early harvests of alfalfa and corn were finished, farmers began reporting half-sized potatoes from their test digs. Most people began preparing for the worst. "We'll have to nurse each other's wounds," Mary Walker had said, even though their family was not nearly as affected as most. "We'll pray we can make it and help those out where we can."

Exactly one week earlier, Mrs. Hutchins had come in to buy all the molasses Cassie had in stock along with a long list of other supplies. "We're headed for the Klondike—well to the Washington coast first," the woman had said. "We're hearing about gold up that way, and Albert is apparently betting we can get there before the rest of the world does."

At least two other families were tempted by rumors of gold in the Klondike and left off farming for what they hoped was a better opportunity panning for gold.

Beginning in mid-July, most farmers in the western half of the valley were making trips to Willow Creek—the creek itself—or the river beyond to fill barrels with water and cart them miles back to their homes, all to care for their livestock, water what remained of their gardens, and have some to drink for themselves.

When people began saying the mighty Snake had been reduced to a trickle, the townspeople and neighbors for miles around had organized a day of fasting and prayer the past Sunday seeking relief, even miracles.

Which caused Cassie to wonder how bleak things might get. She finally had to see for herself.

...

AS SHE RODE THROUGH TOWN, Cassie glanced over at the recently finished rock school Eugene would be attending that fall and then rode past the bank and townhall. Leaving town, she urged her horse to a trot with a "Yip!"

After a mile or so, she neared the Dry Bed and immediately noticed how dry the air was, along with the absence of birdsong. She had expected to come upon the dank smell of water, something regularly present when she walked along Willow Creek. The air only smelled dusty and thick. The abundant chittering of grasshoppers filled the air. Her horse cracked dry branches as she urged it down into the riverbed, letting it bend and drink from a large puddle there, one fed by a slow trickle. Whenever she had previously come, Cassie had seen water running anywhere from a few feet deep early in the summer to a few inches deep by fall. Never as dry as what she was seeing now.

"Back to work," Cassie said, turning her horse upstream. She followed the course of the Dry Bed for a few miles, her horse splashing in occasional small puddles at first and then nothing as the riverbed became less defined, wider and increasingly cluttered by rocks and trees. Cassie had never ridden this way before, but after a few miles she recognized she was now on what her father regularly referred to as "the flood plain."

The day was hot and dry, and she had seen irregular signs of water for the final mile or so. Nearing the Snake River, Cassie's horse whinnied at the smell of water. The pair came up a small rise, and Cassie could hear a gentle hum from the river's flow. Shallower than usual but nothing like the townsfolk were describing, the Snake still ran a few feet deep and a hundred or so feet wide.

Surprised by her sense of relief, Cassie rode along the riverbank, spotting evidence from man-made attempts to turn water out into various ditches and gashes. At one point, someone had dug down several feet below the natural level of the river, but this turnout was now filled entirely with mud and debris. Further along, the remains of an earthen jetty that must have been an attempt to turn some of the river toward another ditch was mostly eroded. Behind her, the rocky contours of the wooded flood plain made it clear why this effort had been abandoned—it was too rocky and covered with trees to make ditch building anything but terribly complicated.

Being near the river gave her a sense of power, life, and abundance. Turning to look back, she felt a profound sadness for the suffering the recent drought had caused. Praying was all many people now could do—a lot of folks were on their knees more than usual. Remembering her mother's easy smile, Cassie bowed her head and said, "I miss you, Momma."

Despite the late setting sun, Cassie could see the horizon to her left beginning to glow as the sun eased its way west, bathing the hills to her right along the north side of the river in hot light. Here each spring for centuries, those hills obviously turned the runoff south, forcing the river over its banks and down across the plain behind her.

Cassie turned the horse back toward the small rise where she had first come up on the river. From there, she could see the Snake turn and straighten for a mile or so upstream. She could see the nearby head gates of other canals to her right upstream along this side of the river—the Farmer's Friend, Enterprise, and Eagle Gate—all that carried water along the eastern half of the valley, including connecting into Willow Creek a few miles away. There was water for sure, she concluded, if you were fortunate enough to draw it from one of those canals.

Looking behind her Cassie could see across the valley and the thick mass of cottonwoods that traced the flood plain and then thinned to where spring run-off would collect into the Dry Bed and meander toward town. After several hundred yards, the Dry Bed became better defined, making it a logical channel to carry Snake River water due west across the valley—if only somehow it could be diverted. She had overheard her father say that it was the first mile, maybe even the first half mile of "catawampus boulders and willy-nilly flood plain" that prevented a more natural and well-defined connection between the two. She could see the impossibility of it all for herself now.

It was getting late. With a "Haw," Cassie urged the horse toward home.

…

DOZENS OF FAMILIES LEFT BEFORE WINTER, most heading back to what now seemed like better opportunities left behind in Utah. As the days grew shorter, Cassie regularly pressed Simeon for any ideas that would reverse the situation at hand.

"For the first time, we have ten accounts that can't be collected—there's no one to contact."

Simeon countered with, "We're blessed, Cassie. No reason to believe people wouldn't have paid if they could have. We have sufficient for our needs, and that's something."

Cassie was persuaded by her father's thinking. "Anything we can do 'upstream' from the problem?" Collecting her thoughts, she added, "I mean, it mostly comes down to water, right?"

"It all comes down to water," Simeon said. "This desert has blossomed like a rose in good years, but as we have now experienced, it returns to its old desert ways almost too quickly. Perhaps a bit like each of us," he said, waxing philosophical. "Good when it's easy, and quickly spoiling when it's not."

"We can only pray for a good winter, I figure," Cassie said. "And stay good ourselves. They say, 'Comfort and ease'…," she rehearsed with a wink.

Simeon finished with, "…'don't bring you to your knees.' A mighty fine notion. Let's get the Almighty's attention somehow—and have Him send storm-laden clouds this direction all winter long. I'm all for the good *and* the easy."

"Until then, I'll go easy on some of our debtors," Cassie said.

"Go easy on all of them," Simeon said. "No one fared well this past growing season. Some just hide the fact better than others. All are on their knees, literally or not."

"Thanks, Pa. I will." Cassie hugged her father before going to her room for the night.

…

THAT DECEMBER WAS TERRIBLY COLD. Late one afternoon, Cassie's best friend Sarah hurried toward the Rapps' barn. "Where's Cassie?" she excitedly asked Eugene who was outside pushing a skiff of snow with his boot to clear the ground and scatter feed for chickens. He looked up, shrugging his shoulders. She said, "I knocked at the house, but no answer."

Eugene shrugged again and said, "Pa might know," pointing at the large open doors of the barn.

"You're not much help for a nine-year old," Sarah said, tussling his dark hair and hurrying into the barn. The smell of hay mingled with other farm smells to make the barn seem warm. Sarah spotted Simeon tending a cow in the corner. She excitedly said, "I have some news for Cassie. Where is she? Aren't Fridays her day off?"

In his heavy jacket and wrapped in a scarf, Simeon looked up from the milk cow standing there chewing its cud. "Why, hello, Sarah. What brings you around?"

Her breath producing clouds of vapor from the cold, Sarah rubbed her hands together and squealed, "I need to see her. I have news!"

Simeon started to say slowly, "Well, I had a few other matters today, so she's covering for me at the mercantile," pointing toward town with his chin, his hands too busy to use otherwise.

"Oh, good. Just so much to tell her…" Sarah ran off without another word.

"I'm glad you girls have each other," Simeon shouted after her, shaking his head.

As Sarah closed the mercantile's tall glass door behind her, she breathlessly gushed, "I'm getting married!" No longer alone in the small store, Cassie stood in a bright blue dress behind a long counter, turning away from the fabric she was wrapping in brown paper. Everything else in the store was muted but in perfect order, with gunny sacks lining walls along one side, barrels stacked at the far end, and a cast-iron stove as the only source of heat in the front corner. Labels marked the items on the shelves. This was all Cassie's doing.

Cassie looked up at Sarah, her eyes betraying more concern than congratulations. "Is it that Swenson boy, Jens?" The Swenson family had arrived just as winter began, a few weeks earlier, and settled on land previously being worked by a family forced out by the drought.

"Of course!" Sarah's eyes were more pleading than happy.

"You're sure?"

"Cassie!" Sarah looked away and stammered, "Why can't you...just be happy for me?"

The answer seemed obvious to Cassie. Sarah was a year older, but for the past few years now seemed to have little more on her mind than getting married and moving to a place of her own. She was not too young to marry, but with only a few young women in the area and a much higher number of young men, being a little picky had been Cassie's regular advice to Sarah, which had not usually been well received and often ended in a debate of sorts.

Cassie searched for something clever to say. Straightening a row of jars, she finally said, "You know how the first hot cake always burns and gets thrown out." She looked over her shoulder and smiled at Sarah, expecting a smile in return.

Sarah wasn't smiling. "Cassie! It's not the first offer." Sarah heard her own protest, and then more honestly added with a grin, "Well, I guess it is. But Jens is..."

"...just a boy?"

"He's 19!" Sarah looked at her sideways and went on. "And he already filed for land across the river up north by Moody Creek. A canal system went in, off the Henry's Fork so there's little risk of drought, and he says his filing is close to a head gate. He's going to be a farmer!"

Cassie wanted to ask, "What else could you be around here?" but instead felt the futility of her line of thinking so asked, "Do you love him?"

"I do...I will!"

The Meadowlark

Despite her regular advice that Sarah wait for the right man, Cassie had grown to expect that once Sarah's heart was set on something, she usually stuck with it. They had grown up together, watched their families move from houses made of crooked cedar logs to two-story homes made of milled lumber. Two years back, they had cried together for days after Sarah's younger brother Samuel died tragically in an accident that had involved her older brother, Erastus. Erastus had left the area a few days later without much explanation, and Cassie and Sarah had talked about how he must not have been able to bear the guilt.

The two women had attended every grade in school together in a one-room schoolhouse with all ages in attendance. They had studied together. On so many summer nights, they had watched the stars, naming every constellation in the sky they could. They had braided each other's hair, sat side by side making quilts with double wedding-ring patterns, and assembled hope chests filled with linens, crockery, boneware sets, and a few serving pieces of silver.

They were inseparable, generally—that is until Cassie began managing the mercantile.

In her mind, Cassie knew it was time for even her to consider marriage. With few prospects of any interest to her, Cassie became introspective at Sarah's joy. She was now seventeen and not getting any younger. Around there, most girls married at about this age, some even younger. She had to wonder if she was waiting for the right young man to come along or merely keeping herself busy. There was her father to care for, of course, a widower at not yet quite forty. Couldn't a man at his age still find another companion, or was she simply playing that role?

Cassie loved running the mercantile and did not mind the extra work involved in taking care of family matters, including being a bit of a mother for Eugene. Perhaps she could do all of that and would still have time to be a bit more available.

Over the years, Sarah had teased Cassie that she should marry Erastus so they could be real sisters, but Cassie felt she knew him too well—he was more like a brother than someone she would ever consider having a different kind of relationship with. Further, he had now been gone for two years, evidently not coming back.

Swallowing hard, Cassie walked over and held Sarah. "I truly am happy for you. You are my dearest friend. But you must know I'm most happy for Jens. He is getting the best girl ever." Sarah hugged Cassie tightly. They chatted for another hour, with a few customers coming and going. Sarah openly shared her hopes and worries but was energized that now was her time for marriage and that Jens was her man.

Cassie had seen Jens at church but knew nothing more than that he was tall, handsome enough, and came from a large family. "I know I've met him but never really talked with him. When can I really meet him?"

"Will you be coming to the Christmas dance next Friday?"

Cassie knew about the dance. It would be at the new townhall, and people would come from miles around for almost any occasion that afforded the opportunity to mingle with friends and newcomers alike.

"I will be there."

"You had better!" Sarah smiled, giving Cassie a hug. She walked out the mercantile door and then rushed back inside to share something important. "Oh, and Erastus will be there. He's coming home!"

Erastus? Surprised at the news, Cassie had not thought much about him in quite a while. She had known Erastus nearly her entire life and wondered if all this time away had changed him much. Would he be better? Smarter? Taller?

She smiled at the thought of seeing him again.

Chapter 11

Petroglyphs

Only hours after returning from Paris and far too early the next morning, Emma awoke to a string of texts and missed calls from her mother. On any other day, she would have noticed her vibrating phone—sleeping or not. How she had slept through all of that could only be explained by the profound fatigue she had felt the night before.

Emma called her mother immediately. Her mother answered but said nothing. "I'm so sorry, Mom. I'm so sorry I'm not already there."

Emma could hear sobbing.

"He's gone. He passed…away in the middle of the night," her mother said. "He so badly…wanted to see you…one last time. He told me…just after dinner that…something inside of him told him…he wouldn't…wake up in the…morning. I just don't…"

Emma cried out loud. "NO! He was…I just talked with him…NO!" Sensing a profound loss, Emma wept inconsolably. She could hear her mother sobbing as well. After crying together for minutes, Emma looked at the time and realized she needed to get to the airport. Between sobs, Emma asked, "What…happened?"

"He wasn't breathing well all day yesterday. The doctors and nurses said he just needed a breathing treatment…and some IV… antibiotics and…would probably get better." Her mother was nearly hysterical.

"Mom…Mom." Emma couldn't stop her own tears as she waited patiently on the phone. "Mom?"

"Oh, I don't know what…," her mother said and then paused. "I don't know what to do."

"Oh, Mom…" Emma knew her mother was devastated.

Between sobs, Emma's mother said, "We were on a lifelong date. He always held my hand and opened doors for me. He was my best friend. It was so sad to see him suffering so much." And then after a long series of sobs, she asked, "What will I do?"

Emma knew she couldn't answer the question and was overwhelmed by her own sense of loss. She had absolutely no idea how she could be of help let alone process any of her own thoughts or emotions at such a distance. Glad she had already booked a flight, she said, "I'll be there around noon today" before adding, "We can talk all the way to the airport and until they close the cabin door. I'm here for you."

Emma quickly repacked her roller bag and left her apartment—all while talking to her mother. She was halfway to the curb before she realized it had snowed enough to cover everything in white—and was still snowing. Her Uber driver arrived on schedule, and Emma saw next to nothing on her way to the airport. Clearing security and hurrying to her gate, it wasn't until the plane was taxiing down the runway that Emma finally said, "See you in a few hours," and removed the Bluetooth earbud she had been covering with one hand to avoid detection. It was only then she realized she was in a window seat and looked around to take in those around her.

For the first hour of the flight, Emma faced the window and silently cried. She wiped at her tears, but they kept coming. The rush of emotions was overwhelming.

As tears began to slow, the older man sitting next to her tapped her on the arm and said, "I'm so sorry to intrude, but are you okay?"

Emma wiped at her eyes, took a deep breath, and said as honestly as possible, "Not really." She then thought just how not okay she was and said, "Actually, I hate baring my soul, but my father passed away last night, and I wasn't…" Her voice trailed off as emotion overwhelmed her.

"Oh, I'm so sorry." The man hesitated and then added, "It's impossible to fathom loss. And hearing about someone else's loss doesn't soften the blow in the slightest. I know." He reached for her hand and gently squeezed it. Letting go, he said, "It's okay to feel."

Emma wasn't sure why, but his words or just the comforting presence of a kind person next to her took some of the edge off. "Thank you," she whispered. She reclined her seat and began to reflect on her favorite memories of her father.

…

A FEW WEEKS AFTER EMMA HAD TURNED SIXTEEN, her father had approached her and said, "It's the Autumnal Equinox this weekend—let's go somewhere!" she was thinking about little more than that Tyler Brown had asked her to homecoming, which wasn't until the weekend after. The entire world was reeling from the fact that terrorists had flown two jetliners into the World Trade Towers in Manhattan. Getting away by automobile seemed safe enough.

Her upcoming weekend had been free—mostly. A friend, a girl named Jessica, had talked about going to the movies or bowling that weekend, but Emma knew the plan would likely change before Friday afternoon.

Emma's father had sensed she was wavering and said, "Just the two of us. Mom has book club Friday night and wants to have a spa day on Saturday. And I have a place I want to show you—Nine Mile Canyon just outside of Wellington. There's an amazing pictograph of a pregnant buffalo!"

"Pregnant buffalo?" At the time, Emma had not been able to imagine why that would be interesting to see at all. Weren't all buffaloes large? Would a pregnant one be any larger? And an ancient drawing or carving at that?

Her father had said, "Good. So, we're good then? Let's leave Friday right after you get home from school. Three o'clock sharp. Be there or…"

Emma had finished the line. "…be square." Her father said a lot of funny things that always made her smile.

As he walked away, he had turned and asked, "So, you know what the difference between a petroglyph and a pictograph is, right?" He had waited for her answer.

Emma had thought. "They're both rock art, right? Native people created them and…" She had been playing with him a bit. Of course, she knew. They'd generally done a trip like this every year for as long as she could remember. "Petroglyphs," she said, emphasizing the "pe" sound at the first of the word as her father had taught her, "are pecked or scratched there by some tools like a deer horn or something. And pictographs," she had said triumphantly, "are pictures painted with plant dyes or something like that."

"Good! You're my little rock art expert after all!"

On that trip, they had traveled south from the Salt Lake area toward Spanish Fork Canyon. It wasn't a long drive, but they had stopped at, the Little Acorn, her father's favorite hamburger joint—at least the one in this part of the world—at the mouth of the canyon for dinner. Emma remembered eating the best French fries she had ever tasted. After, they had grabbed a few other snacks from the convenience store across the parking lot and drove the remaining miles to Price, Utah.

As usual, Emma's father had scanned the main street as they drove into town to see which of the two or three hotels looked best—before pulling into a Best Western, his usual selection. Pointing to the nearly empty parking lot, he had joked, "I wonder if they have any availability." Emma walked in with him to check on room rates. Her father had talked the desk clerk down on price. With the key in hand, they grabbed their duffle bags from the car and found their way to their newly booked upstairs room with two queens.

Once settled, she remembered her father asking if she wanted to see a movie that night. "I have no idea what's playing, but let's go check." Emma couldn't remember what movie they had watched at the Price theater that night, but she did remember that he had called the theater "the sticky shoe" because of how long it must have been since anyone had mopped the floor in front of the seats. "Years and years of soda pop drips and dropped candy," he had exclaimed. "But you've got to love the taste and smell of freshly made popcorn!" And she remembered her shoes sticking a bit as they walked out of the theater that night.

The next morning, they had traveled due east. Emma remembered asking, "So when is the Autumn Equinox?"

"Technically, it was yesterday. I track it to September twenty-first, but there's an exact date and time of day when the earth is essentially straight up on its axis and facing the sun." He had held his hand vertically as he spoke. "And technically, it's called 'autumnal' and not just 'autumn.' As a budding rock art expert and explorer, you want to get things like that right."

"Autumn...nal," Emma recalled saying, tripping over the last syllable a bit. "Autumnal," she had said correctly.

"You've got it! And what's it called in the springtime?" He was always quizzing her.

"Vernal equinox?"

"Exactly. And why?"

Emma said, "Named after a guy named Vernal…" They had both laughed. "Okay, because 'vernal' in some language means spring."

They stopped at a gas station in Wellington and picked up a printed guide before turning the car onto a dirt road with directions to Nine-Mile Canyon. They drove along a creek another thirty miles before finally entering what looked like a canyon.

"Not sure where the petroglyphs are, but let's keep our eyes peeled," her father said. "And look for granaries as well—mud and basket structures stuck up in the edges of the cliffs around here, usually under an overhang of sorts to keep them dry. Native Americans stored their harvest in those."

Emma recalled looking and looking as they drove before coming to a pull out with a sign, where they had pulled over and got out of the car. Both had scanned the cliffs that lined a narrow side canyon for what might be a granary but could see nothing. Her father walked over to the sign and studied something with his finger before looking up to the right and pointing.

"There it is," he said. "See that gray basket'y thing?"

Emma walked over, and he held her close so she could follow his arm and see exactly where he was pointing. "I see it," she said, finally able to make out a mud structure about the size of a five-gallon bucket tucked under an overhang. "How did they get up there?" she asked. "It was clearly where animals couldn't get it…or people too!"

"Some things we will never know," her father had said.

Back in the car, Emma used her map to guide them toward the Great Hunt panel, before spotting another small sign that said, "Big Buffalo Petroglyph," and Emma's father said they had to stop. As they hiked through the brush, she spotted a flat surface on the cliff face that had a variety of petroglyphs—all whiter in contrast to the sandstone cliff where they had been inscribed.

"Well, that's clearly the big buffalo," her father said, pointing to a petroglyph the size of a large watermelon. "Isn't the pregnant buffalo supposed to be nearby?"

Emma unfolded the guide and read it. "It's up that way." They hiked up along the sandstone cliff before arriving at another panel. They both scanned until Emma spotted what looked like the outline of a large cow with horns. It's hollowed-out middle had a small blob in it. She asked excitedly, "Is that it?" and pointed.

"Show me," her father had said, drawing close and looking down her arm to see where she was aiming. "I see it! That has to be it!" He looked around like he had just spotted an alien spacecraft or won the lottery. He even talked about it multiple times on their way home.

He had seemed so excited, so alive that day.

...

IT HAD TO BE ON A DIFFERENT TRIP that she drove one-hundred miles per hour for the first time. They had been driving a stretch of lonely highway when her father had pulled over and asked if she wanted to drive. She remembered having her driver's license, so she must have been at least sixteen.

Her father had said, "This is the longest stretch of freeway in the entire country without any services. No phone. No gas stations or convenience stores. Nothing. For over a very long way." Then with his trademark wink, he added, "So go as fast as you want."

Emma knew that driver's license or not, her mother would have objected to the idea. She asked, "You're sure?"

"Positive," he said. Smiling, he added, "Just don't tell your mother."

Emma had pushed the pedal all the way to one hundred and five before backing off—her first and only time ever driving that fast.

...

EMMA WOKE UP AS THE FLIGHT ATTENDANT asked what she wanted for lunch. Emma waved her hand and said, "Nothing…Actually, can I get a bottle of water?" The sun at thirty thousand feet streamed in the window next to Emma, comforting but leaving her very thirsty.

After drinking the entire half-sized bottle of water, Emma turned to the man seated by her side and said, "Thanks for your words earlier. You were my miracle today."

"Oh, I'm glad you were able to get some sleep," he said. Hesitating, he added, "I lost my wife just over six months ago. Today isn't any easier than that first day, but I'm somehow making it."

"I'm so sorry. So, so sorry. Do you have family?"

"Oh, yes. I was just out to see my daughter and her family in New Haven. We had a delightful time together. My family is a blessing that fills my life with joy—they save me every day," he said, smiling in a way that reminded Emma of her father. "We're very close."

Emma's eyes glistened as she said, "I can see your happiness. You seem like a very blessed man." Emma was grateful for the time she had spent in Paris chatting with her father. She was grateful for so many memories. She was grateful they had talked about taking one last trip even though it would now never happen now. She resolved to find out where he had wanted to take her and committed to make that trip someday without him. Perhaps she could even convince her mother to come along. She smiled at the thought of carrying on the trip tradition together.

She had so many good memories with her father. Time in the Utah deserts. Time on the beach in Carlsbad. Time. Thoughts flooded her mind like waves crashing on the beach at first and then taking over like a high tide that covered everything.

Emma must have dozed off again because when the pilot announced they were preparing to land, she shook herself awake and wondered how the flight had been so quick.

Chapter 12

Jetlag

Emma landed shortly after noon and quickly found her way to the rental car area. She texted her mother that she was on the ground and would be at the hospital soon. As she drove toward Scripps Memorial, she was overcome by an even more profound sense of loss. Tears began to flow again, which made it hard to see. She pulled over on the freeway shoulder and searched for the button to turn on the hazard lights. She sat sobbing for a few minutes, worrying that she couldn't show up like this for her mother. Another rush of emotion had her half expecting to arrive and find her father alive and well, which was followed by an irrational urge to run, come up with some last-minute reason she couldn't make it. She wiped her eyes, convinced the rush of emotions had something to do with loss. She reminded herself she was grieving.

Wiping her eyes and collecting herself, Emma knew her mother was likely feeling everything she was and more and needed Emma's support. She had to be strong for her mother. As she so often did for her speeches, Emma drew a deep breath and said, "Time to focus, Emma Rose. Only present thoughts from here. The time for prep is over. It's time to light this place up!" and then reframed her last statement with, "You mother needs you."

Taking a deep breath, Emma pulled out into traffic and drove on.

When she arrived at the hospital, Emma quickly found her mother, who nearly fell into Emma's arms. There was little to say other than there was some paperwork to finish before they could leave. "They've already taken your father," pointing to the empty room nearby where the two of them must have spent the past day and night, answering some of Emma's unasked questions. Attendants were already changing sheets and cleaning the floors.

Emma tried to hold back the tears. She couldn't remember ever feeling so empty, so lost. "Oh, mom, can I see him?"

"At the funeral home, they said."

Emma and her mother held each other and cried while they waited. A woman in a business suit finally brought a folder with several sheets for Emma's mother to sign and then said crisply, "Okay, you're finished," before registering the overwhelming sadness the two women in front of her were experiencing. More softly, the woman added, "I'm so sorry for your loss. Please do let us know if there's anything more that we can do for your family."

The two women sat together, and then at the same time they leaned slightly apart, looking each other in the eye and saying, "We really should get going."

As they walked toward the parking garage, Emma's mother said, "Oh, do you have a car? We came by ambulance last night…Of course you have a car—how else could you get here!" They both laughed at the momentary comic relief.

Emma drove to her parent's condo in Carlsbad. Her mother wandered around the single-story flat overlooking the beach and asked, "What now?"

Emma wasn't sure if the question was about doing something or feeling something. "Nothing, Mom. We don't need to do anything."

"I feel so lost."

Emma prepared sandwiches, and after eating encouraged her mother to rest for a bit, realizing she probably hadn't slept the night before or possibly even the night before that. Emma walked her into the bedroom despite her protests.

"You know I won't be able to sleep," her mother protested.

"Just try, Mom. Even lying down will help." Emma helped her get comfortable and drew a blanket over her mother before saying, "We can talk later."

…

EMMA CLOSED THE BEDROOM DOOR behind her and walked to the large glass doors with a view of the beach and ocean. The ocean looked cold, as though it was gearing up for winter swells from storms somewhere else. People off in the distance walked the beach in both directions. She saw a lone beach comber, an older man with graying hair, tall and slim, and caught herself leaning forward and mouthing, "Dad?" What had happened in the past 24 hours still didn't feel real.

Turning, Emma bumped into the easy chair where her father had frequently read and spotted Dickens' *A Tale of Two Cities* on the side table, a book she hadn't read since her high school English class. Her father had been a voracious reader and usually marked books with brackets around paragraphs or checkmarks alongside text that he found significant. He had often written comments in the margins for reference. She realized this must have been the book he was reading before going to the hospital and sat in his chair, desperate for any kind of connection with him. She opened to the metal bookmark he had placed early in the book, presumably where he had left off. Two quotations were marked in both pencil and pen, as though they had been highlighted on separate readings.

> "O, sir, at another time you shall know my name, and who my mother was, and who my father, and how I never knew their hard, hard history. But I cannot tell you at this time, and I cannot tell you here."

Her father's handwriting next to this quote said, "Someday." Skipping a few lines, Emma could see he had marked another section.

> "If you hear in my voice—I don't know that it is so, but I hope it is—if you hear in my voice any resemblance to a voice that once was sweet music in your ears, weep for it, weep for it! If you touch, in touching my hair, anything that recalls a beloved head that lay on your breast when you were young and free, weep for it, weep for it! If, when I hint to you of a Home that is before us, where I will be true to you with all my duty and with all my faithful service, bring back the remembrance of a Home long desolate, while your poor heart pined away, weep for it, weep for it!"

Next to this in the margin, he had written, "WC."

Emma could see these were spoken lines but could not remember which characters said them or much else about the story. She shrugged and put the book down. She walked to the table where only a few weeks earlier she had enjoyed Christmas dinner with her parents. It was now covered with stacks of books and paper—photo albums, medical bills, and insurance statements.

To her surprise, on top of one stack was a sheet in her father's handwriting with "Funeral Plan for Steven Rose" across the top and a bullet-pointed list down the left side. She was shocked that he had been this thorough in advance, wondering if what everyone else thought was a routine trip to the emergency room had registered differently for him. Had he known he was dying? Emma shuddered at the thought and quickly accepted the fact that there was more going on here than she might understand.

She scanned the list.

- *Memorial service in Carlsbad (let Emma know).*

Emma smiled that her father had noted to remind her. Was he worried she would be forgotten? She chuckled at the thought but loved his thoroughness.

She continued reading.

- *Sing "Nearer, My God, to Thee"*
- *Thoughts from Bishop Caldwell*
- *"Goin' Home" (if you can, find someone to sing a solo)*
- *Closing song: "Families Can Be Together Forever"*
- *Prayer*

She smiled at the title of the closing song—a song she had frequently sung in church when she was younger. She hadn't spent much time in church for years, anticipating she would return someday but unsure when. She looked away, remembering the tune and humming it a bit. Reflecting, she knew her father had been deeply religious although not in a pushy sort of way. He believed what he believed, had never been embarrassed of his views on this life and the afterlife or love for God, and yet had carried along as though the most mature way to conduct himself was to walk rather than talk his beliefs. Looking back at his funeral plan, she wasn't at all surprised by how straightforward and simple the program was—a testament to his character.

There was a fair amount of whitespace and then one more note that caught her by surprise. It was even underlined.

- *<u>Burial in Idaho</u>*

Idaho? Why not Utah, where Emma had been raised? Or maybe Carlsbad now that this was their home? Emma had only ever been to two or three cemeteries in her life, mostly around the Salt Lake area growing up. She had never thought about where her parents wanted to be buried or heard them discuss it. But Idaho?

Her heart protested. She had never been to Idaho! And then she remembered one family trip to Yellowstone Park when she was very young—with crossing Idaho as the most obvious way to get there—but remembered nothing more about the drive than that.

Emma couldn't recall her father ever mentioning Idaho—in any specific way or especially with even a remote affinity for the place. She knew she had some Rose cousins who lived somewhere in Idaho, Jennifer and her husband, John, but had only met them at family gatherings in Utah.

Why Idaho?

...

AN HOUR LATER, EMMA'S MOTHER emerged from the bedroom smoothing a sweater she had put on. Emma was brimming with questions but knew she couldn't plow into those and instead held most of them back, asking just one.

"Were you able to sleep?"

"Maybe. I'm not really sure, but I do feel refreshed." Then she became fully aware of all that had happened recently and began crying. Emma guided her mother to the couch and held her.

"Oh, Emma. Dad said just last night, 'Make sure Emma is okay. This will be hard on her.' He was so concerned for you. I guess he thought I would be the tough one." She sobbed and looked up from Emma's shoulder with a slight smile, "Well, I'm not right now."

"You don't have to be tough today. Just cry."

Emma waited patiently until she could no longer resist the question blazing a freeway through her mind. She blurted out, "Mom, why Idaho?"

Her mother looked up, surprised. "How do you know about Idaho?"

Emma explained what she had found on the table and read, apologized for being snoopy, talked about how surprised she was her father already had a funeral plan, said it was nicely put together, but wondered why "Burial in Idaho" was underlined. "It really stood out!" She once more excused her snooping with a shrug, saying, "It was on the table!"

Her mother clenched her hands and looked around the room as though relief would come from the kitchen or over by the fireplace.

"I'm not sure I'm ready for this, Emma."

Later that evening, after a call with the funeral home in Carlsbad, eating a dinner delivered by some friends from church, and a shower for each of them, they sat together again on the couch.

"I'm ready to talk now," her mother said, taking Emma's hands in hers. Emma could tell she was carefully thinking over what to say next. In an uncharacteristic manner, she looked Emma squarely in the eyes and cleared her voice, saying slowly, "Emma, your father…was adopted. He was going to tell you. He wanted to show you."

At first, Emma didn't know what to say but eventually asked, "What does that have to do with Idaho? We're talking about his burial, not…" Her confusion trailed off as this second bit of news registered and then registered again.

First 'Idaho' and now 'adoption'? It made no sense. Why the secrets? She began having a violent reaction to what her mother was saying and stood up. Pacing the room, Emma said in a gush, "Adopted? Mom, how can this be? How do you even know? Why didn't Dad ever tell me? How did he feel about all this?"

Her mother sat back, folding her arms across a pillow. "He knew you hated surprises and wouldn't take this well. That's why he wanted that last trip with you, one you'll never be able to take." She broke down sobbing.

Emma reached to comfort her mother, wondering why her father had kept all this a secret.

Her mother finally looked up. "It was a burden he carried with him his whole life. Well, 'burden' isn't the right word. It was something he didn't learn about until he was a young man. It never really concerned me all that much, but he thought it might not sit well with you."

Emma protested. "Sit well! How…I'm…what?" Her thoughts were jumbled. Rationally, she knew whatever the real story was didn't alter her life. Her upbringing was solid. She remembered her grandparents were all about family with their extended family always around. They were gentle and loving, always calling her "Miss Emma" and holding her close and giving her ice cream after dinner. They had both passed away the year Emma turned ten. And that her father was an only child had never concerned her since she was an only child herself.

A series of less rational, newly forming questions raced within her like a wildfire. They weren't really his parents, right? Did her father ever meet his birth parents? Did he have any biological siblings? If he did, then she would have other aunts or uncles. Did she have cousins? If so, where did they live?

And what did this have to do with Idaho?

Emma reached over for *A Tale of Two Cities* and scanned the marked lines once more.

Why had he written "Someday" in the margins? Was Idaho the mystery destination her father had in mind? If so, she recalled it being a big state on the map, so where in Idaho specifically? Clearly, her mother had connected the question of her father's burial with a completely different category of questions about adoption, questions she had not once thought to ask. Not once.

Emma pointed out her father's notes in the margins. "What's WC, Mom?"

Her mother took a deep breath. Tentatively, she said, "It might stand for 'Willow Creek.'" She looked around nervously. "Probably does. That's where."

"'That's *where* what?" Emma tried to mask the slight annoyance building in her. She added apologetically, "Sorry, Mom. This is all just so strange. You spend your whole life thinking one thing and then find out it's something else." She immediately thought of the goldfish sequence from her speech and felt like one of the younger ones asking, "What's water?" She was worried she was being inappropriately pushy but was also feeling overwhelmed by news that was already challenging her own sense of identity. For Emma, this news was simultaneously unraveling but enhancing everything she stood for, spoke about, and was now planning to write a book about. The revelation that her father was not who she understood him to be, that he had roots she never previously knew about, had her feeling a bit unhinged.

"That's where he wants—wanted—to be buried…a little town in Idaho called Willow Creek, one that I know nothing about." Her mother looked around the room, tears welling in her eyes and seeking answers from the air. "We talked about it once or twice only. The cemetery there, that is. It only came up a few years ago. I just thought I'd have more time to…"

Emma sat wringing her hands, sensing her mother was emotionally exhausted. She had a hundred more questions but knew pressing the matter wouldn't produce answers—at least not right then. She told herself to give it some time. She would have to wait and wonder—and patience was not one of her strengths. She wondered about Willow Creek, intending to look online for more about it later.

Emma drew in a deep breath and felt she was breathing something new, heavy, and unfamiliar—like stepping out of a spaceship on otherworldly shores and testing the new planet's atmosphere for the first time. Once more recalling her goldfish trademark, she began to relate to the image in a new way. "You're still breathing, Emma Rose," she reminded herself, simultaneously astonished, shocked, stupefied, and variety of other synonyms describing how totally unsure she was of just what her next step would be.

She mused out loud, "Maybe what I thought was water isn't something else after all."

"What's that?"

"Oh, nothing," Emma said. On one hand, she felt a challenge to her professional platform. She had worked so hard at this! The new facts about her father didn't literally change anything really—or did they? That her father had been adopted brought a whole host of questions to mind. And that an Idaho town called Willow Creek factored into all of this was as confusing as it was intriguing. Family roots she had long since accepted were now perhaps only a figment, with other roots in the Steven Rose family tree she had never remotely considered! And potentially her true roots at that. Were they good roots? Bad roots? For Emma, this was culture at its core. "My culture," Emma mumbled, her mother not hearing, her mind racing to support the news.

Emma worked to calm herself before turning to her mother and saying, "We're still swimming," getting a puzzled look in return.

...

LATER THAT EVENING, Emma's mother said, "Oh, there's one more thing he wanted me to give you," looking startled but happy she had remembered it.

Not one more thing! Emma's mind protested at the surprises so far.

Her mother walked to the side table by her father's reading chair before turning toward the bedroom. Emma could hear shuffling until her mother returned to the table empty handed. She moved papers aside on the table before locating a small, white gift box. "He really wanted you to have this," she said, handing Emma the box.

Emma wasn't sure what to think but smiled, grateful he had remembered her.

"I have no idea what it is," her mother said flatly, as Emma opened the box.

Inside was a thin bronze-colored pendant shaped like the left half of a heart with a serpentine edge along the left side. Emma picked it up and could see it was quite ornate. Underneath was a piece of paper still in the box. Unfolding it, she read it aloud. "Life will continually teach you that we don't always get to choose what happens to us or why—it just *is*, but we do get to choose what we do about it."

Emma looked closer and could see the heart was inscribed with "IS." Looking to her mother, she reflected, "Interesting," running her finger over the surface of the heart. "It just is," she repeated softly, her father's encouragement through most of her life to accept what *is*, love what *is*, work with what *is*, and not let what *is* keep you from growing.

Her mother reached for the pendant. "It's quite pretty—and quite old. I think I have a chain that will work perfectly with it." Looking at Emma, she added, "I don't know where he got it or when. But the day before we left for the hospital, he was adamant I retrieve the box from his dresser drawer and be sure to give it to you." Pointing toward his reading area, she said, "He kept it right there by his side till before we left. I can't tell you when he moved it over here."

"Is…" Emma mused out loud. Before going to bed, she looked again at the pendant hanging from a chain her mother had found. Smiling, she said, "It just is" in the same straight-forward tones her father had used.

Chapter 13

Willow Creek Townsite, 1894

With chores finished, and while Cassie cleaned up from dinner, Simeon sat down at his rolltop desk in the front room. Eugene reclined against a wall by the family's new potbelly stove—one that distributed the heat more evenly and used coal rather than wood. He was reading a book and asked, "Pa, how does a steam engine work?" when Cassie walked into the room drying her hands on a towel.

"Ask Cassie," Simeon said. "She's a good, smart girl."

Cassie began explaining what she knew about steam power, that the inventor James Watt called it "horsepower" based on the number of horses his innovation was replacing in order to pump water out of coal mines in England.

Turning back to his desk, Simeon frowned as he tallied his losses from that year. Sure, his Willow Creek farm had done well, but his two farms to the west and south of the Dry Bed had been scorched by the summer sun. Crops had died for lack of water.

Looking at a map of the valley, he wondered about the reliability of water from canals on the eastern half of the valley, like the newly expanded Willow Creek canal and others. He contemplated how farmers willingly paid fifty to seventy-five cents a year for a water share, enough to regularly water an acre of land. He traced the map with his finger, wondering how to bring enough water to farms to the west. The dry channel of the river was the most obvious answer, one mother nature had built eons ago. But the first mile or so was problematic, one the Snake River used to tease farmers for a few months each spring and then punish them severely in years like the one now nearly finished. And that notwithstanding the prayers and near-constant fretting of so many across this wide valley with no miracles yet.

Simeon had a reputation for doing many things well. As a ditch builder, other homesteaders regularly enlisted his help. He was a diviner of sorts, not the type who could identify where to dig a well by using a couple of twisted sticks but as a man who could walk the contours of a cleared field and with his natural eye declare the run for any ditch. He had saved many neighbors the cost of hiring a surveyor and the associated delays that came from finding and convincing one to come around.

Sorting through papers, he found a clipping from the *Eagle Rock Post*, the local newspaper that a neighbor had dropped by a few days earlier. Based on his shifting eyesight, he held it at a distance and read it over again carefully, not sure whether to feel flattered or frustrated. It was a short article entitled, "The Law of the Harvest."

> *The Idaho landscape is rich with potential but backbreaking when it comes to the law of the harvest. Here, "as you sow, so shall you reap" begins with multiple conditions, precursors, as it were. To begin sowing upon arrival would be foolish, for the common farmer knows that planting must wait while many other strenuous activities are performed. Clearing the land, ensuring access to a steady supply of water, and then plowing.*
>
> *Many residents in our valley are fortunate to be near one of our good canal systems. Only then would any intelligent man, woman, or child plant their first seed.*

Simeon snickered at how well this described his own experience in the valley. Before pinning it to the wall above his desk, Simeon took a pencil and underlined, "a steady supply of water."

He sat contemplating the point for a moment before reading aloud, "…a steady supply of water."

Cassie asked, "What did you say, Pa?"

Simeon said, "Oh, I was wondering why everything anyone has tried so far to keep the Dry Bed full year-round has not produced one single permanent solution."

Listening, Cassie said, "Hmmm," as her father carried on.

"Old Tom Jenkins was talking the other day about a hair-brained aqueduct to carry water from the Snake River across the Dry Bed. At least the take-in would never last. The Snake is just too powerful—especially come spring."

Cassie nodded.

"We don't only have our land here to care for. We're dependent on the farmers themselves being successful. Without them and a small amount of success, the mercantile would not survive. Our other land, the two farms over by the Dry Bed—well, they are about to take me down. If it gets any worse, I'll have to take on more work hauling freight or something." Simeon stroked his beard. "And I'm not alone. There are fifty other farmers—perhaps more—over that way that are about to go belly-up too. And that does not include those who already did." Out of despair, he put his head in his hands. "Darn it all, we just need a reliable supply of water. I'd pay tenfold to get water to my farms on the west."

"Pa?"

Simeon sat for a moment without saying a word.

Cassie looked at him tentatively and asked again, "Pa?"

Simeon looked up slowly.

Raising her eyebrows, Cassie said, "If you really would be willing to spend ten times more for water, wouldn't others also?" Pausing, she then went on. "You have always taught me to look past the obvious problem. Perhaps you're not looking far enough." She smiled at her father.

Simeon shook his head and said, "A fair reminder. I often think we men have come up with all the good ideas there are. You're right. I can probably look higher a bit as well, to see perhaps if there are other thoughts we should be thinking." He looked wryly up at the ceiling, pointing with one finger.

"Oh, and Pa?"

"Yes?"

"Sarah's getting hitched. To that new Swenson boy, Jens."

"Well, I'll be darned," Simeon said, studying her mood. "You don't seem so happy for her."

"I am," Cassie said. "And I guess I'm not. Maybe a little jealous, I suppose."

"Well, jealousy won't get you very far," Simeon counseled.

"I do know that," Cassie replied.

Simeon turned back to his work.

"And, Pa?"

Turning back to face her, Simeon raised his eyebrows expectantly, waiting for her.

"Erastus Walker is home again."

Simeon rose in his chair. "Well, I'll be. And good for Will to have his firstborn around again." Sensing there was more, Simeon continued looking Cassie's way. "And?"

Cassie blushed slightly. "And nothing. I suppose we can only wait and see."

…

EXHAUSTED FROM HER DAY at the mercantile and evening chores, Cassie put off sleep in order to write in her journal.

I haven't written much lately. It's been so busy. Pa is concerned about how we will make it, what with the drought and all. To me, I see nothing but good—we have the mercantile and good farm here. Eugene is doing well in school. Pa must be dealing with bigger problems than I understand, though. He seems desperate about finding water for our other farms. I figure God made all of this, so taking our problems to him seems like a good idea. I hope he prays about it.

Today, Sarah told me she's getting married. I wasn't too surprised since it's all she ever talks about. Jens Swenson is her boy. I guess I'm happy for her. And sort of jealous. None of the boys around here are all that interesting to me. Most have the gumption to farm, which is admirable. Heavens, Pa is a farmer. But I think I'm looking for something different, someone different.

If I look into my own heart, I think I'm hoping for a man who can see beyond planting seeds, watering, weeding, and waiting. Pa has done that, but then he's done so much more as well. Perhaps I want someone like him. But not someone who wants to take me away from Pa and Eugene, but someone who wants to stay in Willow Creek, or at least nearby. Is that too much to ask? I think it might be.

Thinking about that last line I wrote, I guess I should swallow a bit of my own medicine and take that question to the Almighty.

…

EARLY THE NEXT MORNING, SIMEON BURST into the house smelling of morning chores. "Cassie, you're brilliant!" Simeon said, pulling off his coat and grabbing a piece of toasted bread from the pile Cassie had put on the table.

Cassie looked up, confused. "That I made toast? Brilliant? I'm not seeing the connection."

Simeon paced the room with his hand on his beard, making it clear he was thinking about something. "No time to sit! I have to check something out. An idea came to me in the night and keeps getting better," Simeon said as he put his coat back on. "I need to ride out to the river. I want to see something for myself. With enough resource…" His thoughts trailed off.

Simeon left the house, tearing at his toast, and pulled the barn door open. His horse must have already been saddled because moments later he came riding out on Milo, his favorite quarter horse. He pulled up and said, "Can you get Eugene to school this morning?" Simeon drew his coat around him and tucked his scarf up and under his hat to keep his ears warm.

"It's Saturday, Pa. No school today." Cassie couldn't help but laugh.

"Ah, yes," he said, smiling. "Too much on my mind."

"What about the mercantile?"

"It can stay closed for a few hours. This," Simeon said, emphasizing with his hands, "is far more important." Slowing for a moment, he went on. "I just might know a way, daughter. It will cost more than we've ever invested in a project like this and be harder than anything we've done, but you sounded so much like your mother last night. It reminded me to pray—and I did pray, long and hard, probably more than since your mother took ill. And I woke up with a jolt in the middle of the night with a new idea. The word 'tenfold' kept going through my mind. Like I said, it may be the hardest and most expensive work any of us has done, but with some good talent—if we can find it—and tenfold the cost, we might find a way!"

"I'm so happy, Pa!" Cassie added, "Eugene and I can go open the mercantile this morning. You be safe!"

"That sounds about right. Thank you!" Simeon smiled at his daughter and then turned his horse toward the gate. With a "Giddyap," he prodded Milo and galloped toward the bridge over Willow Creek.

Racing at full speed, Simeon had a clear idea of where he was going. He rode the five miles west toward the river—toward a slight northward bend of the Snake. Slowing to a trot through a rocky area, he mulled over several questions—questions he knew he wasn't the only one trying to answer. But his thought in the night was shaping into a plan to handle the annual problem of spring runoff and still keep the Dry Bed full the entire growing season. The details coming together in his mind could bring water to not just a few hundred acres but thousands, perhaps tens of thousands. With what he was thinking, the river could still crest its banks each spring and wash out the mile-wide flood plain to the south—all past the point where the river turned. Stop working downstream, he thought, and work upstream a bit, rethinking the Dry Bed as the river it once was.

Simeon urged his horse back to a gallop across the frozen landscape toward the spot he had in mind, an area right before the flood plain where the entire force of the river banked and turned north. He had to see it again for himself.

Within the hour, Simeon guided his winded horse along the banks of the Snake River. Looking upstream, he could see the drought-proof head gates of the other canals—those that supplied water to the eastern and southern parts of the valley. Their open mouths faced upstream and took water from the straight, narrow, and steady flow of the Snake along the rocky riverbank upstream to his right. The problem was that the northern arch of the river was literally blocked at every turn by the Dry Bed's lazy line uphill and due west across nearly the entire valley. Water wouldn't flow up and over the dry bed, to be sure, but with sufficient volume the Dry Bed could feed any number of canals to the south. In Simeon's mind, consistent volume was the one and only problem.

Simeon came to the exact spot he had in mind—a specific bend and a short stretch of land at the earliest part of the bend. He dismounted and dropped the reins as he walked to the edge of the river. Here, the Snake drove straight at the bank before turning almost abruptly north. He stood atop a natural, flood-proof rise twenty to thirty feet higher than the course of the river. Following the river with his eyes, he could see the flood plain downstream covered by a mass of cottonwoods. He quickly abandoned the idea of using any portion of that section of land. Looking from where he stood toward the west, he plotted a new channel—a river-sized channel—to connect from where he stood into the Dry Bed's well-defined watercourse about a mile off to the west.

In a flash, the rest of the plan emerged in Simeon's mind. It would take everything he could collect—money, tools, know-how. They would do their work here, a few hundred yards upstream from the flood plain. With his hand, he imagined removing all that dirt—hundreds or possibly thousands of tons.

The Meadowlark

They could form a new, mile-long ditch that would connect the Snake with the Dry Bed to the west. The widest and deepest yet.

Add to that a diversion dam dwarfing anything seen in these parts to regulate the water entering this new branch year around—during the heavy spring runoff and slower times as well. The final step would involve blasting away the riverbank at that point, allowing as much as half of the river to be turned down this new channel rather than its current course. If engineered correctly, the river would flow straight through—reliably and permanently.

They would have a permanent solution to a vexing problem.

It had all been inspired by praying over the word "tenfold"—and Simeon's inspiration was backed by the idea of doing something on a scale much larger than any previous project.

…

As Simeon remounted his horse, it occurred to him that someone else owned this land—a gentleman named Walter Bonham, who was known by all simply as "Bonham"—and he was the next obstacle. Simeon knew he needed Bonham to join up—as a partner, since buying the land outright would make the project impossibly expensive.

Bonham might come along. It could work.

Simeon dropped to his knees on the riverbank. "Oh, Lord," he said, "Thanks for the good idea and what feels like a clear path forward. Thanks for your mighty river and for your fertile land. And thanks for a daughter who would guide me back to you for what I see so clearly now."

Looking up, Simeon felt an urgency to move forward with the plan. He rode immediately back to town, straight to Bonham's home. After a brief conversation, Simeon found Bonham warm to the idea of partnering, and the two thought others might be willing to invest capital and labor as well. They shook hands on an enterprise that paired Bonham's land holdings with Simeon's know-how and commitment to organize, fund, and operate an enterprise. They would handle the paperwork later. The Snake River Canal Company was born.

Simeon now had more than a mere proposal to make at the meeting coming up the next week. He had a partner and a plan.

Chapter 14

Townhall, 1894

Water users set a meeting for the following Thursday to discuss matters, particularly any proposed permanent solutions to the Dry Bed problem—regardless of cost. Water was the lifeblood of the area, as the previous year had shown. Rumors circulated that Simeon Rapp had a proposal—and quite costly one at that. Chatter about what he had in mind drifted much like snow across the fields.

That evening, fifty men gathered at the Willow Creek townhall. Most were from Willow Creek and the new nearby communities of Lewisville, Grant, and Rigby to the west and Clark and Poplar a bit to the southeast—the areas most reliant on the Dry Bed and those most affected by the recent drought. Several men came from nearby Menan, Annis, Ririe, Lorenzo, and Iona, some standing to benefit any improvements and others simply curious.

When he arrived, Simeon took a seat next to his new business partner, Walter Bonham. Both eagerly awaited the opportunity to share their plan.

"Gentlemen!" Carter Johnson stood next to the pot-bellied stove that warmed the room and called the meeting to order. He began by raising the general concern over water and was immediately drowned out by a chorus of opinions. It was clear that everyone shared the need, but no one had much of a vision.

Bonham waited for the group to settle in before confidently raising his hand to quiet the group. Clearly holding back his own enthusiasm, he stood and asked Simeon to join him in front. Bonham put his hands in his coat pocket. All in attendance waited to hear from the two men.

"Between us all," he said looking around the room, "and every other farmer from here to Pocatello, we might have ten or twenty thousand acres under ditch. A few canals run out across the east—the successful ones tie into the Snake above my property and follow the contours. As you all know, the upper and western parts are the valley are too high for these canals to reach and any hope of running water to them is blocked by the old dry channel that works maybe seventy percent of the time—not a high-volume proposition," he said circumspectly before finishing with, "more like a weak ditch this time of year."

A few men laughed, and most looked around the room, those with land fed by the "successful canals" smiling while the others looked much more serious. Several began discussing how seventy percent was too generous a rate of success for the Dry Bed. A few could be heard suggesting that any other land claims should be stopped since any newcomers were creating too much pressure for the already scarce water the Dry Bed delivered.

Bonham continued, "While that has generally been fine, last winter wasn't, and we all know what that has meant. We can no longer count on snowpack in the nearby hills to do the job. And when the snowpack upstream in mountains around the Jackson Hole and Yellowstone areas is thin, our lives are especially affected."

The men in the room nodded, still rubbing their hands together as the small stove in the barn worked to bring it up to a more comfortable temperature.

Bonham paused for a moment. Pulling on Simeon's arm, Bonham continued. "Our good neighbor Simeon here and I have a plan to produce a steady flow from east to west for those dependent on the Dry Bed, a solid plan we think will improve all our lives." The room quieted completely, everyone eager to hear more. Bonham raised a finger and added, "And bring water to not only a few thousand acres—but rather a hundred thousand acres or more!"

Bonham waited for a moment to let the point register. The room immediately came to life as the men looked at each other and began exchanging opinions.

Carter Johnson raised his voice and said, "Let's hear from Simeon."

The group quieted back down.

Simeon brushed his black hair back with one hand and then began stroking his beard. He stepped forward to speak. "My plan…err…my proposal has two parts. Neither will work on its own. So, hear me out before you form your opinions." He used his hands to create a picture in the air. "Part one, a diversion dam and new breach. Part two, a new run. Both will take everything we have to make them happen—and be quite costly. Tenfold whatever number you might already have in mind," he said, emphasizing the last point. "Tenfold, I say."

Simeon then explained his plan—a giant diversion dam about one hundred feet wide at the strategic bend he had recently scouted. Made of rock, concrete, and iron gates. He was careful to contrast this with largest one he had seen to that point, which was maybe twenty feet wide. Add to that a new channel upstream from the flood plain that would by-pass it altogether and be wider and deeper than any previously dug. This new channel would carry Snake River water to where the Dry Bed finally became better defined. The work could all be done during the winter, while the river was low, leaving perhaps only a twenty-foot section of riverbank between the floodgate and the river until the project was complete. The final act would be breaching that remaining section of the riverbank with dynamite to let water through.

"It will be the end of droughts for the ten ditches I'm aware of that are currently fed by the Dry Bed."

The men in the room sat quietly, contemplating Simeon's proposal.

Simeon added, "No more wasted crops, dead animals, and bad years."

A few of the men chuckled uncomfortably at the memories of their own losses and neighbors who had packed wagons in late August and headed "back home" to Utah, Colorado, and other places of origin.

Wrapping up his proposal, Simeon said, "With a steady flow of water, this will triple the draw for each of the current canals in Shelton and Clark as well as allow us to run several new canals well above the grade of our eastern canals to bring new water to the northern areas like Willow Creek and Ririe, and then west to Rigby, Lewisville, and Grant. Those can likely be dramatically increased in size. We could install five to ten diversion dams along the channel for other new canals as well."

Simeon stepped back toward the stove, signaling to the group that he was finished outlining his proposal. The gathered men began discussing with each other, a few tentatively raising hands before turning to men on the right and left, most with looks of consternation. Some were smiling at what felt like progress.

The immediate reaction was that this was an oversized dream for a group of men accustomed to scraping sagebrush from one acre at a time and praying for rain. Many had cultivated a few acres at most much of their homestead claim remaining and little motivation to clear those because of the lack of water.

Simeon could hear several men voicing how valuable their uncleared land would become if they could get water to it, catching on to the idea.

Carter rose and faced the group, shouting to regain control. He stammered to form one simple question repeatedly until the group quieted. "How?... How?... How?" All eyes were on Carter as he said, "The Snake has to run five to ten feet higher than it is right now to put even an inch of water into the Dry Bed." He glanced sideways at Simeon before sitting back down.

The men's voices grew loud again, anticipating Simeon's answer.

Simeon spoke above the noise from the group.

"Remember, my proposal has two parts!" He continued, "With the exception of its first mile, the rest of the Dry Bed is already a well-defined, twenty-mile-long ditch capable of holding at least a quarter of the Snake River's supply. It's the first mile that is unpredictable and unreliable. To your point, Carter, its problem is just what you describe—that the natural mouth of the Dry Bed sits near the second bend ten feet too high and is really only a flood plain. But if we dig a new, straighter line upstream at that first bend, we can bypass that and make the Dry Bed a more natural river course from beginning to end. We will have to remove thousands of yards of dirt over that first mile to the depth of the riverbed before cutting the bank away." Pausing, he added a point previously not made, "Which is across private land."

Men looked at each other, puzzled. Each listened as Simeon described how Bonham's land provided the most direct and least rocky line between the Snake and where the Dry Bed resolved from a flood plain into a well-defined channel.

Repeating his earlier point, Simeon said, "We will dig a ditch, three-quarters of a mile long or so, one hundred feet wide and twenty feet deep. We will fortify its banks, and connect in just north of Anderson's," he said, pointing at John Anderson who sat off to the left.

Will Walker stood to speak for the group. He held his hat to his chest as he spoke directly and with concern. "Simeon, my friend, I so appreciate what you are doing here. But, are you saying Bonham will control this?"

The room bustled again with protests and side conversations.

Simeon stepped forward, holding his hand out suggesting Bonham stay seated and not answer. Simeon squared his shoulders and looked at Bonham for reassurance.

"Yesterday, Bonham and I formed the Snake River Canal Company. His land is already deeded to the company."

A few men looked around the room, mouths open in protest. The immediate reaction was that they were being set up, cut out of an opportunity, snookered.

Simeon held up both hands, attempting to calm the group before continuing. "Men! Men! We all know this works only if everyone sees this as an opportunity."

Fairness was the unwritten, unspoken code of the West and had generally prevailed in this part of the Snake River Valley. It took in the forces of nature, the health of a man and his family, and a man's good fortune. Rarely was anyone truly taken advantage of, but people frequently opted out of opportunities for any number of reasons—from accidents and bad health to overextending themselves during good years with life-altering reversals from a drought the next. Often, one man's losses could appear to be another's opportunity.

Simeon's words reassured the men in the room that despite the business tone of his proposal, he was not forgetting the fact they were all interested in the greater good of the community. Clearing his voice, he added, "We're looking for shareholders—both cash and labor on the project. We will let anyone in who wants to help make this a reality."

Bonham nodded his agreement and stood to add, "This may be the largest irrigation project ever undertaken…anywhere in the world! And it won't be cheap."

Simeon nodded and said, "It will be our most expensive water yet. We are projecting five dollars a share."

The room erupted in discussion and protests. One man shouted, "That's ten times what we're paying for any other water!"

Simeon defended with, "I told you 'tenfold'! Think about it—this is for water you can't currently get! And for acreage you can't predictively water or in many cases water at all!" Others nodded as the reality of the situation and the sensibility of the plan set in. One man beamed, saying to his neighbor, "My north forty might finally be worth something after all!"

Bonham spoke again. "Mark my words. Even though this water will be our most expensive yet, five years from now, those farming any part of these one hundred thousand new acres *at a profit* will wonder why they ever resisted and why we didn't do this sooner."

Simeon and Bonham both worked to calm the room and answer questions. Once the group settled, Simeon explained the timeline and the exchange rate for anyone who worked on the project. No one disagreed that this would be the biggest irrigation project ever undertaken by anyone in the room—or anyone they knew. The costs eventually made sense. A well-engineered diversion dam. A new, permanent channel. All to deliver a sure supply of water. All to open new land for farming. All to create more opportunity.

Everyone agreed that it was an oversized dream but one that just might work. It made more sense than anything previously discussed. Simeon looked at Bonham with a smile as he overheard several men using the word "tenfold" positively.

With little else to do but chores for the months ahead, a project like this would give many men work over the winter—especially if that work could be in exchange for ownership. And even though Bonham wasn't as well known to the group, the fact that his land was already deeded to the company added a layer of safety to the idea of joining this new irrigation company.

Carter raised the final question of the evening. "When do we start?"

Knowing his answer would make everyone instantly cold from the deep winter already upon them, Simeon looked around the room and said, "Two weeks after Christmas."

...

After a lengthy discussion, the meeting ended. Bonham left quickly. Simeon talked with a few of the men and then turned to get his horse. As he walked toward the tack side of the barn, Will Walker approached with his hand extended.

Will pumped Simeon's arm in a handshake and said, "Great presentation, my friend. But on a more personal note, how are you getting along?" Will regularly checked on Simeon to see how he was handling matters as a single man, even though it had now been quite a few years since Esther had passed on.

"I'm getting by, Will. Thanks for asking."

Will cleared his throat and looked Simeon in the eye. "You know I trust you, Simeon. But you may have bitten off for yourself a bigger project than either of us has ever chewed—tenfold!" he said, teasing Simone a bit with the word on everyone's lips that night. "Likely much more than you or anyone around here will be able to swallow!"

"We will see. A little hard work—well, a lot of hard work—has accomplished much in our lives so far, Will. Hasn't it? It's not comfort and ease bringing us to knees, mind you. None of us has acquired anything for nothing."

"That's so true, Simeon. Truer words were never spoken."

This gave them both pause, memories filling their minds from a decade that had produced good lives for them and their families—despite some heavy losses and now near-constant pressures from the lack of water.

After a pause, Will looked up, a new forlorn look indicating he was changing the subject to something distressing to him. "My son, Erastus…," he said, pausing. "Erastus is coming home in the next few days—for good now. It's been hard since Samuel died—for both of us—but we're going to try to live together again."

Simeon looked up at Will, sensing hesitation. He knew the accident had ripped the family apart but wasn't sure why Erastus got the blame. Simeon had written it off to grieving parents. The known facts were that Erastus had been careless with a pitchfork which had caused a terrible accident. That Erastus had left the area shortly thereafter led Simeon to conclude that blame can be harder to live with than sorrow.

Unsure just what had happened, Simeon continued to resist the urge to pry into his good friend's affairs. All out of respect for a family's privacy, of course. Supportively, he said, "That's good, my friend, right? Always good to have a grown son return to help with things."

"Well, we will see."

Simeon nodded. Tempted by the moment, he began to ask, "How's he been getting along…?"

Will reflected. "Well, he's a land engineer now. He spent the last year in Pocatello with my brother. He learned to survey. He's only twenty, but I'm told he can build bridges." Will seemed guarded as he said it. "Would you be able to use him?"

With a thousand decisions yet to be made, putting together the right team was foremost on Simeon's mind, something he knew would be his constant focus until this project was finished. He knew his own abilities to measure grade, gauge contour, and manage the flow were limited. He had built small head gates but nothing remotely close to the scale of the diversion dam he was now planning, especially working with that amount of concrete during the winter. He was instantly pleased at the thought of a known talent helping with the complex task of keeping every aspect of this new project leaning in the right direction.

Having an engineer who was a surveyor on the project felt like a gift, even a miracle!

"Absolutely! You bet I could use him." Simeon was almost breathless at the thought. In a more measured tone, he asked, "You think he would be willing to work in trade for you…and some equity for himself?"

They discussed a role for Erastus. Will confessed he had thought to use Erastus to improve his own bridges across canals that winter but had immediately become intrigued by Simeon's new plan. Simeon gave Will an easy way out if he needed one by agreeing that bridges were important, since going from town to town and even farm to farm usually involved several dry crossings in the winter but wet ones each summer. Will thanked Simeon for his consideration but countered that Simeon's project would improve the lives of hundreds, perhaps thousands—and might be a better use of someone like Erastus. After a brief discussion, Will gave his support for this new project, offering Erastus for hire and committing to purchase three hundred shares.

Simeon had himself an investor and a foreman! If Erastus would agree, that is.

As Simeon rode through the cold night across town and toward home that night, he whistled the entire way. Overall, he felt his proposal had been very well received. And his candidate for foreman was also a trained engineer! He couldn't imagine a better start to something so big. "Tenfold," he muttered to himself as he unsaddled Milo in the barn. "Why, I never…!."

Within two days, Simeon and Bonham, the two largest shareholders of the Snake River Canal Company, were backed by fifteen new minority shareholders.

By the end of the next week, the company was seventy-five shareholders strong. A public notice was posted in surrounding towns on January 5th of the new year, and work on the project commenced the next week on a day when the snow blew sideways, and the edges of the river were already thick with ice.

Chapter 15

Winter Like Never Before

The funeral service went well, with great support from friends and her mother's extended family from around San Diego county. Even Emma's cousin Jennifer and her husband flew in from Idaho. Emma spoke with them briefly about Willow Creek and her father's request to be buried there, but they were from the western half of Idaho—Boise area—and had heard of the town but knew of no family connection to it. Emma desperately wanted to ask Jennifer what she knew about her father's adoption but resisted, deciding this wasn't the day.

As planned, Bishop Caldwell conducted the service and said a few words at the end, and Emma jotted down one of his lines. He said, "The only way to take sorrow out of death is to take love out of life." Emma turned to her mother and whispered, "You loved him. We both loved him. That's the good news. But I have a feeling we're going to be sad for quite a while." Pulling her mother closer, Emma continued, "I miss him so much!"

At the lunch following, Emma overheard her mother telling a friend of their plans to fly to Idaho the next morning for the burial. The man shook his head knowingly and said, "Been there. The winter wind there will make you forget you've ever been warm."

Jennifer and John apologized that they wouldn't be able to make it to the burial service. Finally connecting with Emma's earlier question, Jennifer asked with a quizzical look, "And why Willow Creek?"

Emma shrugged. "It's what he wanted."

...

LATER THAT EVENING, Emma held her mother's hands while they sat together on the couch and reflected on recent events.

"Is it okay that I don't want to move on?" her mother asked.

"There's no hurry, Mom."

She looked into Emma's eyes and said, "But we do have to keep moving, right?"

"Only when you're ready." Emma felt the sheer burden of dozens of new decisions and unfamiliar events that were sort of governed by a clock—at least the events associated with a funeral and a burial. Even though her father had previously chosen a casket and planned his own funeral service, it had fallen on Emma and her mother to let people know he had passed. There was the task of getting her father's remains to a place they'd never heard of in Idaho. All tasks Emma had never previously considered and now hoped she would only ever have to do once more when her mother passed—only sometime well in the future, she told herself.

And the now necessary trip to Idaho worried Emma. Having packed for the balmy, year-round seventy-three-degree temperatures of Carlsbad, Emma read online that January highs in Idaho ranged from below zero to twenty-five degrees at best. She hunted through closets for anything warm, not finding much. She had made a trip to a surf shop in nearby Encinitas earlier that day to scout for items—and ended up purchasing a pair of black leggings that seemed thick enough, an orange puffy down jacket that made her sweat when she tried it on, as well as a black beanie and the only pair of gloves they had.

"You work with what you have," Emma told her mother as they packed for their trip.

"And plan to suffer a bit," her mother teased. "Heaven only knows what this trip will bring."

Emma was no stranger to cold—she had been cold before and often let everyone hear about it. The fact that winters in Manhattan were icy, snowy, and blowy—with added high humidity—would produce statements like "bone chilling" and "frozen to the core" from uptown to downtown. Emma would jokingly scoff at her fellow New Yorkers and brag that her years of skiing in Utah as a teenager had shown her worse. Who was the most miserable from the cold was an argument no one could win.

Waiting for their flight to Idaho Falls through Salt Lake City the next morning, Emma wiped her bleary eyes, purchased pastries and orange juice at an airport burger joint that happened to serve a few breakfast items, and sat down to check her email. Other than a few texts with Lacy, Emma hadn't looked at anything business related for a few days.

"I have to catch up on a few things, Mom. Just a few minutes on this," she said to her mother.

"No problem. Do what you need to, sweetie."

...

EMMA OPENED AN EMAIL from Sean McKilroy sent the morning after her Paris trip, one with a quick note in typical "Sean" style.

Emma, you haven't peaked yet. Check your next email. Sean.

Emma deleted several spam emails and then came across another from Sean, a glowing introduction to Amelia Whitehouse, Sean's book agent. Amelia had also responded with a slightly longer email:

Hi Emma,

Nice to meet you. If you are as good as Sean says you are, I want your book. Almost feel like I don't need to see it. I'll get you a healthy advance and strong publisher. Likely Harper Business or Portfolio. I will need an outline. I can pull your online articles as writing samples. Oh, and build a list of assets—social media followers, # of email addresses you have, etc. That's golden.

Best! Amelia

The book! Emma had forgotten entirely about the idea of writing a book and instantly felt the pressure of doing something that she hadn't officially committed to in her own mind. Realizing it had already been four days since Amelia sent the email, Emma felt she owed a response—but still wasn't sure how committed she was to a book just yet. She quickly typed a non-committal email explaining her family emergency, thanking Sean for the introduction, saying she would get back with Amelia shortly.

After boarding the plane and settling into her seat, Emma made sure her mother was comfortable and then decided to take a pass at a book outline—to see how much material she really had. On her laptop, she combined points from her recent speeches with some of her latest thinking. It was such familiar turf that it didn't take long at all and actually seemed to flow better than she expected. She had the realization that if she could turn each major topic into an article, she might be able to then extend each article into a chapter. With twelve topics, she could have twelve articles. Expand each to five thousand words, and she would have twelve chapters—and sixty thousand words! Add an introduction and a conclusion of about the same length, and she might have seventy thousand! It seemed more doable than she had anticipated.

Before landing in Salt Lake City for their connecting flight, Emma decided to take what she felt was a huge risk and outline her thoughts in an email to Amelia, with a promise to provide the rest of her requested items soon. Her hand shook nervously as she hit send.

Emma's mother asked her, "What are you working on, dear?"

Emma looked up, a bit breathless from her foray back into work matters, and said, "I think I'm going to write a book."

Her mother smiled and said, "That's nice, Emma. Your father would be proud of you."

Emma felt swept up in the idea of writing a book—a more welcomed distraction than she had expected. While waiting for their connecting flight, Emma emailed Lacy with the outline of assets needed: number of Instagram and Facebook followers, Twitter followers, LinkedIn connections, the number of email addresses in their database, and anything else business related that Lacy could think of. She knew they had been deliberately collecting email addresses from webinar registrations and more recently as people went online to take her short "Does Culture Own You?" seven-question assessment. It hadn't exactly gone viral, but thousands of people had now taken it—"paying" with their email addresses to get access.

While they were sitting at the next gate waiting for the connection, Emma's mother fidgeted with items in her purse before asking, "What are you working on now, sweetie?"

"Oh, just more work stuff—book stuff," Emma said, surprised at how committed she already felt to the idea of a book but realizing she should give her mother some attention.

"You can work like this, right here?"

Emma smiled. "I can work pretty much anywhere, Mom. Except when it comes to speeches. Those have to be given wherever the client needs me to be." Closing her laptop, Emma reached for her mother's hand. "Sorry to be talking all about me. Tell me, how are you feeling? What's going on in your head and heart right now?"

Her mother's eyes were moist. She squeezed Emma's hand and said, "It's hard to say. I think I will be okay—eventually." Looking over at Emma, she added, "I'm so glad you're with me."

...

LANDING IN IDAHO FALLS BEFORE NOON, Emma and her mother saw they would be taking an outdoor staircase down from the plane and hurried to put on their warm clothing. Wearing her puffy coat and beanie, Emma felt winds buffeting from every direction.

"Oh my gosh," Emma said, pulling her jacket tighter as she walked toward the airport building. "Oh my gosh!" Guiding her mother by the elbow, the two followed directions through the airport to the rental car area. "I should have brought two puffy down jackets!" she said to her mother as they left the building for the outdoor rental car area. An icy blast of wind hit her in the face and instantly chilled her lips so much they became stiff. Her speech slurred almost immediately. Emma envied her mother's long coat with a fur-trimmed collar and her tall boots. Only her mother's knees were showing, but that was better than Emma's long legs wrapped in a thin layer of a fabric she began to think had to be made of plastic. She kicked at some tiny piles of snow here and there with her running shoes trying to shake warmth into her legs.

As the clerk held out the car keys with a gloved hand, Emma said, "There's not much snow—how can it be so cold?" His smile revealed a certain cynicism as he said nothing but hurried back to his post in the warming hut. Once in the car, the two women drove for miles before the inside temperature climbed high enough that Emma could comfortably grip the cold steering wheel even with her thin gloves.

...

EMMA'S MAP SHOWED WILLOW CREEK was ten miles from the airport and five miles from anywhere else. She used the satellite view on her phone to guide them across what appeared to be a flat, white frozen tundra dotted with farmhouses and barns. As they drove, they saw leftovers from snowstorms clumped against fence posts and buildings or piled two stories high elsewhere in strategic spots, clearly made by the huge, orange dump-trucks-turned-snowplows parked near them. After ten miles, Emma turned off the highway and drove straight into town. Just then, it began to snow.

At first glance, what she saw was unlike so many of the small towns she had visited with her father. Instead of lines of mostly abandoned two-story buildings on both sides of the main streets, this little town seemed different—all stores were occupied, and she didn't see one thrift shop or antique store. Most had regular names and looked like they were in business and doing fine. Because of the light snowfall, and finally warm again from the car heater, Emma said with delight, "Feels like we're in a snow globe with a cute little cityscape. Isn't it charming?"

Her mother smiled and said, "I guess so," curious about this town that had been so important to her husband.

They drove directly to the Willow Creek Best Western, the only hotel in town.

"One night here and home tomorrow," Emma said.

Once in their room, Emma retrieved the contact info provided by the funeral director in Carlsbad and called Quentin Waldrup, the director of the Waldrup Funeral Home in Willow Creek, to discuss her father's burial arrangements, all planned for later that day. Very professionally, he confirmed her father's casket had already been "secured at the airport" and that the plot at the cemetery was "being prepared." He confirmed that Bishop Thompson, a local church leader, would be there as well for the final service. He offered a tour of what he called "our funeral parlor" if they had time or interest and then encouraged Emma to invite anyone she knew to meet at the cemetery at three o'clock that afternoon for a short service.

Emma was relieved things were going as planned. After settling into their room, Emma said jokingly, "Want to go shopping?"

Her mother was sitting on the edge of her bed and looking out the window that was mostly fogged over with condensation. She looked back at Emma through tears, clearly not having heard Emma's question. "Why here? Why so far away? And somewhere as cold as this? And why a place where we know no one?"

"I don't know, Mom. I wonder if we'll ever know."

"It's just so far away…"

Emma looked out the window at a large black bird perched on a nearby post, wondering how a bird could survive such cold. She wasn't in a hurry to get things over but was beginning to feel relief that the afternoon service would mark the end of so many planning discussions over the past few days.

"We're here," Emma said softly. "It's what Dad wanted."

Checking the time, Emma called the front desk for a recommendation for lunch. The clerk said, "Try Carter's on the corner of Main Street. Great coffee shop. Good scones."

Emma hadn't heard "coffee shop" for at least a decade, and the mention of scones conjured a recent purchase from the Levain Bakery on 74th on the Westside in Manhattan, a delightful English blueberry scone, the memory of which made her mouth water. She asked the clerk, "Do we have to drive?"

"I would. It's only about five blocks away, but it's cold outside."

As if she didn't already know.

Chapter 16

Scones and Honey Butter

S itting in a booth at Carter's a little before one o'clock, Emma and her mother munched on scones made from what looked like pieces of bread dough that had been fried and were now smeared in honey butter that was melting before their eyes, nothing at all like the New York biscuit variety she had expected.

"These are really delicious," Emma said between bites. Her phone vibrated in her pocket. She checked to see who was calling. The area code was 208, which she now recognized as an Idaho number and knew it likely had something to do with why they were in town.

She quickly swallowed what she could before answering. "Hello?"

"Miss Rose, this is Quentin Waldrup, director…"

She finished chewing. "Of course. Sorry. We're just eating." Swallowing again, she saw honey butter dripping down the side of her hand and rotated her hand as she licked at it. "What's up?"

A few men drinking coffee at the walk-up counter gave her a look that said, "Shhhh!"

"There's been a discovery…an issue…with the burial. Would you be able to meet here at the funeral parlor?"

"Now?"

"Well, the sooner the better. Officer Jones is here now." He said that as though she knew who he was.

"Officer Jones?" Emma tried to lower her voice a bit from the stares.

"Yes, ma'am."

Emma waited for him to explain further but got nothing.

"Okay, we're at the coffee shop…er…Carter's right now but can drive over in a few minutes."

"No need to drive, ma'am. We're right across the street."

Emma looked up and out the window and could see a sign that said "Waldrup Funeral Home" on a mint green building directly across the street, curious that she hadn't noticed it earlier. She said good-bye and put her phone down. "Mom, there's some kind of problem at the mortuary. They want us to come there…"

Her mother shook her head, tears instantly forming, looking down. "I can't…"

Emma thought for a moment and then said sympathetically, "No problem, Mom. I can go alone. Apparently, it's right across the street," she said, pointing out the window. "Do you want to wait here? Our lunch is on its way. Tell them I'll be right back."

Her mother nodded. "I'd feel okay about that."

Emma nearly ran into the waitress as she walked out and explained that she would be right back. On the back wall, she noticed a variety of pictures with marching bands and decorated parade floats. Opening the first door of the breezeway, she saw a large poster with pictures of covered wagons in a line and men riding large bulls that was advertising what appeared to be a rodeo from the year before. She smiled at how small towns were so different from her usual experience.

Emma reflexively drew her coat up around neck and looked all ways around the intersection before crossing the street to the funeral home. The traffic was light but the parking slots up and down the street were full. People were coming and going into the stores lining both sides of the street. Wondering what drew people to town, her immediate question was whether it ever got warm around here.

A bell jingled as she opened the door to enter the Waldrup Funeral Home. She was met by a wave of warm air and could hear soft music playing toward the back.

A bald head poked out from an office at the end of a large open room. "We're back here, Miss Rose." Then he emerged, a short man with round glasses and a bow tie, with a sort of courteous urgency, extending his hand. "I'm Quentin Waldrup, director of—"

"—Pleased to meet you, Quentin," Emma said, shaking his hand.

"Well, of course, we met on the phone, but it's good to meet you finally in person," Quentin said.

As Emma entered the office, a tall police officer wearing a thick overcoat that matched his uniform turned her way.

Quentin said, "This is Topher…"

"I'm Officer Jones," the officer said, extending his hand.

"Emma Rose," she said, taking his hand and nodding. Shaking off the cold from her short walk across the street, Emma asked, "So, what is going on?"

Officer Jones took off his hat and brushed his dark hair back with his hand, looking at the ground and then sort of sideways up at her as though he was swallowing hard and had something complicated to say. He was closer to her own age than she had first thought or expected for a police officer in a small town—and surprisingly good looking. He filled out his overcoat nicely, his uniform underneath tight against his chest. The mud on his shoes seemed out of place given how put together he seemed.

Squinting a bit, Officer Jones said, "We have a situation, ma'am."

His words brought Emma around. Looking up, Emma said, "Okay, Officer?" waiting for more details.

"Well, you can call me Topher."

Emma smiled. He seemed confident, even educated, which made him seem a be a bit out of place given her prior experience with small towns. Always slightly intimidated by the police, Emma had a hard time calling him Topher. Automatically, she said, "Okay, Officer. What's the situation? Topher, I mean."

Topher nodded and squared his shoulders. "Ma'am, the situation is this. Alan Jones, the caretaker at the cemetery—and no relation—who does the digging there, found some bo…err…something disconcerting while removing dirt for…what I'm told is your father's grave." He looked down and quickly up again. In an official tone, he said, "I really shouldn't…can't say more." Knowing the next part further complicated matters, he hesitated before adding, "We have taped it off for further evaluation. For now, it's a crime scene and—"

"—Crime scene? What are you saying?" She looked to Quentin, her look protesting as though he might give her the straight scoop on what was happening. Quentin shrugged his shoulders helplessly.

Topher leaned forward. "It's going to take us the rest of the day to process the scene. To be thorough. Department regulations. We don't know when…"

Quentin's thoughts seemed to resolve. He clarified. "We can't hold the service today, Miss Rose. Maybe tomorrow. Even though we really don't know for sure," he added, looking sideways at Officer Jones, who nodded. Turning back to Emma, he said, "Could you be okay with that?"

Emma's thoughts raced. Of course, she wasn't okay with that. What about her grieving mother sitting across the street at Carter's melting down with her honey butter? And their flight scheduled for early the next afternoon? Would she make her Bentonville speech in two days? "Darn you, Dad!" she whispered, blaming him for the new mystery on top of the original mystery that had brought them to town. Agitated, she unconsciously retrieved the pendant hanging from her neck, rolling the half-heart in her fingers. She had worn it every day since receiving it so far. As she fidgeted, she wondered if Topher hadn't been about to say "bones." After all, isn't that what they had at cemeteries…except wouldn't those be in a casket or box of some type?

If it was bones, then a crime scene of sorts made sense. Slowly accepting the complexity of the situation, Emma hesitated before awkwardly saying, "Well, we do have a reservation for tonight at the Best Western since we couldn't get a flight out later today. Think we can clear things up by morning? That way we might be able to catch our one o'clock flight."

Quentin and Topher both looked up, relieved, and took her response to mean "yes."

Topher let out a breath. "Good plan," he said.

Emma continued fidgeting with her pendant and asked, "What all is involved?"

Topher raised his hands and said officially, "It's police business, Miss. An investigation. I'm not at liberty to comment at this time."

With a resigned look, Emma accepted the circumstance and sighed. "Okay, so what's a girl and her aging mother to do around here?" She immediately felt like she was asking the wrong people.

Quentin perked up. "We do have a movie theater, right next to Carter's. Not sure what's showing," he mused. He walked toward the front window, looked out, and shouted back, "Lion King."

Topher looked like he wanted to help and offered, "The bowling alley over by the rodeo grounds can be fun." Pausing, he added, "If you're into bowling, that is, apparently like the rest of us around here." He smiled and said, "I think they're open 'til eight."

"Thanks." Emma signed. Knowing she needed to reset her mother's expectations, she asked, "So, best case...any idea when we might be able to do my father's service tomorrow?" Tears forming, Emma said, "This really stinks. It's just really inconvenient—this crime situation, that is..." She put her hands to her face. "Sorry," she said, turning away.

Quentin said, "I'm so sorry, Miss Rose. We'll call you the minute we know anything." He gave Topher a pleading look for confirmation.

"We're doing all we can, ma'am," Topher said, sounding more sympathetic than he had. "This was a surprise to us, too." Emma saw him rock forward with his arms coming up either out of personal frustration or to somehow console her. He put them down. She could have used a hug but realized she was among total strangers and that this was a complicated situation in more ways than one.

Emma wiped her tears away and folded her arms tightly. "Thanks," she said before turning to leave. Her feeling was almost surreal, leaving what had been called a "funeral parlor" in a small Idaho town waiting for a police investigation at the cemetery to wrap up before she could bury her father. Oh, and that she had recently discovered he had been adopted. "Expect the unexpected," she mumbled with a sigh as she walked back across the street.

...

EMMA AND HER MOTHER ATE AGAIN AT CARTER'S that night. They had the same waiter as before, a plump blonde woman with an up-do wearing a too-tight striped dress with capped sleeves and an apron where she kept her order pad. She welcomed them back and introduced herself this time as Connie before asking what had brought them to town.

"A funeral—well, a burial."

"Who passed, sweetie?" Connie asked, looking expectantly as though she of all people in the area should have known this already.

"My father, Steven Rose."

"Well, Steven Rose...hmmm...not from around here, was he?" Weighing this and noticing the strain in Emma's mother's eyes, Connie went on. "This must be Mrs. Rose." She reached an arm toward Emma's mother and gave her a hug. "I'm so sorry for your loss, sweetheart. Nothin' harder than losing your man."

Connie tapped her pen against the edge of their booth and then squeezed in next to Emma. "Well, dear, I haven't heard the name Rose around here."

"I don't think…No, it's just…" Emma caught herself, resolved not to get into the details. "It's just where he wanted to be buried." She raised her eyebrows and lifted her hands in silent protest from the table, suggesting that she had resigned herself to this and was merely going along.

"I'm so sorry for your loss, hon." Connie waited for something else to be said before adding, "I know just what you need." She stood and returned a moment later with a plate bearing a large slice of apple pie and two scoops of vanilla ice cream. "On the house, you two. If I can do anything more for you while you're in town, please come back in. I'm nearly always here."

They smiled at Connie and then enjoyed the pie.

As they left the restaurant, Emma pointed to the marquee of the Regal Theater next door, sort of suggesting they see a movie. Her mother pulled her coat tight around her, shook her head slightly, and said, "I think I'd rather go back to the hotel." Even though they had an entire evening ahead of them, Emma knew she could come up with plenty to do but was happy to support her mother any way she could.

At the hotel that night, Emma did a little work while her mother watched the news. Checking her email, she saw an email from Lacy answering the list of questions she had sent earlier.

> E,
>
> *526 Twitter followers*
> *3,253 Facebook Page likes*
> *1,657 Instagram followers*
> *15,558 connections on LinkedIn (wow!)*
> *28,451 email addresses in our list*
> *186,712 TED talk views (but no names captured)*
>
> *Now, stop working and focus on your mother!*
>
> L

Emma added a bit and then forwarded the list along to Amelia Whitehouse, the agent. She watched television with her mother for a minute when her computer chimed with a response.

Hi Emma,

Great list. I think Harper Business will want in. Not sure who else may want to play as well. I'm going to push for a $125K advance, 15% royalty once earned out (meaning after they have made back what they advanced you)—which would be amazing for a first-time author! You'll have to guarantee 5K books can be sold (easy-peasy with your list). Draft by July 1st. Final by end of August. In stores by late October. NYT bestseller in week 1 (because of your list) with a reprint by December.

I want to have this under contract within three weeks.

You're going to be a star!

Amelia

Emma felt her heart rate rise. She wanted to cheer, dance, and shout. She was clearly buying into the idea of writing a book. Her enthusiasm quickly subsided as she looked around the recently remodeled room—dark laminate flooring, a flat screen TV above a mid-century modern wall attachment, a textured headboard at her back, her mother watching TV.

"Mom…?"

Her mother had dozed off but stirred when Emma spoke.

"Mom, wanna go to bed?"

Sleepily, her mother asked, "Oh, no. I'm awake now. Is everything okay?"

Emma started to explain how this book idea had come about and was moving toward publication when she noticed her mother's eyes closing again. When Emma grew quiet, her mother jerked awake and said, "I'm so sorry, Emma. What were you saying?"

"Oh nothing. Work is going well."

"I'm so happy for you!" her mother said, sleepy but still enthusiastic.

Then, remembering why they were staying at this hotel after all, Emma thought about the burial—an event still ahead. She looked at her phone, hoping she had missed a call from the funeral director, but nothing. Would they be able to bury her father the next day? Would it take longer?

"Mom, can I ask you a question?"

Her mother nodded.

Hesitating a bit, Emma asked, "Did Dad ever tell you anything about Idaho or this place, Willow Creek?"

Her mother shifted and sat up on the bed. "Not much at all. He rarely talked about Idaho, and if he did, it was the same way he would have talked about Washington or Montana. Just a place. I know the Roses had some Idaho connections, like Jennifer and John over in Boise. But his parents always said they were from Utah, so I figured as much. When your father announced a few years ago he already had a burial plot at the Willow Creek cemetery, I thought he was being sneaky for the first time in our marriage. He had never even so much as mentioned Willow Creek. He didn't say much more at the time—and I didn't ask. Perhaps my fault for not wanting to know more." She sighed. "When he was writing up his funeral plan a few weeks ago, he said he had known about this since just before his mother had died twenty or so years before."

"Willow Creek or the burial plot?"

"The burial plot, I guess. I probably should have asked more questions. I guess I never thought he would leave me—leave us."

As she tried to sleep that night, Emma sorted through things, wondering if all this new information was simply that or if there was more going on with her father's story, life details that defined him—and possibly her—more than she knew. These were things she didn't know she didn't know—a category she regularly told her audiences was the hardest one in life to figure out. She could hear cars drive by every few minutes. It was nothing like the traffic and all-night sounds of police sirens in Manhattan but still distracting enough and left Emma wondering why she had left her white-noise speaker behind.

...

FAR TOO EARLY THE NEXT MORNING, Emma's phone vibrated on the nightstand next to her. From a comfortable position on her stomach, Emma reached for the phone and saw it was only seven o'clock. She sat up, careful not to disturb her mother sleeping next to her in the king-sized bed they were sharing.

She cleared her throat to try to sound like she had been up for a while, but her voice still came out raspy.

"He...hello?"

"Miss Rose...Emma?"

"That's me."

"This is Topher…Officer Jones…from the police department." He paused. "We met yesterday," saying that as though she might have forgotten.

"Good morning, Officer. What's up?"

In measured tones, Topher said, "We've finished processing the scene. You'll be able to bury your father…sorry, that doesn't sound right…you can proceed with the services today at your convenience."

Emma felt a wave of relief and said, "Thanks so much. What did you find?"

'I'm not able to say, ma'am. That's a matter of police business—actually the medical examiner is involved."

Emma next called Quentin, who confirmed he could make things happen. They agreed to meet at the cemetery at ten o'clock, which would give them plenty of time to make their original flight out of Idaho Falls. After checking out of the hotel, Emma drove her mother along Main Street, once more noticing the orderly nature of the town as they drove. They noticed two- and three-story adjoining buildings lining both sides of the street—a furniture store, two drug stores, a "Five and Dime" that looked like a small general store, a hardware store, a jeweler, clothing shops, a salon, a barbershop, a couple of bars, a bank on the corner, and a gas station opposite that. And of course, Carter's Cafe, with Waldrup's on the other side of the street. They drove past the theater and saw a doctor's or dentist's office, a pizza parlor across the street, and finally a medium-sized grocery store on the right.

"What a cute little town," her mother said repeatedly as they drove, warming up to Willow Creek from the day before. She looked around with wonder as the snow began to fall again. "You're right. It does feel like we're in a snow globe. Or the movies!"

Emma said, "I have to admit, Willow Creek is more put-together than I expected. Perhaps this is why Dad wanted…" She stopped herself at how random it sounded to be buried somewhere because it was cute.

A short distance later, they reached the edge of town, where Emma spotted rows of tall evergreens in the distance that reminded her of massive Christmas trees. Following directions, she realized the trees marked the cemetery. Unlike the bare yards and fields around it, the entire cemetery was covered in an inch of snow. All was quiet as they drove toward a blue pop-up canopy near the middle, passing headstones with names like Ball, Hunter, Ellsworth, Simons, Archibald, and Murdoch. Some were tall and very ornate. Others were marked by snow-covered depressions in the grass. The line she had read in her father's book came back to her: *I never knew their hard, hard history.*

Her mom echoed the sentiment Emma was feeling. "I wonder what all their stories are," she said softly as her eyes swept the area.

Emma recognized Officer Jones carrying an armful of yellow police tape toward the police car. He put the bundle in the trunk and then got in and drove toward them, waving as he passed. Emma waved back.

"Officer Jones," Emma said preemptively, realizing her mother had not met him. "He was investigating the scene here—one of the men I spoke with yesterday."

As Emma parked the car, she saw Quentin standing next to another man under a black canopy, both wearing black overcoats with their hands deep in their pockets. Quentin wore a black fedora that sat a little too high from the ear band he wore beneath. He looked happy to see them. The other man had to be the local bishop who had agreed to come and dedicate the grave.

In the winter light, the entire scene was shades of gray except for the casket propped over the freshly dug grave, bright green artificial turf covering a pile of dirt to the right, and a foot-long piece of yellow police tape left behind and flapping in the wind. The long white hearse parked off to the left almost disappeared into the gray landscape.

Emma parked the car and got out. She hurried around to open her mother's door. Realizing she was the only burst of color on the scene, she hurriedly pulled off her orange puffy jacket and left it in the car. She would brave the cold in the only black clothing she had remembered to bring, leggings and a hoodie. Despite the freezing temperatures, Emma thought she could handle anything for a few minutes.

The other man introduced himself as Bishop Thompson. Emma's mother thanked him for being there since they knew no one from the area.

The ceremony was brief. At Emma's mother's request, Emma said a few words.

"Dad, thanks for being such a good man," she began through shivers. "We will always remember who you were, how you lived, and how you loved." She looked at her mother, recognizing Quentin and the bishop didn't know her father at all but still used the word "we." "We will love you forever," she finished.

Emma's mother squeezed her arm.

Bishop Thompson stepped forward and said a line she had heard at the funeral in Carlsbad. "The only way to take sorrow out of death is to take love out of life." Emma smiled at her mother at the coincidence. He said nothing more before offering a brief prayer.

Then, they each laid a white carnation on the polished casket. Bishop Thompson thanked Emma's mother for allowing him to participate and excused himself, hurrying to his car with his coat pulled up around his ears. Quentin shook both of their hands, telling them to take their time and that he would be waiting in the hearse.

The two women stood there looking at the casket, huddling together to find warmth.

"Your dad was a good man," her mother said softly.

Emma nodded and pulled her close.

"And you're a good daughter, Emma Rose. You're all I have now."

"Oh, thanks, Mom," Emma said, drawing her mother close and kissing her cheek. Looking around the cemetery, she asked out loud, "Do you think we will ever understand all of this?

Chapter 17

Main Street, 1894

The townhall was already too warm by the time Cassie and Eugene walked through its familiar doors. Cassie had promised her father to bring Eugene with her on the condition that he could mostly be with his friends. She knew he wasn't a troublemaker, but she really wanted to enjoy the evening without much responsibility.

Members of the town council greeted everyone as they came in. Along the far wall, a man sat alone at the piano playing familiar songs while members of a brass band milled around nearby waiting for their turn to play. Eugene stomped the snow from his shoes and immediately spotted friends, his look up at Cassie asking if he could join them. At her nod, he cut directly through the small group of people already in the middle of the floor.

With her long hair pulled back just so and wearing one of her finer dresses, Cassie looked around the room expectantly, unsure of who was already there but secretly hoping she might see Erastus Walker. She wondered how he had changed. He had always been the hard-working type and able to fix nearly anything. But she knew he wouldn't be the same young boy she had tossed sticks into Willow Creek with so many years before—any more than she was still that same young girl. She couldn't imagine the result from his two years away.

As Cassie crossed the room, Sarah surprised her from behind. "Cassie, he's here!" she shouted above the music. Cassie's heart raced. Sarah grabbed her by the arm and turned her toward the doorway.

"He" was Jens Swenson along with a few other young boys. Slightly disappointed, Cassie followed Sarah's lead across the dance floor toward Jens.

Sarah greeted him and said, "Jens, this is my dearest friend in the entire world. You know Cassie Rapp, right?"

Jens looked around shyly and said, "We have met, briefly…at church. Still trying to get oriented around here. And remember names! Yours is easy because there's no one Sarah talks about more. Good to see you again, Cassie Rapp."

"Likewise. I hear…"

Sarah interrupted, bouncing with excitement. She released Cassie's arm, took Jens by the arm, and said, "We're getting married!" Jens looked around bashfully. Sarah drew him to the dance floor, and Jens gave off a helpless but happy look as he began to move his feet awkwardly, clearly not much of a dancer.

Cassie laughed out loud before realizing the other boys had already moved off. She was left alone standing near one of the tall poles that supported the roof. "I'll just help hold up the roof…," she whispered to herself.

A deep voice behind her asked, "Cassie?"

She turned expecting to see someone from the town council and gasped with surprise. It was Erastus. He *had* changed. Taller now, he wore a beard, one not quite as thick and dark as his father's, but trending that way. He was more handsome too, his high cheekbones and dark eyebrows accentuating his deep-set eyes. Gathering her wits, Cassie smiled and said, "And you are?"

"I'm Eras—"

"Oh, I know. So good to see you!" Cassie couldn't help but smile.

"It's good to see you as well," Erastus said confidently if not a bit stiffly. He asked, "Would you like to dance?"

"Of course…I mean, yes," Cassie said.

Cassie took Erastus's extended his arm as they walked out onto the dance floor. As they started to move, she said, "Still not one for small talk."

"I just didn't expect…you've grown up," he said, laughing a bit.

Cassie said, "You've changed too." Something compelled her to add, "And quite nicely, I might say." She looked away, realizing what she had said probably sounded very forward.

Erastus laughed warmly and then stammered, "Why, thank you." Then, awkwardly, he added, "And you as well. I know I said you hadn't changed, but I meant…" Realizing he was saying more than he wanted to, he stopped himself.

Cassie smiled at the quiet.

After a short pause, Erastus said barely audibly, "I guess I always thought of you…as my little sister's…err…Sarah's friend, but now…well…" He stopped talking and danced.

After two dances together and despite the double doors being wide open to let in the cold air, Cassie felt flushed from the heat and said, "Whew! Someone put too much wood on the fire!" Looking around, she asked, "Would you want to walk outside?" She added with a smile, "With me, your sister's friend? I hope that's not too forward."

"I'd like nothing more," he said, more at ease because of her invitation. He offered his arm.

…

CASSIE AND ERASTUS WALKED ALONG Main Street and down toward the creek at the edge of town. As they passed the mercantile, Erastus asked, "Rapp Mercantile? When did that open? And who owns the place?"

Pleased, Cassie smiled and said, "I do…Well, my pa owns it, but I generally operate and…uh…manage it. It's what I do."

"Well, Cassie Rapp, I figured as much from you." Erastus added, "You've always been a smart young wo…lady…beaut…" He was clearly searching for words.

They walked on without saying much. As they neared the creek, Cassie worried for a moment about leaving Eugene behind but then thought there were plenty of other adults around to watch over a nine-year old. Turning to Erastus, she asked, "So, what have you been doing all this time away? And where have you been?" Her puzzled look searched for answers.

"I learned to survey," Erastus said proudly, finding it easier to talk about himself. "From my uncle in Pocatello. I'm a licensed surveyor now, what folks are calling a 'civil engineer.'"

"You have really become somebody!"

Erastus said, "Well, I'm trying. Still sort of working on the 'becoming' part."

They talked and talked as Willow Creek bubbled under the ice in front of them from their perch on the bridge. Finally chilled from the winter air, Cassie shivered and said, "We best be going back."

"Here," Erastus said, "Take my jacket. I'm still at least a hundred degrees." He put his jacket around her shoulders.

"Oh, that's much better," she said, feeling his warmth still in the jacket as she drew it close.

Cassie looked down at the dark waters of the creek where it showed through the ice, unsure of what to say next. At the same moment, they both said, "So…" and laughed together, looking back toward the water flowing beneath their feet.

Erastus looked up at the night sky, smiling, and said, "You first."

"Well, okay," Cassie said, shifting in place. Softly, she asked, "So, what took you away after all?"

Erastus looked over with a pained smile. "Well…"

"—If that's too personal, you don't have to answer. I've just known you for what feels like my entire life, and I feel like this is the one thing I ought to know…well, don't know on any account…about Erastus Walker," Cassie said. Then moving a little closer, she said, "And I think I might want to know that too." She thought for a moment about what she was saying, feeling completely at ease with Erastus, before adding, "I don't obviously have a right to know just anything but…"

"It's okay," Erastus said, touching her hand. "I think I'm finally ready to talk about it."

Imagining it had something to do with the strain Cassie sensed between Erastus and his father, she took his arm and said, "All right, but you don't have to."

"I want to. It's important to me." Erastus's voice was unsteady. He cleared his throat, stood taller and turned to face Cassie before beginning. "Most people know what happened, but few ever heard my side of the story. You probably know this already…"

"It's okay. Figure I don't know anything."

"All right." Erastus looked upwards, searching the sky. Sighing, he started. "Well, Sam was late for chores one morning. He must have overslept. And Pa never took kind to anyone late for chores." Erastus paused, looking down. "Momma said he left the house still pulling on one boot. I was busy throwing hay to the milk cows. Sam's job was to break the ice from the watering trough." He took a deep breath and let it out as he said, "I was walking toward the barn to feed the horses and carrying a pitchfork over my shoulder like I always do…did—I don't anymore—and Sam came around the barn behind me at full speed…He…he…didn't…"

Cassie pulled his arm tighter and tried to comfort him. "I had no idea," she said as tears came to her own eyes.

Erastus stood again suddenly, pulling away a bit, and looked at Cassie exasperated. "He didn't even see it!" Pointing to his neck, he bit his lip and then said shakily, "One tine went in here and hit a major artery. There was blood…everywhere." He cried into the night, "The poor kid never even saw it." His head dropped onto his arms, now resting on the bridge railing.

Cassie didn't say anything, wiping at her own tears.

After a minute, he spoke again. "Pa never wanted to hear the full account…my version of what happened. All he wanted to talk about—back then and even now—is how I should have never been carrying a pitchfork over my shoulder in the first place."

Cassie felt helpless to the pain he was feeling, unable to think of anything to say. Speechless for what felt like an hour, a few words finally came to her mind. "No doubt you could have done things differently, but it was an accident—nobody's fault. You didn't set out to hurt your brother," Cassie said to his defense.

Erastus sniffled. "I know it was an accident. But it was sort of my fault—and it wasn't all at the same time. I was carefree then—not exactly careless. It's not like I was the first to carry a pitchfork that way." Erastus wiped his eyes with his sleeve. Grimacing, he added, "It's remarkable how something like that changes you—maybe in more ways than one."

Cassie couldn't think of anything to say but opened the coat he had loaned her and put one side over his shoulders, feeling his strength against her side.

Wiping once more at his eyes, Erastus looked directly at her and said, "The most important realization I've had over the past while is that all this wasn't Sam's fault either. He just came running…carefree too, and even he didn't have any time to react." He sniffled a few more times. "I wish I'd realized that before I left, but then it was too hard to face Pa every day and see his sadness. Too hard to hear Ma talk about what could have been. Too hard to feel so much blame all while missing Sam so much." Between broken sobs, he said, "He was…my best friend. And he…was gone. I held him…right there in my arms, and he was gone."

Cassie couldn't imagine what that felt like. Her own experiences didn't come close to an accident like that followed by such great loss.

Erastus stood, wiping his eyes. "You must think me odd to go there after all this time away. At least telling you right after seeing you again."

"I'm glad you told me." Cassie measured her next words. "I feel like I know you better now. I don't know what I thought before, but I…" She stopped herself.

"I'm sure everyone thought something about the matter. I can only imagine. After a while, it just felt right to get away. When my uncle talked with me about surveying, it was an easy choice. Good for everyone."

Looking in his eyes, Cassie saw a boy who had grown into a man—in part from the hurt he felt and in part from the way he had learned to handle it. She saw a person who took responsibility for the aftermath of his life experiences and didn't blame others.

"I'm past the guilt," Erastus said. "But when I tried to bring up the idea of moving on when I got home today, and Pa just turned away, I wasn't so sure what to do next." Shaking his head, he went on. "He looks at me like I'm broken…"

Cassie's immediate thought was that Erastus's father, Will, had been hurt by losing Sam as well. Perhaps they were both broken a bit by the experience, or at least their relationship was.

"We best be getting back," Erastus said, turning and offering Cassie his arm. They turned away from the sound of Willow Creek and walked back toward the music coming from the townhall. Along the way, Erastus released her arm and reached for her hand. Cassie looked up at him with a smile and found his eyes aimed upward at the starlit sky, a big smile on his face. He seemed far less nervous, perhaps even relieved to have shared.

Cassie felt him shiver next to her and gripped his arm with her free hand, unwilling to let go of his other hand. "I love Polaris, the North Star," she said, pointing with her free hand, not wanting to let go with her other hand at all. "Travelers the world over use it to find their way home. When I look at it, I always think of sailors and explorers on rough seas or wide-open plains, all dreaming of home." Smiling, she added, "Or surveyors."

Erastus laughed. "I've always just thought it was part of the Little Dipper. But that's a nice thought…home." He turned and looked directly into her eyes and said, "I'm glad to be home again too."

Cassie smiled. As they neared the townhall, she handed him back his jacket and then dodged a snowball thrown by a group of younger boys that included Eugene, all chasing a dog and throwing snowballs in every direction. She was relieved he seemed to be having such a good time.

Walking toward the townhall doors, Erastus squeezed her hand before releasing it, clearly not wanting to make a show of their reunion. "Thanks for the talk. I guess I'll be seeing you around," he said with a wink.

Cassie smiled and said softly, "Welcome home, Erastus Walker

...

AFTER SEEING ERASTUS EVERY DAY at the mercantile, Sundays at church, and most evenings over the next two weeks, Cassie began to feel a certain confidence she had never previously felt. One evening after dinner, she approached her father at his rolltop desk.

"Pa, how did you know?"

"Know…what?"

"That Ma was the girl for you?"

Simeon sat back in his chair and smiled before asking, "Is it Erastus?"

Cassie flushed a bit and nodded. "Maybe, but…" She repeated her question. "How did you know?"

"Well, in my own case, it had always seemed obvious." Simeon reflected, "I'd known your mother for several years. One day, I was at the feed store and saw her walking along the other side of the street in town, and it was as though an angel sitting on my shoulder said, 'Simeon, she's your girl.' Before that, we had been in groups together and our families were well acquainted. But in that moment, I saw her in an entirely different way for the first time."

"What did you do then?"

"I walked right over, took her in my arms, and asked her to marry me," Simeon said with a serious look. Then he began laughing. "Not at all. I waited for the right opportunity and then asked her to go with me to the Pioneer Day celebration that year. Two days later, after humiliating myself at the pie-eating contest, we somehow became a couple and were married a few months later—in October."

Cassie smiled.

Simeon went on. "But I do remember that day in town like it was yesterday. She was vibrant and beautiful. She turned from the little girl I had always known into someone I knew I could love forever." He began wiping at his eyes.

"Oh, I'm sorry, Pa. I didn't mean to bring up something so emotional."

"Don't be, dear. I still think about her every day, but I haven't thought about that day in town for years. Thanks for helping me remember that." Pausing, Simeon bowed his head and added, "I do miss her so."

"Me too."

Looking up, he said, "So, tell me about Erastus."

They spent the rest of the evening talking about what Cassie was experiencing. "Butterflies," she called the sensation. She talked about how she felt something maybe like her father had when she saw Erastus that first evening at the dance. "He's different now—in the best of all possible ways," she said, smiling. "I didn't hear any angels, though."

Simeon chuckled. "Well, he's a man now, Cassie. And a good one at that. I'm seeing that with him in our planning discussions on this water project. Even though he's a good man, someone like you will make him even better—that's if things continue between the two of you. Any man would believe fortune was smiling down on him to find a wife like you, Cassie Rapp. I'm sure of that."

Erastus stopped by one early January morning with a wagon full of tools and supplies. Cassie met him in the yard and asked questions about what he was taking.

"Mainly picks and shovels, what we call a 'tongue scraper' for the horses to pull…oh, and three cases of dynamite," he said, pointing to some smaller crates on the back. "I keep those as far away from me as I can," he explained with a wave of his hand, laughing insecurely that the back of his wagon wasn't far enough.

"So, how long will you be gone?"

"We will see," Erastus said. "It's only five miles, but the project has so many unknowns. As the chief surveyor, I need to be there nearly always since the crews will require regular measurements and direction."

"So, is this good-bye," Cassie said, leaning toward him.

Erastus hopped down from the wagon and took her in his arms. He kissed her cheek and looked into her eyes, saying, "For today. But I will find a way to come see you. Since it gets dark so early, we won't be able to work much after five o'clock, until spring that is. So, you might only see me come evening."

Pouting playfully, Cassie asked, "Think I could visit you once in a while?"

Erastus pulled her closer. "Please do."

Chapter 18

South Fork Snake River, 1895

Most days, Cassie kept herself busy at the mercantile to distract herself as much as possible from thinking about Erastus and their developing relationship. With the project on the river advancing, Erastus was no longer coming home at night and only occasionally on weekends. She missed him sorely.

Simeon could sense her mood, and since he saw Erastus frequently during the week at the job site and heard as much from him decided to take matters into his own hands. As any good father would, he told himself.

On a clear but cold morning, Simeon rode over to the store on a roan mare named Socks and walked in. "Go see him," he urged with a sweeping gesture, her instant beaming accurately revealing her mood. Pointing to the horse tied to the hitching post in front of the store, he said, "I'll take over from here and can walk home later tonight after closing."

Cassie hugged him and said, "Thank you so much" before grabbing her coat.

Her father followed her to the door and said, "You'll freeze in just that. Best take this too." He helped her with his own long coat and scarf. "Now, off you go," he said. She darted out of the store, slowed only by the extra layers she was now wearing.

Cassie rode the five miles to the construction site in a little over an hour. Upon arriving, she could see that so much had already changed. A wide hole had been dug near the river with a deep gash behind it that headed back toward town, toward the Dry Bed. A boom in the distance suggested dynamite was being used somehow, which wasn't immediately clear to her.

Erastus hurried up out of the wide ditch but then slowed a bit, greeting her more formally than she had expected. With the crew from towns all around, Erastus introduced her as "Simeon's daughter." Which was true, she knew, since they had only become reacquainted a few weeks earlier. Cassie so badly wanted to rush into his arms but resisted based on the small crowd that gathered to meet her.

After introductions, Erastus showed her around the project, and when they were alone, he said, reaching for her hand, "I know it seems like I'm busy here—which I am—but I think about you."

"I miss you—" noticing his broad hands were more calloused and rougher than she remembered.

Erastus pulled her close. "—I think about you day and night."

"Me too," Cassie said, feeling his strength and warmth. She gave him a long kiss.

...

THE NEXT WEEKEND, Erastus came home. His first stop was the mercantile, where he hurried in to find Cassie alone in the store. He swept her into his arms and announced, "I have to do some wash!"

Laughing, she pulled back and said, "Well, you smell like you brought the barnyard with you—so go!"

"Can I see you tonight?"

Cassie nodded.

Erastus arrived in a buggy early that evening. When Cassie looked out the door, he was holding up two pairs of ice skates by their laces. He shouted, "The slough out south of Menan is frozen solid. Grab something warm!"

Once there, they skated across the bumpy ice, big clouds of breath going everywhere as they laughed and turned circles well into the night.

On her next trip to the work site, Erastus seemed more at ease and introduced Cassie as "my girl" to the new crew that had rotated in. Cassie was amazed at how well the men worked together and Erastus's detailed plans for the work underway. He even showed Cassie how to level a transit on its tripod with a plumb bob and then use the device to check the level of the land being graded by crews with horses and plows. He would call over and say, "Take more dirt to your left," and other instructions. The men heeded his every command.

As they walked upriver to the much smaller head gates of the Enterprise canal, Erastus reached for Cassie's hand and said, "I'm so sorry but I won't be getting home for the next while. It has been so very busy here. We're building big fires to keep us warm and provide light to work as late as possible. The days are getting longer, fortunately—for the work that is. I miss you so."

Cassie reminded him that Sarah and Jens were getting married the next weekend. "I'm so happy for Sarah but sad a little since she's moving. Jens has been building a house for them north of the South Fork over toward the Henry's Fork. It's just so far away—well, across the Dry Bed and Snake," she said. "I'm going to miss her."

"I heard—all but the move part, which makes sense, I suppose. What she sees in Jens…I'll never know." Smiling, he added, "He's a good man. If Sarah loves him, I will accept that." He looked around. "Now I've got to find a way to make it home for the big day—with the ground thawing, we are starting the biggest part of the dig so far over the next few days. That's going to make it hard."

"You mean I get to see you again in town?"

"Of course, I wouldn't miss my own sister's wedding!"

"And my other best friend's wedding…"

"What are you hinting at?" Erastus said with an innocent looking smile.

Cassie denied any hinting at all. "Merely sharing the fact that I'll be losing my best friend," she said.

"I know someone who might be willing to take her place," Erastus said with a wink.

…

TWO WEEKS AND ONLY TWO DATES LATER—one being the ice-skating trip and the other Sarah's wedding at the townhall—Cassie wondered what would come next.

One morning while she was refilling barrels of beans and oats at the mercantile, a younger boy rode up quickly and tied his horse off before hurrying into the store. She didn't recognize him.

"Good-day, ma'am," he said, taking off his hat. "I was told to get here as quickly as I could ride, and then get back to the site. I have a note for you." He cleared his throat as he pulled a note from his pocket and handed it to her. Very respectfully, he added, "I'm Nels, ma'am. I've been asked to wait for your reply."

"Well, thank you, Nels. You're what—twelve or thirteen?" Cassie asked.

"Nearly thirteen, ma'am," the boy said, walking toward the stove to warm himself.

Cassie looked down at the note. It was a bit crinkled and had "Cassie" written on the front. Her heart began to race as she unfolded it and read.

Cassie dearest. Could you possibly arrange to meet me at the site today around three o'clock? If you can, dress warmly—it's been very cold here. I'm positive you will be able to make it home before dark. I would prefer to come to you but cannot at this time. I apologize if this causes you any inconvenience but promise it will be worth your while.

Yours truly,

Erastus Walker

Cassie looked around the store, her breathing quickening as several questions raced through her mind. What could Erastus want? Would her father be able to come to the mercantile for the afternoon? How would she reach him? Then, a peace took over as she looked up at the boy.

"Yes. Tell him I said yes."

...

When her father came in just before noon, Cassie asked if he could stay at the mercantile. He smiled and nodded. "I sure will."

"What could he want, Pa?"

"Why don't you take him that pie you made yesterday?"

"I don't think this is about pie," Cassie mused.

She raced home to dress for the ride. As she hurried to the barn, she was surprised to find Socks there waiting and already saddled. It all seemed a bit coincidental, but she decided not to overthink the matter and mounted and quickly rode out to the project site.

As Cassie neared the site, she slowed the horse to a walk and looked at her timepiece—it was exactly three o'clock. Groups of men glanced her way and then turned back to their work. A few chuckled, and she recognized the boy from earlier that day running toward the river. She walked the horse along the edge, amazed at how much had been accomplished since her last visit—a huge gash extended from near the river away toward the dry channel and was already deeper and wider than the two side-by-side wagons waiting below to be loaded with dirt.

As she drew toward the camp, Erastus came up the rise from the flood plain downriver with the boy following him. He hurried toward Cassie, taking the reins from her hands and handing them to the boy at his heel.

When Cassie climbed down, Erastus hugged her and said, "I'm so glad you came."

Surprised at his warm greeting and no introduction this time to the crew still busy at his back, Cassie suddenly remembered her father's recommendation. "I forgot the pie!"

Erastus looked puzzled. "I only asked you to come. I didn't mention anything about a pie."

Cassie started to explain and then realized he was guiding her away from the work area and downstream toward the river. "Where...what?" The entire scene quickly became eerily quiet—no sounds of horses, no sounds of men shouting or laughing. Only the sound of the river.

As they walked, Erastus held onto her hand, sweeping his free arm across the scene and saying, "We've begun calling this project 'the Great Feeder,' believing this will open up agricultural possibilities on a massive scale, watering new crops that will feed thousands and possibly millions."

"A fitting name," Cassie said, unsure why she felt nervous and looking behind her to see if anyone was following them. They were alone. Downriver in a cluster of tall cottonwoods, Cassie spotted a red blanket spread evenly over the ground along the riverbank and surrounded by the little snow that remained.

Erastus guided her toward it and asked, "Will you join me?" pointing to the blanket. Sitting by her side, he drew her close and said, "I've grown to appreciate this place—it's probably the prettiest place I know, when it's quiet like this. Even though this entire flood plain is the entire reason for the Great Feeder. Sort of a living contradiction, I'd say, to have something so pretty create so much hardship past town and beyond."

Cassie nervously said, "It's really amazing what you and the crew are doing here. It has the potential to change lives."

"It does. It does." Erastus leaned back on his hands, shifting in place before mustering courage to continue. Leaning forward he said, "Cassie?"

"Yes?"

He cleared his throat. "I couldn't wait to see you. I really am so glad you came—I know it was an unusual request."

"Not a problem at all. I wanted to see you too," Cassie said, wondering why he was so nervous but sure he had more to say.

Erastus chuckled lightly. "And heaven knows, I need a shower..."

"You're fine as it is. Not a smell at all," Cassie said trying to put him at ease.

Shifting in place, Erastus looked toward her with full resolve. "I couldn't wait to ask you something." He smiled as if he had arranged for it to be as quiet as it was. "I couldn't think of a better time to do this than today."

Cassie's heart began to race for the second time that day.

Erastus reached in his vest pocket and pulled out a small gold ring. He reached for her hand and looked into her eyes. With glistening eyes, Erastus asked, "Cassie Rapp, will you be my wife?"

Cassie looked down at her hand and whispered, "I do...I mean, yes!"

Erastus slipped the ring onto her finger and then pulled her into his arms. They held each other tightly.

Looking at her hand, Cassie asked, "When did you...?"

"...Your father helped me," Erastus said. Smiling, he went on. "I wanted to say that some men found it when they were blasting rock across the river, but that didn't seem right for the occasion. Your pa and I talked at Sarah's wedding, and he said he knew my predicament and would help me with matters. After Nels rode in and talked with you this morning, he stopped by your pa's place to alert him and to pick up the ring for me."

"A plan made with precision," Cassie said proudly. "Exactly what I would expect from you."

"Were you surprised?"

Cassie smiled, coyly. "Sort of, but I was also getting a little impatient..."

Erastus kissed her. "Well, it's been a complicated season—one that has kept me away from you longer than I can almost manage."

Around four o'clock as the day was drawing on, the newly engaged couple walked back toward the work site where Cassie's horse was tethered. Coming up over the rise, they found the entire crew gathered in anticipation. Cassie looked at Erastus, wondering what was happening.

This time, he climbed up on a pile of logs and said to the group. "Men and brothers, I'm pleased to introduce you to Cassie Rapp, my fiancé!" He let out a big, "Woo hoo!"

Cheers erupted from the group.

...

BECAUSE OF A SLIGHT SPRING THAW IN MARCH, the couple moved their wedding up from their original plan of early April. At the work site, the men had been waiting for weather warm enough to pour concrete for the gates that would control the flow of the Snake into the new channel they were finishing. Hoping this thaw was a sign of an early spring, Erastus took the opportunity to leave for a weekend and "get hitched."

His crews hooted and hollered loudly as he left alone for Willow Creek one Friday in March.

"You're a lucky man!"

"Don't be gone too long!"

"Happy honeymoon!"

Erastus shouted happily in return, "Keep working, men. I expect significant progress by the time I return."

Because the new church was still weeks from being finished, they were married in the townhall which doubled as their church. Their honeymoon that weekend was set for a newly opened log hotel on the riverbank in Eagle Rock.

On their first night together after the wedding, Erastus asked Cassie, "Why do we call it that? Getting hitched? It sounds like I'm hooking up horses to my wagon or plow."

Cassie chuckled as she ran her fingers through his hair. "Husband, you have that backwards. *I* am the wagon. *You* are the horse! You're getting hitched to me." They laughed together.

The next morning after breakfast, Cassie asked Erastus why he always seemed to hang his head whenever his father came around. He thought for a moment before reflecting on how things had never been the same since the day of Samuel's accident.

Cassie said, "I don't think it's about the accident. It's got to be about unresolved feelings. Blame and guilt like this eat at people and ruin relationships."

"You're right," Erastus said. "I've never been able to talk to Pa about it—I have brought it up, of course, but he always turns away."

Cassie asked, "Do you think you could ask him to hear you out? To work through this thing standing between you?"

Erastus wiped at his eyes and said, "I would really like that. If he would. I hope it's not too late."

Recognizing this would be hard for Erastus, Cassie drew him close. "I think your pa is hurting more than you realize—possibly from his own guilt and a long stretch of blaming the best man I know—my husband—for something that was clearly an accident. It's hard to be the bigger man here, but I think you should talk with him. Tell him you are sorry for his pain."

When they got back to Willow Creek, Erastus went straight to his father and asked if the two could speak. Cassie watched the two men go outside and walk toward the barn. When they came back in, Will had his arm around Erastus. Their heads were bowed, each wiping away tears. Will took Cassie in his arms and said, "I've always loved you, Cassie. Thanks for helping my son—this fine man here—help me see what I've been ignoring all these years. He's already a better man because of you."

Unsure what Erastus had said, Cassie said, "You've always been family to me—but now it's official. There's no turning back from here!"

Will turned to Erastus and smiled. "From that day way back at Willow Creek, I sort of saw something like this turning out—you two together. I didn't want to bring it up then," he chuckled. "Of course, we were all looking for Cassie all, as it were, but I did see you looking at her even then with a twinkle in your eye." He winked at his son.

...

WITH ERASTUS BACK AT THE WORK SITE, Cassie remained at her father's place and set out one evening to draw a picture of her new family tree. She turned to the final pages of her journal and began to outline it there. At its base, she put her name. And next to that, Erastus.

Catherine Esther Rapp Walker
Erastus William Walker

She drew a line connecting each to their parents and listed siblings.

Simeon Walter Rapp
Esther Ray Bingham (deceased)
- *Catherine Esther*
- *Eugene Simeon*

William Erastus Walker
Mary Jane Taylor
- *Erastus William*
- *Samuel Brigham (deceased)*
- *Sarah Jane*
- *Thomas Robert*

Next, Cassie drew lines connecting each group of parents to their own parents and realized she needed more information before she could finish the picture. She would add birth dates and the death dates for her mother and Samuel later.

A tree of sorts had emerged. The picture gave Cassie the feeling her family was already growing.

...

IN THEIR FIRST TWO WEEKS OF MARRIAGE, Cassie made six trips to see Erastus—up from once a week when they were dating and twice a week while they were engaged. Erastus was the busiest he had been so far with the Great Feeder, a name that was now being used by folks in town. Her father generously agreed to cover for her at the mercantile when she went and hadn't complained at all that the frequency of her trips was increasing.

"Give Erastus my regards," Simeon said as he saw her off. "He's a good man who is lucky to have you." As if finishing a thought, he added, "I can see how happy he makes you. A happy marriage is a blessed way of life."

Cassie could tell how much he missed her mother, and while he spoke frequently of her, this was the first time Cassie was beginning to understand how lonely he must feel. "Thanks, Pa," she said. "I'm a lucky girl to have two good men in my life."

As Cassie rode for the fourth time in one week, she carried with her a plate of hot biscuits carefully stored in a box tied behind her on the saddle. The trotter would get her there in a little more than an hour if she could withstand the constant jarring and didn't encounter too much mud from the melting snow. She knew the biscuits would cool by the time she arrived but hoped they might still be warm since the weather was warming.

Cassie's thoughts drifted from her own work to progress at the worksite. The buzz about the Great Feeder was constant at the mercantile and everywhere she went in town. It was viewed as "salvation here on earth" and "a permanent solution to a vexing problem" by most. No one didn't want it, but a few people worried that the entire river would miss the turn and instead race straight into the Dry Bed and flood their lands. Comments like "too much force" and "do these men really know what they are doing" struck close to home as Cassie felt her new husband's judgment and ability being questioned. And her father's as well! While Simeon spent less time there now than at first, he still went weekly to ensure the plan was on track. The rest of his time was spent managing the canal company, selling water shares, and laying plans for new canals to be developed downstream along the Dry Bed to finish the job of the Great Feeder.

By early April, the new mile-long channel across Bonham's land was finished—a straight ditch one hundred feet wide and twenty feet deep. It stood dry with only a narrow strand of riverbank keeping water from flowing out of the Snake River into this new stretch and on to where the Dry Bed became well defined. Wooden forms were being used at the site of the diversion dam to hold freshly mixed concrete in place while it dried.

With teams of horses and wagons, the men began hauling rock from the nearby hills to create a peninsula that jutted out into the river to direct even more of the river's force at the spot where the new opening would eventually be.

On each visit, Cassie marveled at the progress. What they had accomplished during the cold of winter was remarkable. The idea of a steady source of new water for hundreds of existing farms and potentially hundreds more was raising the level of hope everywhere. Folks were moving into the valley and onto land previously out of the reach of canals in anticipation. Farms on the west side where the water would create entirely new possibilities were already getting twice the asking price they had fetched the prior fall.

At the project site, there were usually twenty to thirty men working at a time. Add to that the twenty teams of horses and oxen pulling scrapers and wagons full of rocks, and the area was beginning to feel like a small town.

Cassie arrived one afternoon and noticed a newly constructed log building near the river, away from the cluster of canvas tents where the men slept. Smoke drifted from the shiny tin chimney pipe coming out through the shingled roof.

Noticing the quizzical look on her face, a man who was standing idly looking toward the river came toward her and said, "It's where the guard will live—once we're done, of course. Someone will have to guard this around the clock to prevent a disaster were someone to vandalize it," he added, guessing at her thought. "We're using the hut for meetings now."

He unfolded his arms, pulling off a glove before extending one hand and introducing himself. "Excuse me, ma'am. I'm Cloy Bonham. What brings you to 'the Great Feeder'?" His tone was slightly off-putting, almost cocky.

Cassie shook his hand, surprised at how soft it was, and said, "I'm Cassie…Walker." She was still getting used to her new last name. "Erastus Walker is my husband."

"Well, I'll be darned. Erastus is a lucky man," Cloy said, looking her up and down. Cassie squirmed beneath his lingering gaze. "I'll be darned! I'll be gosh darned." Rubbing his chin, he went on. "That would make…umm…my father and your…er…father, the main partners on this here project." He added with a wink, "That almost makes us family." Cloy settled into a stance, his arms folded, looking like he was willing to talk for as long as she was. "And, I'll tell you…" His eyes wandered.

Cassie turned away, asking, "…where Erastus might be?" She was eager to see her husband—and to escape this moment.

Cloy sounded disappointed. "Oh, sorry ma'am. Was it 'Cassie'? Of course, you want to see Erastus." He pointed his gloved hand. "He's there in the new hut, poring over plans for the head gate. Always working! Always working, that Erastus. Must be hard for you," he said, drawing his hands together and feigning a pout.

"Thank you," Cassie said, not wanting to engage any further. She walked toward the building and knocked on the door as she opened it.

"…we have to get more dynamite," Erastus was saying as he looked up, noticing his new bride. With a big smile, he said to the three men gathered around a table, "Let's take a break."

As they walked toward the river, Erastus ate the biscuits Cassie had given him and listened to her tell how Cloy made her uncomfortable.

"Old Cloy, he's not all bad. Not a lot of experience with this type of work, though."

"I don't like him at all," Cassie said.

"Just ignore him. That's sort of what I do. He's been coming around since he arrived from Salt Lake City. Guess he lived with his mother there. New to the area. Green, I'd say."

"Well, I don't need any more of *that*," Cassie said. "Green or any other color."

Erastus laughed and then asked how things were at home and listened to Cassie explain how Eugene was raising his own brood of chickens and had just taken on a yellow Labrador puppy he had named Rusty. "Pa says he's learning responsibility. But he's leaving all the other chores for Pa, who isn't getting any younger."

As they crossed over the land bridge holding the Snake back, Erastus looked down at his feet and asked, "Feel that? It's the Snake rumbling against this bank as the spring runoff begins to build, ready to break through and fill this new ditch." He pointed to the other side of the bridge where the wide concrete diversion dam was being built and explained, "We're only weeks away from completion, Cassie. Only a few more weeks!"

Warmed by the thought that Erastus would be able to come home, Cassie began to imagine the new house they would build, one with a yard and maybe hollyhocks and gladiolas, even a picket fence. Next would come a family and happy days ahead.

Her thoughts were interrupted as a team of horses pulling a wagon loaded with rock plunged directly into the river a hundred feet below where they were standing.

Startled, Cassie asked, "Oh, no. Will they be okay?" Then recognizing from the whoops of the drive that this was intentional, she added, "Wow, what are they doing!"

"We're building a jetty," Erastus shouted. "It will help in low-water years to give our waterway the supply it needs. Any earthen versions have all washed out in the past, but a big pile of boulders will be hard for even the mighty Snake to push aside!"

Looking again at the wagon, she realized the drivers were very young. "But those are just boys!"

"It's the Briggs boys," Erastus said. "Sixteen and twins. They joined us a few weeks ago—sent by their pa to work in trade. Some of the hardest workers we have."

"Why are they driving directly into the river?"

"There's nowhere to turn around," Erastus explained. As the rock was dumped, the wagon began to float in the deep current and the horses swam back toward the shore, making a turn mid-stream as though they had done this before. Cassie heard the men yell "Hurrah!" as the water splashed at the wagon beneath them.

...

ON JUNE 22, 1895, THE GREAT FEEDER was ready for operation. With another hot year already underway, a thick covering of dust hung in the air, replenished by every cart and buggy as people arrived. Tufts of cottonwood seed floated through the air like snow as over a thousand people gathered to watch as the final embankment was blasted away to allow river water to pour into the new channel.

A full celebration had been organized. The morning was filled with songs by a choir, speeches from local dignitaries, and even the canal company's secretary taking to the makeshift stage to report on all that had gone into this project—almost exactly tenfold any prior project, he recited. After his presentation and an announcement that the main event would come shortly after noon, people broke into groups for lunch, with picnics laid out on blankets spread everywhere.

Cassie had looked forward to spending the day with Sarah and Jens—she was always looking for a reason to get together. And she was especially relieved that Erastus would finally be coming home that night for good after being stationed here at the Great Feeder for months. She hoped.

While eating lunch, they sat cross-legged on a quilt and caught up on recent events. Sarah announced in clinical tones, "I'm going to be a midwife."

"How exciting!"

Sarah continued. "I'm learning about sanitary ways to prepare for birth and bring children more safely into this world. We can prevent most infant deaths if we do things right." She explained how only three more daytrips south to Eagle Rock for training would complete her certification.

Eugene came running over. "Hi, Aunt Sarah," he said before grabbing a roast-beef sandwich and running off again with friends.

"He's a handful," Cassie said in motherly tones.

Sarah said, "You're a good stand-in for his mother."

"Aw, shucks," Cassie said. "Oh, Sarah, and I'm so happy for you. We so need a midwife around these parts. I remember your good work when Eugene was born…so, I know who I will be having help me with my babies!"

"Oh, right. We were sure good at handing my mother those towels," Sarah laughed. "Speaking of babies," she said in hushed tones. "Jens and I are…"

"…pregnant?" Cassie whispered back, leaning forward to hug her friend.

"Oh, not yet. But we are wanting to have a baby." She looked up, smiling at Jens, who stood off to one side visiting with an acquaintance. Jens nodded nervously as if he knew what was being said.

The two women visited, watching groups of people milling around with children running in every direction. Wondering when Erastus might join her, Cassie looked over and saw him in a discussion with a group of men over near the head gate. Cassie's spotted her father there as well along with a man she recognized as Cloy Bonham. Based on all the gesturing, the conversation looked a bit heated. She saw Simeon shaking a rolled document of some type with one hand. As Cloy reached for it, Simeon pulled it away. After more words, the men began nodding and eventually, albeit somewhat reluctantly, shook hands. When the group dispersed, Erastus walked toward Cassie and Sarah. Cloy seemed to notice and followed a few steps behind.

"All right…" Erastus began, rubbing his hands together in what looked like anticipation of lunch.

Cassie stood and greeted her husband with a kiss.

Noticing Jens coming over as well, Erastus said, "Well, hello, Jens!"

From behind, Cloy interrupted. "Mrs. Walker, good to see you again." He shook her hand longer than was necessary, and then extended his hand to Jens and said, "I'm Cloy Bonham, Simeon's new partner in this project." At the mention of partner, Erastus shrugged his shoulders.

After a brief exchange, Erastus pulled Cloy aside. Cassie couldn't hear what they were discussing. Eventually, Cloy tapped his hat and said, "Good to meet you, Jens and Mrs. Swenson. Great to see you again, Mrs. Walker." He nodded toward Cassie and the group before walking away.

When Cloy was at a distance, Cassie looked at Erastus with relief and mouthed, "Thank you."

"No need," Erastus said with a scowl. "I see what you meant about Cloy. He won't be coming your way any longer."

After lunch, the crowd gathered to hear a poetry reading, a few more solos and duets, an upbeat dance number by the recently formed Iona Brass Band, and then what had been billed as the main event, a speech by a Mr. Webster who had just been appointed president of the Snake River Canal Company. Webster took his place on the newly constructed diversion dam. People gathered along the banks and down into the empty channel below to hear him.

Webster shouted as he spoke so all could hear. "Capitalists dubbed this country a howling sagebrush flat. A group of honest sons and daughters of the soil have removed that stigma—we have proved them wrong. We have built the grandest piece of irrigation work ever accomplished in the West—in the world!" He stepped forward. "Ladies and gentlemen, it gives me great pleasure to…"

Webster jumped as a loud explosion signaled that the dynamite charge embedded in the riverbank had been prematurely ignited. A tremendous cloud of dirt and rocks rose skyward and began raining down around the area. Everyone ran for cover, people ducking their heads to avoid being hit by debris. Webster flailed his arms frantically, urging those standing in the new channel below the dam to get out. The miner who had set the charge off shrugged his shoulders at the angry look from the event's organizing committee huddled near a tree off to the side of the speaker.

Cassie saw Eugene among the first to climb out of the new channel with a scared but relieved look on his face.

In rushed the foaming stream, a great wave of water passing through the head gate before the speaker could utter another word. The crowd standing along the newly finished channel cheered, the sound of which was muffled by the river rolling over rocks and filling this new section of Dry Bed for the first time.

Chapter 19

Along the Hudson

Five weeks after her father's burial, Emma had a signed book contract and a new problem. Or opportunity, as Lacy reminded her. Emma's pace of life was intensifying—with frequent calls to schedule her as a speaker and the demands of a growing business.

For the book, Lacy had calculated that Emma would need to write ten thousand words a week for twelve weeks to keep the first draft on track—which at first sounded easy, doable. Lacy pulled transcripts of Emma's speeches and compiled thirty thousand words into a rough manuscript, but after one full week of writing, all Emma had only changed a few words and reordered some paragraphs. Expanding this was harder than she had expected.

Emma's agent had committed to check in weekly but sensing Emma's struggle had now called her twice in the second week. All Emma felt was pressure.

"Any progress?" Amelia Whitehouse waited for a response and reacted to Emma's silence as anything but affirming. Amelia finally said, "I'm not saying speaking is easy but being a great speaker doesn't always make someone a great writer—even though your articles made us think otherwise."

Feeling defensive, Emma bristled at what Amelia's "made us think otherwise" statement might imply and remained quiet.

"Emma?"

Finally speaking, Emma said, "This will probably sound like a whine, but framing a three- or even five-thousand-word article is so much easier. On top of that, I feel like I am droning on and on about the smallest points. Coming up with five thousand total words for each chapter is tough!" Emma realized she was complaining to the wrong person—as though the castle Amelia was helping her build had become more like a prison. She was feeling trapped, stuck.

"Got writer's block?" Amelia paused. "Do we need to use some of your advance to engage a ghost writer? It's not uncommon at all to do so. If so, now and not later is the time to make that move."

Emma couldn't imagine handing her material to anyone else. The idea of a ghost writer was totally foreign to her. She had always been able to write and couldn't for her life figure out why words weren't pouring out of her mind onto paper, well her laptop, that is. Emma stared at the screen in dismay, lacking any response. Use a ghost writer? This was worse than having someone else raise your baby!

Emma knew she couldn't just walk away from Amelia's question. She, not Amelia, was on the hook to deliver a book, having not only signed the contract but already cashed the first check from her advance. The next installment would come when she delivered the first draft—a fete she was beginning to compare to climbing Everest, despite never having climbed to the top of any mountain.

The final payment from her advance would come when she delivered the complete manuscript to the publisher—a distant goal, time, place, moment, and meeting that Emma had initially imagined would have her showing up nicely dressed carrying a tall-but-neat stack of paper tied with a red bow at her publisher's office downtown near Madison Square Garden. She imagined presenting the stack in a grand gesture to a group of men and women who would applaud and gush congratulations her way, assuring her this would be a best-seller.

Now, that dream had gone *poof!* and her delusions were replaced by a dreaded sense of plodding—day after day reaching into the ether for something to say.

Emma couldn't recall ever having taken on anything so hard. A light sweat collected on her cheeks. Her heart raced.

Emma blurted out. "No ghost writer. I've got this. I just need to find my rhythm."

"Okay. We'll give it another week." Amelia paused. "But send me what you have, okay?"

Emma agreed. After hanging up, she jotted down a list of daily actions that would get her "in the zone." Still frustrated at the suggestion of using a ghost writer, Emma swung her chair around and shouted through her open office door, "They want to give my baby away! Who would ever do that?" She caught Lacy's look and instantly knew she had said the wrong thing.

A bit red in the face, Lacy said, "Wow! I don't think it's at all like that. I know you're talking about something else—but being given away worked out great for me!"

Lacy was familiar with this type of mood—the times when Emma seemed to acquire power from a negative moment—but she never really understood why. Lacy had tried once to pin it on the plastic wrap incident, something Emma rarely talked about.

In their time together, Lacy had shared about her own adoption, how she knew about it from an early age and felt so surrounded by love that she had never really felt anything negative about being adopted. "I knew I was loved, and for me, little else matters."

Still, Lacy thought there was something to Emma's own early experience, that feeling powerless was too much for Emma—deadlines often being the worst version. Too confining. Too subservient.

As Emma's colleague, and also close friend, Lacy had learned that responding calmly and listening generally helped diffuse the situation. But Emma's poor choice of words this time had really pricked Lacy. Walking into Emma's office, Lacy tried her best not to come across saucy and said, "How's that metaphor working for you? 'Give your baby away?' You sure you want to keep running with it?" A bit flustered, Lacy added, "Because I'm pretty sure *someone else* raised your dad, right? And me too. And we turned out okay, didn't we?"

The two office interns peeked up over their cubicles to see what was going on.

Emma instantly realized her words were reckless and had stung. Hands to her cheeks, Emma said, "I'm so sorry. It wasn't at all what I meant—and yet it means exactly what you're pointing out. Can we talk?"

Lacy knew that meant "in private" and reached to close the door. She walked over to the large window, standing hands on hips. Emma fell on the couch along one wall, head in hands.

Lacy paced while talking, looking out over the Hudson at sculling crews gliding along. "Ok, I'm going to ignore your bad metaphor for now. This book thing doesn't have to be so hard. Emma, you're brilliant. Not that long ago, you didn't even have a speech in you. Think about it."

Emma knew she owed Lacy a better apology. "That was insensitive of me—and unkind. Searching so hard for the book in me has taken me to a weird place, I guess. I sit here looking at my laptop screen, and after cutting and pasting a bunch, I'm left with the conclusion that I'm really just a poser, an interloper. I hear voices saying 'You have nothing to say—at least nothing important. You out of your league. You'll never finish this book.'" Looking away to the window, Emma added, "I'm totally slamming myself!" She leaned forward, covering her face with her hands.

Lacy sat down and reached for Emma's hand. "Emma?" She waited. "Emma, look at me."

Emma looked up, sheepishly.

"It's still your baby—we can stick with your bad metaphor for now. You need to identify the obstacle and then decide whether you're going to go around it or over it. Stop trying to power through it—an approach we both know almost never works." Lacy reflected briefly before adding, "Actually, it never works. Boulders are much easier to go around than through."

Emma looked up, realizing Lacy's sincerity. "Oh, Lacy, I didn't mean anything personal. Blasted metaphors." She shook her fist at the heavens in mock anger.

Lacy chuckled, reflecting. "Remember the time you talked about 'not wanting to throw anyone under the bus,' and the guy came up from the audience after and said that had happened to his sister? It wasn't funny then and probably shouldn't be funny now, but then it can be comical the way metaphors can often make points far too literally. You should stick with mixed metaphors—like Gloria Steinem's feminist opinion that a woman needs a man as much as a fish needs a bicycle."

Emma laughed, adding, "Well, you know I don't exactly agree with that one, unless he's the wrong guy—or it's a fish that knows how to pedal."

From the stress they were feeling, they both laughed harder than the joke warranted.

Recovering her composure, Emma said, "In all seriousness, Lacy, you of everyone I know did turn out more than okay." She looked over at the picture of her parents on the credenza. "As did my dad."

...

THEY TALKED FOR ANOTHER THIRTY MINUTES, shifting into problem-solving mode along the way. They concluded that getting Emma away from the office and possibly even Manhattan might be the right thing to do.

"Every breakthrough requires a 'break with'," Emma said, rehearsing a line she had heard Sean say several times.

They quickly came up with a few starters for working around Emma's writer's block—spend time somewhere sunny like Florida, a chilly but cozy stay in the Hamptons, or even a three-day writer's retreat at Cornell, one that Lacy had received an email about the day before.

"Okay, let's park that for a minute," Emma said. "Can I ask you about one more thing? Something personal? It's been on my mind—subconsciously, I guess."

"Sure."

"When did you know?"

Lacy's wasn't following. "Huh?"

"I mean, when did you learn you were adopted?"

"Oh, I always knew. My parents talked about it from the get-go. I have a memory of seeing my birth mom when I was three or four. She came to all my birthday parties until she passed away right after I turned twelve. Some kind of sudden illness." Lacy shrugged.

"So, you knew?"

"Knew what?"

"You never had to wonder if your parents would come looking for you or if you looked like them?"

"Well, my dad never came around. I still have no idea what he looks like—no photos, nothing. I figure he looked more like me since my birth mom had black hair. Her parents were from somewhere in southeast Asia, and...," she said, brushing her hair back and smiling. "I have her to thank for my mysteriously dark locks. My dad was clearly not white," Lacy added. "How else do you explain this?" Lacy pulled up the sleeves of her cardigan and her pointed to her olive skin.

"You're so modest—and lucky!" Emma smiled but was suddenly confused about her own hair color. Her father's hair had been almost jet black until it had finally grayed in his seventies. And her mother's hair had always been darker brown—no longer kept that way by nature but by her hairdresser. That Granny and Gramps both had lighter hair in pictures from when they were younger had provided enough of an answer for Emma along the way. She had been entirely resolved about the source of her blonde hair until that moment. So, if not them, who?

Musing for a moment, Emma added, "I've been wondering if my dad's parents ever came looking for him or even if they knew he existed—of course, at least his birth mother knew—but did they ever wonder how he had turned out? I'm sure they would have been proud, like your birth mother would be—even your father if you knew him. Have you ever wondered…?"

Lacy leaned forward. "Emma, I came to peace with this long ago. My parents—adopted or not—are the most amazing people I know. They have loved me every day of my life. I'm more like them than not. Well, except for this," she said, drawing her fingers again through her dark hair again. "That I'm taller and more olive than each of them is barely a detail—I'm who I am because of them. Sure, there's a bigger story, but they are my world."

"Lacy, your mom had to be so pretty."

"Aw, shucks," Lacy said, deflecting the indirect compliment. "You know, I figure you get what you get. From there, it's all about what you do with it."

Emma smiled, something still on her mind. "Did your biological parents have siblings? Do you have cousins, aunts, uncles, grandparents?"

Lacy sat upright. "None that I know. I have all of those with my own family. I'm okay that others might see them as my adopted family and encourage me to go searching. To be honest, I don't want to look behind that curtain. No need. Not me."

Emma stopped pushing. "Sorry, I know things like this can be awkward. I don't mean…"

"It's not awkward for me, Emma. It just *is*—using your words. It is part of my reality—not all of who I am. I didn't choose it, but I don't want to *un*-choose it. No big deal, really."

Lacy was right. Emma instinctively reached for the pendant hanging from her neck, remembering "is" engraved on its surface, remembering she had taken it off after returning from Idaho and put it in a drawer at home. While she loved the gift, the pendant was heavy and a bit old-fashioned.

Before leaving, Lacy said, "I need to return a couple of phone calls. That said, I'm happy to talk about this more anytime you want." Pointing to the list on Emma's whiteboard, she urged, "Now, get back to finding a way around that huge boulder in your trail. You've got this. And remember, we both want this book to become reality. I'll be by your side the entire way."

…

BY LATE AFTERNOON, EMMA HAD MULTIPLE OPTIONS on her whiteboard, with stars next to those she liked most and a plus or minus sign indicating how conducive she felt the environment of each option might be for writing. Florida was out because she knew she would spend every day sitting at the pool, even though it had become her go-to when she needed to escape from work. But she needed to work. The second option, the Hamptons, made her cold at the very thought, a place that could get stuck in winter until May some years. But the thought of cozying up next to a warm fire and walking on a beach, however windy and cold, was still quite appealing. So, the Hamptons got a plus.

Emma even read Lacy's forwarded email about the writer's retreat in Ithaca, and it sounded more like a workshop on learning how to write than developing a book. Picturing a dorm room at Cornell didn't sound relaxing at all, so she gave it a minus. No single option had received both a star and a plus sign.

Emma did, however, find the email from Cornell very informative. She quickly typed a second list of ideas she gleaned from the writer's retreat overview. She wrote, "Add multiple stories to make a point, insert contrasting examples that portray both the right and wrong way to do something for effect, and color your writing by retracing how your own thought process brought you to this point."

Emma inserted a few notes in her outline for Chapter 2. Her working heading for the chapter was, "Swimming But Don't Know It?"

Story ideas
- *People with accents based on where they were raised (Dad always said "eench" for inch and "dee" for Tuesday or any day of the week, now I'm wondering why)*
- *Growing up actively "religious" without really understanding what the religion was all about*
- *Preferring peperoni pizza and why ham/pineapple don't belong on a pizza*
- *Finding out you're adopted—and how that changes your worldview*
- *Thought process dev—be sure to write about "goldfish in water" and how I came up with that.*

Lacy poked her head in Emma's office. "How's it coming along?"

"Not there yet but closer," Emma said, looking up from her notes, feeling very productive. "I haven't written much, but I am writing about writing."

Pointing to the whiteboard, Emma laughed as she said, "Nowhere is winning. Is that a place?"

Lacy smiled. "Hey, I'm heading out for drinks with some friends. Wanna come along?"

Emma thought for a minute, feeling like a distraction could be fun but feeling on a roll. Stubbornly committed to powering through her writer's block, she answered, "Thanks so much for the invitation. I think I should stick with this a bit longer."

After Lacy left, Emma couldn't get their earlier conversation off her mind. She wanted to text Lacy another apology but instead drafted an email.

Lace,

For a long while, I thought I was a goldfish—but one totally aware of the water around me. With my father's passing, the news that he was adopted and with his burial in an Idaho town I never even heard of before, it's like I went from the kiddy pool to the deep end. So many new thoughts, new experiences. New water. I knew there was water all along, but this is a new type altogether.

And new topics—like adoption, death, and burial, and who my people might be. I know that may not intrigue everyone, but the idea of an aunt or uncle or cousin out there I haven't met before is both exciting and a bit scary.

That doesn't excuse my insensitivity. Please forgive me. The way you handled our discussion today was as awesome as always. You never disappoint. You're always there for me—a true sister, the only one I have! I appreciate that you help me dial back my crazy and communicate better—sort of like a bull giving candy to an old person (haha), you're always there for me. (And I know that anyone who messes with you does get the horns.)

I'm an inch away from breaking through on this book writing project. I think I feel the barrier disappearing—thanks to you. I'm excited about what's next.

Hugs,

Em

P.S. Want to do one of those DNA test kits with me? Maybe we really are sisters—a girl can only hope!

Emma hit send and walked over to her window. She felt like she was on the verge of getting unstuck. Even her Chapter 2 notes were coming along. Looking back at the whiteboard, she wondered where else she could get away to focus on her book. As she looked out over the Hudson, her phone vibrated loudly on the glass covering her desk, and Emma reached over to see who had texted her.

Emma. Topher Jones here. Officer Jones. Willow Creek. Sorry to intrude. Please call. If you can.

Officer Jones? Now that was out of the blue! Emma couldn't explain why the text made her smile. She read it over a few times and smiled again when she compared it to what she had seen in movies depicting telegrams from the 1800s. "Officer Jones. Stop. Willow Creek. Stop." Counting back, she realized it had already been three months since she was in Willow Creek.

What could Officer Jones possibly need now?

Part III

Chapter 20

A Secret Heart

Emma deliberated whether to respond to Officer Jones's text or ignore it altogether. What could there possibly be to discuss? He wouldn't be calling about headstone engraving or anything else related to her father's brief graveside service. She asked Lacy about it. "Should I call him or just text back for more info?"

"Is he cute?"

"Cute enough, I guess." Emma wondered why she was going along with this line of questioning, puzzled at what that had to do with whether she should respond or not.

Lacy didn't let up. "Why invest in a long-distance relationship unless he's cute. Otherwise, it's not worth it."

Emma looked dumbfounded. "'Invest' is a very big word for what's happening here. It's only a *text*."

"You seem to be making more of it than that," Lacy retorted with a smile. "Trust your inner advisor," she added, turning back to her work.

"Ha," Emma said. "I will." Deciding to do nothing about the text, she opened her book outline and began typing.

Emma woke late Saturday morning and decided to jog to the office, intending to take advantage of the peace and quiet there to focus on her book. She grabbed a bagel and orange juice at the deli on the first floor before taking the elevator up to the third.

It was a perfect morning—spring was well underway. The morning sun streamed through her window and made it nice to be alone in this setting. She wondered how she could make every day at the office this peaceful.

Settling in, she glanced up at the list of places on her whiteboard and immediately concluded that even a week of Saturdays here at the office would never be as quiet as one of those places or feel as "away"—yet none of them struck her as the get-away she was seeking.

Remembering the unresolved text from Officer Jones, something within her told her to make the call. She resisted at first and then reread the text.

Emma. Topher Jones here. Officer Jones. Willow Creek. Sorry to intrude. Please call. If you can.

It had to be eight o'clock there. Without further hesitation, she dialed his number, instantly feeling a tinge of regret. Even though it was already May, she pictured him still wearing his oversized blue police overcoat and standing in Quentin's office at the mortuary where they had first met, which made no sense at all.

And, yes, he was cute enough!

The line barely rang once before he answered.

His "hello" was different than she expected.

"Hell…o?"

Emma started to say who she was when he interrupted with, "This is Officer Jones."

For a moment, she wondered if the call had gone to his voicemail. She waited for a delayed beep, like some people do as a trick, but it didn't come.

"Hello…Officer Jones?"

"Yes, that's me." He paused. "Sorry, I couldn't get my earpiece to work. Okay, there. Can you hear me now?"

Emma said, "Yes, I can hear you just fine. This is Emma Rose, returning your call…I mean, message…whatever."

"I'm glad you called. You can call me Topher, ma'am."

Emma was surprised at how giddy she felt on a call with someone she had barely met two thousand miles away in the West. She waited. "You said I should call?"

"Uh, yes." He paused, background noises sounding like he was sorting through papers. "Miss Rose…Emma, right?" The way he said "Miss Rose" made her smile. His voice was rich and warm.

"Yes?" Emma half-expected him to say he was calling about something she had forgotten at the mortuary or that he had written her a speeding ticket and now needed her address to mail it to her.

He cleared his throat. "Thanks for getting back with me. I can't say much right now, but there was something at the cemetery…you know, the police investigation…that you may find interesting. Something we weren't in a position to talk about while you were here."

Her thoughts raced. What can you find at a cemetery that might be interesting? Especially something connected to a police investigation? Or interesting to her, for that matter?

"I can only tell you that in addition to a few baby bones, we have a box with some personal affects you may find interesting and might want to see for yourself."

Emma was startled. "Those were baby bones you found?"

"Uh, yes." He hesitated as though he was saying too much. "And…near those was a small box…of personal affects."

Emma interrupted, "Personal affects, Officer?"

"I'm not able to say, but you could see them for yourself if you'd like to come in." Topher talked a bit about the fact that he could not send the box to her. That it needed to remain in the evidence locker at the police station, and she could only see it in person at the station. He indicated what was found at the cemetery was quite old and so any concern that there had been a "murder situation" was immediately resolved. "It's a closed case. No further investigation. By us, that is," he added somewhat ominously, almost hinting that someone else, possibly a higher authority, could further investigate. He said he wasn't at liberty to describe the box's contents.

"By you?"

"Yes, by us," he repeated quickly.

"Okay, well, Topher, if I ever make it to Willow Creek, I'll call."

"That sounds nice."

After Emma hung up the phone, she began to wonder about the so-called personal affects. Why had Topher said she might be interested? Could they in any way explain her father's connection to Willow Creek?

And had he said, "That sounds nice," in response to her statement about making it to Willow Creek or was it simply a small-town way of saying good-bye?

Putting her phone down slowly, Emma found herself staring up at the whiteboard. Looking over the list of places with stars and plus or minus signs, the strangest thought hit her, one that immediately felt perfect on many levels. Willow Creek! She could write her book in Willow Creek! She jumped up and wrote "Willow Creek" with a marker and gave it both a star and a plus sign. In no time at all, Willow Creek found its way to the top of her list of places.

Impulsively, Emma quickly searched online for places to stay in Willow Creek—anywhere but the Best Western again! Only a few nightly rental places showed up. One described as "on the only golf course in the area," looked nice but also very small and cramped. The host said it was on "the Dry Bed," an odd-sounding name that made no sense to her at all.

Scrolling further, she passed over a few other options before spotting a one-bedroom studio apartment above the drug store in the middle of town, one with views looking up and down Main Street. Emma flashed back to her snow globe memory from the winter before. "That could be cute," she said out loud. The apartment was "recently remodeled," the host said—and the accompanying photos included some of the annual summer parade and farmland outside of town. Emma felt like flood lights had turned on overhead and angels were trumpeting from heaven. The place seemed perfect.

Three minutes later, Emma finished entering her credit card information and booked the room over the drugstore for thirty days. Upon hitting the confirm button, she recalled the coffee shop there in Willow Creek—what was it called?—and could already taste the hot scones with honey butter.

Looking up, she beamed with excitement over her plan. It all seemed so perfect—a great place to write and then wander around town whenever she needed a break. Oh, and to check out the box of personal items at the police station.

She wouldn't forget that.

...

SORTING THROUGH HER INBOX THAT MORNING, Emma encountered a reply from Lacy she had somehow missed.

Thanks for your note. Apology accepted! And yes to the kit. Woot!-- Lacy

Not remembering what she had written, Emma scrolled down to read what Lacy was referring to. She saw the P.S. at the end with "Want to do one of those DNA test kits with me?" She wrote back to Lacy to have her order two kits, and before hitting send added a few sentences.

Okay, I'm being totally impulsive—and maybe even irrational—but I'm going to take the next month off and go write—in Willow Creek of all places. It meets all my criteria. I can't believe I'm saying this, but I already booked a place to stay. It looks like I only have the CIO speech in Denver in mid-June, which can't be that far away, so this should work. Oh, and I called Officer Jones back this morning (cute enough!) and have to tell you about the strangest thing when you get in on Monday.

Feeling energized and surprisingly free, Emma went back to work, framing up ideas for her remaining chapters. Looking over at the print hanging on her office wall, some ideas for the introduction came to her, and she began to write.

On my office wall, I have a photo of a pretty but small goldfish swimming in a deep blue pool of water. A friend saw it not long ago and asked, "While you and I can see the water, does the goldfish know it's there?" The question struck me as more profound than not. I asked myself, "What am I swimming in and don't realize?" I followed that with two more questions: "If I'm swimming in it without knowing, how much does it affect the way I am, how I think, what choices I make, and everything else? Who is in charge here? Me, or the water?"

Emma wrote for an hour, rarely even hitting backspace on her keyboard. Satisfied, she stood and stretched as she walked toward the window before one final thought hit her. She hurried back to her computer.

We're all swimmers—we're all goldfish. And, newsflash: that stuff you're beginning to see around you? The water? That's culture. You don't get to choose any of that—it just is. But you do get to choose how you swim.

So, in a way, this is a book more about swimming than staring. I call it "Staring Down Culture" rather than "Swimming In Culture" since it's a book about awareness and choice. For me, the word "staring" suggests that once I begin to see culture, I can begin to more deliberately and intentionally choose what I want to do about the forces around me.

An ancient philosopher put It this way: "Life Is like being In a stream. You can swim upstream or float downstream. There is no standing still."

When it comes to culture, I invite you to join me in swimming!

Chapter 21

Dry Bed, 1900

Water gave life. And water could also take it away. Late one Saturday afternoon in late May, Cassie hitched their horse, Polaris, to a buggy to drive her three children—Samuel, Henry, and five-week-old baby Esther—to hunt for asparagus, what locals called "Ditch Weed" based on how tall and spindly it looked once it went to seed as spring turned to summer. It grew abundantly along ditch banks lining the dirt roads outside of town. She pulled out of the barn and down the drive past the rock house Erastus had built for them, a home into which they had welcomed three babies in four years of marriage—a marriage she frequently described to others as blessed.

Cassie shifted in the seat, snapping the reins and clicking her tongue. "Yip, Polaris," she said to get the horse moving. Polaris trotted through town—past the bank and then the mercantile, a place she had worked at every day until Samuel was born. After that, she tried working a few days a week, but that had grown harder. She finally told her father she couldn't work at all any longer. At least for a few months. That had turned into a few years. After Henry came and then baby Esther, Cassie realized returning to the mercantile anytime soon was highly unlikely. Simeon had since hired a few others to work there but was never quite as happy with their work as he had been with how Cassie had run things.

The buggy carried her past a row of new houses under construction, a development that was expanding the town to the east beyond the original townsite. A group of businessmen had recently come together with plan for new, bigger buildings along Main Street, buildings they said were needed for their own enterprises and to make Willow Creek a "respectable" town. Further along, a crew was busy inserting tall poles into freshly dug holes with a second crew stringing wire between poles already in place—bringing telephones and electricity closer to her own home every day. For a few years now, she had read much about how electric lights were changing life for people in the East and eagerly awaited this experience for herself. Even better, Cassie anticipated plumbing improvements she had urged Erastus to install—well water running to the kitchen with an indoor flush toilet to replace the outhouse in the backyard.

Nearly twenty-three, Cassie felt like civilization was changing before her very eyes—and for the better.

After several blocks, Polaris pulled up at the Rapp home. Because the pasture next to the house was empty, Cassie knew her father had ridden his horse to town or on another errand. Only yesterday, she had heard from a neighbor that he was seeing Ruby Poole, a woman who was newer to the area—perhaps he was off visiting her. Pulling away, Cassie formed several questions she intended to ask her father when she next saw him next.

As the horse clopped across the Willow Creek bridge at the edge of town, Cassie reflected on that winter night only a few years earlier, the night she and Erastus had stood on that very bridge talking. "After knowing him my entire life, that was the night we became truly acquainted," she frequently told others. "I'd never really paid him much attention at all until then."

Life with Erastus had been so good. Earlier that morning, he had gone to repair a steam thresher on the Swensons' north forty. It didn't matter the part—a Belle City thresher or the Case steam engine that drove it—this newer farm equipment needed constant attention. Barely over a year into selling and servicing farm equipment, Erastus had even hired a repairman to help him keep up with demand. And Jens and Sarah Swenson were family, so Erastus took that job himself.

"She's a high priority," Cassie had instructed him that morning.

"Of course," Erastus said. "Always good to see my only sister."

"And do bring back any news from my only sister as well, will you? We have precious little time together as it is."

"Of course. And I'll pay attention to the details." He chuckled as he rode away that morning.

...

The Meadowlark

ON THE OUTSKIRTS OF TOWN, Cassie began to smell the dankness of wet fields being irrigated—a smell that prompted so many memories. She knew the window for asparagus opened for only a few weeks this time of year and hoped she had timed it well. No one could explain how the asparagus got here, and despite efforts to transplant it into home gardens, no one had succeeded much there either. But the plant was abundant enough in the wild and brought a welcome addition to any homecooked meal.

A few miles outside of town, Cassie shouted, "Whoa!" as they neared her favorite picking area. Polaris drew the buggy to the edge of the road alongside the Missionary Canal, the source of water for farmland set aside to feed the families of men who had gone off to preach religion in other parts of the world. Cassie walked her children down the slight shoulder of the road, crossed what locals called the "borrow pit," and then up the ditch bank to where asparagus grew in clumps by fence posts. Across the entire valley, ditches and roads alike were built the same way, by scraping up or borrowing dirt from the flat valley floor to form the base of a road or canal banks, all of which generally sat higher than the grade of surrounding fields.

"Careful on the ditch banks," Cassie instructed as she held baby Esther in one arm and a basket on the other. Nudging Henry with her foot to move along, she heard a bird call and said, "Listen, boys! Do you hear that?" The bird trilled again, and its call was answered by another across the way. "Meadowlark," she said. "I need more of this—it sooths my soul," she sighed before noticing Henry wandering too close to the ditch. "Henry, stay right here by Momma's side."

As she looked around, she spotted a few asparagus stalks, the bright green contrasting starkly against the darker orchard grass. Samuel was busy picking up sticks and pulling at the grass, holding up a piece and asking, "Is this 'appargus' momma?"

"No, that's a nice piece of grass. Asparagus looks like this," she said, holding up the single stalk she had just picked.

On their way back to town, Cassie noticed her father's black quarter horse in the pasture so pulled to a stop under a tree in the front yard. She hopped down and tied Polaris off to the hitching post. After turning her boys loose in the yard, Cassie carried Esther toward the house, eager to hear more about this woman her father was said to be seeing.

As the front door squeaked, Simeon woke with a start from where he was napping in a corner chair with the sun coming through the window and breaking across his lap. Rubbing his eyes, he stood and greeted Cassie, reaching for baby Esther. Taking the baby in his arms, he announced, "I'm selling the mercantile… to the Zion's Cooperative Mercantile Institute out of Salt Lake City."

Feeling protective, Cassie asked, "You don't seem so sure. Is that…a good thing?"

"Of course, it is. I'm not getting any younger, Cassie."

"Pa, you're not even forty-five!"

Simeon ignored her comment and smiled at little Esther. Cooing, he put his finger in her tiny hand and said, "What a sweetheart…and what a precious name."

Returning to the subject, Cassie asked, "So, it's a good thing, then?

"Sure is," Simeon said, looking up from his granddaughter. "And at a profit that would take us five years to produce. I'll have more time for water company matters."

"Then I'm happy for you, Pa"

Simeon didn't seem to have more to say on the matter, so Cassie asked about her brother. "Where's Eugene?" He was usually there, so she assumed he was out feeding the horses or changing irrigation somewhere in the nearby fields.

"I let him go fishing with his friends. Got his chores finished first thing." Smiling as baby Esther began stretching in his arms, Simeon added, "That boy is a good worker."

"Hmmm," she said, moving around the room restlessly. Picking up a framed photo on the side table, Cassie finally blurted out the question on her mind. "So, I heard you have a lady friend?"

His cheeks turning slightly red, Simeon said, "Oh, that. Well, she's just a friend."

Cassie said, "Pa, since Ma passed, you have never even so much as noticed another woman! This is so unlike you! Who is she?" Cassie wanted him to start from the beginning and not leave out any details.

Smiling, he explained, "Ah, you probably know this already. But her name is Ruby Poole. She moved here just a few months ago." He paused before adding, "You know we knew each other when we were young—long before moving here to Willow Creek."

"You've never mentioned her."

"Well, back then I only knew her as my friend John's little sister. They lived a short stretch down the road from my family. How time changes things," he said, picking up the book he had left on his chair and folding it closed with one hand, still holding the baby. He placed it on the table next to him and sat back down. Changing the subject, he said, "*A Tale of Two Cities*. Makes me glad I live when and where I do!"

"I hear it's a fine book," Cassie replied, courteously, unwilling to change the subject altogether. "Come to dinner tonight, will you? And bring Eugene, of course." Taking a chance, she added, "And Ruby, too. We would all like to meet her."

Simeon squirmed. "I'm quite sure Eugene can make it," he laughed uncomfortably. "I guess…I'll…I can see if Ruby is available." Changing the subject again, he asked, "Did you hear about the outbreak over in Hamer?"

Cassie looked surprised. "No, what's happening?"

"Not sure if it's consumption or the flu. It's already taken two entire families."

He clearly didn't want to say much more about Ruby.

…

As Cassie was preparing to leave, a knock came on the door, which quickly turned to banging as someone shouted, "Mr. Rapp!"

Simeon rose quickly and went to the door. It was Eugene's friend Robert. Through the open door, Cassie could see Eugene's dog Rusty barking behind him in the yard.

"We can't find Eugene," Robert said, his arms hanging down and hands on his knees to catch his breath. "Dry Bed…"

Simeon's eyes widened as he looked around.

"Take my buggy," Cassie said. "Go!"

"Keep Rusty here," Simeon urged.

With the demands of so many farms at this time of year, the Dry Bed was operating at its fullest. Trout came downstream through the Great Feeder and upstream as well where the Dry Bed re-entered the river miles below, and it was on one particularly deep stretch that the boys routinely fished.

On the ride over, Robert cried as he told what had happened. "Rusty started barking at mallards when we got there. Eugene tied him to a tree so he wouldn't chase them but then finally gave in and turned him loose. Rusty went right after one into some faster water…. And I guess Eugene thought the dog was struggling and so waded in as well—into a stretch deeper than any of us thought. He was wearing his hip waders…"

Simeon instantly knew what had happened. Hip waders could be dangerous. Worn properly, Eugene would have tied them to his belt to hold them up. The flaw in the design was that they were meant to keep your legs dry. Anything deeper, and they would fill quickly and were nearly impossible to undo without getting out of the water. In deep water, they would drag even a strong man under. At the thought, Simeon snapped the reins and urged Polaris to a gallop. The buggy raced through town and toward the Dry Bed.

A small crowd was beginning to gather along the near bank of the Dry Bed, likely there as Robert had run back through town sharing the news. Simeon was grateful to see two men in a flat boat already in the water and rowing out into the current. Others walked the banks shouting Eugene's name. Here, the Dry Bed was wide and deep. Simeon could see the water moving at a faster pace than usual, a flow rate the canal company had only approved the day before to support downstream demand from farmers for more water, a decision Simeon instantly regretted.

Thinking practically, Simeon ran downriver and waded out into the waist-deep current. He spotted a large clump of thick willows and yelled for the men upstream to paddle that way. It prompted memories from years earlier of searching for Cassie in a similar situation. Fear overtook him, and he clawed at the water to move through it, frantically hoping for a few more precious seconds of life for his son.

Within the hour, men had walked the banks to where the Dry Bed went through a diversion dam a mile below, much of the water diverted to adjoining canals with some flowing over a spillway that seemed unlikely for body to pass over. Several searched among the logs and debris hung up on headgates along the way, while others wearing work clothes probed the river bottom from boats or walked waist deep or even deeper.

An hour later, they resigned themselves to the fact that their search was now for a body.

Just before nightfall and five miles downstream, they found what they were looking for.

…

CASSIE LEFT THE CHILDREN late the next day with Erastus and walked across town to see her father. The sun was setting when she arrived, and Eugene's dog Rusty was asleep on the porch, relaxed and unaware of the commotion he had instigated. People around town had been talking about how "the dumb dog had rescued itself barely a few yards downstream" and "why would anyone risk their life to save an animal." Clearly, all sentiment was against Rusty.

Cassie scratched Rusty behind the ears and said through her tears, "Oh, Rusty. I'm so sorry. You don't even know what happened. Eugene was such a good friend to you."

She entered the two-story home and found Simeon standing by the stove, striking match after match. Cassie moved to hold him, but he pulled away.

Angrily, he said, "The boy was barely fifteen but should have known better."

"He loved his dog, Pa."

"But why didn't he…" Simeon checked himself and then lit another match. Emotion welling up again, he sobbed, "How is it right that…the dog—his dog!—is sitting on the front porch and Eugene is gone?"

They talked late into the evening about what had happened. Simeon's regrets mounted. "I should have never let him go fishing with those boys." After a series of reflections on why fishing poles and waders were such bad inventions, Simeon's face reddened as his guilt mounted. "And why did we increase the flow rate—just the day before! Even I voted with the board to support downstream farms. Confound it!" Beating his fist on a table, he asked, "Why did I ever encourage the whole Dry Bed project at all? What a waste of life the Great Feeder has been!" His shoulders shook as he buried his face in his hands.

Cassie listened to her father sobbing knowing she had little to say that would comfort him.

Simeon looked up with red eyes and cried, "Why would I ever propose turning that washed out area into a raging river! Why would I create something that would take my son!"

Cassie sat next to him in the front room and tried to comfort him. "Papa, it wasn't your doing. Nothing any of us can do will bring Eugene back." Confused as emotion clashed with logic, she decided now was not the time to remind him of how many lives the Great Feeder had improved and how cash crops from tens of thousands of acres were now feeding people in places around the world.

Because of him, and several other hard working and ingenious men. Still, was it worth a life? She couldn't reconcile any of what she was feeling.

Back home, Cassie brought the topic up to Erastus in bed. "Do you feel the Great Feeder is responsible for Eugene's drowning?" Moonlight came through the bedroom window and made the room an eerie white.

Erastus folded his arms behind his head and said circumspectly, "You can't know what bad might come when you believe what you're doing is so good. That's a complicated question, though. We had accidents while we were building it—but nothing so personal as this. I know it sounds overly practical, but sadly, it can't be undone." Reflecting for a minute, he added, "Perhaps this had nothing to do with the Great Feeder at all. If not there, the boys might have been fishing on the Snake. We'd have been lucky to find him out there."

Through tears, he added knowingly, "We've all made the mistake of rushing after something without thinking it through. I am sure Eugene was just trying to save his dog. Lapses in judgment can be costly."

"Yes, we have," Cassie said with her head on his chest.

...

Two days after the accident, the funeral for Eugene paid a touching tribute to life. Folks came from miles around to show respect for Simeon and the family. Many stayed on after the burial to visit and eat together at tables that had been set up on a patch of grass in the backyard.

Cassie heard her father talking to her father-in-law Will Walker and a few other men. Simeon was still harping on how the Great Feeder was a big mistake and how he should have never encouraged it. Most nodded politely, understanding how hurt he was at losing his son. She saw Will pull him aside and overheard him saying, "Simeon, now, what has happened to Eugene has broken all of our hearts. Many of us know what it's like to lose a son—I certainly do. I know it's little consolation, but you can't ignore just how much the Great Feeder has blessed the entire western half of the valley—a godsend, as it were. How can we ignore that?" He gripped Simeon's hand and added knowingly, "What happened is tragic, nonetheless. No father should have to bury a son."

Simeon nodded, realizing that Will of all people understood this kind of loss. He reached his arms up to embrace Will and sobbed.

From a distance, Cassie caught Will's relieved look.

After folks had gone, Cassie walked onto the front porch to watch her children playing. Across the wide yard, she could see the white fence her father had built the year before that lined the edge of Willow Creek. Where the cottonwood from her childhood had stood until a few years earlier, a line of tall and narrow Lombardy poplars now grew—already tall enough to provide good shade for the front yard toward sundown on hot summer days and a much-needed wind break to slow the build-up of snowdrifts in the winter. At this time of year, the creek flowed full, delivering its life-giving contents to dozens of farms downstream. The sky began turning a warm orange as the sun slowly descended in the west.

Despite the recent tragedy, Cassie felt a momentary peace from the sound of flowing water and the stunning sunset. She picked up a small branch from the ground, one bearing a tiny leaf, and tossed it into the creek, smiling at the distant memory as she watched it float away.

...

SIMEON AND RUBY WERE MARRIED in the rock church a few weeks later. It was a second marriage for both—Ruby's first husband had died years earlier while hauling logs for fence posts. It was said that he was driving downhill when the load on the wagon shifted, slipping forward, and crushing both him and his double team of horses. Single for the past twenty years, Ruby had raised two children on her own in Utah. She had recently followed her daughter and family to Willow Creek.

When Cassie approached Simeon before the wedding and told her father how abrupt this all seemed, what with Eugene's recent passing and all, he said, "Sweetheart, I've been lonely for years—something I wish to no longer be. I would have it all back if I could. But that hasn't been a choice I get to make. Rather, I only have today. And I hope you'll come along and support me in making the most of it. I believe you will grow to love her as I do."

It was the first and only time she had felt him stand apart from her—a strong statement of self-preservation from someone she had only known her entire life to be selfless. It took only seconds for Cassie to offer her blessing to a man she had always considered wise, strong, and loyal. That day more than ever.

The celebration for the new couple that evening in the new church was splendid. Simeon was happier than Cassie had seen him in years. He stood there tall and proud next to a woman that wasn't at all like Cassie's mother—Ruby was frillier, fancier, and wearing more jewelry. Compared to Esther's blonde, Ruby had dark hair that showed hints of gray, the base color being almost as dark as Simeon's. Cassie could see they were happy together but didn't imagine Ruby could ever be the perfect complement for her father she felt her mother had been.

Cassie took a deep breath and committed once more to give it a try, to "come along" as her father had requested. "I'm happy for you, Pa," she whispered.

Erastus came up from behind and tugged at Cassie's arm and said, "Would you like to dance?"

"Of course," she smiled. "Do you always sneak up on your girl like that?" Out on the dance floor, Cassie leaned into Erastus and said, "I know Pa deserves a companion after all this time alone. I so miss Ma, but I guess I can be fine with my pa having a companion. I hope Ruby always makes him this happy."

Cassie felt eyes on her. When she looked up, she saw Cloy Bonham in the doorway across the room. Since his father's passing the year before, Cloy had assumed the role of half-majority shareholder. Cassie still grew squeamish every time her father or Erastus mentioned Cloy's name. A few days after Eugene's funeral, Simeon had made it clear that his interests in the canal company would eventually pass to her, so now was a good time for Cassie to get more involved—which meant attending meetings with Cloy. Unable to stomach being around Cloy, Cassie had been sending Erastus in her place, making it clear to her father and Erastus alike that this would be the course of action so long as Cloy remained on the board.

"Why so tense?" Erastus asked her as they danced.

Cassie shrugged, turning him toward the door.

When the dance was over, Erastus took her gently by the hand and walked toward Cloy, knowing his wife would have preferred to go a different way, whispering, "Will you trust me and give him another chance? He's changed from what I can see."

Cloy walked forward with his usual energy and pumped Erastus's hand before turning toward Cassie.

"Well, hello, Mrs. Walker," he said. "It's been a long..."

Cassie felt his gaze linger longer than she felt comfortable but tried to follow Erastus's request.

Cloy's eagerness didn't dissipate. "Mind if I have the next dance?"

Erastus gave Cloy a stiff look and took him by the arm. "Now, Cloy, as we've been discussing…" Leaving his wife, Erastus walked Cloy toward the door.

Cassie took the opportunity to collect baby Esther from a friend, needing a distraction while waiting for Erastus to return. When the baby began crying, she went out another door and felt instant relief as she found a quiet room where she could deal with the fuss.

Chapter 22

Idaho Green

A week before leaving Manhattan, Emma asked her mother to express mail her father's copy of *A Tale of Two Cities*, imagining he had somehow left additional clues for her in his highlights and margin scribbles. When it arrived, Emma flipped through the pages and found the quotes she had first read back in Carlsbad. She now recognized that the "WC" next to one of his earlier highlights likely stood for "Willow Creek" and thought that "someday" may being referring to the trip he had been planning for them. She flipped through the book and found other highlighted sections with accompanying handwriting, including one section that seemed important to her father.

> *A wonderful fact to reflect upon, that every human creature IS constituted to be that profound secret and mystery to every other. A solemn consideration, when I enter a great city by night, that <u>every one of those darkly clustered houses encloses its own secret</u>; that every room in every one of them encloses its own secret; that every beating heart in the hundreds of thousands of breasts there, is, in some of its imaginings, <u>a secret to the heart nearest it!</u>*

Next to this, her father had written, "Knowing would mean everything. But how do I find out?" And next to that, he had drawn a half heart. Emma began to wonder if he was simply making notes or leaving clues.

Regardless, she decided to take the book with her to Idaho.

...

Driving her rental car toward Willow Creek, Emma couldn't believe how unreal Idaho seemed this time of year. Already the middle of May, everything she saw was greener than anything she ever remembered seeing. Unlike Manhattan where cherry blossoms had already burst into a rich pink, or her childhood home in Salt Lake City where she remembered trees blooming and lawns turning a nice green, Emma saw a green here that was deep, dark, and indescribably rich. The contrast with the massively wide blue sky and billowing white clouds overhead was exhilarating. Emma hadn't felt this way for years—her closest memory being a drive she could remember taking with her father to some high mountain lakes.

She called Lacy along the way. "I'm here," she said. "And you won't believe how green it is. I have no idea what they're growing here, but Crayola needs to make this a color in their crayon box."

Lacy sounded unimpressed. "Okay…?"

"No, Lacy, I'm not kidding. It's so freakishly green… It's impossible to describe." Catching onto the idea that what she was seeing was impossible to describe adequately to anyone not there, Emma said, "I guess you have to be here. I'll stop trying. So how are things at the office?"

Lacy responded with, "Great. Very quiet." She paused before saying, "Your agent called. Doesn't she have your number?"

Emma said sheepishly, "I forwarded my phone to the office."

"You what? Can you do that?"

"I thought a few days without interruptions would be best." Not asking what her agent had wanted, Emma chatted with Lacy a bit longer before hanging up. Driving along, she noticed men in fields off to the side dragging long pieces of pipe. In other fields, very long lines of pipe on wheels were automatically watering. In some, tractors were cutting a deep green plant and laying down long narrow rows behind them.

The entire area was a hive of activity.

Emma's mind jumped to her mother, so she called to check in. After catching up, Emma asked, "Are you getting out for your walks? Still seeing your friends?"

"Yes, I am getting out. Spending time with Barbara—you know she lost her husband a few years back too."

"I'm happy you have a friend," Emma said. They shared a few memories and Emma told her mother how different Idaho was on this trip compared to last time. She repeated much of what she had told Lacy. "You won't believe how green it is. I have no idea what they're growing here."

Her mother sounded distracted and only said, "That's nice."

Emma repeated her earlier statement to Lacy. "Mom, it's so freakishly green. It's impossible to describe. Maybe this was why Dad chose Willow Creek for his final resting place." Despite how far it seemed from everywhere, Emma was happy for him.

...

WHEN EMMA PULLED INTO TOWN, she drove across a wide bridge she had not noticed before, one with a sign that said "Willow Creek" next to concrete barriers lining both sides. She concluded it had to be the town's namesake, the actual creek itself. As she passed over, she noticed the wide, uniform canal that flowed under the bridge and beyond.

A four-story apartment building flanked the canal to her left, and she recognized from directions her soon-to-be host had given her that she was to turn right just past the apartments. She turned as directed and found her way to the back of what had to be the drug store and to the parking spot in the alleyway marked "Guest." The staircase up to the third-story apartment and the key under the mat were exactly as he had described.

As Emma turned the key in the door, she worried the place would be a dump or entirely unlike the pictures she had seen online but was delighted that it was nicer than she had expected—hardwood floors, tastefully painted walls, and beautiful countertops. She said, "This is going to work out just fine!" as she walked into the bedroom and fell back on the king-sized bed.

Within the hour, Emma unpacked, opened her laptop on the kitchen table, and began working on chapter three. Standing to take a break, she walked over and glanced out her front window, spotting Carter's Cafe on the corner less than a block away. Her stomach growled. She decided to go there for lunch—and make a trip to her father's grave after that.

At midday, Emma took a break and walked toward Carter's. She already felt a lightness she hadn't in months. And a really good decision! Her book seemed to be moving along. She was finally "in the zone," she felt. As she strolled, she caught her reflection in the windows of the Five and Dime store along Main Street, tossing her hair back before making eye contact with a clerk on the other side of the window—a woman sorting what looked like garden implements and beach toys. The woman smiled and waved casually at Emma. Emma waved back awkwardly and hurried along.

The early summer air was cooler than Emma had expected—now glad she had grabbed a jacket before leaving. She passed cars neatly parked diagonally along the way. Main street was lined with fabric, clothing, and craft stores across the street. So many places to visit!

Before crossing at the corner, Emma completed her visual sweep of all four corners—there was a hardware store to her left, the mortuary on the opposite corner, Carter's with its "Family Dining" sign, and a bank to her right. Emma crossed toward the bank. Opening the door to Carter's, she told herself she would be eating here for the next thirty days. The rodeo sign she had seen on her previous visit looked different—or at least had a date: "Willow Creek Days" coming up June 20-21, it announced. She was intrigued by pictures of a parade and rodeo on the sign, quickly doing the math and confirmed that was the weekend she would be leaving—with a finished book, of course, to put in her publisher's hands!

Emma looked at the bar stools along the long counter to her left but opted for a booth instead, one of five or so that ran parallel to the counter and under the windows facing the street. Sitting down, she noticed for the first time the tiny jukeboxes at each of the booths and along the counter. Looking for a volume control, she was delighted by the smell of fresh scones as a basket was placed in front of her. She momentarily closed her eyes, taking in the blast of the familiar warm, doughy smell. She looked down in gratitude at the honey butter in its small tub looking like it was already melting and then up at the waitress, recognizing her as the one from her trip there last winter.

"Miss Rose, right?"

"Wow, you have a great memory!"

"Will your mother be joining you, Sweetie?"

"No, just me today. And what was your name again?"

"Connie."

"Nice to see you again, Connie!"

"You too, dear!" Connie said, smiling and nodding. "So, what brings you back to town?"

Emma considered telling her about her book project and the box Officer Jones had talked about. She thought better about saying much at all and instead said, "I came to visit my father's grave."

"All the way from...?" Connie said, her voice raising slightly to form a question.

"From Manhattan," Emma said. "New York City."

"Oh, I know Manhattan, dear," Connie said. "Been there twice. Saw *Phantom of the Opera* and the Statue of Liberty," she said proudly.

Emma wasn't surprised. To her, Manhattan was a town of millions—a constant mix of residents and tourists. Unless the person was wearing business attire, which was becoming less common all the time, she often remarked that you couldn't tell who lived there and who was visiting.

Emma said, "Well, I'm taking some time off. I haven't done that in quite a while."

"Well, you look too young, darling, to need much of a vacation—or one in Willow Creek for that matter. Why, I'm the one who should be taking a break, at my age in particular," Connie laughed as she spoke. She confessed, "I remembered your last name because it stood out to me. By the way, after your last visit here, I asked around town, and no one had really heard of a 'Rose' family from the area. Not much in that department." Changing the subject, Connie said, "But your long blonde hair did catch my attention," adding with a wink. "It's beautiful."

"Why, thanks." Emma pulled her hair back as she took a bite.

"What's your first name, young lady?"

"Emma."

"What a beautiful, simple name! I love it. Mine...Connie...sounds like it's been around for a while. Even though I guess 'Emma' is equally vintage—my great-grandmother was named Emma—but it's also very fresh and fun. The name probably fits the person. It sure fits you."

Emma smiled at being called "fresh and fun" and looked at her scone before tearing another piece off and smearing it with honey butter. "I've been dreaming about these," she said, pushing the piece into her mouth.

"Folks come from all around just for this. We serve them with every meal. My boss would tell you the first basket is free, but you'll always get as many as you want from me as long as I'm helping you out—and at no extra charge."

Emma smiled.

...

Connie made Emma smile, including how she recommended three separate dishes. "Plenty of folks order the chef salad," Connie said. "Never had it myself. There is the shrimp salad, which comes with bay shrimp in an avocado half and no lettuce. Not really much of a salad if it doesn't have lettuce. To me. I'm just saying…But if you're willing to branch out a bit, I'd get the patty melt myself," Connie urged, adding with a wink, "It's one of our lighter dishes."

Emma went with Connie's recommendation and said, "When in Willow Creek, do as…I'll go with the patty melt." Waiting for her order, she decided to reply to Officer Jones. She wanted to be clear that seeing the box wasn't her only reason for coming to town. After another bite of scone, she wiped her hands and typed.

Emma Rose here. How can I arrange to see the box?

Emma hit send just as her meal arrived. What Connie brought looked basically like a hamburger patty topped with cheese and sautéed onions—not a light looking dish at all, and definitely not small. When Emma took her first bite, the rich, oniony flavor and the cheese took it in an tasty direction. It was so radically un-vegetarian but delicious!

Emma ate about half of her meal before sitting back, peering out the window down the street toward what looked like a couple of fast-food places. She saw Quentin Waldrup walk out of the mortuary next door in a light jacket with round glasses and fedora but otherwise dressed down a bit—no bow tie. It had to be him. She felt glad she knew at least one person. Quentin. Well, there was also Officer Jones. And now Connie.

As she watched Quentin walk down the street, her phone vibrated on the table. She looked down to see an unusually long text.

Good to hear from you. As I said before, you'll have to come to Willow Creek. I can't ship it. It can't leave the evidence locker. We have a strict policy about evidence, even though it was determined that this wasn't a crime scene. Or at least it is so old that whatever the crime, and if it actually was a crime, it was likely committed so long ago that we won't do much more about it. I shouldn't say more. Anyway, let me know if you're ever in Willow Creek, and I can put something together.

Emma smiled at the length of his text and his assumption that she was anywhere but Willow Creek. She wondered how surprised he would be as she typed a response.

I'm here.

Almost immediately, she got a response.

?

...

ON HER WALK BACK TO THE APARTMENT, Emma resisted the urge to cross the street to the other stores, something her father would have jumped at. Instead, she was committed to visiting the cemetery, to visit her father. And then write more, as she had planned. She would take in the rest of Willow Creek another time.

Back in her apartment, Emma dove back into her book, writing feverishly about how so much of who we are is shaped by the cultural forces around us—making notes about upbringing and family heritage and then writing several paragraphs about fake news and the pressures exerted by social media to compare and compete. "That's the water," she wrote. "Once we become aware enough of what those forces are doing to us, then and only then do we have the option of doing something with them or about them and not simply being swept along by them."

Nearly breathless as she wrote, Emma reflected on her father's oft-stated line that "You don't get to choose what brought you to this point in life—what has happened or why—but you do get to choose what you do about it now." She wrote about how it all boils down to awareness of your reality—what *is*—and then choosing what to do about it.

Emma spent the next two hours writing about the "plastic wrap incident" from earlier in her life and how it had shaped her. Finally, she slid her chair back and remembered her original plan. She still wanted to get to the cemetery before dark. Not knowing when it would get dark, now was likely a good time for a break. And rather than drive, Emma felt like going for a run. She recalled her wintry drive to the cemetery not taking all that long and knew she could make it there and back.

After changing clothes, she set out for the cemetery, hoping she remembered how to get there and glad she had her phone just in case.

...

GLANCING AT THE MAP ON HER PHONE AS SHE RAN, Emma followed directions down Main Street and then south to the edge of town where she turned down more of a country road. Jogging east past more of the greenest fields that continued were even more stunning in the late afternoon light, she could see the tall evergreens outlining the cemetery in the distance. Like a homing beacon had been guiding her.

Emma entered the cemetery and jogged toward where she remembered her father's grave was. Her mother had assigned her to inspect the new headstone when she could, something they were both eager to see how it had turned out. They had been working on it for several months now via email with Quentin Waldrup.

Emma slowed to a walk to catch her breath. The cemetery was empty of any living people. As she neared her father's gravesite, she felt a rush of emotion that nearly overwhelmed her. The beautiful granite headstone matched exactly what she had seen in photos—her mother would be so happy! Both parents' names were inscribed on it, despite her mother's lack of commitment to being buried there. Adorned by a simple mountain scene with evergreens, the inscription read, "Steven Ray Rose, May 15, 1935-January 4, 2019" with "Cheryl Darlene Hampton, July 7, 1945."

Emma took a few pictures and texted those to her mother. As she did, the finality of her father being buried at this spot hit her, and the possibility of her mother ever passing caused Emma to tremble—looking back at her mother's blank death date brought tears in anticipation of a day Emma dreaded. She rubbed her fingers over her father's name and said, "Oh, Dad. I miss you so much." It felt good to cry again. She laughed a little as she cried. "I can't believe I'm talking to a headstone, but it feels okay so I will." Wiping at her tears, she said, "So, is this what your big plan was all about? Were you wanting to bring me to Willow Creek, Dad? Was this the trip you were planning?"

Emma reflected. "It is a pretty little town. And I'm here again for the second time—for a month unless things go better than expected. I have so much I want to tell you." It felt good to talk, and Emma told her father about her book and what she had written about that day. She caught herself rambling. "Honestly…as though I would ever not be honest, that is, I'm struggling with the idea that we can ever really know all that is at work around us—the stuff that makes us who we are. In my work, I use a metaphor of a goldfish swimming in water. Do you think the goldfish can ever be fully aware of all going on around it? I mean, water is its lifeforce and all it knows, or doesn't know, for that matter. It can't ever leave the water any more than it can choose that it was born into the water, right? I know it's philosophical, but this entire notion that I've hatched—of people becoming aware enough that they can choose which cultural forces they let influence them and which they reject—well, it's complicated at best. At a simple level, the idea of staring all this down works. But at another level, it opens up mystery after mystery of what makes us who we are." Looking back at the headstone, she added, "Well, of who I am. I have so many questions for you, Dad."

Emma looked around at the tall evergreens thinking they had to be a hundred years old. Glancing back at her father's grave, she said, "Like this, Dad. I didn't even know about Willow Creek six months ago, and now I'm here for the second time. Something tells me there is more at play, more going on here. So, now what? What did you know that you wanted to tell me or show me but couldn't?"

Suddenly aware of how loud she was talking, Emma realized she had taken a seat on a bench facing her father's grave, embarrassed at how comfortable she had made herself. She quickly stood and looked around to be sure no one else was in the cemetery or could hear her.

Looking down, she discovered the bench was actually a grave marker as well. She read the names. "Swenson—Jens Nicholas and Sarah Jane Walker" were inscribed with dates. She walked around and saw a few other Walkers, along with names she hadn't really heard before such as Rapp, Hutchins, Simons, and Smithies mixed in with Poole, Ellsworth, and Hunter.

Emma felt a tingly sensation as her mind flooded with the impression that some of these might be her people—her father's people. "These are probably our people," she whispered at first. Then, standing on the bench wearing her tights and running shoes, Emma swept her arm in front of her and announced loudly, "You might all be my people." Clearing her throat, she added, "And I'm Emma Rose. I'd like to get to know you!"

Chapter 23

Willow Creek Cemetery, 1910

On the twentieth of April, Halley's comet moved slowly across the sky, a streak of light and white cloud of dust in its wake. "It won't come again in our lifetime," Cassie told her children as they bundled together on a quilt under the cold, clear sky that night. Out past the barn to the hayfield, they were away from the new floodlight Erastus had installed on a barnyard post earlier that week. All were glad to be outside after being cooped up indoors for days.

On what she had hoped would be an unforgettable, once-in-a-lifetime evening together, Cassie had been forced by the recent winter fever outbreak to shift her plans made only a week earlier—to have Sarah and her sons over to watch the goings on together. Earlier that evening, Sarah had committed over the phone to come together soon. "Phone calls are okay," Cassie had reminded her, relying on often twice-daily phone calls, "but a visit on the front porch is even better." The two even occasionally still wrote and mailed notes to each other despite living only a few miles apart yet fortunate to share a postman who delivered directly without as much as a postage stamp.

The outbreak was more widespread than in the past and too vicious to take casually. Unlike when her mother had passed, people had learned to avoid contracting the illness by now to isolating themselves as much as possible. Like times before, no one understood where this outbreak had come from or when it might pass to them. For well over two weeks now, Cassie had kept the children home from school, effectively quarantined from friends since the fever attacked willy-nilly. Stories circulated about men and women, healthy until not, some passing within days. Still others considered weak or less hardy were afflicted but surviving, somehow holding on and emerging as ashen, thinner versions of their former selves. Most weren't going out at all.

The children had finished their evening chores before dinner because their mother had promised a great surprise that evening after dark.

Staring up at the cold night sky, Samuel asked, "Is this the surprise, Momma?"

"Yes, it is," Cassie said, pointing toward the one bright dot traveling across the heaven above. "So, what's a comet?"

Samuel looked toward his younger brother, Henry, who shrugged his shoulders. Samuel offered, "That bright, moving star?"

"Yes!" Cassie had been waiting and watching for weeks. The newspaper had described the comet's roughly seventy-five-year orbit, even quoting Mark Twain as saying a few weeks earlier, "I came in with Halley's comet in 1835…. It will be the greatest disappointment of my life if I don't go out with Halley's comet. The Almighty has said, no doubt: 'Now here are these two unaccountable freaks; they came in together, they must go out together.'" Every time she thought of Mark Twain since, she had laughed that he considered himself an unaccountable freak.

She hadn't been able to come up with a useful connection between the comet and the author of *Huckleberry Finn* that her children would understand and so had dropped that part from her intended lesson.

Young Esther repeated the original question. "What's a comet, Momma?" Already reminding Cassie of her own younger self, Esther was a tiny person, one with great questions most of the time and too many sometimes.

"It's a chunk of ice and rock—almost a small planet. Some call them 'long-haired stars' because of the gas trail you can almost see with your naked eye," Cassie said, squinting. "This one is a 'periodic comet.' That means it has a regular orbit of less than two hundred years. It's called a short-period comet because it comes by our planet every seventy-five years or so. They say it won't be seen again until 1986."

Henry looked at his hands, counting with his fingers. "I'll be eighty-eight that year. Pretty old," he said, leaning forward and pretending he was holding a cane.

They all laughed. Esther said, "That's easy for me. I'm ten in 1910, so I'll be eighty-six in 1986."

Cassie continued the lesson. "So, why is seventy-five years a 'short period'?"

Esther and Henry glanced toward each other and shrugged. Samuel lay with his arms behind his head, arching back to see the brilliant sky behind him.

Since no one answered, Cassie continued the lesson. "Seventy-five years may seem like a lifetime here on earth—and that's longer than most people live. But when it comes to the planets and the stars, like the dirt and rocks around us, it's no time at all." She snapped her fingers to emphasize the point. She continued. "For instance, how long has the Snake River been running its course?"

Henry said tentatively, "Forever?"

"You're probably right, Henry. At least much longer than seventy-five years. And when Halley's comet returns, that river will still be running—likely the same course it does today."

Samuel hadn't said much. "Unless it cuts a new channel and goes somewhere else."

"You've been hanging around your papa too much," Cassie teased, tousling his hair. Erastus's worries about small changes in the river and necessary adjustments to canal systems to increase capacity had led to a plan to expand the Great Feeder to double its flow. Others worried that would lead to breaks in ditch banks and washed-out fields, worse than when someone forgot to shut off head gates. The common theme was that water had been "hard to direct to begin with," something he often emphasized.

Henry and Esther shifted toward their mother, and Cassie drew them into her arms. Reaching for Samuel, she whispered, "Seventy-five years is no time at all…," kissing her oldest son's head.

…

FOUR DAYS LATER, winter fever streaked through the Walker household as quickly as Halley's Comet had come and gone, taking Samuel with it after only one day and leaving grief in its wake. Cassie was devastated after having done all she could think of to protect her family.

Equally distraught, Erastus spent the early hours of the day building a pine box to carry his oldest son's body to the cemetery that afternoon. Earlier in the day, Cassie had reluctantly left her two other children at home sick with slight fevers, so she could join Erastus for the burial.

At the cemetery, fresh mounds dotted the wide lawn. Erastus pulled the buggy alongside the plot where Cassie's mother and brother were buried, the rock headstone inscribed with, "Esther Ray Bingham – May 21, 1860-July 2, 1895," already weathering. Next to that was another headstone with the image of a dog etched on it that read, "Eugene Simeon Rapp – June 20, 1885-May 25, 1900."

Erastus finished digging the hole and then lifted the pine box out of the wagon and placed it down in the hole. Cassie sat quietly, shocked at the loss of her oldest son. It had happened so quickly, and she wondered why she couldn't cry. She felt so numb.

Erastus offered a prayer. "Dear Lord, please take good care of my son. He was always yours, but he's now only yours. Samuel was a good boy, nearly a man. Please raise him to manhood in your care. Please hold him for me and tell him once more how much I love him. Please comfort my grieving wife. Please spare our other children, Henry and Esther, from this dreaded contagion. Thy will be done, dear Lord. Amen."

Cassie looked away, her lips beginning to tremble, barely able to utter her own "amen." Her heart was breaking. She knew Erastus felt the same as she watched him shovel dirt into the hole. Before leaving, Cassie pinned a handwritten note to a stake to mark her son's grave. It read, 'Samuel William Walker – A good son – April 25, 1910.'

They wept together as they rode home.

When they arrived, all was eerily quiet. Cassie panicked and rushed into the house to find Henry and Esther lifeless.

It was all she could bear. She broke down and shrieked hysterically. Erastus knew what they had to do. Emotionally spent, he set out to make two more pine boxes and then took another trip to the cemetery to dig a second hole. Cassie felt a deeper exhaustion than ever before as she washed the bodies of her two children and dressed them in their best church clothes for burial.

Near dusk that day as they drove again to the cemetery, Cassie sat in the back of the wagon with her hand on the boxes, shifting and shaking at a reality she was struggling to accept. After Erastus placed the boxes carrying the bodies of Henry and little Esther into a hole next to their brother, Cassie lowered herself into the hole to sit on one of the boxes. Erastus had to beg Cassie to come out of the grave.

"Please just bury me with them," Cassie cried. Erastus looked around, searching for a way to comfort his grieving wife. She wailed, "I want to go with them! Why them and not me? Why not me!"

Erastus climbed down into the hole and sat next to her. Trying to reassure her, he said, "We will see them again. It will not be long. You will be with your children again."

Cassie looked up into her husband's eyes, her wet face revealing a crushed and angry woman. "You can't really know that? You can't promise me that!" She beat her fists against his chest.

Erastus held her tightly, her fists quieting. Brushing her hair back from her face with his finger, he added, "In no time at all."

Two nights later, Cassie took out her journal and turned to the back pages. She added new entries with dates she had never expected to endure.

Erastus William Walker – April 3, 1873
Catherine Esther Rapp – June 1, 1877
- *Samuel William – January 12, 1896-April 25, 1910*
- *Henry Erastus – March 25, 1898-April 26, 1910*
- *Esther Catherine – June 3, 1900-April 26, 1910*

By the end of the week, the apple trees burst into blossom and the contagion all but disappeared.

Chapter 24

White Out

They were driving along a desert road in near white-out conditions. She looked around and could see only snow flurries dancing in the air ahead of them. The snow covering the road ahead was marked by only one other set of tire tracks. "Follow those," she said. How she knew they were in the desert wasn't entirely clear until they stopped near a hoodoo, a medium-sized rock formation sculpted by erosion that looked more like someone had squeezed wet sand into an oddly shaped pile. Her father said nothing. He looked upset—no, like he had something on his mind, something he wanted to tell her.

"What, Dad?" she asked.

Her father started to say, "Emma, I need to tell you a few..." and then stopped. She sensed he was wincing at a collection of memories. Looking ahead, it was suddenly night. The car's headlights struggled to pierce the blackness, highlighting only the snow flurries ahead of them, like countless moths fluttering in the cold.

"Dad?" She felt the seatbelt pulling tight against her chest making it difficult to breath. She fumbled near her hips to release but couldn't find the latch.

Panicking, Emma asked, "Where are we going?" She looked over and found she was now alone in the car—no one was driving, and yet the car continued to follow the single set of tire tracks as the snow flurries thickened and turned into a wall of white.

Emma awoke abruptly, sitting up and momentarily disoriented by her unfamiliar surroundings. She hazily remembered she was in Willow Creek. She was sweating—from falling asleep in a hoodie, something she quickly removed and then sat still, listening. No Manhattan sirens passing by. No constant whirring of vehicles coming and going or the rumbling vibration of passing subways blocks away. All was quiet.

Checking her phone, Emma saw it was two-fifteen in the morning. She walked to the kitchen to get a drink, clearing away the remnants of her dream. She opened a window at the back and felt the rush of cool air. Recalling her visit to her father's grave, she moved to the couch in the living area and sat down, pulling a blanket over her knees and to her chest. He was gone, she knew. Gone. Even her dream had made that clear.

A light outside the window changed from white to red, not so bright but altering the color in the room around her periodically. The refrigerator hummed slightly when it turned on and made a light thumping sound as it worked on something.

In her dream, what her father been about to say? Details about his adoption? Willow Creek? Advice? Her thoughts rambled. Who am I really? Do my new discoveries make much of a different?

Emma began to feel entirely alone, wondering if being in a new place was the cause of her loneliness until she began to tremble. She drew the blanket around her shoulders, but the shaking only increased. Tears dropped on her clenched hands, surprising her. The strange sensation continued to build.

She felt the urge to say something but couldn't think of what to say. More jumbled questions formed. Why? Mom? Alone? This town? The box? Writing? Goldfish? The light in the room was now getting much brighter, going nearly black before turning from white to red and back again.

She began shaking and sobbing. Her internal dialogue spilled out. "What am I doing here? Why did I think this would work? Why did I say yes to a book?" And then a very distraught sounding laugh. "Oh, if anyone could hear you now," she continued. "They'd walk right into your New York loft and take that crystal trophy away. 'Poser,' they'd say. 'No breakthrough award for you. Go find yourself a corner somewhere and see who cares then!'"

Emma tucked her body against the corner of the couch, holding her knees and rocking. She remembered Connie's question from the diner earlier that day. "What brings you back to town?" The question echoed repeatedly in her mind. "So, what?" Emma asked herself. "What exactly? Go home," she told herself. "Do your thing there."

Emma could hear her own muffled, mournful sounds. How could this be happening? Always so put together, so composed, she suddenly felt hot again and flung the blanket off, knocking over her water on the side table. She felt like she was going crazy. Bonkers. Minutes later, cold and shivering out of control, she found the blanket again. She rocked for a long while, not sure what was happening. She felt empty, like everything meaningful had evaporated and was lost forever. She tried to make a list in her mind of what was lost but couldn't think of anything specific. Disconnected. Numb. Flat. Empty.

Her chest felt heavy. "Panic attack" popped into her mind. For some reason, she found herself disagreeing with the notion but then decided to take stock. Her breathing was shallow. Her heart actually hurt. She told herself to breathe in and out. She cupped her hand over her mouth. Her nose was chilled, and the warm breath against her palm somehow felt reassuring.

Remembering her prescription, she hurried to the bathroom and took one of the pills. She knew she had to wait twenty minutes for any effect so curled back into a ball on the couch, still crying about something she couldn't understand.

When Emma awoke, a warm light had begun to fill the room. She was relieved it was morning. In the next moment, rays of morning sunlight burst through the front windows of the apartment and birdsong came through the back window she had opened in the night. The display on the microwave registered six-thirty. Emma realized the blanket she was holding to her face was wet with her tears. Her chest still hurt from the panic episode but otherwise she felt calm and relaxed.

"You're here now. Let's work with it," she whispered, walking toward the bathroom for a shower.

Chapter 25

Upper Snake River Valley, 1920-21

For years, Cassie thought about having more children but remained fearful and felt broken after losing her three children. She wondered if she would ever laugh again let alone love another child. She busied herself around the house, attended periodic community meetings and joined the local historical society, and visited Erastus more frequently at work.

When Cassie received an invitation from the historical society to write a book on the history of irrigation in the area, she could not imagine anyone wanting to read such a book at first before feeling entirely overwhelmed by the idea. The society board members valued her pioneer background and deep connections to the area, they said, along with the fact that she seemed to know anyone and everyone across the valley from St. Anthony to Firth.

Hoping to take her mind off her losses, she agreed. As she began collecting tidbits on the history of the area and interviewing the boards of each of the canal companies, the project began to come alive. Starting out with only a collection of legal-looking organizing documents and charters, the project gradually turned into a passion when Cassie began interviewing women, particularly the wives of many early homesteaders, many of whom were still living. At first, she thought they might be able to straighten out some of the facts she was learning, but when they began telling rich stories of how water had shaped and even redefined their lives, she knew she was on to something. She unearthed a treasure trove of stories—tragedies and triumphs—all in anecdotes that had much more to do with pioneer living than the ingenuity of irrigation.

Sitting on Ann Jenkins' front porch one morning, Cassie became intrigued by Ann's description of the way the land had naturally changed as water was introduced. Like Cassie herself, Ann was one of the earliest settlers still living in the area.

"Endless miles of sagebrush were replaced by lush fields," Ann said. "Fortunate for me, we still have a few acres with native sage over toward the hills. And the birds that had previously only lived along the rivers and streams—along with the few natural meadows that existed—found their way inland. They flourished."

At that a bird trilled from a fence post. "Take that meadowlark just now. Birds like that would never have been seen this far inland before we arrived. Only where the rivers meet the sage." Ann looked steadfastly as the bird took flight. "It's all the canals and ditches. And the farmland. Water is what brought birds like that here." Ann looked off into the distance as she mused.

"In a way, I guess we're all birds—water brought us as well," Cassie mused.

Ann smiled. "Some of us are meadowlarks. And some are just old crows." The two women laughed together.

From visits with women like Ann and so many other people, Cassie's collection of letters, handwritten notes, and sketches quickly formed a tall stack on her desk. She enlisted the help of a small committee of other women to travel up and down the entire valley and along its edges to meet with anyone they could find who had an irrigation story to tell.

Two years into her research, Cassie had never felt more complete. Having met people far and wide, she heard stories that seemed far-fetched at first, except for the fact that she was hearing them firsthand from those who had experienced the events personally.

And family life was good as well. Erastus's businesses were doing well enough that he was home most evenings by dinner time. They even found time to take a five-day trip guided by Erastus's brother Tom to see the geysers and wildlife of Yellowstone Park. They boarded the Yellowstone Special which stopped at Willow Creek and rode the train three hours north to the new town of West Yellowstone. There, they switched to Tom's new auto stage, a vehicle with four rows of seats that had replaced his stagecoach and six-horse team only a year or two earlier. They camped comfortably in teepee villages along the way for four nights, seeing all the major Yellowstone wonders in a trip that would have taken ten or more days by horse.

Life was full of blessings.

...

BY OCTOBER OF THAT YEAR, Cassie began struggling with bouts of nausea. At first, she thought she was merely working too hard and simply run down. She temporarily put the book aside in order to make it through the daily discomfort, secretly worrying she had some kind of illness. Rather than see a doctor about it, she chose to rest when she could.

By mid-November and feeling familiar changes in her body, she finally visited the doctor, who confirmed her suspicion. She was pregnant. It was a bittersweet realization. She was tentative when she told Erastus, who fell to his knees and sobbed. "Oh, blessed day! Thank the Lord for one more opportunity to raise a child," he exclaimed.

When Cassie first shared the news with Sarah, Sarah reacted circumspectly and advised Cassie to stay as healthy as possible, eat well, and take in some exercise now and then. Cassie begged for the particulars of pregnancy for a woman her age, and Sarah spoke frankly as always. As the attending midwife in now hundreds of deliveries, Sarah had experienced nearly every imaginable circumstance related to childbirth.

"Your situation is different," Sarah said. "Most mothers I have assisted were between the ages of eighteen and forty. You're forty-three—and that puts you among the few older women I have previously assisted. Five, to be exact," she said. "Three delivered healthy babies, but two of those women died from infections within days. One mother struggled with a breech delivery, and she lived but the baby did not survive."

The facts were sobering. Cassie took Sarah's counsel to heart.

...

LATE ONE EVENING IN THE LATTER PART OF APRIL, Erastus left the house with Cassie screaming, "Get Sarah!" Sarah and Jens still lived a few miles to the north across the river over on Moody Creek, and Cassie urgently needed a midwife. Erastus had tried several times to telephone his sister Sarah, but the handset was quiet, indicating some bigger problem with the network of wires that now extended across the valley and regularly experienced outages—a situation probably made worse by the freezing rain over the past few hours. His first inclination was to take his new Model T, but as he ran toward the makeshift garage that he had recently erected, he remembered that the main bridge on the Snake was under repair and impassible. Someone had mentioned the old ferry was temporarily back in operation, and he thought for a moment about whether his car could cross that way before concluding otherwise—he had not heard of the ferry carrying cars across the river. He considered his horse Boots, at the same time recalling a route across the Dry Bed that would get him to Sarah's even faster by horse anyway, a path he had ridden many times before. After the crossing, he could be at the Swensons' in no time.

Milo and Polaris were both long gone, both good horses, and Boots was just as good a horse and probably his fastest quarter horse yet. One named for the three white stocking feet that contrasted nicely with his black coat. Erastus saddled Boots and guided the horse out of the barn, glancing over at the Model T and momentarily reconsidering his plan. Shaking his head as Boots snorted, Erastus knew this would be the fastest way to reach the ferry and likely the only way across the river.

As Erastus checked the cinch, he heard Cassie scream "Saraaaaah!" He quickly mounted and leaned forward, teasing the horse with his heels, urging Boots to trot out the gate and then into a gallop as they turned onto the long flat stretch of road that ran along the west edge of town and toward the Dry Bed. The surprise, late-winter storm had coated the trees with ice—which reinforced why the telephone system was down. After a mile or so, Erastus took a shortcut over the southern bank and down into the nearly dry slopes of the Dry Bed, barely a small stream at this time of year with iced-over puddles and yellow grass laying sideways from the downstream current of last year's flow.

Nearing a flat swampy area, Erastus slowed the horse to a walk to pass through before urging him back into a gallop with a "Yip!" Cutting upstream through a stand of cottonwoods, Boots leaped over fallen logs and flipped near-frozen mud high into the air behind him. Leaving the Dry Bed, the pair cut across fields and past farmhouses in a race toward the mighty Snake to the north.

Aside from the icy air and the sound of horse and rider breathing hard, the night was noticeably quiet. As they neared the crossing, Erastus hoped the ferryman was still awake—and better still, he would have just dropped travelers on this side of the river and would be ready for a return trip—the most ideal case he could conjure up. In the moonlight, he arrived at the river's edge and was disappointed to see only an icy cable stretching fifty or more yards away into the blackness on the other side of the river. All was dark except for the single porch light at the ferryman's house on the far side, which gave Erastus concern—straining, he made out the ferry moored near the house as well. It was extremely late, but Erastus rang the brass bell repeatedly to wake the man before noticing a hand-written note tacked to the cable post nearby.

Wife took sick. Off to Rexburg for doctor. Sorry for your troubles.

With no other way to get the ferry to this side, Erastus paced and then pondered for a moment and then bowed his head.

"Dear God," he prayed, "Please help me discover a way across this river. I need to reach Sarah and bring her safely back for my wife. Lord, you know we have already lost much, and perhaps this baby can comfort Cassie. Please save my wife…and our baby."

Looking up, he saw pieces of ice slipping off the ferry cable into the dark river below. The night was warming a bit, and the thought occurred to climb hand-over-hand across the cable and bring the ferry back to get his horse. Giving it no further thought, he tied his horse to the post and grabbed the cable, lifting himself and hanging from it by his arms with his legs crisscrossed over the cable. Going headfirst, he drew himself slowly toward the other side, knocking ice off as he went.

After fifty feet and still less than halfway there, Erastus's hands began to burn from the cold. His arms tingled. Holding onto the cable by the crook of each arm, he rested. Tears of desperation dripped from his eyes into the river. Failure wasn't an option, so he collected his strength and continued the slow crawl.

Near the middle of the river, the cable drooped down within a few feet of the dark water below. Nearing that point, Erastus could feel his coat dragging below him in the water, growing heavy as it soaked up water. After a few more pulls and his arms on the verge of failing, he held on again by his elbows, slipping one arm out of his coat and then the other before dropping it into the dark waters only a foot or so below him. He hung there breathless, watching it float away before sinking.

Nearly exhausted, he finally reached the far shore and landed feet first on the ferry itself. Shaking his arms to restore feeling to his numb hands, he fumbled at the rope that secured the ferry before releasing it. Then, he began to turn the hand-crank of the pulley system to draw the ferry along the cable back toward the side where his horse was waiting. In the middle, the ferry began bucking as the nose caught the current, alternately submersing and rising. The crank grew stiff in his hand, immovable. Almost completely spent, Erastus mustered strength from somewhere and leaned into the crank with his entire weight. It finally turned again.

Upon landing, Erastus bent over, hands on knees, and breathed deeply for a few moments before reaching up to untie Boots and guide him onto the ferry. He tethered his horse to the post at the back end, hoping this arrangement would keep the nose of the ferry from digging into the river as they crossed back over.

Working to warm his hands somehow, Erastus reached for the crank and began to work the crank, surprised his energy wasn't completely gone. Within minutes, he reached the far bank again, looking around and smiling.

With a "Giddyap," he raced the final mile.

...

SARAH ASSISTED CASSIE through the night, with contractions at first, then the pushing and exhaustion. Cassie admitted this time was more painful than she had experienced with any of her other children. At times, she cried out their names. "Samuel, Henry, Esther," knowing they were gone, buried. Sarah stroked her head and tried to comfort her between contractions.

After eight hours of hard labor, Cassie lay motionless, exhausted. Minutes before seven o'clock the next morning, the sun broke over the hills to the east.

Sarah seemed concerned. "Cassie, I need you to be awake. You can sleep later." She nudged Cassie and placed a damp cloth across her forehead.

Cassie's weak reply said everything. "I don't...know...how to...do this."

"You do know how. You have done this before. I just need you to be part of it. This baby won't make it without your help."

Cassie said, "But I just want..." Her eyes rolled back.

"Cassie," Sarah urged her again, shaking her lightly. "We need to get this baby to come! On the next contraction, we will both push."

Sarah placed her hand on Cassie's stomach. As the pain built, Cassie bit her lip and Sarah said, "Push," while gently pressing down. "Push!"

Cassie lay back, beads of sweat dotting her forehead, her breathing growing shallow. Sarah yelled for Erastus to come in. She gave him instructions, and then the next contraction came.

Erastus helped lift Cassie up on her elbows. "Now push, Cassie. Give it all you have."

Bearing down with what energy remained, Cassie pushed as Sarah assisted. Moments later, a baby's head emerged, and a soft cry filled the room. A baby girl! Sarah cleaned the baby with a towel and then handed her to her weeping mother.

Simultaneously exhausted and filled with joy, Cassie said, "I'll never let you go, sweet one." She looked up at Erastus who had tears in his eyes and said, "We have another child!"

Erastus sat next to his wife, stroking her hair. "What will we name her?"

Cassie said, "I want to call her Iris."

…

AFTER PUTTING THE BABY TO BED one evening, Cassie began sorting through books on the shelf in their front room and came across her journal. Holding it to her chest, she sounded surprised. "I haven't written in this for a while!" She opened it to the last few pages she had written.

October 19, 1917

We are at war. We have been for some time. Many men from the area have been called up—starting with the young men, but now they are calling up men in their thirties. If my boys were still living, they would likely have been sent with the first groups from the valley to battles across the world in Europe. Samuel would be twenty-one and Henry nineteen. I miss their smiles, but I can't imagine the pains of mothers whose sons won't ever come home. Why, there must be more than fifty blue stars up in front windows across town, but sadly at least ten have been changed to gold. Johnsons lost their boy. So did the Lowders and Murdochs. Frenches out in Roberts area lost two sons. It doesn't seem right.

A mother shouldn't outlive her children, but at least I know where my sons are buried.

Erastus's brother, Tom, is somewhere in England. We hear from him only occasionally. I pray he remains safe.

Cassie reflected on what had been a tragic and hard-to-understand war. Even though crop prices had been good for a few years, they had now dropped based on what newspapers were reporting as oversupply. Tom had returned late early the next year, discharged honorably as an officer in the U.S. Army from a war that had finally ended.

She flipped to the next page, instantly recognizing the date. A strip of paper marking the page slipped out of the book onto her lap as she read.

June 27, 1919

We will have a parade tomorrow! The canal company's float will have real trees on it and blue cloth draped in a way to look like a canal. We will add fresh flowers from our yards just before the parade. Our theme is written in large letters, "This desert blossomed like a rose." It will be good to get outside and see folks gather again in town. It's been so long.

Papa passed away in May from that outbreak of Spanish flu. It was an awful season of loss for folks everywhere. The doctor told Pa he had a bad heart and to be more careful than usual—that he was highly susceptible to this wicked flu. Pa had always been so strong and carried on as usual. The sickness took him in two days. We were told not to go near him. Losing him without being able to say good-bye was one of the saddest days of my life. We had a simple graveside service. No gathering. No one has been able to gather. The quarantine was lifted only a few weeks ago.

I don't know why I'm writing this, but Ruby says she found him relaxed in his chair when she came in from the yard. She knew he hadn't been feeling well but thought he was only resting at first. He didn't wake up when she nudged him. Sixty-three is too young to go. Needless to say, we will miss seeing him on the float this year. He was like a fixture in the parade.

Ruby has been so good to all of us these past years.

I will write more later.

Wiping her tears with the tissue she almost always carried, Cassie put the journal down on her lap and reflected. She missed her father, a man who had been instrumental in nearly every aspect of her life—and life for so many countless others. Celebrated for a time for his pioneering work with irrigation, Simeon contributions had more recently remained unheralded, taken for granted by city and country folk alike.

As she lifted the book to locate her bookmark, she found the piece of paper on her lap, one with a quote from Thomas Jefferson that she had first read years earlier.

Cultivators of the earth are the most valuable citizens. They are the most vigorous, the most independent, the most virtuous, and they are tied to their country and wedded to its liberty and interests by the most lasting bonds.

"He *was* a valuable citizen, an original pioneer," she whispered, smiling at the memory of her father and all he had accomplished. Cassie inserted the bookmark before turning the page, expecting it to be blank. She spotted one line she remembered hurriedly scribbling months back.

November 10—going to see Dr. today. I might be pregnant. Book set to be published soon.

"My, how life can be so sad one minute and take you by surprise the next," she said aloud, holding the journal to her chest. Sighing, Cassie put the book on the table, thinking she would write about baby Iris and so much more the next chance she got. She peeked in on her baby before turning out the lights.

Chapter 26

City Hall

After such an awful night, the shower helped. Emma stood under the steaming water for the longest time before finally getting out. Swiping at the condensation on the mirror, she caught her own reflection and felt embarrassed that she had spent so much of the night thinking so many random thoughts and crying.

"This is so not us," she said to her reflection in the mirror. "We don't freak out, Emma Rose." Laughing that she was talking to herself this way, she looked at her puffy eyes in the mirror and pointed, saying, "Well, you did, but you pulled yourself together, right?" The tears began to flow again, and she looked away. She remembered the panic attack with Jake—so very different than the night before—and wondered what she could do to prevent something like that in the future. Or at least see it coming.

As she pulled on leggings and a t-shirt, Emma thought briefly about talking things over with Lacy but then didn't want to sound defeated after only one night in Willow Creek. This was supposed to be a month-long writing retreat, not a one-night stand. She smiled, happy she didn't feel any of what she had the night before.

Emma found a loaf of bread in the refrigerator and some tea bags in the cupboard next to it. She made toast and tea and then sat at the kitchen table. "Textbook," she said out loud, reassuring herself that her panic attack was over and that it was okay to move on.

Sighing, Emma retrieved her phone and saw it was already eight o'clock. She suddenly remembered Officer Jones's text from the day, a "?" She typed a response, not wanting to go into detail.

Just here. Can I see the box today?

She had barely put her phone down when it vibrated. He was speedy!

Would 9am work? What brings you back to Willow Creek?

Emma decided to answer his question about when and ignore the other one. An hour from then was too early—she needed a little more time before taking on the mystery of the box.

Too early. Busy until noon. Noon?

Sure. Thx!

Wondering at how Officer Jones had made the connection between whatever the box contained and her, she smiled as her phone vibrated again with the address to City Hall.

As Emma put on her favorite hoodie with the Columbia University logo on it, she worried she wouldn't be able to write after such a hard night. But as she opened her laptop, she was surprised that her ideas from the day sounded so clear and knew exactly where to pick up. Words began flowing. At eleven-thirty, she ran a word count and was pleased she had already written over three thousand words. Just before noon, she checked herself in the bathroom mirror, pulling her hair back into a ponytail and putting on some mascara.

Emma linked from the address Officer Jones had texted to open the maps app. She reached for her car keys and began hurrying down the stairs before realizing City Hall was less than a block away. She decided to walk instead.

The day was still on the cool side, so Emma crossed Main Street to be in the sun. The town was so picturesque. She noticed a Chinese restaurant and then what looked like a U.S. post office that she hadn't seen before, smiling at how much her father would have loved it—or may even have already loved it from some past experience.

A deep sound began to build from somewhere—a siren sound somewhere between a foghorn and a tsunami warning that rose briefly and never got shrill before descending. Startled at first, she passed a few people who seemed altogether unaware of the siren sound, and then noticed a few others looking down at their watches or phones. Glancing at her own, she could see the time was exactly noon. Another fun small-town thing, she thought, smiling as she hurried along.

Turning left at the next corner as directed, Emma immediately saw the three-story City Hall building just ahead, a very traditional looking government building. As she approached its glass double doors, she caught her own reflection and pulled a strand of hair back. Inside, she saw a large sign at the end of the hall that said, "Police." She walked through the office door and approached the receptionist. She heard a shuffle behind her, and turned to see Officer Jones standing up from his seat behind along the wall. He must have been waiting for her. He was taller than she remembered, and without his winter coat had broader shoulders than she had been able to detect before. Tan and neatly groomed in a tailored uniform, he seemed confident as he came forward, his hand extended.

"Emma?"

Only a little surprised, Emma replied. "Well, hello, Officer Jones. I didn't see you there." She reached to shake his hand, instantly feeling a little self-conscience about what she was wearing.

"Just 'Topher,' ma'am. Sorry to startle you…it's good to see you again. Really good." He let go of her hand and looked at the hoodie she was wearing and muttered, "Columbia, hmmm."

Emma wasn't sure what to make of his statement, straightening the waist of her hoodie. Smiling, she said, "My mother is 'ma'am.' Let's go with 'Emma,' okay?"

"Sure thing, Emma." Topher looked around like he was making things more complicated than necessary. "Did you come all this way…to see the box?"

Emma thought for a moment, and then a little cautiously replied, "Sure—to see the box." Convinced about her answer, she shrugged her shoulders and added, "I guess I needed to know what's in it."

A twenty-something woman behind the counter was smiling at their exchange. Emma smiled back at her and said to Topher, "Well…"

"Come with me," Topher said, pointing down the aisle to his left.

Opening a half-height swinging door with one arm, Topher gestured for Emma to go ahead of him. As she passed, she caught a hint of his cologne and smiled. "Thanks," she said.

"No problem. Right this way." Topher guided her down a long hall and indicated a room at the end with "Evidence" written on a sign jutting out from the wall. "We keep all the evidence there," he said.

"That would…make sense," Emma said playfully, realizing she might have sounded too amused based on Topher's serious tone. He seemed not to notice.

"So, before I show you what we found, I need to fill you in on the particulars of this case. Take a seat," Topher said, pointing to two chairs in the hallway outside the door.

Emma sat down, curious at the hint of drama that seemed constant in Topher's voice when they talked—even the first time she met him. His chair squeaked on the linoleum floor as he turned it to face her. Two police officers came down the hall and squeezed by with "Hi Toph." Both looked back at Emma and smiled as though curious to see a stranger.

Topher waved them on. "We're a little tight on space here." Then, rubbing his hands together, he began to explain, "Okay…here's the situation. When they began digging the hole for your father's grave, the backhoe operator noticed a small bone sticking out of a scoop of dirt. He did the right thing and stopped digging. He called us in. I was patrolling the area at the time and so took the call. That's how things get assigned around here."

In her mind's eye, Emma could see the backhoe operator jumping down from his digger and pulling a bone out of a pile of dirt. Had he swept the dirt around to see if there was more?

Topher continued. "Back then, I couldn't tell you or even the funeral home much about this because we just didn't know. When I arrived at the scene, I could see several more bones down in the hole, all fairly small and maybe a foot below the surface in unfrozen ground. Bear in mind that this was still early winter—it can take until late January for the freeze to penetrate past a foot or so. Anyway, I taped off the scene and called over the ME—the Medical Examiner." Topher looked up. "And that's when I went to Waldrup's." He clapped his hands together as though finished, and added, "Where I met you."

Emma nodded and said, "Right. And?"

Topher took a breath and said, "The ME took pictures and spent the rest of the afternoon gathering evidence. Apparently, they finished exhuming the remains. I had other police business to attend to, so it wasn't until the next morning when I heard they were baby bones. We all began looking at open cases for anything related. We found nothing on a missing baby."

Emma asked what she knew might sound like an obvious question. "But wouldn't there have been a casket?"

Topher touched his nose. "Bingo. We all wondered exactly that—why would there be bones without a casket? We looked for signs of rotted wood or any other container. The cemetery caretaker said all bodies interred there from the beginning were in at least pine boxes. So, it made no sense…at first." He wet his lips and continued. "Along with the bones, which the ME by then had concluded were very old, possibly decades old, the ME also found something metal alongside the body. At first, she thought it may have been part of a casket but dug it out and realized it was a small, rusty tin box. We all wondered if it was a tribute that someone had left somewhere over the years—you know, these things do happen. The caretaker there said people quite often leave very personal items—not only flowers but mementos like tiny race cars, framed family photos, and even garden gnomes."

Emma shifted in her chair, wondering momentarily about garden gnomes, before saying, "I have a question."

"Yes?"

"So, just baby bones and a box, right?"

"Yes?"

"And yet you called me about the box and not the bones, right? How do you figure the box has anything to do with me?"

Topher said, "That's what I'm getting at. We don't know how old the bones are or if the box has anything to do with the bones. They could be two totally different matters." After a brief pause, he stuttered. "There was something in the box that made me think of you…uh…I noticed about you…that I think you should see." He beckoned toward the door and said, "You'll see."

…

TOPHER UNLOCKED THE DOOR. Inside the room, the walls were lined with shelves loaded with white file boxes all neatly arranged and labeled. Emma assumed the markings correlated with various crimes. On a well-lit, tall table off to one side was a small rusty object shaped like a box. The flat top was propped along one side. A variety of objects were spread in front of it on the table—a decayed piece of tattered cloth, a tiny wooden object shaped like a dumbbell, a dark glass bottle with tiny yellowish rocks around it, and a clump of light-colored hair tied with a ribbon.

Topher swallowed and said, "At the funeral home, I noticed you touching your necklace. The thingy hanging from it…what are they called?"

Emma supplied the word. "Pendant?" Her mother had told her many times that Emma played too much with any necklace she wore. She reached for the necklace before remembering she had left it in her drawer back in New York.

"Wow, a man who notices jewelry!" she exclaimed out loud.

"Generally, not," Topher said. "Well, we all do some detective work around here, so I try to pay attention to details. I normally don't notice jewelry much, but you were touching yours now and then. I remember you seemed nervous. The shape caught my attention." With no drama time, Topher added, "Anyway, look at this," reaching behind the box and picking up a rust-encrusted pendant. "This is what I thought you should see."

Another half heart! In his palm was a grimy version of the pendant from her father. It seemed like a perfect match to her other half!

"Wow…!"

"I've noticed a few like this before. Most are usually shiny and thin. This one, like yours, was different enough that I filed it away in here," Topher said, tapping his right temple.

"My half heart," Emma whispered, touching the spot where the pendant would have hung had she been wearing it. She regretted leaving it behind.

"Can I hold it?"

"Sure."

Emma felt a chill as she lifted the pendant from Topher's hand. She ran her finger along the edge, straighter than her own. Cleaned up, it might be the same bronze color, but it felt thicker and larger than hers, possibly from being so encrusted. Any details were crusted over. She shifted in place, resting her elbows on the table. "This is amazing!"

"I hoped you might think so." Topher seemed relieved.

Emma held the heart toward the light, turning it in her hands to see it more closely. "Just curious about this…so similar. Feels so much heavier," she said, testing its weight with one hand. "I'll have to get my own to see if they match."

"Want to run grab it? I mean, I can meet you back here later this afternoon?" Topher seemed interested.

"Wouldn't that be convenient," she said, looking disappointed. "Except for the fact that it's in my dresser drawer—back in Manhattan."

"You're from Manhattan?"

"Now, I am."

"And also here in Willow Creek?"

"Now, I am as well."

Topher looked as though she might say more.

Catching his look, Emma shrugged and said, "I guess I can have my partner send it to me."

…

EMMA ENTERED THE DRUG STORE below her apartment and asked the clerk at the front if there was any way she could receive mail there, that she was staying upstairs. The clerk told her to talk with the pharmacist at the back who was also the owner.

Emma walked toward the pharmacy, past a soda fountain on her right with its long white marble counter and row of red and white stools, turning down a row of sundries.

"Can I help you?" The pharmacist was an older man with white hair that matched his white coat.

Emma said, "Hi, I'm staying upstairs."

"Oh, hi, I'm Richard Swenson. I'm your landlord…err, your 'host.' You must be Emma. Nice to meet you! I noticed the car out back yesterday and thought it must be yours and wondered when I would meet you."

"Nice to finally meet you as well—outside of email, that is."

"I hope you're comfortable up there," Richard said, pointing at the ceiling overhead.

Playing with words, Emma replied with a smile, "It's heavenly," looking up as well. They both laughed.

"Emma, how can I help you?"

She asked, "If I were to have something sent via overnight mail, could I use this address?"

"Absolutely."

Chapter 27

North Forty, 1921

Erastus was busier than ever—with a new baby at home causing more sleepless nights, having added automobiles to his farm equipment dealership, and still farming a few acres himself—except for the planting. He had recently leased out the rest of the nearly five hundred acres Cassie had inherited from her father to three other farmers, along with the two hundred or so he brought with him to their union. On Tuesday, his hired man plowed and tilled five acres for planting. On Wednesday and Thursday, he brought in another crew to handle the back-breaking task of planting cut pieces of seed potato into mounded rows. In a few days, the bright green tips of newly sprouting potato plants would emerge from the neatly furrowed rich, dark dirt.

Late one afternoon, he slipped away from his dealership to walk the ditch banks and double-check matters before turning the water out onto his newly planted potato fields. He wanted to keep some tasks for himself as long as time allowed—things he could do on nights or weekends. The past Saturday, he had lit the ditch banks on fire to clear off the tall grass and other plants that had grown tall during the past year and tipped over into the ditch—the fire had removed strainers that would slow the flow of water and create inconvenient dams during the growing season ahead. While burning, the smoke had climbed straight and black into the sky without a breeze to turn it. Now only a few days later, Erastus spotted similar columns of smoke from farms all around and could smell the rich, dankness of burning plant matter wafting around him. Farming full time brought with it so many joys, but he had grown to appreciate the steady income coming in from his dealership, income far less affected by the weather, pests, and seasonal output.

Erastus climbed down into the dry ditch in a few places to remove blackened rocks and charred wood. The fire had burned a few fence posts to the point that he would have to repair or replace them later. Near the top of the field, he took a heavy canvas tarp tacked to a long pole along one edge and placed it across the ditch bank-to-bank. Once he turned the water down the ditch, this would dam it up and force it over the bank into well-planned furrows in the field.

Once in place, Erastus walked toward the headgate of the Willow Creek Canal which ran along the opposite edge of his property. As he turned the heavy iron wheel to redirect his share of water, he looked upstream as far as he could, seeing in his mind's eye where this water flowed from the Snake through the Great Feeder miles to the east before entering a network of canals and eventually making its way to this head gate. With great pride in his own contributions over the years, he smiled at how well it all still worked now nearly twenty-five years later. With regular annual repairs and one major overhaul six years earlier, the Great Feeder had been an overwhelming success. Hundreds if not thousands of farms now had water for cash crops like potatoes and alfalfa on land where only sagebrush had ever thrived.

Pulling the gate that let water into his own ditch, he spotted a newer car from a distance driving his way. When it got closer, he recognized the Touring Model T he had recently purchased for Cassie. It was one of the first designs with a backseat for children—the perfect family automobile. He smiled at the thought.

The water flowed quickly through, prompting him to hurry back to the canvas tarp and wait for water to race its way there. As the water arrived, the tarp held it back, acting as a dam, catching it and bowing downstream while backing it up to fill the ditch upstream. With a shovel, Erastus packed dirt around the leaky edges of the tarp and cleared a few old troughs in the ditch bank upstream, letting the water flow over into a furrow that ran along the top of his field and drain downhill into smaller, perpendicular furrows to water row after row of potatoes down the entire length of the field. He hurried from one to the next to make sure the water flowed as planned.

Cassie parked and made her way across the field toward him, setting down a basket she had carried, all while rocking baby Iris.

"Well, hello!" Erastus hurried over, kicking mud from his boots.

"I brought my man some dinner," Cassie said, giving him a kiss. "And a surprise."

"Well, I'm a blessed and lucky man!" Erastus took baby Iris from her, continuing the rocking motion.

Cassie opened the basket and removed a light blanket that she spread along the ditch bank.

"You should sit," Erastus said. "Are you feeling any better?"

"A little. I thought this would be like my other babies—up within a few hours and back doing my chores the next day. This little one…" she said, opening the swaddle and peering at Iris's face. "…this little one has changed my life in so many unexpected ways."

"Well, not many women have a baby in their forties." Erastus sat down beside her and looked through the basket with his free hand before pulling out a roast beef sandwich. He spotted a plate covered by a cloth that he knew contained a piece of Cassie's tasty apple pie. He leaned forward periodically, glancing toward the ditch and field to make sure the canvas dam was still holding, and water was not pooling across the field.

"I'm definitely not the same woman I was." Cassie looked over the field, wondering for a moment how things would be if her two sons and daughter had survived. By now, they would be in their twenties and likely here helping their father on an evening like this or running farms of their own. She had learned not to spend too much time looking back.

Erastus rocked his baby and cooed. Looking at her face, he asked, "How's my little Iris?"

Cassie teased, "I think she would say, 'perfect in every way,' if she could talk. She never cries, which Sarah says shouldn't worry me like it does."

Sitting together on the blanket, Cassie leaned to put her head on Erastus's shoulder before sitting up with a start. "Oh, I almost forgot!" She reached into the basket and lifted the apple pie out. Erastus acted surprised, even though he had already seen the pie.

"Pie!" He played along.

"No, not that, silly." Cassie pulled out a rectangular object wrapped in brown paper. "My book! It came today!" She handed it to Erastus who carefully opened the wrapper to reveal a green-covered hardbound book.

He rubbed his finger over the gold-foil title. "'Pioneer Irrigation in the Upper Snake River Valley.' Cassie! Congratulations! It's so real—finally!" He jumped up. "Speaking of, give me a moment to check a few things." He walked over and worked his shovel at a few spots where the water was backing up. Cassie watched him walk the length the field, adjusting here and there with his shovel and occasionally bending over to remove plant matter or rocks. Wiping his hands on his pants as he walked back toward Cassie, Erastus said, "All right. All is okay. First water of the year always requires more tending. Should get much easier from here." Taking a breath, he sat down and said, "This is so very exciting. A reflection of so much hard work on your part!"

Cassie shifted in place. "I wasn't expecting it for a few weeks. Mina Dunn brought it over this afternoon—actually ten copies, that is." Giddy, she exclaimed, "I'm an author!"

"Oh, Cassie, it's sure to be popular!"

"Perhaps among farmers," she said, laughing.

Erastus dried his hands better on the blanket before flipping the pages. "Wow, there are pictures and maps. And, oh, here's the charter of the Eagle Rock Canal Company…and where's the section on the Snake River Canal Company?"

Cassie reached over and turned the pages to show him where those details were.

After a few moments, Erastus exclaimed, "This is a remarkable history."

Cassie smiled and said, "It's our history." They both looked around at the land, seeing how the sky reflected on the fingers of water slowly coursing down the potato field. "Enough of the book," Cassie said. "Now, you must eat."

As Erastus took a bite of the sandwich, Cassie remembered another piece of news. "Oh, and they caught the Peeping Tom!" In the middle of the night a few weeks earlier, she was checking on Iris when she looked up at the bedroom window and saw a shadowy face pull quickly away and disappear. Erastus had looked out the window and checked that the doors were locked before convincing her to she could go back to sleep. The next morning, when they found footprints in the flowerbeds by the house, they had called the police.

Cassie said, "It was the Johnson's boy, the odd one. Apparently, he's been reported several times. Alice Johnson was beside herself, frustrated that she had not been able to discipline her son any better. They say he is possessed or something like that—that he is like two or three people in one. And he's too big for her to handle anymore. Apparently, he's had some other criminal behavior as well, run-ins with the law." Cassie breathed a sigh of relief. "But he won't be letting himself out in the middle of the night anymore—they're having him committed."

"Committed? Can they do that?"

"Yes. To Blackfoot...the state hospital there." They chatted about one or two other situations they had heard over the years, how people had taken to calling it the state hospital rather than the insane asylum, and how the courts could take people from their families if they were deemed a public nuisance or risk to themselves. There were people who failed to cope or struggled with the oddest things—collecting skulls, alcoholism, obsessions with dangerous activities.

"And a few others who just went plumb crazy," Erastus added.

"You know, all along I thought it was Cloy," Cassie said uneasily, breaking out into a laugh and leaning gently into her husband.

As the sun began to set in the hills to the west, their conversation shifted back to farming, potatoes, irrigation turns, and a variety of other subjects. The light reflecting on lines of water halfway down the field first faded from blue to yellow, then to pink, then to a deep orange, and then to black. A few high clouds took on the same covers as the sun finished setting. Iris slept the entire time.

Wiping his mouth on his sleeve, Erastus said, "I better get back to work."

...

THE SKY WAS DARK GRAY AS ERASTUS watched and waited. As the moon rose, he walked back toward the heavy concrete head gate on the main canal, convinced in that moment he would rather be home in bed and already considering hiring someone for this job as well. He tested the large iron wheel with both hands, sure it wouldn't turn by itself.

Walking back toward the field, he recalled an incident the past summer between two neighbors—Bill Higgins and Albert Taylor. Both men were in their sixties and original pioneer settlers of the valley. At the time, Bill was serving as the mayor of Willow Creek and Albert was the bishop, a well-respected church leader and man of God.

Whatever pressures they felt, Erastus had arrived to find Bill holding a pocket watch and explaining that Albert had kept the water far too long, while Albert had insisted that Bill was trying to take the water ahead of schedule. Each was fighting the wheel, one turning it left a few times and the other turning it right. "You had the water for six hours longer than you should, Mayor" was followed by "Not so, Bishop! I still have time!"

Neither could resolve entirely who was right. When their words shifted from "taking" to "stealing," their fight over the wheel turned to blows. By that point, enough time had passed that it was now clearly Bill's water turn. The men had brushed themselves off and wiped away some blood before each committed to track the time better and notify the other earlier of any water-turn discrepancy.

The two men shook hands before departing, which wasn't always the case when it came to water disputes. A few cases turned up in the local courts, with a few going all the way to the state court, including one where shots had been fired, which resulted in jail time.

The local newspaper regularly featured nearly anything to do with irrigation on the front page as well—often good news about upgraded head gates and new bridges with frequent photos of the owners of what now had to be over a hundred private canal companies, the "canal leadership" standing on concrete and metal structures near their canals. In these photos, some of the men wore bib overalls, the working man's uniform, while a few of the more business-minded men were dressed in suits and ties. Captions often read, "Men who are responsible for a lot of canals and their beginnings" or "The Enterprise Canal crew expanding the headgate near Shelton."

The code of the west had been rewritten around water with one major clause: don't take water that isn't yours. Which meant a farmer should never take it early or keep it longer than scheduled. From that, emerged notions about the window of time that represented each person's turn or share, your responsibility to open and close their head gate, and every farmer's job to fix any breaches they found in canal banks or ditches routing water across a neighbor's property—to avoid lost water, extra water for anyone in particular, and eroded fields. The concept of sharing was never more pronounced, and use was based on what shares a person owned—all determined by a chart with start and stop times but extremely dependent on each farmer's commitment to follow the chart and turn the water back downstream at the appointed time.

Water meant everything—harvest or famine, it built friendships or eroded lives.

Confirming the water was flowing at the correct rate, Erastus walked to the end of one of his rows and lay on his back waiting for it to slowly flow across his five acres of potatoes and reach him. Reflecting on years of farming and related engineering projects, he took the harmonica he nearly always kept in his shirt pocket and played *Home Sweet Home* and a few other songs while looking up at the starlit vault of heaven. Eventually, he pulled his hat over his eyes, folding his arms over his chest to ward off the late spring chill before dozing. "It's my alarm clock," he regularly told Cassie "I'll wake up when the first water hits me."

Cassie always teased, "What an awful way to wake up!"

"Better than spending the entire night out there," he usually protested with a wink and saying, "And I'll be crawling into bed and kissing your cheek before daylight."

As the first water of spring began to tickle his sleeping head, Erastus sat up with a start, rubbing his eyes and taking his bearings. He quickly stood, wiping his head and shaking away the chill. He walked back toward the head gate. In the predawn light with the water song of a meadowlark on a nearby fence post, he shut off his gate and turned the wheel to turn the water downstream for the next farmer.

Chapter 28

The Edge of Town

Running the country roads surrounding Willow Creek quickly became Emma's favorite afternoon activity—and she was getting better and going farther. After writing most mornings, a quick lunch, and then another stint at the computer, Emma usually ran to the edge of town, past the cemetery, and then across a bridge marked "Burgess Canal" and then several other with canal names. She was growing to love the wall of coolness near flowing water—which was at nearly every turn—along with the dank smell of fields flooded by irrigation water.

One afternoon, with Chapter 6 moving along better than expected, Emma decided to take a longer run than usual and headed out toward some distant mountains. The afternoon was slightly overcast, making the temperature perfect for running.

Emma's thoughts drifted around the topic she was tackling at that point in her book—what happens when you realize the pool you're swimming has suddenly become a much bigger body of water? Or a metaphor like that. She was struggling with how to portray her own recent experiences with adoption and coming to Willow Creek as examples, sensing she was seeing only the tip of a much bigger, metaphorical iceberg. As she ran, she searched her mind for a more fitting description. An iceberg didn't really work, she had already concluded. Sure, icebergs are made of water but not in the same waters as goldfish. Her mind jumped to an absurd image of a goldfish frozen near the edge of an iceberg, blinking at the outside world and wondering how it got into that predicament. Maybe it does work. She imagined a caption like, "Bigger ocean than I realized," chuckling at the thought.

This sort of mental drifting was what Emma described to others as "finding my quiet, happy place," and she often found it while exercising, no matter the place or activity.

She jogged on, crossing several bridges before coming to one with "Dry Bed" marking the waterway. Expecting an empty waterway, she looked down into a wide, deep river flowing slowly beneath her feet. "Dry bed, my…," she began to say, startled by a siren squawking behind her as a police cruiser pulled alongside with its lights flashing.

A voice came over the PA. "Ma'am. Please step to the side of the bridge."

Still startled, Emma knew she never carried any ID while jogging and then wondered what possibly she could have done that was wrong. "I certainly wasn't speeding," she protested under her breath, shocked that a pedestrian could be pulled over this way. She held her hand up to shield her eyes from the flashing blue and red lights before recognizing Officer Jones, well, Topher, as he got out of the car. Topher took off his sunglasses and leaned on the open door, smiling at something delightful to him. His smile was disarming, white teeth contrasting with his dark police uniform.

Emma's began to form a protest over being stopped, when Topher said, "Well, what are you doing this far away from town?"

Recognizing that he was clearly more at ease than before, Emma didn't want to state the obvious but could only come up with, "Standing on a bridge." Then, playing along, she walked toward him, adding, "Isn't this an abuse of police authority?" Suddenly happy he had stopped, she wondered if he had some official police business only or merely stopped to talk with her. "What can I do for you, Officer?"

"Ahh. I'm just having fun," Topher said, smiling and looking around, holding back a laugh. Swallowing, he said, "We do patrol out here, you know." Then, with his face scrunched up, he asked, "So, here I thought you came to town for the box and now I find you out for a run. Are you sticking around? Waiting for your pendant to show up? Or perhaps moving in?"

Emma still didn't want to explain her primary reason for coming to Willow Creek. She was intrigued that he might think she had only come for the box and decided to keep the mystery alive, at least for now. Feeling a little exposed in her running clothes, she pulled up the zipper on her windbreaker. "Well, that's what I'm doing. Sticking around. Waiting for the mail." And then asked playfully, "You? Patrolling?"

Topher laughed a little, nodding and looking around again. "I guess…I'm patrolling." After a moment of silence, he held up both hands and said, "And I'm okay that you're still here—I mean, here, not 'still here.'" Wincing a bit, he asked, "Know what I'm saying?"

Emma replied, "Yes, I think so. And from an officer of the law, at that." Looking up at Topher, she realized she knew nothing about him. He was friendly enough, not unlike most people she had met so far. But he did seem different in ways as well. Something told her he wasn't a local. She smiled as she asked, "Well, as a 'student of the obvious' myself…" adding in her best western drawl, "you really aren't from around these here parts, are you?"

Topher looked relieved, like the ice between them had officially broken—that they were finally meeting in a less formal way. Walking out and leaning against the hood of his car, he folded his arms and said, "That's a long story—perhaps another time." Trying to decide what to say next, he pressed his hands against the hood of the police cruiser and said, "Oh, by the way, Sarge wants me to send for DNA results from the bones and the box. He's thinking they're connected somehow. I don't disagree."

Emma felt unusually playful. "The bones and the box share the same DNA?" She couldn't help but laugh.

Topher looked up, and going along said, "Well, the stuff in the box. We didn't actually sample the box itself—you know, that's not standard procedure—but we did take samples from the teeth and the hair that were in the box."

"Nice." Emma thought for a minute. "Could we…how could we…what would it take to test to see if I'm related in any way?"

Topher looked at her curiously. "I imagine a similar test, but let me check with Sarge. I'm not sure how that would work. We're usually testing crime-related cases only. I have no idea if those tests prove only direct relatives or beyond." Reflecting, he asked, "You okay to spit in a tube? Quite a bit, I hear. That's the best way."

"Ewww."

Topher laughed. "Probably a teaspoon or so. Not a gallon."

Looking around for something else to discuss, Emma finally said, "Hey, so what's with all the canals? They are everywhere. I have crossed at least five bridges on my run so far. Why all the water?"

Topher looked up. "All the water? You may not realize this, but these ditches and canals make the Snake River Valley one of the most prolific breadbaskets in the entire world—well, the potato basket at least. You've heard of famous Idaho potatoes, right? Ever eaten French fries from a McDonald's?"

Emma said, "Yes, but I haven't seen a McDonald's in Willow Creek."

Topher laughed. "You're right. We won't be getting one here anytime soon. But a large portion of the 'taters they use are from this region."

Emma nodded, her eyes narrowing in disbelief. "Hmmm. Interesting." She wasn't so interested in potatoes but was enjoying their friendly banter. Not willing to abandon her earlier question, she asked again, "So, where are you really from?"

Topher reacted to her sudden change of subject. "Who, me?" He held his hand to his chest, looking around and laughing, acting put on the spot.

Emma put her hands on her hips and nodded.

"You don't let up, do you? Well, okay, here goes," he sighed, taking off his hat and smoothing back his thick hair.

Given his reluctance, Emma waited for something complicated.

"I'm actually from here. Born and raised in Willow Creek. And then not from here for the past fifteen years or so. But now, I'm back. So, I guess I can say that I'm from here again."

Emma looked at him. "Simple enough, but still sounds like a mystery wrapped in a puzzle."

"That's what my mother says," Topher said, looking curiously at her as though she had somehow recently spoken with his mother. "And you?"

"Me?"

"Yes, where are you from? Wait! Let me guess." He put his finger to his temple and looked up with bright eyes. "New York?"

Emma said, "Yes! How did you know?"

"212 area code," he said, holding up a finger as if having a realization. "And Columbia hoodie. Oh, and that you said so the other day at police HQ."

Emma smiled. A nearby bird made a sound that interrupted her line of questioning. She asked, "What is that amazing sound? It's the longest bird sound or noise or whatever you call it I think I've ever heard."

"I hadn't really noticed," Topher said. They both listened quietly until the flute-like trill could be heard again, first rising, and then descending.

"There, that!"

The Meadowlark

Topher said matter-of-factly, "Oh, that's a meadowlark. It's probably my favorite bird. Yellow and gray with a black necklace that actually has its own pendant," he said, tapping his chest and nodding at Emma. "Pretty in its own way, but prettier still because of its song. Most birds chirp for a half second or so at most, but this one sings for a good long while. I imagine it's got something more to say than other birds," he added, smiling.

Emma heard another across the way and looked delighted.

Topher swept his arm in front of him. "Stretches of irrigated farmland up against uncleared sagebrush territory is the perfect habitat for them. Not sure why, but they live along the edges."

Then two birds called, one right after the other.

"Such a pretty sound," Emma said.

The day cooled as evening began to creep in. Emma drew her jacket around her.

"You're cold," Topher said. "Can I drive you home?"

Emma thought for a minute. "Sure…as long as we can turn the light on. Just the light—no siren needed."

They both laughed.

As Topher walked her to the passenger side of the car, Emma asked, "So, who made all the canals? I presume some men with backhoes and big diggers?"

"Great question, and one I actually only researched when I came back to town a few months ago." Topher stopped and simply said, "They say it was the original pioneers. Homesteaders. Back in the late 1800s and early 1900s. With horses and plows. That's slightly easier than digging them all by hand, I guess." Topher appeared satisfied with his answer before asking, "Hey, wanna see something pretty cool? It's kind of geeky irrigation stuff that I always knew about but never understood its history. But it's as cool as the Eiffel Tower. Do you have a half hour or so?"

"Here…?" Emma couldn't imagine what Topher had in mind. The thought of the Eiffel Tower really put her off. She asked a little miffed, "Eiffel Tower, really?"

Topher looked at her, wondering why she was so bugged. "No, but something that was built around the same time—the source of all of this," Topher said, sweeping his hand out front before beckoning toward the door he had opened for her.

Emma felt cheeky. "Your police car makes all of this possible? I've already seen the inside of a police car…" She said as she got in.

He laughed. "And, no, my squad car is not responsible for all of this."

Watching him come in the other door, Emma felt a bit too close and said, "Sorry I'm so sweaty and gross. You probably don't want all this…" pointing at the top of her head and drawing her hands quickly down, "…in here," she explained.

"These seats are one hundred percent vinyl. They have seen much worse—not that 'all this' is bad at all." Topher grinned, pleased that she was even considering coming along. "I've wiped them down with great success before. I can do it again should it be as awful as you make it sound."

As Emma put on her seatbelt, she wondered about the adventure ahead.

"It's a very cool place—and not far from here," Topher said semi-triumphantly as he turned the flashing lights off and pulled out onto the highway.

…

DRIVING ALONG, Topher pointed to fields with row after row of alfalfa. "Hay!" he shouted, and Emma looked around like he was calling her out. He laughed. "It's called 'hay.' Alfalfa is what the farmers call it until it's bailed and ready to feed their livestock. Not sure when its name changes—likely soon after it's been cut." He pointed to a large tractor mowing a huge field of knee-high, deep green alfalfa, laying out the cut plant in a single, even row behind it as it moved along. "That's probably his second cutting of alfalfa this year so far. Around here, he might get four cuttings—most parts of the world are lucky to get two or three."

"Well, that sounds like a good thing," Emma said. She mouthed "alfalfa" a few times, remembering how she had said it in high school, extending her tongue with each vowel.

Topher looked over. "You okay…? Need a drink?" He offered her a water bottle.

"Thanks," Emma said, a little embarrassed as she accepted the water bottle.

Topher suddenly lit up. "Okay, can I share some facts with you? I promise they will sound boring but give them a chance. When you put it all together, this entire place will surprise you."

Emma smiled and said, "Well, I'm not exactly a prisoner, but I am sort of captive. I am a big fan of facts. Even un-interesting ones. So…share away!"

Topher slowed and pointed to a tall, gray-green plant growing alongside the road, one with a brittle and dry spindly trunk. "Well, that's the type of sagebrush we have around here. That could even be original…based on its height," he said, sounding a little too delighted by his own observation. "When the pioneers first got here in the late 1800s, there was nothing but sagebrush across this entire valley. It was six to ten feet high in the most fertile places. And thick."

"Wow," Emma said. "We have some back home—just much shorter."

Topher looked puzzled. "Manhattan?"

"No, but that's another story," Emma answered.

"Okay," Topher said, speeding up. "Moving on…the pioneers tore it out of the ground by hand or with ropes pulled by horses. Some probably had other ways. It was long before tractors or even steam engines. What's more amazing is that, back then, they leveled the ground and built all of these canals the same way—with horses and old-fashioned plows."

Emma could see ditches carrying water in straight lines—all reflecting angles of the remaining daylight and tracing the road. Wide fields on either side were outlined by ditches, with wider canals passing under the road periodically and wandering less exactly along the contours of the land. "So much free water," she said.

"Ha, not so. There are over a hundred private canal companies still in the area. The early settlers started them, and these same companies still run everything to do with water this many generations later." He took a breath and added, "Water is a big deal around here—a huge deal and not free at all—everyone pays for it. You wouldn't know since in the East, they've got water everywhere. Ever heard of a drought?" Topher looked amused.

She decided to reveal a bit more of herself. "Well, let me unravel a bit of that puzzle for you. I haven't always been from the East. I actually grew up in Salt Lake but left after high school and have only been back a few times since."

Topher cocked his head and rubbed his chin. "Salt Lake? Really? I had you picked for…well, the Columbia University sweatshirt and what not. You seemed like pure East Coast to me." He acted like he was storing this revelation for exploration later.

Emma laughed. "Even then, we were pure city slickers, our neighborhood had a few big gardens but no farms at all. And definitely no alfalfa," she said saying it with her tongue extended. "And, yes, I have heard of droughts. We had to take short showers one year."

Topher laughed, shaking his head. Emma looked again at his face—he seemed about her age but looked wiser and more experienced than most people she knew. Three little laugh lines turned up from his eyes and away, lost in his thick, dark brown eyebrows.

Topher turned her way, and Emma quickly looked down at her hand, worried he would think she had been staring. She could tell he was smiling.

"Anyway…" he said, turning back to the subject at hand. "Because it doesn't rain nearly enough to keep this land as green as it is, the farmers around here are careful to keep things straight when it comes to water—which is probably true in Utah as well," he added with a hint of sarcasm. "And there have been plenty of fights over water—even shots fired. The story goes that one of Willow Creek's original mayors and a church leader got into a tangle once that landed them both in jail overnight and cost them each a few thousand dollars." He slowed for a tight bend in the road before saying more softly, almost to himself, "From a book my mom has on all of this."

Topher took a quick turn down a narrow dirt road and soon announced, "We're here!"

Emma looked ahead and could see a wide river coming toward them before banking left. A wide, single-story concrete structure stood to her left, one topped with a framed steel contraption and motors. Opening her door, she could hear water coursing through the structure. Topher met her as she got out of the car, having walked around to her side. He closed her door for her, a fact she noticed.

"All right," he said. "Better to see this before dark." He turned and walked quickly. Emma took that as a signal to follow. She jogged to catch up and could suddenly smell a dankness in the air that she took for water. The temperature was instantly cooler, and even the air felt thicker. She was glad for her windbreaker.

Topher walked to a point that jutted out into the river. "Careful about the rocks," he said. Emma tip-toed across rocks behind him. Pointing upriver, he said, "This is the South Fork of the Snake River. Its watershed is the south side of Yellowstone Park, Jackson Hole, and the eastern side of the Grand Tetons. By the time it gets here, the river has been dammed up once at Jackson Lake and a second time at Palisades. It's mostly snow melt and still almost freezing this time of year."

Unsure why he had brought her here or why the history lesson, Emma wanted to hear more. Perhaps it was the cadence of his voice, but his choice of words created a picture in her mind that she was enjoying. He didn't seem to notice, but she began to feel more was going on here for her. Something deeply personal.

He continued. "I have no idea what the total amount of force is here, but I imagine the river always turned here at this bend. But this bend we're standing on is man-made." He pointed down to large chunks of rocks that jutted out ahead of them into the river. The slower portion of the river turned left, while the greatest force of the river ran past them and straight through one of six openings in the tall structure on the right, each big enough to drive a car through.

Emma felt a fascination she hadn't felt since touring the Empire State Building—something she had finally done after living in Manhattan for six years—and then again on that bike tour of Paris with Jake that she was still trying to forget.

"1895," Topher announced, extending his arm in front of him. "I get kind of choked up when I think of the men who built this—during what had to be a very cold winter in 1895. Oh, yes, you've been here in winter," he said with a laugh.

Emma shuddered at the memory of winter, folding her arms across her chest and almost expecting a blast of the coldest air she could imagine.

Come with me," he said and began walking up the bank toward the concrete structure, guiding her with his hand in the small of her back.

He was so considerate!

They walked toward the contraption, which turned out to be a one-lane bridge across the river. "Remember where I picked you up?"

Emma nodded. "You mean, pulled me over?"

Topher laughed. "Okay. Well, that was the Dry Bed—or what previously was only a dry channel—an ancient channel of the river that had dried up." Pointing, he said, "This here is where the wet version of the Dry Bed begins. Right here," he said. Showing her words etched into the downstream side of the huge concrete contraption, he said, "Read this."

Emma adjusted her angle to read the words "Great Feeder." She asked, "Great Feeder? Kind of a funny name for a bridge thingy, isn't it?"

Topher sat on the opposite side of the structure with his back to the river. Emma took a spot beside him, a slight breeze blowing the scent of his cologne her way.

Gesturing with both arms, Topher said, "This is much more than a bridge. Remember, this was built in the dead of winter—by hand—with only horses and some early steel tools to do the job. Concrete was even kind of new then. Of course, this isn't the original—it's been replaced a few times, since then." He pointed to the dates etched in as well: 1915, 1965, 2015. "But it's still doing the same job it did when first completed in 1895."

Emma nodded. The tone of Topher's voice held her attention. And the feeling she was having about this place held her interest more as well. She knew Lacy would never let her live this down and resolved not to tell her about this. Ever.

Topher pointed past the structure at the downstream flow. "The Dry Bed used to be dry most of the year except for a few months of spring run-off when the river overflowed—hence the name. So, the men back then dug this huge canal from here in that direction for about a mile to form a better-defined channel," he explained. "Then they built this diversion dam so they could turn water away during spring run-off. I imagine they had to blast the bank away right out there," he said, turning to where the water from the Snake entered the Great Feeder. "Logic tells me they did that last," he chuckled.

Emma turned to look, rocking back a bit more than she expected. Topher caught her by the arm just as she began to see the volume of water rushing beneath their feet and through the diversion dam—more clearly than she had wanted. Her heart raced, glad for Topher's steady hand.

"Steady there," Topher said.

"Whew," Emma said, feigning a wipe across her brow. "Thanks."

"Don't mention it."

Topher sat with his hands on his knees before explaining, "I read this was the largest engineering project in the world at the time—at least when it came to irrigation. The Eiffel Tower was finished the same year for the World's Fair—and it's clearly quite a bit more famous but is really just a decoration and giant tourist attraction."

Emma winced at her own memories. It was a giant tourist attraction, for sure!

"This here," he said with a sweep of his arm, "is the total opposite—it's entirely functional. You and I may be the only tourists to visit this entire year, and it's hard to fathom just how much this has changed the entire country and shaped generations. It not only feeds this entire valley but thousands worldwide."

Emma said, "Hmmm. I think I'm getting the picture."

"The Dry Bed fills nearly every canal you cross in this valley, and in turn, those canals feed dry ground and make plants grow."

"Sorry, I'm a little slow," Emma teased. "Could you start from the beginning."

Emma couldn't stop laughing—mostly because Topher's laughter was so infectious. After what seemed like minutes, they both sat looking at the words, "Great Feeder."

Emma looked up innocently. "Is this what makes the alfalfa grow?" She couldn't help extending her tongue as she said it, laughing uncontrollably again.

Topher gave her a confused look. "And alfalfa," he went along, mimicking her as he did, looking unsure why he was saying it that way as well.

Emma felt lighter than she had in years.

...

WHEN EMMA ARRIVED HOME, she found a sticky note on her door. "You have a package." She ran down the stairs and walked to the back of the drug store.

"Hi, Richard," she said eagerly.

"Hello there, Miss Rose. I have something for you." He walked to the back. Emma had been imagining a small envelope, but he returned with a medium-sized box, one heavier than she had expected.

Emma looked over at the soda fountain and realized she was still thirsty from her run and all the discussion about water. She asked Richard, "Can I get a glass of water?"

"Sure thing." Richard walked over behind the soda fountain counter. "Take a seat," he said.

As he put ice in a glass and pulled a lever to fill it with water, Emma sat on a round stool that was fixed to the floor in front of the counter and began to twirl back and forth. It all seemed so cute—a working soda fountain, red stools that spin, a cute old man in a white coat working behind the stark-white counter.

Richard slid the glass of ice water in front of her. "Actually," he said, leaning across the counter as if he had a secret to share, "I have something even better for you. Have you ever had an Iron Port?" The smile on his face suggested that her life wouldn't be complete until she had.

Emma assumed because he was holding another glass that he was referring to a drink of sorts. "Never."

"Well, let me treat you to one." Richard kept talking as he turned toward some syrups next to the soda dispenser. "I've been making these since I was a kid. Being a 'soda jerk' was my first job—at ten!" Richard looked up, waxing a little sentimental as he explained. "This was my dad's drug store, and I loved coming here with him. I'd stock the shelves and help wherever I could. He told me I could serve customers from back here once I turned ten," he said pointing to the service area where he stood. "So, on my tenth birthday, I only wanted one thing, and that was to make my dad a drink. His favorite, and mine ever since, was the Iron Port. Even better with cherry. Okay if I add that?"

Emma nodded, watching him pump from two different containers before dispensing liquid from the soda machine. "You've gotta put the soda in last," he said. "If not, the syrups make it almost explode." Richard turned while stirring the concoction with a long spoon. Dropping the spoon in another container and inserting a straw into the glass, Richard's hands did a sort of "ta-da" as he presented Emma with a fizzing glass of dark soda.

Emma could smell a richness as she put her lips to the straw. The ice cubes cracked and soda fizzed as she took her first sip. It was delightful and reminded her a bit of the birch beer she had tasted in Maine once. "It's like a million-dollar version of cherry cola and cream soda combined!" Emma exclaimed, smiling broadly. "What other secrets is this town hiding?"

Richard looked immensely satisfied.

As Emma carried her package up the stairs to her apartment, she found herself burping from the carbonation she had just consumed. Once inside, she opened the box and saw a DNA test kit, remembering her conversation with Lacy. "Good timing," she whispered, walking to the kitchen for a knife to cut the plastic tab that held it closed.

She looked inside and found a large test tube and a sheet of instructions. The top of the box said, "Millions of people have uncovered something new about themselves. You can too." She had originally imagined returning the kit and shortly thereafter discovering she was related to the Pope or Madame Curie. Now her thoughts were more about her father's connection to Willow Creek and the clues from the box. She wondered if taking the test would help answer any of those questions.

In the kit, Emma found a card that warned her not to eat or drink for at least thirty minutes before the test. Still tasting her soda, Emma put the kit down and busied herself. She took a shower, put on comfy clothes, and checked her email.

Finally, it was time. The card gave three steps. "Spit," was the first. Emma's mouth went instantly dry at the thought of spitting to fill such a large test tube. She began working her tongue back and forth inside her mouth in anticipation as she read the other steps. The second instruction described how to insert the tube into a sleeve and then back into the original box, affixing a new mailing label and sealing the box with clear tape that was provided. The final instruction was to "drop it in any mailbox."

With saliva collecting in her mouth, Emma pulled the top from the tube and looked in, relieved to see it half-filled by a plastic insert of some kind. Working her tongue against her cheeks, she emptied what she could into the tube and repeated the process until she filled it up. Completing the other steps, Emma was excited to see what might come next.

As she gathered the extra materials and put them back into the original shipping box to throw away, Emma felt something jostle inside. She looked in and found her pendant at the bottom, shocked that she had completely forgotten about it. She held it up, inspecting it and seeing the familiar "IS" lettering. She quickly put it around her neck and then typed a text to Lacy.

Thanks for sending the package. Got it today. You're a dear.

A moment later, Lacy texted back.

"Dear"? Have you gone native?

Emma looked back at her text and realized what she had said. She laughed as she typed again.

So much to tell you about.

Emma so badly wanted to tell Lacy all about Topher and her trip with him to the Great Feeder. "The Eiffel Tower of the west," she whispered, smiling at the thought. "And alfalfa." She followed with one final text.

I spit in the tube. Did you do your DNA test yet?

Emma looked at the test kit and reflected on her experience in Willow Creek so far. She felt her world expanding—excited for the first time in a while with the idea that her carefully curated pool of water was being inundated with an ocean of new risks and discoveries.

"Look at you now, Emma Rose."

Chapter 29

Act Busy

Early the next evening, Emma went out for a walk, thinking to explore over toward a water tower she had seen from her front window, one that rose above other buildings a few blocks away. She had seen similar structures in movies and some of the small towns she had visited on drives with her father. This one looked like a silver alien spacecraft, an oblong orb with five-story legs. She had no idea what purpose towers like this served, only that they were called water towers, and thought walking near it might be revealing.

The air was chilly, and Emma was glad she had grabbed her hoodie. She crossed the street to the bank and walked past. Coming up on a rock church, she smiled at the marquee out front that read, "Jesus is Coming. Act Busy." Past the church, she turned and saw what looked like a fire station. A white truck turned down the street at the far end. As it neared, the driver honked lightly and slowed alongside her going the wrong way.

Topher leaned out the window and said, "Evening, ma'am." He wore a baseball hat and golf shirt. He seemed relaxed.

Emma had only seen him in his police uniform and laughed. "You're clearly not arresting me this time—wearing *that* at least. I never thought you might have other clothes." Smiling, she plunged her hands into the pocket of her hoodie and asked, "Were you following me?"

Topher protested. Looking back at where he had come from, he gestured with his hands. "I was actually driving toward you just now, not coming from behind. I was…"

"…patrolling?"

Topher realized she was teasing. Feigning ignorance, he said, "No, ma'am. Just going to drag Main Street." He laughed. "Oh, wow! I can't believe I just said that. I used to do that all the time in high school. What an enormous waste of time!" He could see that Emma had no idea what he was talking about. Explaining himself, he said, "We used to spend nearly every summer evening driving from one end of Main to the other. It's only like four blocks. With a grocery store on one end and the post office on the other, we would just park there and wait for our friends to show up. If they didn't come soon enough, we'd drive slowly to the other end and look for them there."

Emma looked around and said, "Interesting..."

Topher asked, "So, where are you headed?"

"I was just going to check out the water tower thingy." She pointed with one hand. She began walking slowly toward the tower, and he put his car in reverse and began backing up with her as she walked, his arm resting on the door of his truck and the gravel crunching under his tires.

"Can I join you for your walk?"

Emma nodded.

"I mean, I already exercised today, so I plan to drive—if that's okay." Topher added, "Backwards."

"Backwards is good," Emma smiled. She pointed toward the water tower and asked, "So, what's it for? I've always wondered." Beaming, she said, "You're the man with the facts on water. I'll bet you know!"

Topher adjusted imaginary glasses with one finger and responded matter-of-factly. "Water pressure." Letting it register, he added with a smirk, "Got any hard questions?"

Emma chuckled.

Topher went on. "There isn't enough slope around here to make the water move through a pipe let alone come out the faucet in your apartment above the drug store. Even the canals barely flow downhill."

"Well, aren't you a fountain of knowledge." She laughed and added, "Pun intended." She wondered how he knew about her apartment.

From the look in her eyes, Topher realized he had let on to something that she may not have told him. Preemptively, he offered, "Remember, I'm a part-time detective. I'm paid to know things like this. And...just maybe I am checking up on our Columbia University girl." He smiled, beckoning at her hoodie.

The Meadowlark

Emma played along. "Okay, well since I'm 'sticking around,' I figured I should know about things like this. Like…that a water tower is for pressure."

Topher said, "'Sticking around?'" and then smiled. "Well, depending on how long you're here, there may be a quiz at the end of your stay." He continued backing up alongside her, the crunching sound fading as the pavement widened near the water tower. Topher waved to an older man holding a hose and sprinkling his lawn. "That's Dr. Smith."

Dr. Smith waved back, unphased by the sight of a truck backing down the road on the wrong side with its occupant conversing with a pedestrian.

Emma waved as well and whispered to Topher, "He's such a cute old man…" She was enjoying the company and began forming a question. "So…," she started.

Topher interrupted. "Hey…," he said. "I was going to go bowling tonight." He emphasized the last part. "It won't be as boring as you might think," hinting that she might want to come along.

Emma raised her eyebrows and playfully said, "Okay…?"

Topher looked around as though he realized he should have asked her and framed his thought differently. "Since you're 'sticking around,' wanna come along?"

Without any hesitation, Emma said, "Sure!"

Topher looked delighted and then glanced around expectantly.

"Now?" Emma asked.

Looking down at his empty wrist, Topher said, "No time like the present. Climb in!"

Emma laughed. She walked around his truck and got in.

As she fastened her seat belt, Topher pointed to his shorts. "I golfed today. Day-off thing to do. I blew up on the fourteenth but ended with a birdie on eighteen," he said. "And a birdie makes a good day."

"My dad was a golfer," Emma said. "I went with him a few times but could never really get the knack. So, I mostly rode along."

"It's never not a tough game," Topher said. "More like life, I guess, with good days and bad days." Smiling he added, "Plus a few really glorious moments."

…

AT THE BOWLING ALLEY, only three of the six lanes were occupied. Music blared from overhead speakers but didn't quite drown out the sound of rolling balls knocking over pins. "Wow, no waiting! It's usually busier," Topher said loudly, sounding surprised.

Emma pulled off her hoodie and spotted Connie from the diner with a small group. Connie waved and then looked up, puzzled. Emma couldn't tell whether from the look if she wondered why Emma would be there bowling or why she was with Topher.

Emma's first six rolls were gutter balls before she finally connected for a strike. "It's like that for me," she told Topher above the noise. "I'm sort of an all or nothing girl—well, nothing and then all," she laughed. She watched Topher, dressed in golf attire and bowling shoes, knock down most of pins with every roll.

"I'm always all in," he said just as the music quieted, looking around sheepishly from talking so loudly.

They both laughed. Between rolls, Emma found the opportunity to say, "So, you say you're from around here, then not, and then back again—and not so long ago at that. Something tells me you weren't planning to come back."

"You got me," Topher said as he picked up a ball from the returner. "I moved back..." He rolled the ball down the lane and this time got a strike. "...by choice."

Connie walked over and greeted them. "Topher, I see you've met Emma Rose, our newest short-time resident. Isn't she sweet?" Connie waited for an answer until both Topher and Emma were uncomfortable.

"Uh...yes," Topher said, motioning toward Emma. "How are things for you and Chuck?"

"Well, Chuck couldn't make it tonight—his knee is killing him, you know." She looked at Emma and said, "He's a carpet layer. Been that his whole life, I declare. Too much time on his knees. And not the praying kind of time," she explained, chuckling. Looking Topher in the eye, Connie said, "We're so glad you're back. Most people move away for good." She chuckled. "And I'm so sorry for how things ended up with you and that girl Monica. She didn't deserve you anyway." Connie leaned toward Emma and said confidentially, "He's a good one." She pinched Topher's cheek before walking away.

Topher rubbed his cheek.

Emma smiled, waiting for Connie to move out of hearing before asking. "Monica?"

"It's a long story," Topher shouted above the noise.

As they switched back into their street shoes, they laughed at how their scores totaled 200—150 from Topher and 50 from Emma. Leaving the noise and heat of the bowling alley behind them, Emma carried her hoodie in one arm and immediately felt the cool of the night, still the warmest night so far since her arrival in Willow Creek. Emma leaned toward Topher and said, "I have time for a long story." She was curious to hear more about Topher's life.

As they neared his truck, Topher began talking. "I told you I grew up here, right? When I left for college at Boise State, I knew I'd come back for holidays but otherwise planned to grow old somewhere else. My parents own the car dealership at the other end of town, and after selling and servicing cars my entire life, I was ready for something else. I mean, I did okay in college and then miraculously got accepted to Stanford Law School. Long story short, after a law degree and a decade of doing trademark law in the Bay Area, I was burned out."

Topher had lowered the tailgate of his truck down and motioned for Emma to take a seat with him.

She hopped up and teased, "So, you're a cop *and* a lawyer?"

"Yes, ma'am."

"Okay, cut the 'ma'am'." Emma pushed him on the shoulder. "Isn't being both a contradiction?"

"Well…"

Emma didn't wait for his answer. "So, what brought you back?"

"I'll confess, it was Carter's scones and honey butter," he said, winking. Emma laughed, knowing it was half true for her as well. "Actually, it's a bit more complicated than that."

"Okay…and Monica?" Emma reached for her pendant and began twirling it in her fingers. She could see him wince at the question.

Changing the subject, Topher said, "I see you got your pendant!" He drew closer, inspecting it and saying, "Wow, it looks a lot like the other half."

"Oh, yeah. It came yesterday. I'm dying to see the other half again."

Topher seemed relieved that the conversation had turned. "Maybe tomorrow? It's Saturday, but I can see if Sarge will loan me his key to the evidence room."

"That would be nice," Emma said, eager to compare the two pieces but suddenly more curious about Topher's life. Letting what they had been talking about simmer a bit, she said, "Look, there's Cassiopeia." She pointed to the lazy W-shaped constellation. "And there's Orion."

"Wow! Pretty impressive for a city girl…Columbia," he said, nodding at the hoodie she had spread over her knees.

"I'm a constellation nerd," Emma said. "It sort of runs in the family."

Topher smiled. "Like being an irrigation geek, right?"

They both laughed. Emma swung her legs.

"Okay, so your turn. Why are you 'sticking around'?" Topher made quote marks in the air with his fingers.

Lowering her voice to mimic his earlier words, Emma said, "It's a bit complicated. Maybe another time."

He laughed. "Touché," he said, still looking at her expectantly.

"Okay. Want the long version or the short version?"

Quoting Emma's line, Topher smiled and playfully said, "I've got time for a long story."

"Well, when I was young…okay, maybe not that long ago. Shorter version is, I have a book deal. I was a management consultant for a group called Pilot Consulting…" Emma looked at Topher wondering if he would know.

Topher looked up knowingly. "Heard of them. Pretty reputable. Sweatshop for new college grads, right? Did you work twenty-hour days?"

Happy they shared some common ground, Emma nodded and said, "No, but it's not far from the truth. It was a great experience—with many long days. But I went out on my own about two years ago."

Topher looked up respectfully. "That's brave," he said.

Emma smiled and nodded before continuing. "Anyway, after I got this book deal, I got totally stuck. Writer's block. Ever had it?"

Topher nodded. "Always. I have it right now."

Emma laughed and said, "Really?"

"Oh, yes. Writing is almost painful for me."

Emma looked puzzled. "That's usually not my problem—I love writing but had never written anything quite this long. Anyway, I felt like I was writing the same things over and over. Chapter two sounded like chapter one which sounded like chapter three. My assistant Lacy, who is amazing, beautiful, and someone you really should meet sometime, suggested I go somewhere—to write, that is. 'Take a month off and go,' she said."

Topher looked puzzled.

Emma added, "So, I thought of all the places I could go to and struck out. Plenty came to mind, but most sounded like vacation spots, and the last thing I needed was relaxation." Emma paused before looking up, sheepishly. "And then you texted."

"What!" Topher teased, "So you came to Willow Creek because of me?"

"Not even!" Emma laughed, and bumping his shoulder with hers said, "Really, I came for the scones…and the bones." She laughed at her own joke. "Well, sort of. It wasn't until our conversation a few weeks back that Willow Creek even made the list. But when it did, it all made sense. Seemed like the perfect place to go for some reason I still can't explain. When I added it to my whiteboard list, it looked sort of backlit and all sparkly. I didn't exactly hear angels trumpeting from heaven, but it's one of those rare moments of clarity that I've grown to appreciate—however infrequently they happen." Emma looked around at the night sky.

Topher waved at Connie and her group as they walked to their cars.

Emma noticed their legs were swinging together. "It's worked out well…so far," she added, smiling.

Topher nodded, contemplating something. "So, you're here for a month?"

"Well, a month total. I now have only a few more weeks—I leave the middle of June," Emma said.

"Nice." Topher looked away, counting. "Three more weeks?" he asked, expectantly.

"Sounds about right." Emma added, "Either the night is cooling or it's me," putting on her hoodie.

Topher sat up. "Okay, not sure why, but here's a bit more of my story. Here's why I came back." He put both hands on his knees. "My older brother Kyle wanted to be a cop more than he wanted to breathe, it seemed. He was a week short of graduating from the academy when he stopped at a rest area on his way to waterski at Palisades and was shot by an angry truck driver. When they caught the guy, his only explanation was that Kyle had not pulled his trailered boat far enough ahead to make room for this guy's truck—that he was 'hogging' the pull out. It was the lamest excuse I have ever heard for shooting someone. Fortunately, the guy is doing twenty-five-to-life for what he did. But that won't bring Kyle back."

Emma shook her head. "I'm so sorry."

He looked up. "It probably doesn't make much sense. But that's why. When all that went down, I realized I was burned out chasing intellectual property issues for Silicon Valley companies. Totally burned out. My marriage had failed. The day I made my last student loan payment, I decided I needed to finish what Kyle started."

"So, you were married?"

Topher squirmed. "Deal killer?" He caught himself as he said it, not wanting to assume any interest on Emma's part.

Emma gave him a puzzled look.

Topher looked around awkwardly. "Okay, wrong choice of words. I feel like I'm about ten right now, like that boy in elementary school who likes a girl but has no way—no courage—to tell her. So, he lamely asks a friend to ask her if she likes him." He looked up again and said, "Darn, that didn't sound any better, did it? It's just that I…"

Emma looked at her swinging feet, smiling at his awkwardness.

Topher gave up on whatever he was trying to explain and then looked at Emma. "Yes, I was married. I blew it. I got too wrapped up in my work. Monica—my wife at the time, who you've heard about from Connie—she probably felt ignored. When I found out she was seeing another guy, I lost it." He rubbed his hands together. "It's been over for a little more than a year, but I wonder sometimes if I—"

"…Do you miss her?"

"Not really. But, honestly, I do wonder if I'd taken things more seriously…if I had…would they have worked out?" His words began spilling out as he counted fingers on one right hand. "We grew apart—from what had been a pretty good fit—well, enough to…Well, anyway, she wanted money way more than she wanted kids. She was all about glitz and swanky high-rise apartments." Wringing his hands, he looked up at Emma and said, "And there's no way she would have moved here—that was never in the plan. After a couple of visits to Willow Creek early in our marriage, she refused to visit at all—not even to see my family! I played along at first, but then I realized how much Willow Creek was a part of me. Looking back, I can see now how we gradually stopped being a match. It still scares me just how it crept up, just how off I was. But it also scares me that I went along for so long like it was working—for seven years!" He looked up with resolve. "It was plain hard."

Emma wasn't sure what to say. She was sure he had unresolved pain from the look in his eyes and his hunched shoulders. She looked at his dark hair poking out from under his baseball hat and glimpsed what she imagined to be a younger version of her own father.

"Yeah," she said, "relationships sometimes aren't what you think they are."

"Truer words were never spoken," Topher said, looking up at the darkening sky.

Emma reached to touch his hand, and he turned his over, their fingers intertwining, his hand swallowing hers up. She began to feel something she hadn't in a long time. She felt instantly warmer, happy. She scooted closer and put her head on his shoulder. He smelled great. She tilted her head to look up at him. "Not a deal killer at all."

…

THAT NIGHT, EMMA COULDN'T SLEEP. She decided to write. The words tumbled out onto the page. "Life, like culture, delivers a mixed bag," she wrote. "Sometimes, you can't see what's in the water around you until you bump into it. The act of swimming is sometimes bruising but often serendipitous. While swimming, listen to your inner advisor, connect authentically, and try to stay awake—since these hard-to-detect forces can erode at us." She looked away for a moment and reflected on her time in Willow Creek so far before adding, "Or can build us, elevate us, and expand our lives."

Looking down at the hand Topher had held, Emma puzzled over how to capture the notion that not all going on around us may be toxic after all—in fact, water is the very force that keeps the fish alive. Take it away, and fish die. Clearly, too much of the wrong stuff makes fish struggle. But in clean, pure doses, water always works—and works great. She made a note to explore later how someone could go about finding pure water.

Before finishing for the evening, Emma added, "Whatever your water, it just IS." She tried tying it all together but decided to do that another day.

Chapter 30

Walker Home, 1935

Once Iris learned to walk and talk, it became clear that she was different than other children. She was quite verbal, very precise and especially precocious, using words such as "fatigue," "burgundy," and "precisely" at a young age. Cassie generally dressed Iris well, happy the small department store in town seemed to stock fashionable clothing for girls.

Iris was often very direct, even harshly blunt, which given her appearance made her look somewhat smart and quite cute. Despite many reminders from her mother, Iris would regularly ask complete strangers why they looked "quite sickly" or when they might "pass away" because they seemed "elderly." She warned plenty of smokers "to have low expectations for longevity." Most would look at the bows in Iris's blonde hair and respond with something like, "Those are some big words for such a cute little thing."

For the first few years, Cassie explained Iris's direct manner from "having too much going on in that pretty little head." At school, Iris's differences became even more pronounced. Where other children her age were interested in playmates, Iris was curious about everything—from the way someone combed his or her hair and why lady bugs had so many layers of wings to where water came from and how it flowed through pipes and into her cup.

She also read voraciously beginning in elementary school, completing all of Mark Twain and then Jack London's complete works by eight. She devoured any science book she could find and regularly spent hours poring over the encyclopedia set Ruby gave her that year.

Never any trouble at school, Iris's teachers insisted that she be moved at least a grade ahead, but Cassie felt Iris's lack of social skills was a better reason to keep her with her age group. Iris's third-grade teacher, Mrs. Morris, had rudely scoffed. "Social skills? The girl hardly talks to anyone…" before catching herself, regretting what she had said. Cassie asked to have Iris moved to Mrs. Anderson's class the next day.

Even at home, Iris behaved oddly, reacting to usual matters in unusual ways, often absorbed for hours in the smallest things, and never really laughing much or crying for that matter. When plied, Iris would shout or even scream loudly to let you know that was enough.

At eleven, Iris became interested in bones, particularly skulls of small animals that were common enough in the fields and groves around the edges of town, frequently bringing home the dried and bleached skulls of birds, squirrels, and once what Cassie thought was a dog or skunk. They fought all day over keeping or throwing that one away, and it wasn't until Erastus came home that evening that Iris could be persuaded that it really didn't smell good.

Cassie struggled with all this, but Erastus would listen to his daughter's descriptions of her treasures for hours. More than enough encouragement, Cassie felt.

Iris began wandering farther from home—usually without permission or explanation. At first, Cassie would find her a few blocks away at the edge of town carrying a small bag, looking along ditch banks down a dirt road or poking at the base of trees with a stick.

Cassie set rules for her daughter to little effect. For a while, Iris didn't go all that far. But one day following Iris's thirteenth birthday, Cassie drove a full mile before she located Iris all the way to the Dry Bed, dropping sticks down from one side of the new bridge and rushing to the downstream side to watch them come through.

Iris protested with, "I followed the ditch…," looking at her mother like it was perfectly reasonable explanation for what had happened.

One day and without explanation, Iris's collecting abruptly ended. Cassie went to empty the garbage pail in the barrel out back and looked in on a macabre scene of animal skulls and bones, abundant feathers that Cassie had never seen, and strips of ribbon that had been kept somewhere out of sight as well. When Cassie asked about this, Iris had looked up blankly before going back to reading.

...

At fourteen, Iris seemed to withdraw from nearly everything. She increasingly kept to herself and her books. Only her father could lift her out of these moods. Iris's awkward questions to strangers also suddenly ended, something Cassie didn't miss. She now barely talked at all.

One evening after the town summer festival that June, Cassie described what she was seeing to Erastus. "This morning, we were seated on the curb in the shade of the bank watching the parade. Ruby had joined me and even commented on Iris's mood. 'Look, she's not even noticing the candy,' Ruby said." Cassie shook her head. "The other children were jumping up as wrapped candy was tossed from floats and cars in the parade, but Iris sat drawing with a stick. She always enjoyed that so much in the past! Even when the Swenson's came by with that wagon and their draft horses, neither Sarah nor Jens could get her attention. Iris didn't even look up."

Erastus listened to his wife before saying, "We both know when she gets her mind on something, it takes its own course. I'm not sure anyone can explain it, but I sure do love her."

"Of course," Cassie said. "As do I. But, dear, you need to know that when the Snake River Canal Company float came by with you on board and waving, I tried to get her attention and said, 'There's your father, Iris! Wave, Iris, wave!' Her own father!"

When Cassie later discussed this with Dr. Hall, he called it "a depressiveness."

"Okay," Cassie said, thinking the idea over carefully and finding it fitting. "It's more like a sadness that seems to last for a few hours and certainly doesn't happen every day." Cassie felt herself minimizing the situation. More honesty, she added, "Actually, it comes most mornings but usually passes by noon."

Dr. Hall said, "This could be juvenile melancholy, something she will likely outgrow." He took extra time to describe how he had observed Iris since she was a baby and found she was unusual in other ways, a manner that seemed quirky to him. "We can only hope it doesn't get more extreme from here," he added. "I've seen this type of personality a few times, and it can go any direction as individuals like this mature."

Discouraged, Cassie probed what "any direction" meant without feeling the doctor gave her much hope for improvement at all.

Later that night, Cassie shared what she had learned with Erastus. "Yes," she told him. "He used the word 'quirky.'" They looked it up in the dictionary just to be clear and were satisfied with the definition, that Iris had a few peculiar traits but considered her more original than odd.

"She's an original," Erastus said with a twinkle in his eye.

"And a handful," Cassie sighed, leaning into her husband.

...

ONE FRIDAY AFTERNOON IN MID-JULY, Cassie was out weeding the garden when she heard the phone ring from inside the house. Her hands were covered with dirt from weeding the cucumbers and zucchini vines that were thriving. Iris was swinging slowly from the tire swing in the backyard, scuffing her feet at each passing.

Cassie began to say, "Iris, will you…" but had second thoughts about having her answer the phone. Instead, she let it ring. It eventually stopped. As Cassie stood to stretch before moving to the next row, the phone began ringing again. "Must be urgent," she said aloud, quickly wiping her hands on her apron and trotting toward the house.

"Hello?"

"Cassie, it's about Erastus. Come quickly." It was a voice she recognized from Erastus's auto dealership. Cassie stood looking at the handset, instantly worried and sensing she needed to move quickly. She shouted, "Iris, come with me now!"

Iris jumped from the swing and came quickly toward her mother. Cassie noted how Iris could comply so well at times.

Arriving at the dealership, Cassie saw flashing red lights from two police cars and an ambulance. Alarmed, she parked among the new cars on the lot and ran toward a group of men lifting a gurney into the back of the ambulance, screaming "Erastus!" as she ran.

Erastus turned his head slowly as his wife approached. "Bad ticker," he whispered, reaching his hand slowly toward his heart. Cassie took his hand and realized her own hands were still dirty from gardening.

"I was weeding… when they called," she explained.

Erastus winced and reached for his left shoulder.

Cassie looked into the eyes of the men attending her husband. "What is it?"

"Could be a heart attack. We need to get him to the clinic in Idaho Falls. We already gave him quinidine and some morphine. It's all we can do here. We will monitor him on the drive."

Cassie kissed Erastus on the forehead and then looked over to see her daughter standing off to the side between two new cars. The puzzled look on her face said enough. As Erastus was loaded into the ambulance, Cassie crossed the empty space toward Iris.

"Oh, Iris, sweetie. I didn't mean to leave you."

Iris asked flatly, "What are they doing to Papa?"

"He's hurt. His heart isn't working well."

"Is it a heart attack?" Iris asked, frankly, clenching her fists. Reflecting, she cited a fact she must have picked up from an encyclopedia, saying, "Eighty percent of people don't recover from heart attacks."

Cassie could see Iris's eyes glistening. It was the first time in years that Cassie had seen any outward display of emotion.

Following two days in the hospital, Erastus was released with detailed instructions. Bedrest for two weeks. He could go back to work at the car dealership eventually but should avoid lifting much at all or strenuous activity of any kind for several months—if not the remainder of his life. A bad heart was likely to get only worse, not better, the doctor said.

Cassie saw Iris smile very briefly when Erastus walked through the front door. An hour later, she found Iris sitting on the edge of her father's bed watching him intently while he slept.

One morning two weeks later, Erastus rose early for a quick breakfast. He had gone back to work the day before and was planning to tour another dealership in nearby Sugar City. While eating, he asked Cassie to rub his right shoulder, a stiffness that quickly turned to pain. Iris came into the kitchen to see her father grabbing at his chest.

Cassie raced to the telephone and worked the lever to get the operator's attention. "I need an ambulance," she shouted into the mouthpiece, not caring who else might be listening on the party line.

Cassie helped Erastus to the couch and got him comfortable. Iris watched from the doorway. By the time the ambulance arrived, Erastus had stopped breathing altogether.

That evening, Cassie sat with Ruby in the front room. Iris was focused on writing in a notebook, turning pages back and forth and making marks of some type.

Cassie was angry and said, "Why would he leave me?"

"I don't believe he would ever choose to leave you," Ruby consoled her. "You were the most important person or concern in his life, Cassie. He would never have wanted to leave you."

"It all makes no sense. It makes no…" Cassie began sobbing.

Iris looked up momentarily before turning back to her notebook and marking the same page over and over.

…

ON BAD DAYS, Iris's mood could be so sad. The bad days far outnumbered the good ones, and Cassie could only fault Erastus's departure for the shift.

"I miss him. Do you?" she asked Iris one afternoon, trying to engage her by the comment. Almost immediately, Iris's moodiness turned to a flat affect, a manner that was more provoking to Cassie than not. Taking another pass at it, Cassie asked, "Iris, darling, would you want to visit the cemetery with me?"

Iris didn't respond.

"Please tell me. You seem so quiet, so withdrawn."

Iris blurted out, "I am working, mother," busying herself with her notebook.

Cassie pressed a bit, knowing full well that Iris would pull further away if pushed too hard. "What can I do for you?"

"Leave me…alone."

"Iris, you know I won't do that. I will never leave you."

"Papa did."

"Darling, you know Pa didn't expect to…die. It wasn't his…"

Iris interrupted and said emphatically, "He left."

"Iris, honey, with all your reading and studying, you should know that your father didn't want to leave you. His heart just up and quit."

Cassie was startled when Iris looked up helplessly, responding with more words than she had spoken in days. "He didn't get back up, Mother. He didn't…"

"Oh, darling…" Cassie reached for her daughter and drew her in. For the first time in weeks, Iris allowed it only briefly, sniffling exactly twice. Cassie snuck a look at Iris's face to see if this rare show of emotion was real. Iris immediately stiffened up, wiping her eyes and pulling away, turning back to her notebook. Cassie watched for anything more but only saw Iris occasionally brushing stray hairs from her face.

Two days later, Iris disappeared. Wanting to give her daughter some space, Cassie waited for two hours before driving out along routes where Iris had previously wandered, even along the country road leading to the Dry Bed. She prayed in her heart to find Iris as she drove. "She's at the cemetery," came to Cassie's mind. Struck by the clarity of her impression, Cassie turned the car around and drove directly there, finding Iris sitting in an array of sunflower heads that she had obviously collected from around the edges of the cemetery where they grew abundantly. The sunflowers were laid out in rows on top of the bare dirt. Iris poked at the dirt with a stick.

Cassie parked the car and walked over. "That's beautiful, Iris," Cassie said.

Iris looked up at her mother. "Pa's in there, right?" she asked, pointing at the ground. The way Iris asked the question, her sincerity, brought Cassie to her knees.

"Just his body is. His spirit is up there," Cassie said, pointing to the sky.

Iris looked up innocently. "How did he get there?"

Cassie thought to explain her own convictions about heaven but after a moment simply said, "I don't know how. I only know he's there."

Iris shook her head before saying, "Hmmph."

Cassie sat alongside her daughter in silence for a few minutes and then walked to the car. She waited for an hour before Iris stood up and joined her.

…

OUT OF THE BLUE, IRIS DEVELOPED a fascination and even slight enthusiasm for birthday parties—even though she had turned down every prior invitation. It was the one topic she would discuss with her mother, and Iris shared every detail she was hearing about such parties. There were games, party favors, and presents. Some kids even dressed up for these affairs, she said.

On a call with Sarah one evening, Cassie said, "She's very preoccupied with these things. We drove by a lawn party the other day, and Iris wanted to know why they were wearing blindfolds and a swinging a stick at a piñata. She had so many questions."

"It's good she's talking about something," Sarah said. "Well, you should get her to one."

"Are you suggesting I angle for an invitation? She's had a few over the years but has always said no."

Sarah laughed and said, "That's exactly what I'm suggesting. Give her another chance. Maybe now is the time!"

Before hanging up, Cassie said, "I miss our time together, Sarah. What with the auto dealership and all, I barely have time to blow my nose anymore."

Sarah said, "Starting with the mercantile, you've always been so good at business matters. You took a break for a good long while. As Jens regularly reminds me, there's a season for everything. This must be your season for a few new responsibilities. So, do come around when you can. I can be patient. Until then, I'll fill that empty place in my heart with baked goods."

They laughed together, and Cassie said, "You're lovely. Thanks for being so good to me."

That Sunday at church, Cassie overheard a discussion about children playing Pin the Tail on the Donkey at parties, and she immediately wondered if she could ever persuade Iris to actually attend one. Could an invitation be arranged?

To Cassie's surprise, Iris came home from school the next Monday with a note. It was an invitation to a birthday party for Sally Bonham, Cloy's daughter.

Iris asked brightly, "Can I go?"

Based on Iris's prior refusal of every invitation, Cassie was surprised that she was even asking. She wondered whether Cloy would be there, but she quickly dismissed that as irrelevant to what she wanted for Iris. Cloy's wife Mercy was kind enough and had even brought several dishes to the gathering after Erastus's funeral that day. Reflecting on Mercy's earlier kindnesses, she eagerly said, "I think you should."

Iris nodded, which surprised Cassie even more.

The Meadowlark

Sally's party was set for the next Friday after school. Iris walked in to find the girls laughing about something they were discussing. One looked up and said, "'That girl Iris is here!'" Iris smiled and tried laughing along with them, not knowing what else to do. She watched the girls interact, feeling tense and wondering how they had so much to talk about.

When it came time for games, Iris wasn't sure how they went but paid careful attention. Sally announced that the first game was called Penny Drop. The object was to kneel on the seat of a chair facing the back and hold a penny to your nose. Leaning over the chair, you tried to drop the penny into a Mason jar positioned on the floor below. Iris waited patiently for her turn as each girl missed. When Iris took her place on the chair, she concentrated for a long while and was satisfied to hear the clink of the penny as it hit the bottom of the glass jar.

Several girls chimed in with "How did you…?"

Iris said matter-of-factly while pointing, "I merely aimed with my eyes and ignored the empty space around the bottle…" She looked up to see the girls rushing into the next room for another game, a few shouting "merely" as they went.

"Pin the Tail on the Donkey!" Sally announced. Iris grew curious, having heard of the game but never seen it, always wondering what type of donkey would be involved. She was struck by its simplicity when Sally's mother taped up a wall poster with a colored sketch of a donkey.

Iris bravely asked, "Can I do it?" clearly nervous in her request.

The girls were quiet as Sally looked around. "Well…I guess. Let me help you with this," she said with a wink to the other girls as she placed a blindfold over Iris's eyes. The girls stayed quiet as Sally spun Iris in circles. Iris could hear "Shhhh!" as she turned. After a moment, the spinning stopped.

"Now, 'pin the tail on the donkey'!"

A bit dizzy, Iris still knew exactly where the poster was. She took two steps forward. Without as much as feeling for the wall, she reached out with the paper tail in one hand and a straight pin in the other before sticking them both to the poster. With a sense of satisfaction, she lifted the blindfold to see that the tail was in the middle of the donkey and not at all where a proper tail should be. She made a quick adjustment to the tail, and turning, saying, "I did it…" before realizing the girls had already tip-toed away. Iris saw them peeking around the corner, a few snickering until they all burst out laughing.

Sally's older brother had come into the room and sat watching from a chair in the corner. "They're mean," he said.

Iris wasn't sure what to say.

"You're Iris, right?"

"Yes." She recognized him from around town and knew he was older.

"I'm Harlin. You're smarter than they are. That's why they don't like you."

Iris didn't understand what he meant by "smarter." It hadn't occurred to her until then that they didn't like her.

"All right," she said before rejoining the group.

Chapter 31

Dry Bed, 1935

Life began settling into a new sense of normal. Without Erastus's familiar and steady presence, it fell on Cassie to manage affairs. She began spending most of her days at the auto dealership to learn all the details that he had previously handled.

And there was the canal board. Before his passing, Cassie's father had regularly reminded her, "When I'm gone, my shares are yours." Of huge relief to her, Erastus had represented Cassie's interests, but now this too had fallen on Cassie.

No small surprise to her, Cassie found her role in the canal company more interesting than she had expected—despite needing to interact with Cloy Bonham, her equal partner on the board. She paid him as little attention as possible, with no real drama ensuing. No longer thin but now with quite a paunch and nearly bald, Cloy was still Cloy—the over-observant, uncomfortably flirtatious man she had met years earlier. Before Simeon's passing years earlier, he often told her to expect Cloy would be fine partner—should it come to that—and to simply ignore his personality. "Stick to business and business only. If circumstances ever put you in the same room alone with him," her father had advised, "I recommend you ignore any personal questions, turn it all back to business, and consider any forward behavior as an odd form of salesmanship. The man always seems to be selling something." Erastus had reinforced the same notion. Still, her early experiences with the man had been hard to shake.

One Tuesday, Cassie attended a canal company meeting for a critical vote that Cloy was requiring, one she couldn't avoid. On several past occasions, Cloy had tried to sell his shares to third-parties, moves both Simeon and Erastus had regularly blocked. This put Cloy in a bind since the original partnership agreement required the other partner's approval. Simeon had regularly insisted that any new partner would never be as good as the one he already had. That job had since passed to Erastus and now Cassie.

With the proposal in front of her and unexpectedly strong support from all other board members, Cassie remembered her father's position and quickly voted against it, effectively killing the deal. She quickly left the meeting before Cloy could corner her with questions.

...

A STRAIGHT-A STUDENT, Iris sat one day in her English class at Willow Creek High School with a copy of Thomas Hardy's *The Return of the Native* in front of her. Intent on fostering a relationship with Iris, the teacher approached. "Iris, I'm delighted to see you've moved on past *Tess*. Have you read about 'redding' yet?" she asked, pointing to the book. Iris nodded and said, "It is the red dye used by sheep men to keep bugs and lice out of a sheep's wool."

The teacher smiled and added, "It's basically 'sheep dip'."

Others in the class looked amused and began whispering in less than kind tones. Two girls at Iris's side whispered, "Teacher's pet" and "odd duck," not in a kind way at all. Still, Iris looked satisfied, the negative tone lost on her. She nodded toward them and said, "Thank you."

After class, Iris saw Sally Bonham in the hall with a few other girls. As Iris walked past, Sally looked up and smiled suspiciously. "Harlin thinks you're pretty," she said before turning back to her friends laughing.

When Cassie came home from the auto dealership that night, Iris asked her, "Am I pretty?"

"You're the prettiest girl I know."

"What is 'pretty'?"

"Well, that's a good question," Cassie answered. "I guess it could be a lot of things. Mostly, I think it's who you are—not just how you look. You're pretty here," Cassie said, touching Iris over her heart. "And here," she explained, touching Iris's head. Working to reinforce concepts she wanted Iris to adopt,

Cassie added, "Smart is pretty. But nice is the prettiest thing of all. You're so, so nice, and that is what makes you so pretty."

Later that night, Iris looked in the mirror and touched the same spots her mother had, repeating, "I'm pretty here…and here."

One Saturday in September, Iris waited at the auto dealership while Cassie met with Alexander Jones, the store manager.

"We will be only a few minutes," Cassie said to Iris as she closed the office door. Iris walked outside to wander among the new cars. She was very interested in a new sedan with a turbine on the passenger's side of the car that someone had explained was used to cool the car during the hot days of summer. She was squinting at the invoice posted in the car's window to confirm that the math was correct when she heard, "Hello."

It was Harlin Bonham.

"Hello," she responded curiously.

"What are you doing here?"

Aware of what Harlin had said about her to Sally, Iris awkwardly said much more than usual. "This is my daddy's car store. I mean, it was my daddy's car store. He died, so my ma is running it now." Then she repeated in the same tone he had used, "What are you doing here?"

Harlin answered, "I'm looking for a new car. Pa is buying me one for my sixteenth birthday."

Iris walked around the car.

Harlin followed her. "Would you want to go together?"

Iris ignored his question, unsure what he meant.

Changing the subject, Harlin asked, "Which car should I get?"

"This one."

"Why?"

"It has a turbine that makes the car very cool in the summer," she said, repeating word-for-word the description the store manager had given her. "It's called a 'swamp cooler.'"

They were interrupted by a salesman walking out from the store.

"Harlin Bonham!" he said loudly, extending his hand. "Good to see you, young man!" The two shook hands and began walking around the lot. Harlin kept glancing back toward Iris as the salesman introduced him to the various models available.

After a few minutes, Cassie emerged from the office with a flustered look, mumbling, "Does finding a business partner have to be so complicated?" She told Iris it was time to leave.

On the drive home, Iris asked, "What does it mean to go together?"

Cassie shuddered at the thought and said, "Oh, you're too young to date. Why, did someone ask you?"

Iris didn't answer.

...

AS SUMMER TRANSITIONED TO FALL, Sally Bonham dropped by one afternoon to talk with Iris. From her chair in the kitchen, Cassie could hear "Huh?" and "Uh-huh" coming from Iris. At one point, Iris asked loudly, "Mom, can I go with Sally and some friends to the Dry Bed on Saturday night? She says there will be boys and girls. They're going to have a bonfire and roast marshmallows."

Cassie had always thought bonfires were fun—from the sagebrush burnings when they first moved into the valley to one someone had started with old car tires a few years back that had burned for days after. She remembered loving gathering around such tall fires, the flames licking at the sky and so hot you had to stand way back.

Despite her fondness for bonfires, her first reaction was protective, group thing or not. She walked from the kitchen. She wanted to ask why Sally's sudden interest in Iris but decided not to dampen Iris's only social prospect in months. "Hi, Sally. How many boys and girls?"

"Probably ten or so."

Folding her arms, Cassie said, "And who will be there?"

"Oh, I will be, for sure. Some of my friends. I don't know quite yet about the boys."

Cassie asked, "What time will you be home?"

Sally said, "Probably by ten or so. We have church the next morning."

Without thinking much more about it, Cassie turned to Iris and said, "Sure, dear, you can go."

...

CASSIE AND RUBY HAD BEEN MEETING FOR LUNCH most Tuesdays for several years—long before either of their husbands had passed away. But after losing Erastus, things had become so busy for Cassie that she had cancelled too many of their planned lunches. With the summer over and Iris back in school, and despite her time at the auto dealership, Cassie was finally able to meet. Ruby had suggested they meet at the new coffee shop called Carter's Café that had recently opened on the corner of Main Street.

Arriving in her new Pontiac coupe, Ruby emerged from the car with a dark fur shawl and bright red lipstick—her typical style. Her heals clicked as she approached the cafe's entrance where Cassie stood waiting. Cassie waited for Ruby's hug, a lean-forward type embrace that had cheeks touching and nothing else.

"You look so pretty!" Ruby said.

"Why, thank you," Cassie replied. "I appreciate that. With everything going on lately, I feel more exhausted than pretty." Sitting down at a booth, she told Ruby, "I'm now running an automobile dealership that still sells farm implements despite trying to get out of that part of the business for the past decade—but now with a partner. There's money in the farm business—something Erastus always understood. I guess farmers are going to farm!"

"Oh, I know," Ruby said, looking past Cassie wistfully. "Simeon, rest his soul, would walk between his new truck and his old threshing machine with equal awe and wonder."

They both laughed.

"How's Iris?"

Cassie looked up from reading the menu. "Iris is still my world—nearly my entire world—but her world is expanding…and it will either take me with it or leave me behind!" Cassie sighed before explaining, "She's having new experiences that I'm not sure she's ready for. Some days, I wish I could go back to the little girl who collected everything she could find and laid her collections out in a row on the fireplace hearth. I miss her sheer delight when she would say, 'Momma, come look.'"

Ruby said reassuringly, "You have the prettiest little girl still. And the smartest." Changing the subject, she said, "Tell me about her little friends." Cassie recognized Ruby's kindness because she could have just as easily asked if Iris had any friends at all, a topic they had explored many times. Ruby added, "While you're thinking about that, let's order."

The waitress approached with a basket of hot scones. "They're our specialty," she said. "Try them with honey butter."

"They look absolutely delightful," Ruby said, moving one to her serving plate and reaching her knife toward the small crock of butter.

After placing their orders and while waiting for their food, Cassie told Ruby about the recent birthday party and sudden interest from Sally Bonham. Ruby frowned at the idea of Iris joining a mixed activity that included boys, even though Cassie assured Sally was Iris's friend.

"Oh, my. She's just so young. And innocent. And she has the most unusual way of being around others—I certainly hope no one teases or is mean to her."

Cassie paused. "I have thought all of that over—many times. If I ever hope to get her out of the nest, we must start somewhere. Further, it's not far or for long."

Ruby said, "Oh, I worry. I'm certainly not trying to tell you what to do. I simply worry about that cute girl."

"I'll be sure she stays close to Sally," Cassie said.

...

THE NEXT SATURDAY EVENING, IRIS WATCHED CURIOUSLY as several boys dragged logs together and formed a tall pile of wood. Led by Harlin, the boys ventured out along the banks of the Dry Bed to find more. They had all ridden there in a pickup parked off to the side. Harlin had come alone in his new Chevrolet Coupe, the cherry red one Iris had talked with him about at the dealership. Sitting next to Sally on a log, Iris gathered her dress around her knees and looked over at the three other girls across the space who were seated less lady-like on another log and whittling at willow branches with pocketknives they had borrowed from the boys.

Sally caught her questioning look. "Marshmallow sticks."

Iris smiled. The other girls seemed a few years older. She and Sally were clearly the two youngest ones there.

Sally said, "Let's help out," and then asked, "How about monkey vine?" Iris smiled and began pulling at the vine extending down from many of the nearby trees. The long stringy vine seemed dry and perfect for a fire starter. Tearing it away from the trees and avoiding the fluffy tufts growing on the vine turned out to be harder than she expected.

"Clematis," Iris said.

Sally gave her a puzzled look.

"It's called 'clematis,' not monkey vine."

"You're funny, Iris," Sally said.

Misreading the situation, Iris began telling Sally how the Dry Bed was not really dry anymore because her father had worked on the Great Feeder years earlier when he was younger.

Sally said, "My daddy worked on it, too."

"Oh." Iris then repeated something she had once heard. "Your daddy makes my mamma uncomfortable."

Sally looked offended and asked, "Why?"

Iris shrugged and continued tugging at a vine. "I don't know. I just heard my momma say that."

"You shouldn't repeat everything you hear, Iris."

After piling on more fuel, and with tufts of clematis poking out from between many of the logs, one of the boys moved around the pile pouring gas from a tall can over the wood. Another lit a match on the zipper of his jeans and shouted, "Stand back!" as he tossed a burning match onto the pile. With a whoofing sound, a wall of flames instantaneously shot up into the gathering darkness for thirty seconds before dying back down.

Iris asked Sally, "Is that all?"

"Oh, Iris. You are so silly for someone so smart. Wait for a minute." Sally stood and moved toward the girls at the other side of the fire, leaving Iris alone.

Iris watched as the flames began to catch hold of the wood. The fire grew again, and soon enough, it once more lit the sky and penetrated the deep riverbank woods behind them. Iris looked around, remembering that her mother had instructed her to stay near Sally. She was about to get up when Harlin walked over and sat next to her.

"So, what do you think of our bonfire?"

Iris felt him looking at her. She didn't know what to say. She hadn't really talked to him or any of the other boys to that point. Iris's eyes and blonde hair glowed in the firelight as she held her hands in front of her to warm them, feeling a need to respond. "I believe I like it."

"Are you cold?" Harlin scooted toward her, reaching his arm around her and pulling her toward him.

Iris pulled away. "Not really."

"All right," Harlin said a bit frustrated, standing and walking back to the group of boys heaving a big log onto the fire. The other girls were shielding their faces and reached toward the fire with their marshmallow sticks before shying away from the heat. As he walked, Harlin shouted, "Give it a little time. It'll die down later."

...

AS THE FLAMES SETTLED, Iris watched across the fire as the other girls began to roast marshmallows and feed them to the boys. Sally stayed with the group, and occasionally one or more of them would burst into laughter at something someone was saying. Iris watched as Sally's first marshmallow burst into flames. She waved it frantically in the air, the flaming blob flinging from its roasting stick into the bushes, starting a small wildfire that was quickly extinguished by the boys stomping at it.

A few minutes later, Harlin walked over and sat next to Iris again. He shifted as he repeated his earlier question. "So, what do you think of our bonfire?"

Iris looked at him quizzically. "I... like it?"

"I like you, Iris." Harlin reached for her hand. "I know I asked you this before, but would you want to go together?"

Iris quickly pulled her hand away. "I'm too young to date," repeating what her mother had told her.

"No need to call it a date," he said matter-of-factly. "We would just go together. Be a couple. You would be my girl."

Since her mother had never mentioned anything more, Iris said, "All right." Harlin reached for her hand. She could hear the group on the other side of the fire laughing and having a good time. Harlin glanced around the fire with a satisfied smile. The two sat quietly for five or ten minutes. Harlin would start to say something and then gaze back into the fire.

With a start, one of the boys looked at his wristwatch and said, "I have to move pipe in the morning before church. Sprinkler pipes don't move themselves." The group groaned and began packing up.

Harlin let go of Iris's hand and said, "I can take you home when you're ready. I have my car."

"All right," she said.

"Stay here for now," Harlin instructed.

Iris watched from the log as the group quickly disbanded. Harlin said something to the other boys. One of the boys grabbed a girl by the hand and the two hurried the truck cab with the rest of the group climbing into the back.

Harlin walked over to Sally, who bent over from the bed of the truck to whisper something to him. Iris could hear the girls laughing as the truck pulled away, revealing a clear view of Harlin's new car, the deep red now dancing in the dying firelight.

Harlin waved Iris over. "Okay, let's go," he said, getting in the car and pushing the passenger door open from the inside. He revved the engine. On the short drive home, Harlin said confidently, "Scoot on over here. Be my girl." He reached for Iris's hand again and pulled her toward him.

This time, she pulled away.

"Are you mad?"

Iris said flatly, "I am not mad."

Frustrated, Harlin squeezed the steering wheel with both hands and pulled the car to a sudden stop in front of Iris's house. "You can go." He waved with one hand dismissively. "Go!"

Part IV

Chapter 32

Bonfire, 1935

Later the next evening after dinner and chores, Iris set out on a walk to the Dry Bed. She still wore her dress from church that day and had in mind to see what the bonfire looked like the day after, wondering if it might still be burning. A few cars passed along the way, and after a mile or so, she turned off the main road and down a short dirt road to the field where the boys had parked their cars the night before. She walked past the smoldering remains of their bonfire—wispy smoke coming up from a few spots around a wide black, burned-over area. She stood facing the log where she had sat, pulling at some clematis vines poking out from behind that she had intended to throw on the fire but had forgotten. She looked down at her left hand, remembering Harlin holding her hand.

She walked on toward the riverbank and began looking around, remembering the boys cheering and shouting from the darkness there the night before. Barn swallows darted along the riverbed, and a few dippers bobbed on rocks along the edges before diving beneath the water to look for food. Magpies flew every which way mournfully cawing. She realized dusk was settling over the river, knowing her mother would want her back home before dark.

As she walked out from the lower area along the river channel, she spotted Harlin's dark red car parked at the bonfire site. She was at first confused, remembering he had driven her home in it the night before. Then she came past a tree and saw him sitting on one of the logs with his back to her, leaning forward with his elbows on his knees and placing a can next to two others lining the log next to him. He reached forward and came up with another can.

A stick snapped as Iris walked forward, giving him a start.

Harlin turned to look and hurriedly put the can down. "Oh, hi, Iris." He seemed different than the night before. Harlin asked in a quavering voice, "What are you doing here?"

"Going for a walk. I'm going home now."

He swatted the cans away and patted the log next to him. "Come, sit by me." He laughed awkwardly, his words a bit slurred. "Like last night."

"I can't," she said. "It's getting dark, my mother wants me to be home." But not knowing what else to do in the situation and seeing a pleading in his eyes, Iris sat down on the log, her hands bouncing on her knees. She could see Harlin's eyes were wet and could smell the beer around her.

Harlin reached for Iris's hand and pulled her toward him. She tried to pull away, but he was much stronger this time. The smell of beer increased as he leaned in and pressed his lips against hers.

Iris drew back, but Harlin pulled her closer.

"You're so pretty," he said over and over as he kissed her.

Iris could taste the beer from his mouth and tried pulling his hands away from her face. Harlin began touching her in other places, pushing her roughly to the ground and pulling at her dress.

"Stop," Iris protested, unable to move. Her heart racing, she plead more loudly, "STOP!"

Harlin covered her mouth with his hand making it hard for her to breath. "You're my girl," he whispered. He briefly let one hand go and began fumbling with his pants. When Iris tried to pull away, he hit her with his free hand. "You're my girl!" he shouted, pinning her to the ground.

Iris didn't know what was happening—she couldn't move her arms and legs. She felt Harlin pressing himself against her and suddenly hurt everywhere.

A few minutes later, Harlin walked to his car, looking back at her angrily before driving away.

That evening, Iris stood in front of the bathroom mirror holding a pair of black-handled scissors and hacking at her hair. Her blonde curls were scattered over the sink, and she was now cutting at the right side to make it match.

Cassie walked by and screamed at what she saw. "What are you doing, Iris, dear?"

Iris sobbed. "I don't want to be pretty anymore."

"Why would you want to change that?"

"I don't want to be pretty."

Cassie knew how hard it was to change Iris's mind when she was in a mood like this. "Well, let me help then." Iris handed her mother the scissors, and Cassie trimmed the hacked line until it became an even, straight cut.

"There," Cassie said. "Do you want to talk about what's going on?"

"No," Iris said flatly.

…

AT SCHOOL, IRIS'S CLASSMATES MOSTLY AVOIDED HER. Iris became more withdrawn than ever. She developed a habit of rocking slightly, at first when sitting alone and then anytime she was sitting.

And then Iris got sick. At first, Cassie thought it was the flu—some of that had been going around town. It would likely pass in a few days. But there was no fever or cough, and then the vomiting shifted from episodic to several times a day—and every day.

It was no surprise when Ruby dropped by with a boxed lunch for their regularly scheduled lunch one Tuesday afternoon. Cassie had said she needed to stay home with Iris.

"So, you think it's the flu?"

Cassie said, "It's hard to say what else it could be. She's been throwing up every day. Can't keep anything down, the poor dear."

Ruby hesitated and then began to ask, "Could it be…could it…"

A new thought suddenly crossed Cassie's mind that made no sense at all and yet fit a familiar pattern at the same time. She didn't want to say it but knew someone had to. "Are you suggesting she could be pregnant? She's barely fourteen!"

Ruby said, "I don't really want to be suggesting anything at all, but very little else explains this kind of nausea. Have you had her checked?"

"Well, I figured I could ask Sarah, but that's nothing to be discussed over the phone," Cassie said, alluding to the party-lines used in their area. "You never know who will be listening in." She wrung her hands and said, "And I could never take her to see Dr. Hall."

Still, the flu remedies she had tried were not working at all. Ruby suggested they switch to seltzer water and saltine crackers to see if Iris could keep that down. She offered to run to the store.

Ruby said, "If she can keep anything down, we're sure to know soon enough whether this will pass or….or…let's just leave it at that."

When Ruby returned, Cassie poured a glass and put some crackers on a plate before taking them to Iris's room. She found the curtains drawn with Iris curled on her side on top of the patchwork quilt that covered her bed. The pillow was as straight as everything else in the room—barely a wrinkle despite the fact that Iris had been laying there for hours.

Iris looked up.

"Here, dearest. I brought you something." Cassie added, "Ruby suggested it."

Iris asked, "Is Ruby here?" Ruby was the only grandmother Iris had known but called her by her first name at Ruby's request.

"Yes, she's sitting out in the front room."

Iris shifted to get up.

"Why don't you sip a little of this first and eat one or two of these, and then come out?"

Iris nodded and then took a few sips of the seltzer water and worked her mouth at the fizz and lack of flavor. "Not good," she said wincing. As she left the room, Cassie could see Iris rocking on the edge of her bed and nibbling the edges of a cracker.

Ruby sat up on the sofa when Iris came out, and she knew the look instantly. It wasn't the flu. The flu left you ashen or gray, a wiped-out look complete with fever and sweat. Iris's now-shorter hair looked bad enough, but the consequences of daily nausea left her looking gaunt in her cheeks and around her neck. Ruby wondered if she had lost weight, which often happened in the first few months of pregnancy.

"Why, Iris, sweetheart, come sit by me."

Iris sat next to her and accepted a hug before starting to rock slightly in place.

Ruby fingered Iris's blonde hair and asked, "What happened to your beautiful curls?" She didn't see Cassie's signal to not ask.

Iris responded. "I didn't want to be pretty anymore. I didn't."

"Why is that, my dear?"

Iris winced at the statement and said, "I just didn't."

...

IN EARLY NOVEMBER, CASSIE MADE THE DECISION to keep Iris home from school—she didn't want the questions. It was clearer every day that this wasn't the flu but much more of a "predicament," she called it, uncomfortable with any other word. If Iris truly was pregnant…well, Cassie didn't have a plan for something like that at all. She avoided thinking altogether about how this could have happened, reflecting on who Iris had been with and concluding there was only the bonfire that one night. But it was a group activity, Cassie's mind protested, searching for any other possibilities, and still unwilling to accept what was getting increasingly obvious. She even called Mercy Bonham to check on when Sally had arrived home that night. Mercy had confidently confirmed it was right around dark, to the best of her recollection. Cassie recalled Iris coming home about then as well on the night of the bonfire.

Then there was the night Iris had cut her hair, which in Cassie's memory was around the night of the bonfire but could have been as much as a week later. Cassie strained to put things together.

Iris's nausea didn't let up. Mornings were the worst, and Cassie regularly expressed her gratitude for indoor plumbing—even though it had been installed two decades earlier. Visiting with Ruby on the phone one day, they laughed when Cassie had said, "Once a pioneer, always a pioneer! Remember running to the outhouse every time or carrying around a chamber pot?" Then, because their telephones shared party lines, she added circumspectly, "Let's talk about this later," since whoever picked up the handset from often twenty or more houses could overhear whatever others were saying on the line. Cassie and Ruby were both careful not to say much more since you could never know who else was listening in—the favorite pastime of more than one nosy neighbor.

Mrs. Gooch, the operator who heard every conversation, could often be the nosiest of all and even break into calls with questions. Occasionally, Cassie had heard gasps while on a call she could only assume came from Mrs. Gooch. To avoid the possibility, Cassie and Ruby worked out a code of sorts to discuss the situation without really naming names and only speaking very indirectly about pregnancy. Just saying "pregnant" once would have lit a wildfire of gossip wondering however it could be possible that one of these two older women could possibly get pregnant—especially since both had lost their husbands. They used "it" when referring to pregnancy or the situation, creating a mystery for anyone eavesdropping. Statements like, "Well, 'it' is complicated" and "It really needs careful attention" and "How is 'it' developing?"

When it came to Iris being the affected party, they had decided they needed a code name for her too. While on the phone one day, Cassie glanced around and spotted Iris's copy of *Huckleberry Finn* on the kitchen table. They decided to refer to her as "Huckleberry" since no one within a hundred miles had that name and it was definitely more of a man's name at that. Cassie had received the most confused stare from Mrs. Gooch at the grocery store one day with what looked like a question forming on her lips that she was mustering the courage to ask.

Unable to resist, Mrs. Gooch had finally blurted out, "Who's Huckleberry?"

When Cassie told Ruby, they laughed until they cried.

Ruby developed a plan of action and drove over one afternoon to discuss it with Cassie. She hoped Cassie would support it. Pulling up to the front of the bungalow-style house, Ruby smiled at her memories of sitting so many evenings on the large front porch. Apple trees framed the front walk, with apples scattered everywhere in the grass and only a few still clinging stubbornly to the branches. Ruby looked beautiful as usual, her hair done up nicely, red lipstick, and a fur coat to ward off the late fall chill. She knocked as usual.

Cassie came to the door and said like she had so many times before, "Hello, Ruby. You don't ever need to knock. We're family. Walk right in!"

"Of course, dear." They sat together in the front room, and after asking about Iris, Ruby pulled her chair closer to Cassie.

Cassie exclaimed with a sigh, "I'm getting too old for this."

Ruby laughed and said, "You're a spring chicken—not even sixty. I'm the one who is getting older, although…" She pulled her chair closer to Cassie, adding with a wink, "…but I will never say my number." Now, knee to knee, she reached for Cassie's hand and said, "You'll want Iris to go somewhere until this is over."

Cassie sighed. "I know, but where?"

"It's obvious, don't you think? Sarah's!"

Cassie considered the idea and warmed instantly to the idea. After all, Cassie knew Sarah would gladly take Iris in, no matter the circumstance. Sarah regularly helped younger women with their pregnancies—especially unplanned or unwanted ones. Sarah never really talked about it, carefully to guard the girls from prying eyes and questions.

"We should ask her," Cassie suggested tentatively, worried about how to even begin that conversation.

Ruby said, "I've already made the arrangement with Sarah. I asked her not to discuss it with you before I got the chance."

As they spoke, Iris emerged from her bedroom rubbing her eyes. She was glad to see Ruby. Iris stretched her slight frame, reporting with a yawn, "I ate dinner tonight."

A week or so later, Cassie and Ruby sat together and again explored the question of how Iris could have become pregnant. They probed every situation Iris had been in—from the bonfire to staying after school a few times. All were in group settings. If Iris had ever been alone, it had been away from people. And she always came home within a few minutes of when she said she would.

Cassie asked Iris in to reconstruct what had happened the night of the bonfire.

Without any emotion, Iris said, "Someone threw a burning marshmallow into the bushes."

Ruby noticed Iris rocking in place and mouthed, "When did this begin?"

Cassie shrugged, turning her attention back to Iris. "Who all was there again?"

"Sally and some older girls."

"And no one else?"

Iris stopped rocking momentarily before starting up again. She shook her head.

Changing her line of questioning, Cassie asked, "Did anyone ever touch you?"

Iris looked up flatly.

"That night you cut your hair," Cassie probed, "Did anything happen to you that day, anything involving a boy or man?" Cassie couldn't remember exactly which day that had been. The best she could recall, Iris had only been off on one of her wandering walks. "Were you ever around a boy or man who touched you?"

Iris's began rocking slightly forward and back again. Cassie could see her eyes flitting back and forth. Still, Iris said nothing. Moments later, she got up and walked to her room.

In whispered tones, Cassie asked, "What will we do with a fourteen-year-old mother with a newborn?"

"I know a couple in Utah who might consider adopting a baby—my niece and husband," Ruby offered. "Would you like me to approach them when the time is right?"

"No need…yet," Cassie stammered. "Let's wait until we are sure the pregnancy takes…and get a little closer to delivery."

…

THE DAY AFTER THANKSGIVING, Ruby and Cassie talked with Iris about what was going on in her body, how a baby was being formed, and what to expect over the next few months. They both hoped Iris would be forthcoming with more details, but Iris only listened before withdrawing quickly to her room once the discussion was over.

The next morning, Cassie packed a bag and drove Iris to Sarah's. Iris had watched before adding several of her books. "It will be for only a few weeks," Cassie told her, knowing that saying "a few months" may have caused Iris stress. "And I'll come see you every day I can."

Part of Ruby's plan was that Cassie would continue living at home and simply explain to people that winter was an especially busy time at the auto dealership, and that Iris had gone to stay with her Aunt Sarah for a bit. "Should it come up," Ruby said. "That way, nosy people won't know any better."

On a crisp and bright early winter day, Sarah drove the ten minutes north and over the big bridge that crossed the Snake into Madison County before turning toward the Swenson's farm along what only locals still called Moody Creek. Like many others, the creek had long since been straightened out and deepened into a canal fed by other canals—one that supplied water for the Swenson's and a handful of other farmers.

As she drove, Cassie realized how unfamiliar this area was to her, despite being so close to home. She realized she had never met many of Sarah's neighbors and only recognized a few by face or by the names Sarah mentioned. The drive clearly wasn't that far, but it was far enough to get Iris away from prying eyes and gossip—the other side of the river, a different county, a different church group, and even a different school district.

Cassie felt a wave of relief as she pulled the car through a log-framed arch with a sign declaring "Moody Creek Ranch" and drove down the long dirt road that led to a single-story, redbrick farmhouse. As she neared the house, the relief she was feeling was replaced by embarrassment over seeing her sister-in-law and lifelong friend in circumstances like this.

Of course, they still talked by phone frequently, nearly every day. And talking about Iris's situation in veiled terms had been better in many ways than visiting about them face to face—indirect and much safer. Now pulling to a stop in front of Sarah's, Cassie hesitated. She felt her face redden as Sarah emerged from the house. Cassie knew none of this was her doing, but she still felt responsible as a mother. It was hard, nonetheless.

Iris looked out the window, rocking lightly.

Cassie got out and gave Sarah a hug. Pulling back, they looked at each other as though to say, "Well, here we go."

Sarah looked through the car and waved at Iris. Iris got out, holding her stomach that was now bulging if only a little. Sarah embraced her and said, "Hi, Iris. I'm so glad to see you. It seems like it's been months and months!"

Iris pulled away, uncomfortably, and said, "Thanks, Aunt Sarah."

Sarah looked back to Cassie. "How's my old friend doing?"

Cassie smiled and said, "Old is right. Times like these make me feel old." Pausing, she added, "Older, that is."

As they walked toward the house, Cassie saw Jens standing on the porch with three mottled dogs by his side. Jens tipped his cowboy hat at Cassie and then came toward Iris and gave her squeeze from the side. The dogs followed and licked at Iris's hand till she pulled it away.

Sarah showed Iris to her room. "My sons used this when they were young, but it sits empty most of the time now." Smiling toward Iris, she said, "Except at Christmas, when everyone comes around. Even the dogs sleep outside then. Otherwise, it sits empty like this." Turning to Cassie, she said, "Lately, with all this extra space, we've begun thinking of getting a place in town—Willow Creek, that is—lot's less to take care of!"

Cassie envied the warmth of her home and the abundant evidence of so many children and grandchildren—lots of extra places to sit, a box of toys, card games and board games on a nearby bookshelf. The mention of a Christmas gathering made Cassie nervous—that Iris would be lost in a group with prying eyes and too many questions. She urgently said, "I can always pick Iris up anytime you need your space. We can spend time together at my house or Ruby's."

Off to the side, Jens was warning Iris about the nearby canal and how that was only a short distance from where it went back into the river. "I heard you like to go for walks," he said, startled when Iris brightened at the idea.

"Momma," she said, sounding happier than she had in weeks. "I can walk to the canal. Over there," she said, pointing.

Cassie reassured Jens that these were familiar places to Iris and that she was glad Iris would have somewhere to go. "Iris has always been safe around water. She goes near but never goes in."

They discussed how Iris could call home whenever she wanted. "Any time," Jens said.

"I'll try to visit every few days, Cassie said to Iris. "I've got so much to do at the dealership, you know, but this will be a good place for you to stay for a while. You take care of yourself—and the little one inside of you."

Iris patted her stomach, very unsure about what was ahead.

Cassie drove away, looking up at her rearview mirror and watching Sarah wave from the porch until she couldn't see her anymore. She felt nervously confident things would work out.

...

ONE EVENING, CASSIE WANDERED AIMLESSLY around the house straightening things. She sat on Iris's bed, reflecting on how happy Iris was as a young girl—extra smart but still a puzzle for most people—and how she had few emotions now.

Cassie walked into the hallway, lingering at the pictures hanging in wooden frames, a few with glass and most without. There was the black-and-white picture of her father Simeon with his arm around her mother and another of Eugene in the yard by the willow tree, likely taken about the time Eugene had drowned. One frame held a sketch that her mother had drawn of the family's first home in Willow Creek, over on the edge of town—a time long gone but not forgotten. There was the picture with Simeon and Erastus together along with other men standing atop the Great Feeder with water flowing beneath their feet. "Not long after we were married," she whispered, Touching each of their handwritten names along the white border below the photograph—"Founders," it declared.

There was a family photo of what she and Erastus had called their "first family"—with her children Samuel, Henry, Esther. Next to it, a photo of Erastus's parents, Will and Mary, in their eighties. She smiled at Will's full head of white hair and a matching white beard. Mary's hair had grayed about then. They had passed years earlier within a few weeks of each other—oh, how she missed them. Directly below that was a color-tinted photo of her father in front of the mercantile looking robust on the day he sold the business.

Then the picture of Tom, Erastus's brother, in his military uniform, a studio photo taken days after he returned from the Great War. Tom's first wife had passed during childbirth, so Tom enlisted and eventually became an officer—the uniform he was wearing in the photo. Tucked into the corner of the frame was a snapshot of Tom and his second wife Ellen.

Then there was the one with her and Erastus on their twenty-fifth wedding anniversary—just the two of them. It had to be her favorite of all. In the picture, she was very pregnant—it was taken only weeks before she delivered Iris. She remembered trying to button her best dress over her swollen midsection that day in preparation for their anniversary celebration. At the time, Erastus had shaved his beard but left a long, droopy mustache. She smiled at how scratchy it had been to kiss and remembered insisting after a few days that if he ever wanted to kiss her again, the mustache had to go too. She could still hear him protesting that she had been kissing the same face with a beard all along, why the absence of the beard meant shaving the mustache too. He had shown up a few days later to breakfast clean shaven—and remained clean shaven thereafter. Cassie remembered Ruby snapping the picture as they were preparing to go to dinner in nearby Idaho Falls that night. She couldn't remember why Ruby had been there.

She reflected fondly on that evening. It had been a wonderful celebration—Erastus had driven her by the site where they had honeymooned years earlier—it was no longer a log structure but had been replaced by a newer building now called the Riverside Motel. She recalled him asking for another picture there by the waterfall, but she had not felt well and begged to go home. Now, she wished she had agreed to take the picture. She missed him so much.

That night, the dozen or so photos took her to a place she hadn't thought about for some time. "You have a story," Cassie whispered. "A story that needs to be told." She hurried to the kitchen and opened the drawer that had a little of everything in it—keys, reading glasses, postage stamps, screwdrivers, and knobs from drawers that had come off somewhere along the way. She searched for a pencil, figuring that would work better than a pen. With a pencil in hand, she went to the front room and found her journal. Returning to the kitchen, Cassie turned on the light over the table and took a seat. The clock on the wall showed eight o'clock.

She flipped through pages she had written over the years and realized her name was missing altogether. On the plain liner page at the front, she wrote an introduction.

My name is Catherine Esther Rapp Walker, but everyone calls me Cassie. My story is one of blessings that have come through trial and tribulation…

Words came easily. Cassie turned occasionally to read pages she had written earlier, adding notes here and there in the margins. Where she needed more space, she inserted blank sheets of paper between the bound pages of her journal to add details of incidents as she remembered them.

When she looked up, both hands on the clock pointed straight up. She shook her writing hand and flexed her fingers, deciding to call it a night.

Chapter 33

Every Beating Heart

Emma tossed and turned for what seemed like hours, thoughts of the day raced through her mind. There was her book with so much left to do. And the conversation with Topher from the evening before. She felt her book was coming along just fine, a reassuring thought. And Topher wasn't like anyone else. At least those she had dated. Still, she worried that she had no time for a relationship. Or did she?

She scolded herself and began making a list. Toper was taller than others she had dated. He was sure of who he was. He was willing to be vulnerable. And strong. And very good looking. She put her pen down, smiling.

Somewhere around three o'clock, she must have dozed off, her thoughts washed away by a dream.

New girl!" said someone. From the edge, Lacy said, "Leave her alone," and then was gone. Everyone looked around for a pole. Someone shouted, "There's a streetlight." Emma felt herself being lifted while several boys—all taller and older, more like men—pushed her against the pole. She was surrounded by plastic wrap and looked down to see a small crystal obelisk.

Feeling immediate panic, she shouted, "I don't need you people!" Then they were suddenly gone.

A police car drove past along the front street and then slowed, backed up, and came around. The red and blue lights flickered around her. The stars above began flickering the same red and blue. "You okay, miss?" It was Topher asking the question. He walked around to help her father out of the passenger side. He seemed so feeble and old. Together, the two men began to cut away the plastic wrap.

At nine o'clock the next morning, Emma's phone buzzed on the nightstand and woke her with a start. Pushing back the puffy down comforter, she rubbed her eyes and picked up her phone. It was a text from Topher.

Thanks for listening to me last night. Sorry to go on about my life.

Smiling, Emma remembered the warm touch from his strong hand. Her heart wanted more, but her head told her not to rush into things. She reread the text and decided there was no harm in being friendly.

No problem. And thanks for bowling. I'm so bad!

She hit send and saw the time. 9:02! She was already behind! She had originally planned to rise at six to enjoy the sunrise through her windows, something she was growing to love. She had imagined a few thousand words by this point and instantly felt disappointed at the lost time.

Emma took a breath. Willow Creek felt like it was growing around her—more familiar places and people. She actually had friends, and now knew what a water tower did. Should she spend more time writing or connecting? She recalled her therapist's advice to be more human, not so driven by checklists and goals, at least not all the time.

Checking her phone to confirm that it really was Saturday, Emma relaxed a bit. She decided to take the day off and have some fun—and immediately wondered if Topher was available. She looked back at the string of texts from Topher. He really was a nice guy. Wondering what else she could say, she felt relief when another text from him came in.

By the way, Sarge said yes to the key and also the DNA test. Maybe around noon?

Until that moment, she hadn't thought at all about that part of their conversation from the night before. She wondered what he meant by "key" before piecing it all together.

To the evidence room?

Topher texted back almost immediately. Then a pause before he texted again.

If today's not good, Monday would be easy?

Emma really wanted to see Topher again—and the pendant. Her head was telling her to take a break from texting and consider her next text carefully. "Darn inner advisor," she said aloud, rethinking her own advice. She felt their relationship becoming very personal. And with her writing moving along so well, along with a very happy agent and publisher, Emma felt she was on track. Plus, she only had five more chapters to go. Her heart told her to have some fun. But with less than two weeks left in Willow Creek, something else told her to stay focused.

Emma felt her inner advisor doing a Jekyll and Hyde dance—to go to the evidence room with Topher, which had a lot of benefits, or to hunker down and write another chapter. "Potato, potawhto," she said, laughing at her attempt at humor but feeling like a hypocrite for not sticking to her goals.

She opened her laptop and began scrolling through her notes from the day before, stopping at "connect authentically." Wasn't that what was happening here? Meeting Topher and now having spent time with him, even putting her head on his shoulder the night before, made her heart beat a little faster. "Plus, I just dreamt about the guy!" she blurted out.

Emma reached for her pendant and twirled it in her fingers. It seemed so much shinier than the one in the evidence room, probably a little smaller and lighter, too. She ran her finger along the serpentine line down one side, questioning whether the other one wasn't straight after all. She had to see the one at the police station, unsure how similar they really were. Something told her they belonged together.

She realized she still hadn't responded to Topher's text. She picked up her phone and put it down again. Wherever things with him might go, she wasn't sure she was ready for a relationship, or had time for that matter.

Emma remembered the box. What would she learn from seeing the box again? In a flash, Emma knew it was an adventure she was already on. It felt right. And this adventure now seemed to include Topher, for the time being at least.

Deciding to take a shower, Emma reflected on her dream wondering why the stuck feeling—she thought writing about it days earlier may have taken her there. Perhaps it was more like a police lineup, with what had to represent most of the men from her life standing before her. Were they all bad guys? As she rinsed her hair, a thought came to her. She knew she had never really let them in. It hadn't really been the right timing. Clearly, Topher bringing her father to her rescue signaled yet another thing. Why was she pairing them, even subconsciously? Wiping steam away from the mirror, Emma caught her reflection and said, "Emma Rose, I think you don't have a man problem—you don't want to be tied down." Reminding herself of how she generally faced problems like this, she whispered, "Lean into it" and then more loudly, "Lean into it!"

After a quick breakfast, Emma spent the rest of the morning writing. At eleven, she looked again at Topher's text from earlier and immediately thought of a trust fall, something she had never done in her life—the one where you fall backward straight as a board into other people's arms. In so many corporate retreats she had attended while at Pilot and even going all the way back to team building exercises in business school, Emma had always been one of the catchers but never a faller. She had always dodged the challenge somehow.

Now, holding her phone again and wondering what to say back to Topher, she felt like she was standing there, arms folded over her chest, and preparing to fall backwards for what felt like the first time in her life.

The thought hit her: maybe there are no rules here. No lists to follow. No specific ways to show up. After all, he was a nice guy. And handsome. Someone with direction in his life. Still, something in her pushed in a different direction. She mechanically typed a response and hit send.

Monday works.

She felt instant disappointment. What was she thinking…or not thinking? Regretting that she wouldn't see him until Monday, and wondering what she would do the rest of the day, Emma felt a wave of confusion.

The words "call Lacy" came to mind. She hadn't spoken to Lacy in days but agreed this time with her inner advisor. Lacy answered right away, and Emma told her about the conversation from the night before.

Lacy reacted with, "Stanford Law School…are you kidding me?"

"Lacy, I can't afford to get distracted by smolder eyes and cologne," Emma argued weakly, hoping Lacy wouldn't disagree but rather tell her to rush out and find Topher that very minute. "I've got to stay focused. I have a huge advance to earn back—got to get this book finished!" She could hear Lacy sigh on the other end.

"You're right, Emma. But I'm pretty sure you are forcing your own hand here, like a few hours off doing something relaxing will compromise everything. You're the most focused person I know, so what's the harm in hanging out with that cop for a few hours?"

Emma weakly protested, "I'm sort of all or nothing—you know that about me, right? Probably best to stay focused on my book." Secretly, she wanted Lacy to disagree.

Lacy shifted the conversation to a speech Emma was scheduled to fly out for the following week—a trip to Denver that she had initially expected to be complicated by a stop-over in Salt Lake City only to find out there was a direct flight from Idaho Falls. She could get there and back in the same day.

Before hanging up, Lacy asked, "Do you really want my advice?"

"Sure."

Lacy laughed. "Not convincing. Why did you call me in the first place?"

Emma sighed. "Lacy, my dearest friend and astute partner, I want nothing more than your advice. My inner advisor is short-circuiting right now, doing a Jekyl and Hyde dance. So, please, advise away!"

"Here you go then." Lacy cleared her throat and said, "Be one of the blondes that really do have more fun. Stop overthinking things. Be a little impractical—maybe even a lot. Take a few hours for yourself and this cop guy. You might learn something valuable."

Emma sat for a while. Thinking about Topher, she promised herself not to get carried away. But she really did want to see him again. She checked the time and saw it was almost noon. Looking at his last text, giving him only a few minutes to find a key didn't seem fair. How should she respond? Emma could hear Lacy saying, "Hang out with that cop" over and over.

She walked to the front window overlooking Main Street and watched as cars pulled in and out of the slots along the way with patrons going from one store to the next. The scene was bustling. She could see people down the street going into Carter's.

"Impractical," she said out loud, repeating Lacy's word. "It's Saturday. I'm going to be impractical if only for today." Emma reached for her phone and quickly typed out a text.

Sorry for the slow reply. Can we do the box on Monday? I'm going for a run in a bit. Want to join me?

She stared at the text before finally pressing send.

Almost immediately, she got a response.

Sure! Noon-thirty?

"Noon-thirty? Who says that?" Emma looked around the room expecting an alien to step out from behind the drapes. She mumbled to herself, "Go with it, Emma" and typed.

Sounds good. Meet where?

Excited, she stared at her phone and waited. The dots on the screen kept refreshing, indicating that Topher was typing something.

Out front of your place. Scones after?

Emma smiled.

...

EMMA AND TOPHER JOGGED NORTH PAST A PARK and through town. Topher talked the entire way.

"There's my elementary school. Miss Marriott was the toughest teacher. I stayed in elementary school until after seventh grade because the junior high had burned down," he said, pointing back behind them. "With it gone, there was nowhere for us to go."

Emma huffed as she asked, "Do you always talk when you run?"

"Always...even when I'm by myself." He laughed. "Those are some of the most interesting conversations of my life. Except, after a few miles I realize I've been having the same old conversation forever." He began laughing uncontrollably and had to stop. "Stop...stop!" His laughter was infectious.

Emma pulled up by him. "What is so funny?"

Topher was wiping at his eyes and still laughing. "I'm just...I'm just..."

Emma began to laugh as she waited for something funny to come out.

Topher finally got control of himself and said in a half laugh, "I just had the thought that my conversations with myself may really not be that interesting."

She smiled. "You are pretty interesting—but then we've barely started running. Let's give it a couple more miles and double-check that before we form any permanent conclusions. Let's go!" She took off running again and shouted, "Beat you to the corner?"

Along the way, they talked about Emma's upbringing in a little area south of Salt Lake City called Holladay and then her MBA from Columbia.

Topher shared how when he was younger, he had loved riding through town on his Schwinn bicycle, one with a banana seat—a completely retro bike his brother Kyle had salvaged from a shed on the empty lot across from his parent's house. "I wish I still had it for summers like this—my favorite time of year. Warm but not too hot with a lot of summer fun ahead!"

Emma wasn't sure when she changed the subject to Jake and the Paris proposal, but she told him the entire story.

"The guy sounds like a romantic."

Emma agreed. "Wrong place, wrong time, though…and wrong guy," she said between breaths.

"Boy, he missed out," Topher said, looking her way. "Ever think of taking him back…," he began saying before recognizing he was working against himself.

As they jogged into the countryside, Topher pointed to an old, abandoned house and said it reminded him of one across from his parent's place where he and his friends had formed a neighborhood club. "We called it the Double-Bubble club, and the rite of passage was to eat a saltine cracker and whistle 'Yankee Doodle' as fast as possible." He had to stop again from laughing. "I was spitting out pieces of cracker and trying to work up some saliva to overcome the dryness in my mouth, an impossible task."

It reminded Emma of her recent DNA test, and she started to say, "I had that experience recently and anticipate having it again with Sarge and the DNA test." After another hundred feet, she asked, "What happened then?"

Topher said, "I guess it's not really that interesting, but since you asked, ultimately, I was able to whistle a few bars. We all got in the club, though. We took turns being presidents and vice presidents—often changing roles during our meetings. The club had no other real purpose." He laughed. "We met twice."

Emma teased. "So far? Job keeping you too busy?"

Sensing her sarcasm, he teased back with, "Right. Actually, our third club meeting is scheduled for next week." They ran further before Topher said, "Okay, race to the bridge?" pointing ahead.

"You're on," Emma said, speeding up.

Stopping on the bridge, Topher said, "We're over the Dry Bed again."

Emma looked down at the water. "It's way calmer here," she said, remembering the volume of frothy water at the beginning.

"Yeah, by this point, most of the water has been diverted into canals and ditches. There are still several canals that come off downstream from here, but most of the valley slopes off that way," Topher said, pointing.

"Fascinating," Emma said, looking up at him.

…

ON THE WAY HOME, they stopped at the park they had passed earlier where Topher promised they would find a drinking fountain. They walked past an old piece of military equipment. "Gun turret from an aircraft carrier. World War II," he said, guessing at her question. "You can only imagine how many games you can play with an oversized machine gun," he said.

Emma laughed and then took a long drink from the fountain. Rising, she wiped her mouth and said, "You're wrong. I've listened to you now for what, three miles. I don't find you boring at all."

Topher gave her a puzzled look as he bent to drink.

"Unless you have a completely different conversation when you're running alone," Emma reminded him.

Topher laughed while drinking and looked up, choking. "All about the Double-Bubble club—top secret until today."

They laughed together. As they walked around the park, Topher pointed to a variety of things. The playground. The firepit. The ballfield. The clumps of lilac bushes along the far side. The pavilion.

At the playground, Emma found a swing and Topher took the one next to her. "So, Emma Rose, when do you head back to Manhattan?"

Feeling the moment, Emma wanted to say, "Never" but knew that wasn't her reality. She reflected on all she had going on and finally blurted out, "My ticket says a week from tomorrow."

Topher took it in stride and said, "Okay. Well, good, you'll be here for the rodeo next weekend. Nothing says 'Willow Creek' quite like our rodeo, parade, and carnival."

Emma interrupted. "…So, 'rodeo,' as in where men ride on bucking broncos and rope cows and things like that?" The first and last rodeo Emma had seen was the Days of '47 indoor rodeo in the Salt Palace as a kid. Her father had convinced her that the horses, bulls, and cattle were much better off than most of the men who rode or wrestled them—many of whom walked off the dirt limping or holding a shoulder. She couldn't watch any of it until a young woman barrel-racer had been announced— paraplegic from a terrible car accident but had recovered enough to race. She went on to cut beautifully with her horse around all three barrels before heading to the finish line—and winning! Just the thought brought back a memory of good seats and eating popcorn with her father.

Emma said, "I didn't know they still did things like that."

"Yup. It's America's sport," he said. "But here, it's more than a rodeo. There's the parade on Saturday morning and the carnival and farmer's market all day." Nearly gushing, he continued, "The Tilt-a-Whirl is still my favorite, although it took me a couple of hours after I rode on that last time to get my head to stop spinning and get my appetite back."

Emma kicked at the bark chips on the ground each time she swung passed center.

Topher asked, "Want to go with me?"

"To the rodeo?"

He grinned as he asked, "To all of it?"

She took his extended hand and smiled. "Ok, all of it."

He pulled her hand making their swings collide.

…

THEY SHARED SCONES AT CARTER'S. After Connie took their order, she looked back at Emma as she walked past with a grin and wink, making a big okay sign with her finger and thumb.

Emma blushed and smiled. Topher looked over his shoulder and asked, "See someone you know?"

"I'm sort of a regular around here."

They took turns playing songs on the mini-juke box at their table. "Favorite songs only," Topher said. "From whatever selection is here."

Emma chose "Take Me On" by Aha—and sang along quietly but really wanted to belt the song out. Topher chose "Live Like You Were Dying" by Tim McGraw and could barely keep his singing to a whisper. The two men at the counter kept looking over as though the place had been invaded by teenagers until Emma finally gave them a scowl.

"Those two guys are always here—I see them every time I come."

"Which means…you're always here too then, right?"

"Topher! Okay, you're probably right. When I first got here, I wanted to try the burger place but haven't yet."

Topher was shaking his head. "Not the burger place. Worst two cases of food poisoning I ever had."

She laughed. "You went back?"

Topher said, "Okay, not by choice. And no, I didn't go back. I went there once, and then Sarge had them cater a training lunch we did. I was down for twenty-four hours both times. Wicked freight train going through…" He slapped his hand down hard enough on the table to make the two guys look over.

Emma held up her hand. "Okay, got the picture. In here," she said, tapping her head like she had seen Topher do. Connie delivered a plate of country-friend chicken they had agreed to share.

"This looks delicious, Connie," Topher said.

"Anything else, you two?" Connie smiled again at Emma and drew her shoulders up. Topher shook his head. Connie leaned toward him and said, "This one here, she's a keeper. I wouldn't throw her back, and…" before adding in a threatening tone, "…if I hear you even so much as…"

Emma smiled up at Connie. "Connie, we're good. Thanks for everything."

As Connie walked away, Topher said, "Wow, I forgot this place puts so much on the plate. Glad we're sharing."

After lunch, Topher asked if they could walk together for a minute. "Really? Like this?" Emma pointed to her running clothes. "Haven't you seen enough 'sweaty' people for one afternoon?" She watched him shake his head and said, "Okay, all right."

They waved to Quentin across the street who shouted "hello!" as they walked past the Regal Theater and a small doctor's office.

"That's only the second time I've seen Quentin since last winter," Emma said. "And in exactly the same spot!"

"He's a fixture around here. Always coming and going. You're sure to see him again." Topher smiled. "And probably exactly in that spot."

Topher took Emma's hand as they continued down the block. She loved how warm his hand felt gripping hers, soft enough but clearly a hand that got to work when needed. He stopped her in front of an older single-story Art Deco-style building flanked by a small grocery store on the other side and pointed to a sign above the door that read "Library."

"This is still my favorite place in town. It's only open on weekdays until five and then sometimes on Saturdays. As a kid, I bet I read every book here. Tom Swift. Tom Clancy, Tom Sawyer. Louis L'Amour. Harry Potter. All the good authors named Tom, and then some," he said with a wink.

Emma dropped his hand and protested. "Tom Sawyer was not an author! In fact, only two from your list were." She tried to look offended.

"What!" he exclaimed, feigning surprise.

The look of victory on her face drew him in.

"I better do some research," Topher said. "Friends?" He held up his little finger.

Emma took his with her own and said, "Friends."

They both held on, and Emma felt him pulling her closer. She quietly protested with, "Here? In full daylight?"

"It's not like we're kids anymore," Topher said, leaning forward and giving her a kiss. He pulled her even closer and kissed her again.

Warm all over, Emma kissed him back.

Late Sunday evening, Topher texted Emma that he was incredibly sick—and no, it wasn't food poisoning, he reassured her.

In bed all day. I'm out for meeting at police HQ tomorrow. Don't want you to get what I have.

Emma texted back.

So sorry.

After a few minutes, Topher replied.

I think I've come down with a serious case of 'like'—possibly fatal.

His text included emojis of two people running.

Emma could only describe how she felt as cringing joy—totally delighted and equally filled with dread all at the same time. Topher was a far better kisser than she had expected. He was kind. He was strong. He was courteous. He was smart. He was more than cute enough. She fit perfectly under his chin when they hugged.

But sitting at her laptop, she felt conflicted over the fact that she was preparing to leave town for good at the end of the week. She didn't regret her few hours of fun but was instantly nauseous over the idea of saying good-bye to someone that already checked so many boxes for her.

After reviewing every heart emoji, she felt unsure what to say without saying too much and finally texted back a smiley face with a heart over one eye. She added one more thing.

Get better for the rodeo!

Moments later, Topher texted back.

Thx! Sarge can meet you tomorrow morning at any time to see the box. I will miss seeing you.

...

THE NEXT MORNING, SERGEANT SMITH unlocked the evidence room for Emma. Out of the blue, he offered, "Topher's a good officer. Smarter than the rest of us put together. We're fortunate to have him here. He's got so much potential. Hope he sticks around."

Emma said she agreed, a bit surprised he was telling her this.

Sarge added, "Topher mentioned you might be willing to give me a saliva sample for a DNA test he wants me to run."

"Happy to," Emma said.

"Great," Sarge said. "Before you leave, I'll get you a tube. The results will take about a week."

Emma walked to the table with the box and its contents still spread out before asking, "May I?"

"Of course, Miss Rose. Of course. It's one of those cold cases where we're ninety-nine percent sure no crime occurred but one where we are required to keep items on file until things like DNA reports come back and we can confirm the case doesn't tie to anything else in our database."

Emma slipped her own necklace off and eagerly picked up the half heart from the table. They were closer to the same size than she expected. She put the serpentine edge of hers against the other, exclaiming, "They might have the same line! How can this…be? Look!" She held the two parts up to the light together for the sergeant to see. Looking closely at the older half, she could see buildup along the edge.

"Sarge, do you have a brush or something I can work this edge with?"

"One sec," he said, turning to leave the room. "Just don't touch anything else in this room." He waved his arm at the shelves with boxes and boxes. "I can trust you, right?"

Emma nodded. As she picked at the edge of the heart with her fingernail, a few fragments broke away.

Sergeant Smith returned with a set of picks that looked like ones Emma had seen her dentist use. "These should do the trick," he said. "I'm no jeweler, but what's stuck on that heart is something we should be able to remove. If not, we can take it to Stan—our forensics guy."

Emma picked at the build-up where the two hearts should connect, breaking away much of the crusty material, revealing a more serpentine edge along the older half than she had expected. When she put the two halves together again in her palm, the fit was nearly perfect.

Emma buffed the surface of the heart with a soft metal brush and found it was mostly coated with hardened dirt, which gave way easily and began to reveal some detail she hadn't previously noticed, including engraved letters.

The Meadowlark

"You're a regular detective, Miss Rose."

Emma smiled, having forgotten there was anyone else in the room. "I think I have this." She first saw a capital "R" emerge from the dirt that had accumulated over the years. Then an "I." Her own heart began to race as she put the two halves together and saw a word that she knew hadn't been seen in decades.

Emma exclaimed, "IRIS!"

It was a name she had never heard anyone in her family mention—one that instantly shifted her mindset about the heart's message.

Chapter 34

Moody Creek Ranch, 1936

Iris was kept quite comfortable at the Moody Creek Ranch. During the days, she immersed herself in reading and was introduced to new books by her aunt and uncle—Westerns by Zane Grey and Louis L'Amour and stories of the frontier by Willa Cather. She read late most nights since she was least nauseated then, sleeping well into the morning each day. Jens made his annoyance known by stomping around and clanging pans, irritated that anyone under his roof would sleep past daybreak.

"Be patient," Sarah encouraged. "She's a young girl who is going through so much, much more than you will ever experience or come close to understanding."

After a few days where Iris spent until well after noon in the bathroom, Jens finally admitted, "You're right. I'll do better."

Most afternoons, Iris would put on a jacket and walk down to a tiny creek she had found, one that didn't have a name. She followed it down the borrow pit along the dirt road, which eventually led to a boat ramp on the Henry's Fork of the Snake River. Iris had seen the Henry's Fork on maps and knew it joined with the South Fork a mile or so downstream. On her first trip there, Iris tossed sticks in, imagining them floating downstream to the confluence and on past where the Dry Bed's waters emptied back into the Snake River. Jens regularly asked about her walks, mostly interested in her safety. They talked about little else, but Iris would talk about the river, reporting each day on ducks landing in the river or muskrat she had seen.

As winter took over, Iris began reporting on how far the ice had grown out from the banks each day. "It's heaviest among the willows and shore plants," she said. "I tested it with my foot."

Jens jumped up protectively. "Iris, you can't do that. The ice can break and—"

"—I only tapped it with my foot. I was standing on a rock only partially submerged." She showed Jens how she had balanced herself while testing the ice.

One February morning, Iris asked Sarah if there might be another coat available. "This one is ill-fitting," Iris said, showing how the coat wouldn't close over her stomach any longer.

"I have the perfect coat," Sarah said. Without a second thought, she reached for one of Jens's coats on a hook by the back door. "Here you go," Sarah said, preparing herself for a protest from Jens.

Jens looked up and smiled. "Iris, you keep yourself warm, darling."

Sarah walked over and gave Jens a kiss right on top of his bald head.

...

IN FEBRUARY, CASSIE LEARNED that the two Bonham children were involved in a terrible accident. On a foggy night, the newspaper said, a dark red Chevy Coupe hit a freight train as it rumbled through town. More than one hundred cars long, the engineer said he hadn't felt a thing but finally heard the sound of screeching metal and stopped the train to explore. Only then had he found the two young people, both lifeless until the girl came to.

The paper said Harlin Bonham had been killed instantly. Sally had been knocked unconscious but since released from the hospital with only a few cuts. The two were driving back from Labelle. The iced-over roads and thick fog coming off the river that night greatly reduced visibility, making the black hulk of the train hard to see at the unmarked crossing.

Cassie attended the funeral and reported back to Iris. "I talked with Sally after the funeral," she said, assuming that would be of interest to Iris. "Terrible thing about Harlin, though—with his whole life ahead of him. But Sally is doing fine."

Iris brightened uncharacteristically before turning back to her book, rocking forward and back as she began to read.

For Iris's fifteenth birthday, Cassie enlisted Ruby and Sarah to surprise Iris late one afternoon with a cake and fifteen lit candles. Jens was instructed to hang a paper donkey on the living room wall.

When Iris returned from her usual walk, she began to say, "My Momma's car is in the driveway…" and was shocked when the women and Jens yelled, "Surprise!"

Confused at first, Iris looked around before spotting the cake on the kitchen counter along with the paper donkey hanging on the wall.

The group chimed in with "Happy birthday!" Cassie hurried to light the candles, waving Iris over to blow them out.

Jens stopped her, saying, "I believe it's customary to make a wish before you blow out the candles."

Ruby urged, "Make a wish! But don't tell us!" Everyone laughed.

Iris looked around, unsure what to do, holding her protruding midsection.

Cassie said, "It can be any silly old thing. Do you a wish?"

Iris nodded.

…

THE APPLE BLOSSOMS THAT SPRING were unusually full, their fragrance filling the air. A killing frost had hit the area the same time the year before and reduced the apple harvest by half. Those with orchards prayed for warmer weather to stick around.

In the middle of May, Cassie arranged to pick Ruby up on her way to "see *it* happen"—code for "the baby is coming." Ruby was prim as usual, her hair nicely done and bright red lipstick. As they drove, Cassie said, "Sarah says we're still a little early but close. The signs are right. Unless we guessed the wrong due date."

The two shared news they had heard and laughed as they drove across town and toward the bridges to Moody Ranch. With the weather changing, the snow had been gone for weeks. Pulling through the gate of the Moody Creek Ranch, they saw Iris walking— "more like waddling," Ruby chuckled—back and forth across the front porch and holding her protruding stomach with both hands. The sweater she wore was buttoned at the top and falling away at the sides.

As the two women approached, Iris said, "Momma, the baby is quite still right now. Is that all right?"

Cassie was pleased with Iris's engagement. Nodding as Sarah came out to greet them, she assured Iris that the time was drawing closer—perhaps even today. "Because the baby is most definitely running out of room in there," she added. The three women chuckled knowingly, each quick to share anecdotes with Iris of their own pregnancies and deliveries.

"Iris, you were still for two days—the longest two days of my life," Cassie shared before realizing how ominous that may have sounded.

Ruby drew Iris close, despite her stiffness, and guided her to a bed that Jens had set up in Sarah's front room, one with a curtain to close it off from the rest of the house. "This is where…" Ruby looked Iris and then at Sarah for support.

"Yes. We can get what we need fastest from here." Sarah motioned around the room. "Plus, the light is good in here." Motes of sunlight streamed through the large picture window.

Ruby continued. "Now, Iris. Things could take a while, but we will all be with you throughout whatever comes next. We love you so."

Iris sat calmly on the edge of the bed. Cassie smiled nervously. Having Ruby with her was reassuring. And having Sarah there was essential.

"I've been through this nearly nine hundred times. It's all recorded over there," Sarah said, pointing to a dark leather book with worn edges on the bookshelf. "A baby is a blessing," Sarah explained. "And a healthy momma is an even bigger blessing."

Iris asked if she could walk again. "I want to move around." Cassie and Ruby walked with her, first walking along the porch and then up and down the lane leading to the main road. Cassie asked Ruby about arrangements for the baby, and Ruby confirmed she had spoken again with her niece in Salt Lake City. Iris had been informed a few weeks earlier of their plan and asked again about Ruby's niece.

"She's a beautiful young woman," Ruby said. "You will like Ruth. And she has a handsome husband, Franklin."

"I don't want to know them," Iris said matter of factly.

"Well, you don't need to, but you can if you change your mind," Ruby encouraged. They had talked about all of this, how much more healing it might be for Iris to hand her baby to someone rather than have the baby simply taken away, never to be seen again. Cassie hadn't really argued but did try to explain how Iris usually had a more practical view of most situations—not having been through anything exactly like this before—but keeping things

The Meadowlark

simple and practical was likely to feel more awkward to them than it would to Iris.

Iris said, "I only want them to nurture the baby." To Cassie's point, Iris had always referred to it as "the baby" and not "my baby."

As they walked, Ruby held Iris by the arm. "Oh, Iris, dearest. The Roses are the most loving people. They have tried for years to have a baby of their own without any luck. This baby will give them greater joy than you will ever know. This is a blessing for them—no, a miracle."

Iris flinched and looked down at water pooling at her feet. "What is happening?"

...

AT TEN-THIRTY THAT NIGHT, Iris delivered a tiny baby girl with a full head of blonde hair—smaller than usual at under four pounds. The three women were encouraging. Ruby held Iris's hand while Cassie wrapped the baby in a warm towel and began cleaning it. Sarah tended to Iris.

"Oh, she is so tiny," Ruby said. "Oh, Iris, she is beautiful. Just beautiful—like her momma."

Iris winced and looked away.

Cassie whispered to Sarah that the baby seemed small for how large Iris had grown during the pregnancy just as Sarah looked up, startled. "Ladies, I think we have another baby."

Cassie hurried back, handling the swaddled and crying baby girl to Ruby. "What now? How can I help?"

Ruby said, "Oh, Iris, you must have twins."

Cassie gave Ruby a puzzled look, instantly concerned twins may alter the arrangement Ruby had made with her niece. Guessing at Cassie's look, Ruby shrugged her shoulders and turned her attention back to Iris. Ruby said, "What a miracle, you sweetheart."

"Oh, my," said Cassie, reaching over to wipe Iris's brow.

Sarah slipped out through the temporary curtain hung over the room's entrance and returned moments later with a stack of folded towels. Over her shoulder, she shouted, "Let me know when that water boils, Jens, and I'll send Ruby for it."

The three women huddled around Iris offering encouraging words. The contractions began to mount again. "It's time," Cassie and Ruby said simultaneously.

"Push," Sarah said.

"I don't want to," Iris cried. "I can't. I don't care anymore."

"Push! Iris, darling, you must push."

Another contraction came, and Iris pushed. Within minutes, she delivered a second baby—a little boy with dark hair.

Chapter 35

A Frayed Knot

That Tuesday morning, Emma landed in Denver and made her way to the convention center, working on her speech while entirely distracted by thoughts of Willow Creek, Topher, and the heart engraved with "Iris." The idea of staying in Willow Creek nagged at her but wasn't really an option.

Upon arrival, Emma learned that Sean McKilroy was speaking ahead of her, surprised to share the stage with him. With only minutes to go, she went over her checklist and worried the venue had ignored most of it. From what she could see behind the curtain, there was no sign of a table. Only Sean standing at a full-sized podium with an attached microphone—something she never wanted. There was a large screen behind him, but Lacy had warned her earlier that organizers for this event had been harder to communicate with than most. "The format for this speech might be a little different," she had warned. "Just setting your expectations."

Intending to give it her best, Emma's thoughts returned to the fact that she had less than a week in Willow Creek. Life there was beginning to feel so real—was it only Willow Creek or Topher or both? Clearly getting to know Topher was only adding to her attachment to Willow Creek. He was different from her exes in nearly every way. She smiled remembering kissing Topher and that he was still home in bed sick. "Note to self," she told Lacy a few days earlier. "Full daylight in front of the city library makes you sick."

"Not your typical make-out spot," Lacy had said before being reminded that a few kisses wasn't exactly making out. "Okay." Still, Lacy had insisted, "Not a make-out, but it was more than a kiss."

Emma reached for her pendant—now a whole heart, and heavier. Sergeant Smith had let her take the old half, "for a bit. See what you come up with," he had said. She now felt a calming influence. Still, the unfamiliar complete shape raised several questions. How did her father get the IS half of the heart? Who was Iris? Was she his girlfriend, a relative, or someone else? How could she ever know?

Hearing the thunderous applause that signaled the end of Sean's speech, Emma's thoughts snapped back to the job she had to do here in Denver. Her typical pre-speech insecurities mounted—that others were better speakers, that she wasn't nearly as funny, and that she really needed to work more on her laugh lines. She talked to the guy checking her lapel microphone, asking him about his family, which made things better.

The applause for Sean continued for what seemed like minutes before he came through the curtain. Seeing Emma, he immediately gave her a big hug. "I saw you on the program but didn't know if we'd run into each other."

Emma wrung her hands. "It's so good to see you!"

Sean said encouragingly, "I always get the jitters before stepping on stage."

With little time to say much, Emma went along with the idea that her concerns were about her speech and nothing more. "I have so many questions I want to ask you. Maybe later?" she said, nodding her head toward the stage.

"Of course, of course. Obviously not now," he said. "But anytime. How long are you in town…here, I mean? Perhaps we can talk later."

"I fly back tonight," she said.

"To Manhattan?"

Emma squirmed as she said, "No. Back to Idaho."

"Idaho?"

"I've been holed up there for a few weeks working on my book. In a little town called Willow Creek. It's been a very productive escape for me."

"Great way to live, Emma! You always do whatever it takes to get focused. You have your priorities straight!"

"Sean, you're as good to me as anyone I know." Emma looked around at the black curtains separating her from the waiting audience. She could hear the emcee introducing her and knew she had only a few more seconds.

"I do need some advice, Sean," she said. "Later…?"

The emcee announced, "Welcome, Emma Rose!"

Sean gestured and mouthed, "Call me!" as Emma pushed the button to turn on her lapel microphone before walking out to very welcoming applause. She was instantly relieved to see the stage had been completely rearranged—the podium replaced by a table with a water bottle in one corner. The entire scene was now bathed in the light blue glow the goldfish swimming in water always cast on the stage.

…

ON THE FLIGHT BACK TO WILLOW CREEK, Emma made a list of pros and cons for staying in Willow Creek before deleting the entire thing. The speech had gone as well as any, and she was reminded of her "priorities," as Sean had put it. She knew she had to go home, eventually. Darn commitments! Willow Creek had been delightful and all, but Sean's brief words had reminded her that it had served its purpose—to focus her on writing a book. Now only inches from the finish line, she really must get back to Manhattan and back to work.

After nodding off briefly, she once more reflected on how much she had enjoyed Willow Creek, smiling at so many new memories. With only a few more days left in town, she committed to enjoy her remaining time and do her best to keep emotions tidy before returning to New York.

Emma began walking through just how she could tell Topher "thanks for everything" and leave it at that, feeling things were already more complicated than had been only a few days earlier. She could not resolve the script in her mind. At thirty thousand feet, she ran through dozens of versions. The rational, cold version included wondering why she even had to thank him. Hadn't they only hung out a few times and kissed once? He was an adult, right? Couldn't "good-bye" be adequate? Keep in touch, perhaps, as friends? It all felt so flat, contradicting something her inner advisor was beginning to count on.

Emma reminded herself not to go analytical. "You had a long day," she sighed, shifting to get comfortable and smiling at all that had happened since Topher had pulled her over in his police cruiser that day on the bridge. "Trust your inner advisor," she whispered as she closed her eyes.

Something told her this adventure was far from over.

It was after midnight when Emma walked into her apartment, exhausted from a long day. When she turned on the lights, she found a very large shopping bag tied with a bow sitting on the kitchen table. She wondered who could have put it there. Richard maybe?

A heart-shaped card on top said, "Emma." Her mouth wrinkled as she concluded it couldn't be from Richard. She opened the card and read, "I hear you have a whole heart now! Here's a little surprise." It was signed, "Topher." She smiled and concluded he must have talked to Sergeant Smith.

She undid the bow and found a straw cowboy hat sitting on top of a pair of dark brown boots. The boots reminded her of some Gramps had given her as a little girl—ones with a square toe. Beneath those was a pair of Wrangler jeans and a shirt with tiny flowers and pearly snaps. She half-expected to find a holster and six-shooter at the bottom but instead saw another note.

Forgetting how tired she was, Emma put the cowboy hat on and sat at the table smiling.

Hi Emma,

I'll take a risk here that all this cowboy garb will come across as too much, but come Saturday, you'll find that it is exactly what you need. I cheered for you all day today—in my heart—especially from two to three when your speech was. (I literally went to the Dry Bed and cheered. I took a fishing pole so no one would think I was totally crazy.) Finally feeling better.

I know you get in late, but wanna meet me at Carter's for breakfast at 9:00 a.m. tomorrow? I'll probably be sleeping by the time you get home, so text me a Y or N about tomorrow. Can't wait to see you again.

Topher

P.S. If I got the sizes wrong, we can make exchanges. I hope I guessed right—remember, I'm a part-time detective...

P.P.S. Sarge told me about the whole heart. So cool! Confirms my hunch from the beginning that there's more to the box than meets the eye. I'm pretty sure you're connected to all this somehow. The DNA test may tell us more.

Emma held the note to her chest, her thoughts racing from a long day. Why Topher? And why now?

For some reason, Emma could imagine Lacy saying, "Get the job done you went there to do and move on. You can always go back later on vacation." She knew it would be something super practical like that, but then she could hear Lacy also saying, "Lightning never strikes the same place twice. Go with it while you can!"

Emma picked up her phone and called Lacy to be sure.

Groaning, Lacy protested, "Emma, it's almost three a.m.!" Then paused. "What's wrong?"

Emma began to cry. "I have no idea why I'm crying. Really." She sobbed for a minute or so and then said, "And I know exactly what you'll say, but I called because I needed to hear you say it."

Lacy said, "Say what?"

"Is it real? Is what I'm experiencing here reality at all?"

"In Willow Creek?"

Emma sobbed. "Yes…here…in Willow Creek." Her sobbing sounded more like wailing, and she worked to quiet herself.

"You really like it there, don't you?"

"Sort of. I mean, there are scones…" Her sobbing mixed with laughter and then escalated for a few minutes. Collecting herself, she finally said, "And the people—Richard and Connie…" More sobbing. After a minute, she said, "Obviously, I'm being hormonal. I have no idea why I'm feeling this way."

Lacy asked, "It's that Topher guy, isn't it?"

Emma bit her lip to avoid saying anything, not knowing where her emotions would take her.

"I knew it, Emma!" Lacy sounded too excited, too happy for Emma at that hour.

Emma sniffled and began to say, "Yes…" but couldn't finish the word before sobbing again. "He is so…" She looked at the clock and saw that it was already well after midnight.

"You there?"

"Sorry, Lacy. Give me a second." Emma got herself a glass of water. "Okay, whew!" Emma said, fanning her face to dry her tears.

Lacy asked, "I know you, Emma. Want to know how I see it?"

Emma said tentatively, "Well…it's why I called… I need to know how you see it…but I'm not totally sure I actually want to know how you see it."

"Well, since you woke me up from an incredible dream where I was paddle boarding in the Bahamas with a very tan and muscley guy, I'm going to tell you."

"Okay?" Emma waited for it.

After what seemed like a full minute, Lacy said, "Take advantage of the moment."

"What?"

"You only live once—you're always preparing for the future, so why not live in the present for a bit."

Emma sat quietly, mulling over Lacy's words. Smiling, she finally said, "It's not what I expected you to say."

Lacy retorted with, "I know you have a book contract and a super-amazing partner and best friend who helps run our super-amazing business. I've been thinking a lot about this—and you probably have seen me flip-flop on your situation there in what sounds like the cutest little town in the world. But I think Willow Creek has changed you."

Emma waited.

Lacy explained. "For the better, that is. You sound like you finally have something everyone wants. You talk about Willow Creek like you actually belong there. Think about it for even a pico-second. You have something we all dream about. Sure, I know Eric at the bagel shop on my corner and Molly my personal shopper. But after Taylor and I broke up, I wondered forever if I'd ever have anything close to that again—even though it felt like a junior high relationship, I have to confess."

Emma laughed. "So, you're finally willing to admit that you and Taylor had a thing going after all?" Her crying stopped as she imagined Lacy sitting cross-legged on her bed with a nightstand lamp on.

"No…well…okay! But that's hardly the point!" Lacy continued. "Anyway, I was rambling. Back to you, I might feel differently about all this in the morning once I'm less cranky about being awakened in the middle of the night, but I think you should do some 'and' thinking here." She paused, letting Emma think about what she was saying.

"And?"

"Run with whatever it is you have there. *And* still finish your book. *And* still be a successful businesswoman. You have possibilities, Emma," she said with emphasis, "possibilities that most people only dream about or watch on the Hallmark channel." Pausing, Lacy added, "It doesn't have to be an 'or.' You may not have to trade what you have there for what you have here, or vice-versa."

Emma sighed. She was surprised by Lacy's middle-of-the-night clarity.

"Oh, and one more thing, Emma. You still have the heart thing to figure out. Think of it, you have a place that feels like home, someone to love, and a mystery to solve! What else could you want?"

"It's so new, so unfamiliar but familiar all at the same time, so welcoming. I thought I had things figured out. And now I'm wearing a cowboy hat and have a bag full of cowboy clothes," Emma said, laughing through her tears.

Lacy asked, "Cowboy clothes? Emma, what have you done!"

Emma told her about Topher's gift and the rodeo plans. She read Topher's note to her and wondered out loud whether she should meet him the next morning for breakfast or not. Lacy listened and commented occasionally. Finally, at one-thirty, Emma apologized one last time for the late-night call.

"You definitely owe me," Lacy concluded before hanging up.

Emma reflected on her writing effort and knew without a doubt that she was on track to finish her book. "*And* spend time with Topher," she said aloud. "*And* enjoy a few more days in Willow Creek." With the items in the box and a pendant that now had two parts, there was still more she needed to learn.

As Emma brushed her teeth, she smiled at her reflection in the mirror. Still wearing the cowboy hat. More excited to see Topher than ever before. He was a complete bonus in all of this and possibly the factor messing most with her emotions—in the best way possible! She had no idea how things would play out from here.

Before going to sleep, she texted him back.

Y

Chapter 36

County Line, 1936

On the day the twins were born, Cassie asked Ruby if she would drive into town on an errand for her. Cassie had planned to give Iris a small bracelet to help her remember her baby, but that no longer seemed adequate now there were twins. Cassie hoped Ruby could find something more fitting considering the two babies wouldn't be hers for much longer. "Or yours," Ruby reminded her. "You're a grandmother, Cassie. Enjoy this moment while you can."

"Oh, hopefully there will be more but just later, under better circumstances—and once Iris is much older."

As Iris slept on and off, Cassie held the babies when she could—changing them and feeding them alternately with the tiniest bottles Cassie had ever seen. She worried over them—which despite their size and early delivery appeared to be thriving. The little girl was the sleepiest, and Cassie had to offer a knuckle to wake her up and get her sucking before slipping in the bottle.

Iris didn't take much notice. Whenever awake, she laid on her side looking out the front window, shifting to get comfortable and rarely glancing toward the crib Sarah had put up for the babies. Cassie asked a few times if Iris wanted to hold the babies, imagining it might be good for her to at least know them a little, but Iris remained steadfastly focused on whatever she was thinking.

Ruby returned later that afternoon with what she called "the perfect memento." Ruby held up a chain with a heart pendant hanging from it. As Cassie held it, she saw "IRIS" engraved on it.

Ruby was pleased with the result. "Farr's had it and Ron was able to engrave it while I waited. It comes apart," Ruby said, showing how the heart could be divided. "And it fits back together."

"It's perfect."

Cassie gave the necklace to Iris that evening. "It has two parts," Cassie said, showing her how it came apart. "Just like your two babies."

Iris liked that it was shaped like a heart. She put it around her neck, pulling it apart and snapping it back together before going back to bed.

...

TWO DAYS LATER, Ruby informed Cassie and Sarah earlier in the day that her niece and husband were on their way from Salt Lake City and would likely be there the next morning—and they were pleased with the arrival of twins, especially a girl and a boy, and had agreed to take them both, urging that it was best to keep the babies together. They had already engaged an adoption attorney and were bringing the necessary paperwork for all to sign.

Between feedings, the newborns slept peacefully in the crib. Iris still refused to hold them. Sarah had encouraged everyone not to press the matter—based on her experience with young mothers, she said.

With things settled down, Ruby left for home for a bath and change of clothes. Not much later, Cassie announced she needed to tend to some business at the car dealership and then participate in a canal company board meeting. She explained to Sarah, "Things are falling apart at the canal company—with the recent accident involving the Bonham children, Cloy has gone off his rocker and is pushing harder than ever to sell his interest. He's twisting my arm—almost physically—to get my agreement. Both Pa and Erastus always said it was a bad idea, so without anything else to go on, I'm sticking with that for now." Taking a deep breath, she added, "And you know how I feel about that man."

"I do. And I don't blame you," Sarah said.

"I'll likely be back late, probably not until after nine or so."

"You may as well go straight home at that point," Sarah proposed. "We will either all be in bed by then," she said, nodding toward Jens with a smile, "Or heading that way shortly after."

"I'll consider that." Looking in at the twins, Cassie said wistfully, "It's hard leaving those two dear ones at all right now."

Cassie pulled her shawl around her shoulders as she walked to the car, sniffling a bit and wondering if she wasn't coming down with something. She felt the temperature had dropped, looking up to see dark clouds on the horizon. All characteristic of an Idaho spring.

With everything calm for the first time in days, Sarah decided things were well enough off that she could leave the house for a bit as well and take a walk with Jens. "We're going to stretch our legs for a bit," she told Iris. "We'll be right back."

Iris lay back on the bed, happy to rest. She could hear Jens talking to Sarah about how cold it was as they got ready. "Grab a coat," he urged. "Cold front coming in. Hope we don't get a late frost," he said. "It would nip everything in the bud. Potatoes, apricots, apples, and peas. Wouldn't want the budding plants neutered—even a ten-minute dip below freezing can do real damage. And pray we don't get hail…" His voice trailed off as they went out the front door, closing the door behind them.

Iris awoke with a start, realizing she must have dozed off. One of the babies was stirring. The house was eerily quiet. She looked around the room and realized no one was home, wondering what to do about the baby. Suddenly curious, Iris sat up on her bed to get a better look, pulling a blanket around her shoulders and loose nightgown.

The little girl was cooing, waving her little hand erratically in the air. Iris could see that her hand had come loose from its swaddle. Walking to the crib, Iris leaned over to see the babies better, feeling the heart-shaped pendant swing against her chest. She poked at the little girl's hand with her own finger as though it was a foreign object. Growing more comfortable, she finally guided it carefully back under the flannel blanket. "There now," Iris said, repeating words she had heard her mother say.

The baby turned toward Iris, her dark eyes fluttering open and closed. Her arm came loose again, and she waved it in a random pattern. Iris reached to put the baby's arm back under the covers. The baby cooed lightly, and Iris thought she saw a hint of a smile.

"Do you like me?" Iris asked, reaching to pick up the baby girl. The tiny baby was almost weightless in her arms. "Oh, you are so tiny. Do you like me?" Standing there with the baby, Iris heard a sound outside and looked out the window to see the wind picking up and dark clouds coming in. A dog barked as it chased a tumbleweed across the yard. Any sign of spring had vanished.

"I'm your momma," Iris whispered, looking around to make sure no one else had heard. She explained, "I didn't want to be a momma just yet—I'm too young. I held his hand at the bonfire. He said I was his girl. That I was pretty. And then he hurt me and…never you mind." Iris felt a little relief from finally telling someone what had happened. Looking at her baby daughter, she smiled and said, "You're pretty. You're my girl. I like that now."

Smoothing the baby's hair with her hand, Iris asked, "What should we call you, sweet little one? What should we call you?" Iris cooed, resting her cheek against the little girl's soft skin. "Should we call you 'Sally?'" It was the only girl's name she could think of in the moment. Iris shook her head, and then with a smile, she said, "No, I'll call you 'Sunflower'."

The little boy began stirring as well, arching his back as he stretched. Both arms came free of the blanket, and he pressed both hands tightly against his face, his face reddening as he stretched. Iris smiled at him and then looked around wondering if she could hold both babies. Resting the little girl on the bed, she reached into the crib for the little boy. Settling him on her right arm, she then scooped the little girl up again with her left. Looking alternately at the two babies, she flipped her braids back and then rested her cheek against one and then the other, feeling a wave of happiness and wonder at the two bundles in her arms. "I did it," she announced triumphantly.

…

Lighting struck off to the north, and Iris could see the sky brighten. A storm was coming in. Moments later, thunder pealed through the valley, shaking the house and rattling the picture window where Iris stood. A light rain began to fall, making a pattering sound on the tin roof. Iris could see poofs on the roadway as the first drops hit its dusty surface.

Feeling an overwhelming need to protect her babies, Iris wasn't sure what to do next. When she heard her aunt and uncle hurry through the back door, she felt a surge of panic. She could hear them in the kitchen, knowing after a walk Jens typically took his place in an easy chair in the bedroom while Sarah worked on dinner.

Iris jumped when Sarah looked in through the curtain and saw her holding both babies.

"Oh, Iris. How sweet." Sarah walked over and tucked the blankets around the babies.

Iris pulled away, protectively.

Sitting down next to her, Sarah said, "It's okay, Iris. You can hold them. Let's make sure they stay warm. And be careful not to squish them too much. They're tiny and a bit fragile right now."

Iris began rocking with the babies.

On her way back to the kitchen, Sarah said, "Be so careful with them. Let me know when you're ready to put them back in their crib, and I'll come help you."

Lightning struck again, somewhere closer. Iris felt worried as she watched the babies sleep. Her room quickly darkened as the late evening light was swallowed by a dark cloud. The noise on the tin roof grew louder, even more staccato sounding as the rain turned to hail. Thunder pealed more frequently as the sky brightened every few seconds from lightning. Iris shuddered. Through the front window, she could see hail piling up in spots around the yard. The babies seemed okay.

When Iris remembered the people were coming the next day to pick the babies up—to take them away—she grew even more nervous at the thought. Why had she agreed to the hand-off? Kissing the little girl's forehead, Iris whispered, "Sunflower, I don't want you to go away."

Chopping sounds from the kitchen added to the clatter. Suddenly, the rain and hail let up a bit. In a moment, Iris knew she needed to act. She needed to keep her babies. "We're going home," she whispered. She spotted some tall boots in one corner of the room and slipped them over her bare feet. She put the little boy down to work the quilt around her shoulders up over her head with her free hand before picking the baby up again.

"All right, we're ready," she whispered to her sleeping twins.

The sound of the rain increased once again as more lightning lit the sky. Iris waited for the thunder, counting "one-one thousand, two-one thousand…" until it cracked and then rolled past. She peeked through the curtain and could see Sarah's shadow dancing on the far wall from the kitchen. Squeezing the babies together, she slipped out of the room and reached for the knob on the front door. Iris felt the urge to go right then. She quietly opened the front door. "I'm sorry for squishing you," she whispered as she walked into the yard as lightning lit the sky.

...

THE OVERSIZED BOOTS MADE CLOPPING SOUNDS down the dirt road that led toward the bridge. The warmth she had felt in Sarah's home was instantly replaced by a chill that got even colder at the end of the lane. Wind whipped at her the skirt of her nightgown and rain pelted the parts of her face not covered by the quilt. Her pendant felt like a cube of ice against her chest. The chill was even worse whenever she looked back at the house, so she decided to stop doing that. The boots were awkward and caused her to stumble, but she gradually got better at anticipating the drag in each step. Despite the quilt quickly soaking through, she found holding it close still seemed to keep her and the babies mostly dry.

Walking along the main road, Iris felt rain dripping into the tops of her boots. She slogged on for at least a mile, doing her best to ignore the cold and the winds whipping everything around her. Toward the first bridge back, she saw car lights bobbing high up into the trees ahead and knew someone was coming behind her. She hurried off the road into the trees to avoid being discovered.

The tree blocked most of the rain and wind. Peering out from her hiding place, she watched a truck pass, recognizing it as Jens's and frustrated that he was looking for her. "Why?" she silently protested. "Doesn't he realize I need to take care of my babies!"

The truck crossed the bridge toward town. As Iris began to emerge from her hiding place, she could see taillights turning red. She stopped, watching the truck back around and come back her way. The wind shifted, whipping rain in her face. She pushed her back up against the tree and waited for Jens to pass. His taillights disappeared down the road just as the rain stopped.

"I'll keep you safe," Iris whispered to the babies, leaving her shelter, and hurrying again into the night. Walking across the big bridge over the Snake River, she looked behind her to be sure no other cars were coming. Midway, she looked over the railing at the dark water swirling far below. Downstream, she could see clouds quickly gathering directly above the trees before breaking up and lifting away.

Iris trudged on, her legs growing numb. There was no telling how much rainwater had collected in her boots. As the clouds around her lifted, she could see stars, but the night instantly grew colder. The wind added to the chill and whipped at the quilt over Iris's head, pressing her wet nightgown against her skin.

Nearing the bridge over the Dry Bed, Iris felt the rain coming down again and huddled under a clump of trees to wait it out. A car coming toward her sped past, it tires making smacking sounds against the wet asphalt as it went by.

Iris waited for the rain let up again, but it only grew stronger. Desperate to get home, she left her shelter, the quilt snagging on a branch overhead. She tugged at it with her chin and shoulder before deciding to leave it. The baby boy began to cry. "I'm so sorry your blanket is so wet," Iris said, glad the little girl was sleeping quietly, her cheek pressing the pendant into Iris's chest. Iris began to shiver as she walked. She began to hope for another car to come by, resolving she wouldn't hide again.

As Iris walked the final blocks toward home, the rain stopped. The moon emerged from behind a cloud and lit up the wet road ahead of her. Both babies were now asleep. "I can be a good momma," she said, looking down at each. The baby boy was restless in his blanket, and the little girl wore a peaceful look on her face. Iris put her cheek against each baby's face, feeling the cold in their cheeks. "I love you with all my heart."

...

THE DOORKNOB SLIPPED in her cold hand as she worked to open the front door. Finally turning it just enough, she pushed it open with her foot. She kicked off her boots before going inside, water draining from each boot as it tipped to the side. She pushed the door closed and hurried to her bedroom for anything dry. Putting both babies down, she retrieved dry towels from the hall bathroom and then pulled away the wet, clinging blanket around the baby boy before wrapping him in a warm towel. Holding him close, she could feel him shivering against her chest, his heart beating rapidly.

Iris wiped the rain from her own face and before setting the baby boy down. Turning her attention to little Sunflower, Iris pulled away the wet blanket and saw the baby girl was listless, her lips slightly blue. Scooping the baby girl up and holding her against her own chest, Iris could feel the baby's chilled skin against her own. Little Sunflower wasn't moving at all.

"Wake up," Iris whispered. "Please wake up." Urgently, she added, "Please move!" Rocking back and forth, Iris wanted to feel how she had with the baby boy. Nothing. She began to wail as she reached for an afghan from a nearby rocking chair, wrapping the little girl in that to warm her. "You have to warm up! You have to move."

On the bed, the baby boy had drifted off to sleep, his light breath puffing at a knot of yarn on the quilt. Her pendant had come apart, the two halves knocking against each other as she rocked. Iris fumbled with one hand, trying to put it back together again before letting it go.

Peering inside the blanket, Iris had a sinking feeling. She knew the baby was gone. "You were supposed to be safer at home! You didn't make it! You didn't make it!" Iris's crying turned to a whisper. Iris rocked the bundle in her arms. "Good-bye little Sunflower," she said, looking up and wiping her tears.

Iris put the baby girl down and kicked away her nightgown. She found a dress and sweater in her closet. She found shoes. She moved quickly through the house, feeling a panic building, knowing she had failed in part and now needing to take care of matters before her mother or anyone came home.

Iris's hands trembled as she ran to the kitchen. The kitchen clock began to chime, making her even more agitated. She needed a container, a small one but still large enough to hold a few things. After frantically searching, Iris couldn't find what she imagined before remembering the tin keepsakes box on her dresser. Running back to her bedroom, she opened the box and scattered its contents. There was the bottle her mother had saved Iris's baby teeth in. And the wooden toy she had used as a baby. There was a small piece from her own baby blanket.

Needing one more thing, Iris ran to the hall closet and grabbed a pair of black handled scissors and cut away the tip of her braid. She carefully placed the items into the box, feeling the pieces of the heart pendant bumping lightly against her chest. She took the necklace off and looked at each piece. Undoing the clasp, she slipped the piece with IR inscribed on it from the chain. "Because you came first," she said, putting it in the box.

Iris covered Sunflower's lifeless body before reaching over to check the baby boy. He was warm and sleeping. That felt right to her, and she knew it was time to go. She lifted the baby girl and rearranged the towel.

"Next to Papa," she said, placing the bundle in one arm. "I'll bury you next to Papa." She hurried to the back shed for a shovel.

...

IT WASN'T UNTIL AFTER TEN TILL CASSIE RETURNED to Sarah's.

"We've been trying to call you everywhere," Sarah cried, panic-stricken. "Iris left—with the babies!"

Shocked by the news, Cassie was beside herself.

"Jens has been driving every road around—to Willow Creek and back several times looking everywhere for you and Iris, whichever of you he could find first." As she spoke, headlights came through the window and lit the room where the babies' crib now stood empty.

Jens shook the rain from his jacket as he came in. "No luck, nothing. I'm sorry, Cassie."

Sarah remembered something. "I telephoned Ruby—she's out looking too. She agreed to drive along the Dry Bed in the unlikely event Iris went there."

Cassie asked, "How long has she been gone?"

Sarah squirmed. "Well, I was making dinner last I saw her—probably three hours ago." She looked unsettled and worried.

Cassie's look revealed real panic. "You stay here, Sarah, in the event Iris returns." She reached for her purse and keys. "We have to find those babies."

As she ran to the car, Jens shouted after her. "I'll keep combing the area around here and down along the river on this side."

Cassie drove frantically toward a specific spot along the Dry Bed, the only place Iris had ever wandered on her own. She mostly worried for the babies, something she knew Iris had no experience with at all. Cassie's thoughts raced. Iris had barely acknowledged the babies so far! Why the sudden interest? That she had taken them was entirely confusing—but not entirely out of character.

As Cassie drove over the bridges back toward town, she spotted something flapping in the trees and pulled over. She drew her jacket around her neck as she ran toward it, stumbling through dead, wet weeds that drenched her legs. It was one of Sarah's quilts! Soaked completely through and stiff from the cold. Clearly, Iris had come this way.

Cassie wondered if Iris was probably taking the babies somewhere she felt was safer—from her limited experience and simple point of view. Nowhere was safer for Iris than home—she had to be going there. Cassie hurried to the car and raced toward town. Pulling into her driveway, she could see a light glowing from somewhere toward the back of the house.

Cassie hurried inside. "Iris!" she shouted as she ran down the main hall. All was quiet. The light was on in Iris's room. Cassie saw the pile of wet blankets on the bed. Iris's nightgown lay crumpled on the floor. Nothing else seemed out of place. Iris had been there. But where had she gone?

Turning to leave, Cassie heard a cry behind her and turned to see a blanket shift on the bed. Relieved to see the baby boy, she lifted every other piece of fabric searching for the baby girl but found nothing. She picked the baby boy up and hurried to the kitchen. She searched with one hand for anything she could use to feed him and found a rubber thimble. She carefully placed the little boy on the kitchen table and searched for a nail to poke a hole in the thimble's tip. The baby began crying.

Car lights flashed through the house as someone pulled into the driveway. Ruby knocked at the door and then let herself in.

"Here," Cassie said, handing Ruby the baby boy. "I know where she's gone."

"Where's the other baby? The little girl?"

"With her, I do believe. What I don't understand is why she would leave the boy." She quickly told Ruby about the quilt she had found in the trees and the wet clothes and blankets in Iris's room.

Cassie handed Ruby the temporary nipple and told her how at one point they had used one to feed baby sheep. "There's milk in the refrigerator. Perhaps you can warm it a bit." Cassie's words trailed off with worry.

"You need to get going," Ruby insisted.

Cassie drove as fast as she dared through the quiet streets of Willow Creek and toward the cemetery—the wheels of her car squealing as she turned onto Main Street. She prayed for the baby's safety as she drove, feeling foolish that she hadn't prayed in some time. "Dear God," she cried. "I'm no saint, but I'm on my knees…in my heart. I'm begging, Father…I'm begging…please protect that baby…and my daughter."

She sped across the bridge on the other side of town and past her Ruby's home, the one her father had built. A half a mile or so past town, she pulled into the cemetery just as the clouds parted and a full moon shined bright that the surrounding evergreens cast long shadows across the wet grass, dark and shining in what seemed like frost. At this late hour and with freezing temperatures, the shadows were anything but comforting.

Cassie drove toward the Walker section, her headlights catching a small figure darting behind a tree. As she parked, she saw what looked like a fresh pile of dirt next to her husband's headstone. Her hunch was confirmed by the shovel standing in the dirt to the side. Cassie turned off the car and waited.

In the moonlight, Cassie could see Iris peering out from behind the trunk of a tall evergreen. Cassie shivered as she got out of the car, pulling her shawl tightly around her shoulders. She walked toward the dirt pile, calling, "Iris, come out."

Iris came out from behind the tree, her arms empty and face streaked with mud.

Cassie moved quickly toward her daughter with her arms extended, wondering what if anything she might say. She knew most any line of questioning would be unproductive and settled on a simple question. In the kindest, calmest tone she could muster, Cassie asked, "What happened?" Pulling her trembling daughter toward her, she felt Iris's wet hair against her shoulder. "Oh, Iris," she said, taking off her shawl and putting it around Iris's shoulders. She could see one of Iris's braids had come loose.

Iris's shaking turned to sobbing. "She's only a body, Momma. I don't know how it happened. Sunflower was so sweet and happy and then got so cold. So very cold."

Cassie pulled Iris closer, shivering together, hoping they could warm each other. Peering down into the shallow hole, she saw a piece of fabric poking up through a layer of dirt at the bottom and began to say, "We should…" and then abandoned the thought. "May I?" she asked, gesturing toward the hole.

Iris nodded.

Cassie knelt down, reaching into the hole and brushing the dirt aside to reveal a towel from home. She pulled it back to have her greatest fear confirmed. Iris's name for the baby registered in Cassie's mind. "You named her Sunflower?"

"Ummm. Yes." Iris said with resolve. "She was so bright and beautiful."

"Indeed, she was."

Clouds covered the moon, and the rain began to fall again. Cassie drew Iris closer, offering a silent prayer for little Sunflower and that the baby boy with Ruby would be all right. Then, working the shovel herself, she finished filling the hole as Iris stood to the side watching.

She had no idea what time it was when they finally turned to leave.

…

UNABLE TO SLEEP AT ALL, Cassie huddled under a blanket at the kitchen table in a robe and slippers, sipping at a hot mug of milk and staring at her journal. Iris was asleep, finally. Ruby had gone home. The baby boy was asleep in a basket on the table next to Cassie.

Her hand trembled as she began to write.

It's been a complicated season. I felt the need to record these details while they were still fresh on my mind. Writing them feels like it could put Iris at risk, but my sense is not telling them would be a bigger mistake. So, here they are. My sweet Iris, barely fifteen-years old, gave birth to twins two days ago on May 21, 1936. A little boy and a little girl. We were at Sarah's. Ruby was there too.

How this all happened is a mystery—we all know how babies are conceived, but we have no idea how Iris got pregnant. Iris hasn't been willing to talk about it. My first clue should have been that she took to making herself look anything but the pretty girl she is. A few weeks after that, it became quite obvious what was going on.

The twins were to be adopted by a couple from Salt Lake City, Franklin and Ruth Rose. They arrive in the morning. That was the plan until tonight. How do I say this? I will just say it. The little girl passed away tonight. It all happened so quickly—while I was away and the others were distracted. Iris must have taken it upon herself to care for the babies, a decision I can see her making but one that I'm sure she will never talk about. Bless her heart. For some reason, she walked the entire way home well after dark and in a storm—with the babies. She was apparently outside in the elements for about three hours, long enough that the little girl likely died from exposure. After searching everywhere, I finally found Iris at the family plot at the cemetery. She was in the process of burying the little girl. I know this wasn't the right way to do things at all. Possibly illegal. But something about it worked for Iris. What with the trauma over the past few days, I guess I went along. I even helped her cover the grave.

There's no way I can tell anyone.

I don't know why, but she named the little girl Sunflower. How will we ever forget her?

The Roses will be blessed with a baby boy in the morning.

My first grandchildren...

Cassie sobbed until a profound weariness overtook her. She rested her head on her arms and tried to sleep.

Chapter 37

First Impressions

The next morning, Emma was eager to get a few paragraphs down before meeting Topher for breakfast. "Becoming is a constant process. Until recently, I thought I knew the facts of my upbringing and family heritage. That is until something was literally unearthed, a small token that points to a much different story and cast of characters than the ones I had previously known. And now it's becoming my story—one I know is part of me but still haven't heard."

She felt the words flowing.

We all have a deeply personal version of this experience. I can say in abstract that knowing those who came before us—our ancestors—what they did, how they lived and died, and the traits they passed along can be vital in understanding more about ourselves. I'm guessing that it will take a fair amount of research and luck before I will ever know the full story. Fingers crossed, right? Who doesn't have a story like this? And those figures from the past that told their stories so their posterity could know it are fortunate indeed.

My assertion? We are shaped more by the past than we realize. The past—our past—is a part of the larger unseen culture we each inherit. In some cases, it's the goldfish's pond. In others, it's wide as the ocean blue.

Emma picked up her father's copy of *A Tale of Two Cities* and found the marked page she was looking for. Turning back to her writing, she inserted, "'their hard, hard history' can teach us so much about who we are," into the paragraph she had just written.

Emma paced the floor of her apartment, reflecting on what she was learning. Sunbeams sliced through her front windows, causing her to check the date on her phone, confirming Friday would be summer solstice, the first day of summer and longest day of the year. The solstice explained why the sunlight was beginning to peek through the windows on the north side of her apartment. All facts her father had drilled into her head.

Emma felt an urge to visit the cemetery and wondered if she could convince Topher to come along for the ride after breakfast.

…

At Carter's that morning, Emma hugged Topher and thanked him for the gift basket. "And, yes, I tried everything on. Overall, pretty good detective work, Officer Jones, but you missed only slightly on that pants and hat size." She laughed, adding, "My head is not so huge despite what some people might think."

After eating, they drove to the Bob's Western Wear at the edge of town. Emma once more tried everything on. The jeans were a bit baggy but they had the right size.

Topher laughed that the cowboy hat slipped over her ears. "You're right—not such a big head after all."

Emma tried the entire outfit on for him to his great satisfaction as indicated by his whistling. She teased, "Isn't cat-calling a thing of the past?"

Topher said, "Not when you're with a beautiful cowgirl!"

The morning was still cool, even though the day promised to be warm eventually. Emma persuaded Topher to stop by her place so she could grab a jacket. Moments later, she hurried down the wooden staircase pulling on her favorite hoodie. When she got back in the truck, she leaned over and gave him a quick kiss.

"Thanks."

"Wow, Columbia!" he said, pleased. He added quickly, "I have another surprise for you."

Emma smiled expectantly.

"I'm taking the rest of the week off."

Emma squealed with delight. She slid across the bench seat to be next to Topher. "Wanna try that again?"

After a long kiss, Topher put his arm around her and said, "A man, a truck, and his girl! The perfect day!"

At the cemetery, the scent of freshly mowed grass and the whine of a weed-whacker filled the air. The groundskeeper was busy trimming around headstones, while a young boy that must have been his son was removing dead flowers from various graves and placing them in a wagon.

Walking toward her father's headstone, Topher began going over things. "So, what we know is that Steven Rose—your father—was not born a Rose. His biological parents were very likely named something else. Here he lies next to…," Topher said, bending down to read the words, "…next to Erastus Walker and Catherine Esther Rapp. Erastus passed in 1935, and Catherine in 1936." He looked again at her father's marker and said, "That would have been the year your dad was born but…Catherine couldn't be his mother—she would have been in her fifties that year—fifty-seven to be exact."

"Good math." Emma took a seat on the nearby bench. "You keep working on that. Would it be okay if I just sit here for a minute and feel the place?"

Emma smiled as Topher walked around before eventually finding his way to the groundskeeper who turned off his weed-whacker to greet Topher. Looking at the headstones around her, Emma reflected on what little she knew. Her father had wanted to be buried here. Right near his grave had long been the resting place of the bones of an infant. No one knew yet exactly how old the bones were—but soon enough. In the same shallow grave, officers had found a box with some clues as to who that infant was—including a half heart that fit with Emma's, now after however long once more forming the word "Iris."

Emma had to know who this Iris was. Excited, she searched the grave markers nearby and found the names of Samuel, Henry, and Esther—all children of Erastus and Catherine and all of whom had died within a few days of each other in 1910. Another marker with "Rapp" inscribed at the top displayed the names of Simeon Walter and Esther Ray Bingham below. These had to be Catherine's parents. An adjacent plot had the graves of William and Mary Walker, with the names of their children—Erastus William, Samuel Brigham,

Sarah Jane, and Thomas Robert—inscribed on the back. She concluded that these were Erastus's parents and family.

Standing to look at the bench, she saw "Sarah Jane Walker" inscribed along with the name of her husband, Jens Swenson. She concluded this was Erastus's sister—these people were all family!

Hurrying back, Topher had news to share. "The groundskeeper…"

Emma interrupted, too excited to listen. "I have something! This Sarah," she blurted out, pointing to the bench, "is the daughter of William and Mary. Over here," she said, walking to their headstone. "And Erastus, here," she pointed, "is their son and Sarah's brother. Erastus married Catherine, a Rapp, and here are her parents—Simeon and Esther. I'm not exactly sure how my father fits into this since Erastus died the year before my father was born and Catherine Walker died the same year he was born, and as you pointed out, Catherine would have been too old to have a baby at that age."

Waiting with his arms folded, Topher said, "Good work! I have something else for you."

"Okay."

"The groundskeeper said that these are family sections. Anyone directly related to the original pioneers of this cemetery can be buried in the family section free of charge—as long as there is room. He said you only have to pay for the burial but not the land. It's like two-hundred dollars or something to dig the hole." Topher looked at her. "Good deal, huh?"

Emma reached for her chin. "So, you're saying my dad had a free plot here, which would make him…" She walked back toward his headstone which appeared to straddle what was clearly an area with two families. "Then he would be…. that would make him either a Walker or a Rapp. What the…! I'm not a Rose at all—I mean, I am. But I'm also a Walker or a Rapp! Maybe both!" Emma jumped up and down with excitement.

Topher looked at her encouragingly.

"What an amazing connection!" Realizing something, Emma added, "We could have probably just asked Quentin at Waldrup's or the groundskeeper when we were first here and learned about the free plot. I guess you can't ask questions you don't have. I should have…"

Topher shrugged. "How could you have known?" He reached for Emma's hand and walked around the grave markers looking at more names and dates.

"They're all so different," Topher said. "I mean the headstones. Just like their lives—different as well. Wouldn't it be cool to know each of their stories?"

Emma nodded, twirling the heart pendant in her fingers. "I've got to find Iris," she said, searching among the headstones. "So, who do you think she is? And how does she fit into all of this?"

They scoured the area looking for any headstone with the name Iris inscribed on it. Topher ran back over to ask the groundskeeper about anyone named Iris buried there. He showed Topher to the cemetery directory.

When Topher returned, he shrugged and said, "Nothing."

...

ON THEIR DRIVE BACK INTO TOWN, Emma asked Topher what he thought when they first met.

"First, first meeting?" Topher shifted in his seat.

"Yes, the very first time."

"First impressions straight up or would you prefer sugar coating?"

"Straight up."

Topher turned the volume on the radio down and sat up, placing both hands on the wheel and clearing his throat. He cautiously said, "Being totally candid, I was overwhelmed. There you were—beautiful, full of confidence and swagger…"

Emma nudged him with her shoulder. "Swagger? Really? Like a pirate?"

"Okay, what's the female version of swagger?"

"I don't know…Charm? Moxy? Poise? Should I continue?"

Topher laughed and added awkwardly, "I'm going to stick with 'overwhelming' for now. You're not exactly non-intimidating, you know."

Emma had heard the word "intimidating" too many times before. She said, "So, I think 'not exactly non-intimidating' means 'totally intimidating' if you go with the double-negative, you know."

"Yeah, that's about it." Topher gave her a big smile, bumping her with his shoulder. "You asked for first impressions. Want a bit more color?"

"Yes, please," Emma said, shifting so she could look at him directly.

"Well, I did say you were beautiful and full of confidence. Perhaps you missed those first two points. Those two impressions were even more intimidating—not non-intimidating, just intimidating." Topher laughed. Looking her way, he confessed, "I instantly wanted to be around you—even back that first day at the funeral home. Well, then, I knew you were leaving so sort of just gave up at that point."

"Well, why didn't you say something then? I might have…"

Topher interrupted with a scoff. "…gone back to Manhattan anyway?"

Emma slowly said, "Probably."

"Anyway…you have turned very quickly from intimidating—into the most amazing, warm human being I think I have ever met. Daunting," he added, using one hand to draw quote marks in the air, "at first—probably because of all the swagger." He laughed.

"Daunting, hmmm." Emma felt delighted by how free he seemed to feel. She leaned into him and kissed his cheek. "Those are nice things to say about anyone."

"You're not just anyone. You're pretty special."

"Okay, this is going farther than I expected. 'Hay,'" she said, pointing at the freshly bailed hay off to the side of the road.

"Don't try to change the subject," Topher protested. "You like to have real conversations about real things. You are pretty darn approachable. Is that too much on my expanded first impressions—because I could go on?"

Emma took his arm and asked, "So, are you saying you like me?"

"Just a little," he teased, at first holding his thumb and index finger an inch apart and then extending both arms far apart. The truck swerved, and he grabbed the wheel. "Whoa," Topher said. "Better watch where I'm going."

"Yes, you should," Emma added, laying her head on his shoulder.

Topher asked, "And yours? Your first impressions?"

"You may not know this about me, but I don't really like surprises," Emma said. "And there have been non-stop surprises since I met you." She looked at Topher warily before smiling. "But unlike any other time in my life, I'm loving them all."

Topher smiled.

...

WHEN HE DROPPED HER OFF, Topher asked Emma what her plans were for dinner.

"Nothing," she said.

"Pick you up at seven?"

"Sounds great! Let's see how much writing I can get done by then," Emma said, hurrying up the stairs. Smiling about her time with Topher, she began craving an Iron Port and hurried down the front steps to the drug store, hoping Richard was still there.

"Is Richard around?"

The girl at the check stand pointed toward the back. Emma saw Richard raise his hand from behind the pharmacy counter. "Back here, Emma!"

Emma walked back and said, "Can you make me that one special drink again—Iron Port with Cherry?"

"Sure thing, give me just a moment to finish up this prescription."

Emma waited on a barstool, swinging her legs as she twisted around. She noticed dozens of historical photos hanging along the walls. Some had teams of horses with groups of men, people standing near old automobiles, men in suits and hats standing near ditches or canals, groups of women around tables filled with food in front of old houses, and one with several children all on one horse.

When Richard came over, he asked, "How's the place upstairs? Wanting to stay any longer?"

"Oh, it's been great," Emma answered. "And no, I can't. I leave Sunday. It's bittersweet," she said.

"Why 'bittersweet'?" Richard slid the finished soda across the counter in front of her with the straw pointing her direction. "Here you go." He continued working, washing and drying a few glasses and an ice cream scoop.

"It's such a charming little town," Emma said, sipping at her beverage. "Wow, this is as good as last time if not better!" She swallowed. "I'll miss the amazing people like you. I've made friends—you, Connie at Carter's, Quentin who, incidentally, I have only waved at since I got here, and others." She decided not to mention Topher. "Bitter in that regard. But I'm nearly finished writing my book—which was my original reason for coming here. That's part of the sweet. Even more sweet is that I've discovered a few wonderful things—that my dad who is now buried here might have originally had the last name of Walker or a Rapp. Now I have other puzzles to solve."

Richard put down what he was doing and looked up excitedly. "You're telling me that your father may have been a Walker?" He added, "My grandmother was a Walker. Her name was Sarah. She married a Swenson."

Emma grew excited. "You're *that* Swenson. I was sitting on your grandmother's bench at the cemetery just a few minutes ago! It's such a beautiful bench. Oh, my gosh! That means we might be…"

"Well, if your father really was a Walker, that would make you one, too. That would potentially make us cousins!" Richard reached his hand over the counter and said, "Nice to meet you, potential cousin!" Richard described his family heritage. "My grandmother had a brother named Erastus that married a Catherine Rapp. I didn't know them, but I always heard nice things about them. My parents talked about Catherine also being my great aunt." Realizing something, he added, "I guess that would make us cousins either way!"

Emma told him more about her first visit to town. She shared about the baby bones, learning her father had been adopted, and discovering the pendant from the box of clues. "I'm so messing up the chronology of all this," she said. "Oh, and this!" Emma showed him how the pendant came apart and revealed the name "Iris" when put together. She shared more about how her father gave the IS half to her and then more about police evidence she had reviewed. She ended with, "And we can't find anyone named Iris at the cemetery. Do you know of any Irises in the family line?"

"It's a beautiful name," Richard said, looking lost in thought. "Doesn't sound familiar. But I can take a look at my genealogy tonight." As Emma finished her drink, he shared one last thought. "With the two parts of the heart pendant, is there any chance your father was a twin? Hmmm. He probably would have known, right?"

...

"Mom, did Dad ever mention any Walkers or Rapps?" From the long pause, Emma could tell this caused her mother some concern. Despite the warm day, Emma pulled a blanket around.

When her mother finally spoke, she said, "Not that I recall. He only ever talked about his Rose relatives. Of course, when he told me he was adopted, we both had so many questions but no way to answer them. I guess his parents never really talked about it much, and he didn't tell me until after they were gone."

"Oh, I wish they were all still here," Emma said, adding, "so we could ask them. There's so much history here. It's becoming clear that the blonde hair and tall part of me both come from my DNA—his DNA—and point to a history that I've never known—maybe Dad never knew either. I'm dying to hear that story somehow—it all affects who I am in ways I don't even understand and know nothing about. There's got to be more out there on of this, don't you think?"

"Oh, Emma. You are so bright. But don't let this tangle draw you in to a bigger mess."

Emma reacted with, "What do you mean by that?"

"I've just heard things. I was watching a television program the other night where long-lost relatives were meeting each other for the first time—a younger man and his sister were meeting an uncle, I think it was. These people had never previously met. Everyone was crying. And the uncle was going to help them find their birth mother who was apparently his sister. And later, the young man and women looked a little scared over what they would discover next. That's all."

Puzzled by her mother's story, Emma asked, "That's all?"

"Yes, that's all I saw." Her mother warned, "Just be careful."

"Okay…" Changing the subject, Emma asked, "So, Mom, you know nothing more about Dad? Swear on a stack of bibles?"

"I know nothing else. Your dad was always a Rose to me, and I took on that name. I couldn't even tell you what other name he could have had. We are Roses, plain and simple. He didn't seem to have the need to be anything or anyone else, or I think he would have told me."

"Did he leave anything else behind from his childhood—adoption papers, legal documents, anything?"

Emma's mother thought for a moment and then said, "I'm not aware of anything at all. I've gone through everything recently." Pausing, she cried, "Oh, I miss him so much!"

Emma felt selfish that she was probing so much, asking about relationships her mother seemed to have no need to explore further. Suddenly remembering her pendant, Emma reminded her mother about the call from Topher weeks earlier and how she had finally seen the box and the other half-heart pendant. She also described how Topher had helped her on this and that, and how today they had been to the cemetery together.

Sounding distracted, her mother was clearly not connecting with Emma's urgency about all of this but rather turned her attention to Topher. "Sounds like you have something going on with this Topher fellow," her mother said.

"Sort of, but I don't what will happen after this week. I have to…go home…" Emma said, struggling to say the word home in relation to Manhattan. "…I have to go back to Manhattan on Sunday. I don't know if I can handle a long-distance relationship." Pausing, she turned back to the subject of Iris. "Oh, and Mom, remember the inscription on my pendant, the word 'Is'?"

"I had forgotten that."

"Well, I thought it meant what it said—'is'—Dad's philosophy to accept what *is*, lean into what *is*, love what *is*, and so on. I couldn't imagine it meaning anything else."

Her mother said, "Well, it is a good philosophy, you know. It's a great way to look at things as they happen. Is there more?"

Emma said, "Sure is. Well, when I saw the other half…how do I explain…I guess I should have known the other half would say something but just what it said was anyone's guess. We brushed some crusty stuff away. Guess what we found?"

Emma waited. Her mother didn't venture a guess.

"The other half had an I and an R inscribed. Put them together, and the pendant spells 'Iris.'" Half-expecting her mother to know who this Iris was, Emma paused before exclaiming, "Who would have thought it would be a name!"

Her mother remained silent for a moment before reflecting, "Your dad never mentioned an Iris….He didn't keep any secrets from me—well, except this entire Willow Creek thing. I can't think of any reason he would keep this Iris a secret. It wouldn't be an old girlfriend—hard to get half of her pendant in a box and bury it in a small Idaho town you've never visited. Unless she was a magician," she said, laughing uncomfortably.

As her mother spoke, Emma wondered if her father had known either. She wanted to mention Richard's theory that her father was a twin but felt like her mother didn't want or need to spend more time on such complicated discoveries.

…

AFTER HANGING UP WITH HER MOTHER, Emma noticed how late it was getting. She had intended to write all afternoon but hadn't expected so many distractions. Collecting her thoughts, she decided to text Topher.

Can you talk?

Sure.

Her phone rang almost immediately.

Topher said, "What's up?"

Emma confessed, "I'm so sorry, but I can't do dinner tonight. I'm running out of time—I only have a few more days here. I really need to write." She worried he would be disappointed.

"Can I bring dinner to you? I promise I won't so much as make a peep. I'll just drop it off and slip away."

"That would be so nice!" Emma said, instantly giddy. "Will you stay for a few minutes and at least eat with me?"

"I wouldn't have it any other way—unless you needed it another way."

They laughed together.

Relieved, Emma turned back to her writing. With renewed focus, she wrote over a thousand words before Topher knocked on her door at seven.

Chapter 38

Willow Creek, 1936

Falling forward into the main canal that flowed through town, Iris felt water all around her, sweeping her downstream. It wasn't deep, she knew, but it was deep enough for what she wanted. She had heard of people drowning and prayed as she floated downstream on her face that her own breath would somehow cease, that fog would take over, that her pain and non-stop thinking about Sunflower and the baby boy would grow quiet as well.

Twenty feet below the bridge, Iris bumped unexpectedly into something and looked up. Pressed against the wood planks that diverted water into ditches to the right and left, she gasped for air before putting her face again into the water. The gentle flow of the canal kept her against the wooden planks, her body bouncing slightly on the small pillow of water that had built up there.

After several failed attempts at drowning, she stood up in the waist-deep water up and trudged home wet.

It had been two weeks since she last saw her babies—one taken away by some people she didn't like and the other gone to heaven. Iris missed them desperately, more every day. The Roses had come early the morning after the storm as planned. When Ruby introduced them to Iris, she assured Iris they were good people and would take care of her baby boy and raise him to be a good person too.

Iris had liked them well enough at first. She had slipped off the necklace with the remaining half heart and given it to them. They said they would make sure the baby boy always had it. Iris had asked them to name him Steven because she liked the name. They had agreed, saying they liked that name too.

As Iris had watched Ruby explain matters, she recalled the man nodding and the woman holding Steven gently in one arm, touching Steven's face, and crying. The memory still frustrated Iris. Steven was her boy, her pretty little boy! She regretted ever agreeing to let Steven go.

She had tried to change that! She had quickly changed her mind when she saw the Rose's brake lights glaring at the stop sign near her house. She had chased after the car, unable to catch them. They were gone now. Steven was gone.

The next day, both Iris and Cassie began sniffling. "Colds from a long night out," Cassie had said. Iris's sniffles went away a few days later. Cassie's continued. Her home remedies hadn't worked, and with summer coming on, she blamed it all on hay fever or some other allergy, until the aching set in.

Ruby came over almost daily to help. At first, Iris could tell by the whispering between the two women that Ruby knew about Sunflower. Iris shuddered that anyone else knew. When Ruby said, "Little Sunflower is all right up there, she is," the pain in Iris's heart only grew, leaving her with a desperate desire to hold her babies again. Without the babies—her babies—she couldn't think of anything that made life worth living. And she couldn't imagine ever not feeling this way.

As Iris trudged back home, she looked behind her to see a trail of footprints getting less wet as she went. Once there, she changed clothes and dried her hair, glad her mother had gone to town. Iris sat at the window watching for her.

Cassie returned, carrying in armloads of groceries and matter-of-factly said, "Sarah says you have the baby blues." Iris didn't respond. "She says they will go away. Now, can you help me with these groceries?" Iris didn't budge until her mother asked again.

A few minutes later, Cassie found the pile of wet clothes on Iris's floor and exclaimed, "What in tarnation is this?" Iris didn't hear her from her seat at the front window, staring up at the clouds.

Iris walked into the kitchen. She saw her mother sipping at a tea of some type and announced, "I would like a sketchpad."

"A what?"

"A sketchpad. For drawing."

Willing to try anything to help Iris, Cassie said, "We will need you to go with me uptown to get one."

Iris agreed. Later that day, she began drawing figures of various types. Cassie looked over her shoulder and asked, "Are those wings?"

Iris nodded.

The next day, the first sketchpad was filled, and the two made a second trip. On the third trip, Cassie purchased extra sketchpads since Iris was going through them so quickly, spending hours each day drawing and yelling for her mother to go away if Cassie interrupted for anything at all—meals, bedtime, or even to visit.

A few days later, Cassie was surprised when Iris presented her with a completed picture. "That's Daddy," Iris said somberly, pointing to an elaborate figure that Cassie thought nicely resembled a man. "And this is Sunflower," she added, turning to a page showing a tiny baby asleep on its side with wings folded across its back.

"You are becoming quite the artist," Cassie said, relieved that Iris was finding something that made her happy, if only a little.

...

CASSIE'S ACHES TURNED into a cough with a more pronounced fever. She decided to see a doctor and took Iris with her. As they entered Dr. Hall's office, they were greeted with the smell of cleaning chemicals.

Waiting for the doctor, Iris walked over to a small aquarium on a table against the back wall and looked at a tiny goldfish swimming purposefully around the tank. "What is it looking for, Momma?"

Cassie worked to clear her throat, coughing before saying, "Probably food, dear." A coughing fit overtook her. Once it stopped, Cassie wiped her mouth and sat back with a look of relief.

"Doesn't it want out?"

"What do you mean?"

Iris asked, "Perhaps it wants to be somewhere besides this tank?"

"I don't think we know what fish want, Iris."

"I would," Iris said, not hearing her mother.

"It needs water to live," Cassie said. "Just like you need air. A fish wouldn't live long outside the tank…with us." Cassie looked away, working to suppress a cough.

Iris began whispering to herself, asking and answering her own questions. "Can it see me? I don't think so. Does it see the water? I don't think so."

Cassie watched her daughter, puzzled.

Dr. Hall wore a white lab coat over dark slacks, a stethoscope draped around his neck with the round part bumping against several pens in his left chest pocket. Cassie took a seat in the room and motioned for Iris to sit down. Iris began fidgeting with hands, rocking in place.

Peering over his reading glasses, Dr. Hall said in a nasally tone, "What brings you in today, Mrs. Walker?"

As Cassie started to speak, another coughing fit took over.

"I see. Say no more. Let me listen," he said, motioning for her to take a seat on the exam table to his side. He listened to points on her chest and back, asking her to breathe deeply each time, which she couldn't do without coughing.

"You have some fluid buildup. I wouldn't be surprised if this is heading toward pneumonia. We can start you on antiserum therapy, but that can take weeks. I'd like to use a new therapy called sulfa pyridine. We're seeing good success with that. Let's get you started on that right away."

They discussed how Cassie would need to spend time in bed until this cleared up. He said she could pick it up at the new drug store in town, the one Sarah's son had recently opened.

"Having a drug store close by is saving us all a lot of trips south to the Falls," he said. Dr. Hall turned his attention to Iris and reached for her hand. "And how's Iris?"

Iris pulled away and said, "Fine…I'm fine." She looked down at the floor.

Cassie so badly wanted to tell the doctor everything that had happened over the past few months—the pregnancy, delivery, death, adoption, and postpartum stress. Instead, she said, "Iris has been a little sad lately."

"I can see that. Iris, you seem distant and withdrawn—not your usual self. Has anything changed for you?"

Iris shook her head. Dr. Hall gave it a moment. Iris touched her chest and added, "My heart is broken in two. They are gone."

Cassie looked at her curiously.

Dr. Hall began forming a question but decided to leave things at that.

…

CASSIE MOSTLY STAYED IN BED as instructed and began to feel a little better. Out of the blue, Cloy Bonham reached out to discuss "incredibly urgent matters" for the Snake River Canal Company. Against her better judgement, she agreed to meet him. Since the company had no formal office, he proposed they meet at the small building located next to the Great Feeder, the one originally used as a guard house now used mostly to store tools.

"If you'll meet me there, I think you'll understand why I need to do what I need to do," Cloy said.

She had little energy to argue, so agreed.

Still an early summer day, Cassie expected a chill and so bundled up before driving the few miles there. The car made thumping sounds on the wooden structures as it crossed bridge after bridge. Pulling up to the over-sized shed, she saw Cloy standing to one side with his arms folded and remembered meeting him almost exactly in that place that winter day so many years earlier.

Expecting a confrontation, she gathered her energy before emerging from the car. A bit dizzy at first, the smell of water invigorated her and reminded her of so many visits there. The loud swishing sound of the river coming through the flood gates indicated the spring run-off was still in force.

Cassie raised her voice above the noise. "Cloy, I've been sick. Can we make this quick?"

As he approached, Cloy held up a hand and said, "Sorry to bring you all the way out here, Mrs. Walker. I thought you would want to see this." "Walk with me," he said, reaching for her arm. She pulled away. Cloy pointed to a plaque on the side of the building. "Your pa and mine—and your husband—were instrumental in making this all happen," he said, pointing to their names inscribed at the top of the plaque and then swinging his arm in front of him to point out the improvements that had been made. "I always admired your father and Erastus—both good, honest men. Some of the best men I ever knew," he said. "They, and others, did amazing things."

Cassie coughed as she waited for him to say something fishy sounding.

He added, "And I've always admired…and appreciated you."

Cassie thought, "Here we go."

Cloy went on. "And I need to make a few things right by you. I'll just say it, but I don't believe I took you as seriously as I should have. From the beginning. Even Mercy has known that—she's a good wife and counselor and has told me so many times to be better about things like this. I guess I didn't think the board of a canal company was a place for a woman. But I've grown to see you as remarkable and intelligent, and I let my own behavior all along keep us from doing business together the right way."

Unsure about Cloy's intentions, she was surprised when he added quite humbly, "And I'm truly sorry for that."

"Apology accepted," she said, still wary about what he was getting at. It seemed to her that something had changed. She couldn't be sure.

"Thank you." Cloy seemed relieved. He swung his arm in front of him and said, "I'm tired of water, Mrs. Walker. Actually, exhausted. My family has been decimated. I have no son to hand this to," he said, referring to his ownership in the company and Harlin's accident the past winter. "I suppose Sally might…" he mused before catching himself. "No doubt, you've thought about that too."

For the first time, Cassie thought about her own prospects. She had Iris, of course, but no one else.

Cloy said, "You know I've pushed to sell my interest for years to any qualified buyer—and you've all blocked that. Well, Simeon and Erastus both blocked it—wisely, I'm sure. And you, yourself, a few weeks back." He laughed. "All wise, I should say." Gathering himself, he said, "But I have a new proposal."

A tickle welled in Cassie's throat, and she doubled over coughing, holding up one hand to suggest he pause for a moment. The cough finally settled, and she wiped at her mouth. "Okay, I'm listening."

Cloy continued. "I'm sorry to keep you out here. I'll make this quick. I've spoken with all minority shareholders about an approach I think will work for everyone. Here's what I propose." He held up a hand, anticipating Cassie's resistance. "I will gift you ten percent of my preferred shares in the company, and the others will purchase the remaining forty percent. That will give you the controlling vote—sixty percent—and I can then cash out and retire to Arizona. No new outside owners. Just the board as it currently sits."

Cassie began laughing uncomfortably, and in a tone that was a little too loud for the circumstances, which triggered another coughing fit. When she finally recovered, she around before asking, "Arizona?"

Cloy smiled and shrugged his shoulders. "It's where Mercy is from, and she hasn't been warm since she left the place. It's what I've been aiming to do all along. I don't need a lot, and I'm stuck here unless I can make it work for you. I figure even a reduced share of what my father and your father started here is worth more than enough to me— if you can support what I outlined."

Cassie surprised at what felt like a workable arrangement. The odd tension she had felt in the past dissipated, replaced by a compassion she hadn't expected. "Cloy, you know how sorry we all are about your family's loss. No one should suffer like you all have." She shook her head and said, "But ten percent is too much. Would the other owners take nine points of that? And I'll buy the one percent, which will give me what I know Erastus and my father would want—to maintain control but no longer with a majority partner, I mean, *the* partner I know they trusted and respected."

Cloy smiled. "You're a better negotiator than I expected, but no need to be quite so generous. Your family deserves it, and I insist," he said with a wink. Cloy extended his hand. "If you'll say yes, my offer stands as is. I don't want to change anything about it. I have the paperwork right here," he said, patting his coat pocket. He extended his hand. "Deal?"

Cassie hesitated and then shook his hand. "Deal."

…

That night, Cassie wrote in her journal.

It's probably because of that awful night a few weeks ago, but I took very sick shortly after and have been laid up until today. Pneumonia, the doctor said. He's trying a new treatment, and I guess I expected to even feel better by now. I've never been so sick and had begun to worry what would happen to Iris if something happened to me. I try sitting outside in the sunshine when I can before it gets too hot. It's good to sit outside and hear the birds. More magpies now than ever. I listened today for the meadowlark but think they've flown out to the country.

I wrapped up business with Cloy Bonham on the canal company. I now control 60% of the primary voting shares. After all these years, we finally let him sell—Erastus and my father are likely turning in their graves. I guess that secures things for Iris. She will inherit it all. When I go, that is. She's the end of my line for now—a good line of good people. I wonder if she will ever marry or who. She troubles me so.

I'll write more later once this pneumonia clears. Just needed to get these few thoughts out of my head and onto paper.

…

A FEW MORNINGS LATER, Iris found her mother cold in bed. Iris ran down the street, screaming "Momma, Momma," over and over. Dr. Hall was home at the time and hurried out to see what was going on. He found Iris standing in the middle of the road looking around frantically.

"What's going on?"

"Momma, my momma is…" Iris broke down.

Funeral arrangements were made. People came from miles around. *The Willow Creek Sentinel* featured Cassie's obituary on the front page with the headline "Original Pioneer Dies" and subheading of "Local Author Leaves Legacy." It was followed by a lengthy tribute to Cassie's life and her contributions to the valley. Two full paragraphs described the importance of her book on pioneer irrigation.

The day of the funeral, more than fifty floral arrangements adorned the church pulpit and surrounded the casket below it. Sarah gave a touching life sketch, paying special tribute to the dozen or so original pioneers sitting in the congregation that day. She quoted from Cassie's book, "She was a woman who could sing 'for hours in rich, bubbling tones.' Cassie always had beautiful, important things to say and was truly one of our loudest songsters. The songs of her life are filled with deep sadness and great joys."

At the cemetery, Iris counted seventy-five cars around the grave site. As tradition held, a horse and carriage with the words, "A noble pioneer," draped along its side transported the casket from the cemetery's entrance to the family plot. The gloomy clouds parted briefly, and the sun peered through.

Ruby held only Iris throughout the graveside service. She whispered, "Your momma's with the angels now."

Iris said repeatedly, "An angel now."

At "Amen," the skies darkened once more, and a light rain caused everyone to scurry to their cars.

At the luncheon after, Iris walked from table to table, interrupting other discussions, puzzling everyone with, "My momma and Sunflower are angels now. Steven is not. He is in Salt Lake City." Ruby tried several times to redirect her, but Iris would pull away. She wouldn't let anyone touch her. Toward the end, Ruby was able to sit her down. Iris rocked in place, more agitated than before, flatly saying, "No one can see the angels. No one can see…"

After most were gone, Sarah and Ruby sat with Dr. Hall to discuss what to do with Iris, an orphan at fifteen. Iris sat away in the far corner rocking in place and tapping the table in front of her. Occasionally, she would look up at the ceiling and say, "Angels" before looking away.

Dr. Hall expressed his concern that Iris was becoming less stable each time he saw her. "It's best to keep people like her where things are familiar," he counseled. "At or near home, if possible."

Ruby offered to have Iris stay with her for a few days until they could come up with a more permanent arrangement. "I'm concerned," she said. When Iris began shouting, "Angels!" repeatedly, Ruby went over to comfort her and returned with Iris by her side.

Sarah said, "If it helps, she can stay with us or one of my boys—we are family, you know!"

"Let's see if she stabilizes," Dr. Hall said.

"Stabilizes? She's gone through a lot! The bab…," Ruby began to say, catching a sharp look from Sarah before correcting herself. "You say 'people like her,' but all that has happened here is no small matter."

…

THE OUTBURSTS ABOUT ANGELS ONLY INCREASED. Making it impossible for Ruby to contain her, Iris began to leave the house unexpectedly and run down the street yelling, "My momma, my babies." Sheriff Johnson was called several times to intervene.

One morning, Iris disappeared altogether. Ruby called the police. After searching the neighborhood, Sheriff Johnson sent his officers on a broader search. It wasn't until afternoon that they found Iris at the cemetery digging in the fresh dirt near her mother's grave site. Sheriff Johnson took her directly to Dr. Hall for an opinion.

Dr. Hall asked Ruby to meet them to his office. There, he expressed serious concern for Iris. "I think she's a risk to herself," he said. Sensing Ruby's exhaustion, he added, "I'm not sure what you can do—perhaps bring in some help?"

Ruby looked toward the sheriff, her confidence was waning. "I don't disagree. Perhaps I just need to lock the doors and keep a better eye on her."

The sheriff also agreed to check in every day to make sure Iris was all right.

Two nights later, Ruby woke with a start and found Iris's bed empty. It was after two in the morning, so she called the police department to help with the search. The on-duty officer found Iris right where Ruby had suggested he look—at the gravesite again. When he brought her home, he said he found her there weeping openly and digging in the dirt with bare, bleeding hands.

Sherriff Johnson came over to relieve the officer. He woke Dr. Hall and asked him to come help clean and bandage Iris's hands. The two men sat at the kitchen table while Ruby got Iris back in bed.

"Okay, she's sleeping," Ruby announced with relief as she joined them at the table.

Sheriff Johnson quietly reported, "Officer Louder said she was shouting things like 'my babies, my babies' over and over. When he told her she was too young to have babies, she slapped him. Rubbing his cheek, he said he's never seen anyone look quite that angry."

Dr. Hall said, "I'm gravely concerned, Ruby. I've been observing Iris for weeks now. It reminds me of cases I've seen like this—where people lose control and don't ever get it back."

Ruby glared at him. "She's not a case. She's Iris. You better not…"

"I'm sorry, Ruby. It's easy for me to get clinical and practical. Sophie tells me to be easier on people with my direct conclusions—a good wife's counsel. But I only know one way, so may I speak openly and honestly about what I think is going on here?"

Ruby fumed for a moment and then said, "Fine. I'll try to relax. That girl is so special to me. And she's got no one now—no one! But she is a handful." She felt a deep exhaustion from the events of the past few weeks. "What *we* do next is more than merely dealing with a temporary problem. And, yes, she's not very stable right now. She's gone through more than you will ever realize—difficulties no man could ever understand. She's lost everything and more. What can we do?"

Dr. Hall collected his thoughts before speaking. "I know this is hard on you, and I know it's probably even harder on Iris. Losing her mother may have tipped the scales, so to speak." He looked up tentatively. "So, hear me out. You say this is a temporary problem. I don't think it is. I know she's lost both parents now, but I think Iris isn't who she used to be. She's been trending this way for years. And the loss of her mother seems to have accelerated her condition quite dramatically." Measuring his next words carefully, he added, "It somewhat reminds me of a few extreme cases of baby blues that I've seen over the years—

but with some other trauma on top of it. I know it's not that, but it's hard to say otherwise. I believe she's literally gone—I mean, going—mad. Hardly a clinical word." He grimaced as he corrected himself. He looked around and added, "And I don't see her coming back."

Ruby began shaking.

Dr. Hall added, "It's hard even for me to say that. I'm sure it's even harder to hear."

Ruby struck her palm on the table. "Are you saying she's crazy?" Ruby realized she was nearly shouting and quieted herself so as not to wake Iris.

"Not exactly, well, maybe I am. What we do know is she does not manage herself well and cannot be contained. I can't see a viable solution that has Iris staying at home or with you. Or with Sarah. We don't want her becoming too dangerous to herself. Heaven forbid she become dangerous to others." Dr. Hall bowed his head.

Sheriff Johnson asked, "So, what can we do?"

...

A FEW WEEKS LATER, IRIS TOOK A NEWBORN from a house a few blocks away. Fortunately, Ruby came home from errands and found the baby boy in Iris's room. The little boy was quickly returned to his mother unharmed but very hungry. The incident forced a discussion no one wanted to have between Ruby, Dr. Hall, the sheriff, and now Sarah, Iris's only next of kin. A plan was set in motion.

Ruby woke Iris early the next day. She busied herself making Iris a light breakfast, happier from the birdsong coming through her open kitchen window. Iris dressed and came to the kitchen, one hand still bandaged from the incident at the cemetery and carrying a copy of her mother's book under one elbow. She seemed very calm as she turned for Ruby to zip her dress.

Ruby tugged at the zipper and began to cry. "You look so beautiful," she said, pulling Iris's hair back. Iris's puzzled look revealed the fact that she had no idea what the day would bring.

"Thank you," Iris eventually said, preferring the word "beautiful" over "pretty."

Ruby wiped at her eyes, asking, "How are your hands this morning?"

"Fine."

They ate scrambled eggs and wheat toast in silence. Iris held the fork awkwardly in her bandaged hand and asked for ketchup for her eggs. Ruby got that and suggested honey for the toast. She had so much she wanted to say but struggled to find the words. As they finished breakfast, Ruby began to say, "Iris, today…" and then a few minutes later started to ask, "Will you…?" Nothing felt right.

Around nine thirty, Sarah and Jens drove up. The day was warming quickly, and Ruby heard Jens commenting about dry spots in Ruby's front yard as they came up the walk before turning his attention to the quality of the house Simeon had built so many years before.

"Good morning," Ruby said artificially as she met them on the front steps, relieved finally to have others around. Iris came to her side.

Sarah drew close to Ruby and whispered, "Let's make this the best morning we can," giving Ruby a knowing look. She touched Iris on the arm and asked, "How are these doing? Healing okay?"

Iris nodded. "Yes. Healing well, Aunt Sarah."

Ruby watched, shaking her head. "I just wish…"

As planned, Sheriff Johnson arrived at ten o'clock in his black and white squad car. His crisp, tan uniform added to the formality of the occasion. Dr. Hall came straight from his office and met the group on the front lawn, still wearing his white lab coat. A few neighbors sensed something going on and came out onto their porches to watch.

Sheriff Johnson walked nervously forward and stammered as he reached up to hand Sarah a letter. "You're…next of…kin. Here's the…court order." He looked away as Sarah read over the letter. Nothing was a surprise as all of this had been previously discussed.

From her place on the steps, Sarah looked away before turning back to the sheriff. "And now what?"

"Well," Sheriff Johnson said, "It's time." He stooped to pick up the small bag Ruby had brought with her to the porch and then reached for Iris, who pulled away, looking toward Ruby.

The confused look on Iris's face evoked emotions Ruby didn't know she had—infuriated, she began walking in a circle.

Sheriff Johnson said, "Now, behave yourself, Ruby. We don't want any trouble this morning."

"But…"

The sheriff looked over at Jens for assistance. Jens and Sarah moved next to Ruby and put their arms around her. Resigning herself, Ruby asked to hug Iris. Surprisingly, Iris let Ruby hold her for a good long time before pulling away. Ruby returned to Jens and Sarah, making a gesture for Iris to go with the sheriff. Iris seemed to understand and walked with him toward the squad car.

Ruby turned away, unable to hold the tears back any longer and beginning to weep inconsolably. As Sarah held Ruby, she cried too. Jens reached up and put his arms around both women, wiping at his own eyes.

The three of them watched as Sheriff Johnson helped Iris into the passenger side of his car. Ruby was relieved Iris would be sitting next to the sheriff and not like a prisoner in the back seat.

Ruby broke free of Jens's bear hug and ran toward Iris, yelling, "You can't take her…" before catching the sheriff's stiff look. She slowed to a walk and reached through the open window for Iris's bandaged hand. She held it, stifling her own sobbing, and said softly, "We will always love you." Unsure whether she could promise anything more, Ruby added, "We will never forget you."

"Time to go," Sheriff Johnson said as he turned the key in the ignition.

Jens had come up behind Ruby and pulled her back. It took all he had to restrain her as they watched the car pull away.

Chapter 39

Second Rodeo

Even though she had always believed her blonde hair had come from Granny and Gramps Rose, Emma now knew better. Other physical traits—like her dimpled chin and height—were obviously from her father's biological line since no one in her mother's family had those.

But so many other qualities had come from her upbringing—nurture, not nature. The Roses were a hard-working, street-smart clan with amazing common sense and impeccable integrity. Even though Emma knew she couldn't fix everything like Grampa Rose had been able to, she certainly tried. That her father had been the first in his family to go to college seemed to build on that—a drive Emma had as well but from where? The questions only mounted from there.

"Maybe that's where you get your OCD," Lacy teased on a call early that Saturday morning. Joking, she added, "I mean, you're probably not clinically obsessive, but you are about as focused as anyone I know."

Emma's phone vibrated. It was a text from Topher telling her he was out front.

"Speaking of focus, gotta go," she told Lacy. "Last day in Willow Creek. Gotta make the most of it. Love you tons!"

...

THEY WALKED TO A SPOT right in front of Carter's on the curb. "Be prepared to do more than just sit at this parade." Looking at her seriously, he said, "And don't let the kids be the only ones going for the candy." Smiling, he added, "We deserve our share too!"

Emma clapped and cheered with the crowd as the first few entries in the parade came by—a float carrying Miss Willow Creek and her royalty and local politicians in fancy cars. Several pieces of saltwater taffy rolled toward Emma's feet—she tried to ignore them at first. When she saw Topher out in the middle of a group of kids collecting candy off the road, she joined him. They both returned with a handful. As more candy was thrown, Emma shouted, "Look, more candy!" She jumped again and ran into the street.

When the candy-throwing let up, Topher sat back on the curb and sighed. "You went for it with reckless abandon." Laughing, he imitated her, adding, "Bumping kids out of the way—this way and that. I'm sort of proud of you."

Toward noon, they walked to the park for the festival. The day was quickly getting hot, and the park was already crowded with food trucks and carnival rides from a full-sized Ferris wheel to the Tilt-a-Whirl that Topher said he loved. There were carnival games with barkers standing in front to draw people in.

"Hey, there's the spudnuts' cart!" he said, pulling Emma by the hand through the crowd toward a red wagon that resembled the caboose of a train.

"Did you say 'spudnuts'?"

Topher looked back at her. "Yah! They're the best doughnuts you'll ever taste." Topher ordered for them. "Six spudnuts...with powdered sugar." He asked Emma to grab extra napkins as they walked toward a bench in the shade to eat. "Tear a piece off and let the heat out," Topher encouraged.

Emma tore off a piece but found it still too hot to eat. "These are huge," she said as she waved it to cool. "What's a spud?"

"Another name for potato—we even have a candy bar called the 'Idaho Spud.'" Working on another bite of his doughnut, Topher pointed and said, "These are made with potato flour. Aren't they good?"

"Very yummy!" Emma said, suddenly remembered something. "Hey, did you ever get the DNA test results back."

Topher nearly choked on the bite he was chewing. "We did...Sarge called me late last night. Sorry I didn't tell you earlier."

"And?"

"You're related."

"That's it?"

"He said there's a full report at the station. Apparently, based on percentages, you can know just how closely related you are. Sorry I didn't mention it earlier. It totally slipped my mind. I'll have him email you a copy."

Emma looked up with a smile. "I knew it. I knew it!"

...

THEY SPENT THE AFTERNOON RIDING RIDES and playing the games. One game offered a large purple dinosaur, and Topher took it on himself to win it for Emma. He was on his fifth attempt to toss all three of the softballs into the narrow mouth of a tall silver can about five feet away.

Emma heard a voice behind her.

"Milk cans."

She turned and saw Richard from the pharmacy smiling at her and standing with a woman about his age who had lightly tinted blue-white hair holding his arm.

Emma surprised him with a hug. "Hi, cuz!"

Richard smoothed his shirt and pointed toward the cans. "My grandpa had a dozen or so of those in his barn when I was a kid. You would have liked Grandma and Grandpa Swenson. Oh, Emma Rose, meet my wife, Bonnie." He turned to Bonnie and said, "This is Emma Rose, our upstairs tenant and new cousin."

"Nice to meet you!" Bonnie smiled and said, "Richard has told me so much about you."

Emma said, "Oh, there's not much to say—but I love your beautiful hair. It's the prettiest hair I think I've seen all day."

Bonnie smiled.

Topher suddenly yelled, "Yes!" as he got the first of three balls in the can. Emma, Richard, and Bonnie watched together as he tossed the second one in as well.

Emma squealed with delight. "One more!" She gave Topher a kiss, "For good luck," she said.

Bonnie said, "I was going to introduce you, but you two apparently know each other quite well."

"Just getting started," Emma said with a smile before feeling bashful at how quickly it had come out. Topher looked back and said, "Hi, Mrs. Swenson," before focusing on his third and final toss.

Bonnie turned to Emma and said, "Christopher is a good man from good stock. The Jones family has been around here since the 30s or 40s. They're good folk. And we're glad to have him back after his time away in California. He might not remember this, but I was his second-grade teacher. He was my best student."

They all watched as Topher aimed and tossed a large white ball in an arc toward the can. The ball hit the rim and bounced straight up in the air before miraculously coming down directly into the mouth of the can.

Topher was jubilant as he took the large stuffed animal from the attendant. "I won this for you, babe!" He handed it to Emma and scooped up three other stuffed animals from the counter in front of him.

As they turned away from the game, Richard took Emma by the arm and said, "Oh, and I found not just one but two books you're going to love. I finally went through some boxes last night and found my Grandma Swenson's ledger, and it starts with a few entries in 1895 that go until about 1940. She was a midwife and always had amazing stories to tell. I still remember sitting on her lap and begging her to tell more stories. She once told me she had delivered over a thousand babies in her lifetime. Amazing!"

Emma smiled. "That is amazing. Much different career than mine!"

Bonnie interrupted. "So, Emma, we are having a big dinner on Sunday with our family—children and grandchildren. Four sons and three daughters along with all eighteen grandkids—they are all so wonderful! You should join us—and meet more of your family." Bonnie looked up at Richard, who was waiting patiently and clearly had more to say. "Five o'clock?" Richard nodded.

"That is so kind of you," Emma said reluctantly. "But I fly out tomorrow morning early—home to New York. I so wish I could come."

Bonnie wasn't satisfied. "Well, now that we're all related, you'll want to come back in August for the Walker family reunion, right? There will be quite the crowd." Bonnie talked on as though Emma would be there for sure. "Great Grandma Sarah was a Walker. And she had five sons—all Swenson's of course—but between her line and her brother Tom's, there will likely be over two hundred people coming. All cousins! It's a delightful time to reconnect—or connect," she added. "You'll be there, right?"

Emma was a bit overwhelmed by the thought of meeting hundreds of relatives. She had no idea what August would bring but said, "Sure…I really don't know…but I might be able to work something out." She remembered Richard still had a second book to tell her about.

Just then, someone came up to Bonnie and distracted her with questions about a social club meeting. Richard turned to Emma and said with a wink, "I found a second book as well. I'll bring them both by tonight. I'll knock first, but if you're not there, I'll just put them on the kitchen table if you're okay with that. You're really going to like the second book—it's Catherine's journal."

"That would be perfect," Emma said. "Thanks so much. You've been such a great help."

...

LATER THAT AFTERNOON, Topher dropped Emma off at home so she could put on her cowboy attire.

"I'll pick you back up in half an hour," he said. "I'll honk."

Emma changed and worked on her hair a bit trying to get her braid to hang below the cowboy hat without tilting it forward. She remembered Topher's statement— "You're related!"—and wondered just how. And how did Iris fit into all this?

Hearing Topher honk, Emma grabbed her hat and hurried out. As she walked down the backstairs in her Wranglers, boots, and the flowered shirt Topher had given her, he rolled the window down and looked her way.

Emma smiled and asked, "What?"

"Wow!" He hurried around to open her door, first grabbing her hand and pulling her toward him. "You look amazing."

As they drove to the rodeo grounds on the edge of town, Emma asked, "So, what's next?"

"Well, we're going to sit with my family if that's okay. They're all eager to meet you."

As they pulled in, Emma saw most of the food trucks from the park earlier that day. It seemed like the whole affair had moved this way, including the people. The grandstand was already full of people cheering at an event in the arena that involved two-wheeled chariots pulled by single trotting horses.

"Chariot racing," Topher said, guessing her question. "I think I spotted my family," he said, guiding her through the ticketing area and into the grandstand. They walked up a few rows before turning down one and toward some people smiling their way expectantly.

"Emma Rose, meet my dad and mom, Jim and Alice."

Everyone exchanged pleasantries and then Topher pointed to the rest. "You'll never remember all their names, but this is my sister Tessa and her husband, Crew, my oldest brother, Jesse, and his wife, Meg, their two boys Andrew and Joseph, my Aunt Donna and Uncle Earl, their sons…"

Emma immediately saw the family resemblance—the same strong jawline and high cheek bones. The same deep-set eyes as Topher's. She nodded and smiled at everyone. They appeared to already know who Emma was and said things like, "so nice to finally meet you," and "we've heard so much about you," their smiles making her surprisingly comfortable.

When the rodeo started, Emma watched the entire group sing the national anthem at the top of their lungs. "Family tradition," Topher told her after they all sat back down. Emma's second rodeo was underway—and so very different than she remembered.

"Timey events first," Topher said. "The best time makes for a winner. Roughie events come later—the crazy cowboys riding the roughstock—bulls and horses. Gotta make it to the buzzer to even be considered."

Failing to understand most of what he had said, Emma nodded and smiled.

During the barrel racing, Emma was grilled by Topher's sister and sister-in-law with questions about where she was from and what she was doing with her life. At one point, Tessa yelled over to Topher, "Topher, did you know Emma's an only child? I'm sure we're overwhelming her!"

By the time the calf-roping started, Topher's Aunt Donna sidled close and asked how many children Emma wanted and whether she liked their small town or not. Donna didn't exactly mention Topher's ex, Monica, but Emma sensed that was on her mind.

Watching barrel racing and calf-roping over the next thirty minutes, Topher periodically looked over at Emma, mouthing, "Are you okay?" When the announcer said bull riding would be the final event, Topher pulled her away from the group. Waving everyone off, he said, "She's mine for the rest of the evening. Enjoy your own people."

He pulled her close and said, "They're just eager and a little protective."

"Really nice people," Emma said.

Topher smiled. "You have to watch this," he said. "Have you ever seen bull riding before?"

Emma shook her head.

"It's a contest of brains, balance, and brawn," he said. "And both the bull and the rider have it all. One moment, the rider thinks he's outsmarted the bull, and the next, the bull has the rider holding on for dear life. All in eight seconds. If the rider makes it that long."

Emma worked to process what he was saying just as more clowns than she had seen all evening jogged out into the arena. The announcer came over the P.A. system. "In chute number one, we've got a huge surprise. I'm not kidding folks, but we have a for real rider named Tim McGraw riding a bull named Fu Manchu." The grandstand broke out in laughter as "Live Like You Were Dying" began playing over the speakers. As a joke, a gate opened, and a clown worked desperately to pull an old milk cow out of the chute. When the cow finally took a few steps into the open arena, the crowd erupted in cheers. The clown hopped on and sat there casually until the timer showed eight seconds and the buzzer went off. The crowd erupted a second time.

Emma looked satisfied. "I finally get it! I never knew what the line 'two point seven seconds on a bull named Fu Manchu' meant until now. I know this sounds naïve—well, is naïve—but I get it that the guy was just happy to stay on the bull for however much time, right?"

"Bingo," Topher said, touching the tip of his nose.

Emma squeezed up close and said, "Thanks for teaching this city girl the ropes!" She was delighted he hadn't teased her about it at all.

Next, the lights dimmed and fireworks went off as the announcer laid out the program. Eight riders on eight bulls. Eight seconds was the goal. Anyone who lasted even close to six was a hero. Less than that, and you were zero. "This is the only event in the world where you can go from champ to chump in one jump," the announcer explained. Emma was curious to see what he meant.

Before the first chute opened, Topher said, "Remember, these bulls are as competitive as the riders. People get all bent out of shape that there's some form of animal cruelty going on here—if there is, it's really just the bulls being cruel to us. We probably shouldn't let our kind ride their kind. You'll see." He jumped to his feet along with everyone in the stadium as the first rider was thrown from the bull but landed on his feet after four seconds. Emma waited for the people standing in front of her to sit before asking what had happened.

"Four seconds," told her all she needed to know when she could finally see what was happening in the arena again.

The second and third bulls outlasted their riders at five and seven seconds respectively. Emma gasped as she watched each rider getting tossed perilously into the dirt, landing on his side or shoulder. By the fourth bull, Emma was cheering along as she watched Jerome Stanley stay on a bull named Party Animal for the full eight seconds. The crowd cheered for Jerome, but Emma sensed their disappointment that the bull hadn't lived up to its name well.

"Too easy," Topher said, turning to Emma. "Jerome got lucky. Some bulls just have bad days." She was puzzled at how competitive he sounded over the matter.

The fifth bull dragged his rider halfway around the soft dirt arena before the rider's hand came loose, and riders number six and seven didn't make it more than two seconds each. When rider number seven didn't get up, several clowns ran around him to keep the bull away while two others rushed out with a siren blaring from one of their helmets. As the cowboy tried to get up, Emma laughed as the clowns worked to get him onto their stretcher before he shook his head at them and walked off the dirt.

With only one rider to go, the crowd was rumbling and began to clap and stomp their feet. The announcer read the moment well and had a lot to say. "Ladies and gentlemen. Let's give it up for our hometown boy and regional champion. It's the one and only, home grown, naturally talented, professional circuit bull rider—Blade Jones." The crowd went wild. Topher looked at her and announced with a big grin, "My youngest brother."

"Your what?"

The announcer continued. "Here we go with our final rider of the night, Blade Jones riding a bull named Pond Skipper. This bull's name says it all. Let's cheer this cowboy on!"

Emma finally understood Topher's earlier statement about Jerome's luck. She saw Topher look over at his parents. His mother sat with her hands over her face peeking through her fingers. His father looked proud, like this is what Topher's brother was born to do. Topher made a gesture like he was skipping a rock across a pond, and Emma looked at him quizzically. "I'll explain later—unless it's obvious from what happens next," he said.

Emma could see the rider and bull banging around inside the tight gated area. When the gate opened, the rider was wearing a helmet and vest that looked more like body armor and was covered with logos. After a very brief pause, the black and white bull snorted as it leaped directly out of the chute. On the first jump, Blade leaned back and was met by the rear of the bull from behind. The bull twisted and then jumped in an impossibly straight line across the arena. She tried shouting above the noise, "How did he get into rodeo? I thought your dad was a car dealer."

It was too noisy, but Topher gave her a puzzled look and said, "Yes, my dad is a car dealer."

Emma pulled close to his ear and said, "I have qestions for later." She felt Topher squeezing her hand as tightly as she imagined Blade was holding onto the rope around the bull. On one jump, the bull threw Blade sideways and to the other side on the next. Blade was clearly the best rider they had seen all night. With two seconds to go, the bull turned, pushing wildly against the far rail before turning back toward the middle.

When the buzzer went off, the crowd erupted and gave Blade a standing ovation. Blade rode on for two more seconds before jumping from the bull and landing on his feet. With the tension of the rope around its flanks gone, the bull turned and trotted around the arena in its own victory lap—glancing over at Blade, each looking proud and satisfied.

Emma watched as Topher's mom finally looked up from her hands and shake her head. She seemed relieved.

Topher said, "He made over a hundred thousand last year. Riding bulls. And from sponsorships. Can't see him doing it much longer, but he's the hot ticket right now."

"He's not single by chance, is he?" Emma said, thinking of Lacy.

...

WELL AFTER DARK and driving back to Emma's place, Topher said, "I want to show you something." He drove straight to the water tower and parked his truck at its base, leaving the headlights shining on the tower's legs. "You never did climb up this thing, did you?"

Emma said, "Up it? Of course not. Why would I want…" She gave him a confused look before adding, "But I have walked past it once or twice and think about it every time I turn my faucet on."

"Well, we're going up," Topher said, walking toward the leg nearest the fire station. "You sort of have to work your feet against the pole, like this," he said, demonstrating with a foot pressed against the inside of what was more of an I-beam than a pole. "A few feet of this, and you can reach the ladder."

Emma shouted up at him as he climbed. "You really think I want to do this?"

"I know you do," Topher said, looking down and sounding challenged by her hesitation.

"Well, okay." Emma could see Topher touching the bottom rung of a ladder about ten feet that rose from there to join a platform that circled the domed tank a hundred or so feet up.

Topher dropped to the ground and said, "Your turn. I'll follow."

"You're sure they want us doing this?"

"Positive. I've been doing it since junior high. Clearly, it's best not to do it in the middle of the day like my first time. That's when 'they' talk to you when you do that."

"They?"

"The police."

"Aren't you 'the police' now?"

"Yup. That's why I'm talking to you."

Emma laughed. "Yes, you are," she said under her breath as she began awkwardly working her way toward the ladder. "Helping me break the law and getting me thrown in the slammer?" Louder she said, "Is this some sort of set up?"

Topher laughed. "Sort of. I'm setting you up—figure that way you can't leave town." He waited for Emma to say anything in response before adding, "Expect to see an amazing view. That's all."

As Emma neared the ladder, she glanced back to see Topher beginning the climb. "And if I fall?"

"I'll try to catch you," Topher chuckled, "But I imagine you'll take us both out. So please don't fall."

Emma gave herself one last push before reaching the ladder and began climbing one rung at a time. "Oh, it's easy from here."

"If you're scared of heights, don't look down."

Emma looked down and said, "Ah, why did you have to say that. It's like saying, 'Don't think about a white polar bear'—I couldn't not look." Talking to herself, she said softly, "Just don't look again."

Near the top, Emma stepped onto the fenced walkway and took in the view. "Wow," she exclaimed as Topher joined her, taking her hand and guiding her to the far side.

"Behold, Willow Creek," he said with a flourish as they walked. "Join me," he invited, sitting down on the walkway and leaning back against the dome.

"Wow, it's beautiful," Emma said as she relaxed, her eyes taking in the streetlights and downtown glow of Willow Creek.

"You should see it in the daylight sometime. The ribbons of trees tracing the course of the Dry Bed and all the canals are stunning."

After reflecting for a moment, Emma said, "This little town has changed me. I'm going to miss it here." She wiped at her eyes. "I'm not sure why I'm crying. I was just thinking about Connie at Carter's—she's a dear. And Richard, my new cousin. Your family tonight was so kind to me."

Topher pulled her close. "Did you just say 'dear'? This town really has changed you!"

They laughed. Emma poked him in the side and said, "You know what I mean. It's so pretty and fun. The parade. The rodeo!" Emma looked out over the valley before speaking again. "I'm going totally native, I guess. There's this fellar that the locals have been warning me about—the law 'enforcer-slash-breaker,'" she said with an accent, making quote marks with her fingers. "A guy named Topher Jones. Officer Jones, I mean." Leaning closer and giving him a kiss, she added, "I'm hoping there's more of him in my future."

A bright spot off in the distance suddenly went dark. Emma jumped.

"Lights turning off at the rodeo grounds," Topher smiled, pulling Emma close. "Locking up for the night."

...

PACKING WAS THE MOST IMPOSSIBLE THING Emma had ever done. She was torn between what was beginning to feel like two lives—a new and vibrant one here in Willow Creek and the older, now less familiar, life she was returning to in Manhattan. She slipped the two books Richard had dropped off into her carry-on bag—the black legal-looking ledger and the other in a large manila envelope—intending to read them on the plane. Richard had scribbled on a sticky note on front of the envelope "You're part of an amazing family now, and we already love you," which didn't make leaving Willow Creek any easier.

Topher watched patiently from the couch, sitting quietly looking at his phone to stay out of her way. He knew there was no staying or changing plans—Emma had to return home.

"So sad to be leaving," she said. "I already have meetings set for Monday morning and with my publisher that afternoon." Holding the cowboy hat, she looked over at Topher and asked forlornly, "How do I fit this in my bag?"

From his spot on the couch, Topher gestured for her to hand it to him. "I'll keep it for you—for next time?" he said, raising his eyebrows to emphasize the question. Then, putting his phone aside, he looked up and asked, "Can I come see you?"

"Silly question," Emma said. "Add 'when' to the front of that or 'next week' to the end of it, and you have a question I am willing to answer."

"Okay…can I come see you next week?" Topher said innocently.

Emma reached for her phone and pushed a button before sitting next to him on the couch. With a kiss, she said, "I'm so glad you asked. Check your email. You already are."

Chapter 40

Going Home

Neither Emma nor Topher said much as they drove to the airport the next morning. As they pulled in, Emma insisted she could take things from there, but Topher jumped out of the truck and lifted her bags out of the back, placing them on the curb.

Pushing them toward her, he said, "I was born not to sit and watch. It's against my nature to let you struggle with heavy bags—or with anything, for that matter." He looked up to see tears running down Emma's cheeks. He took her in his arms.

Emma broke down. "I don't want to go," she said. "I was just beginning to feel at…"

A car honked, and Topher waved the driver on with an emphatic look.

Emma's larger roller bag began to drift down the sidewalk, and Topher turned to catch it before it rolled away. Emma stood looking at him, her arms hanging down with her head off to one side. He couldn't tell whether she was dejected or resigned to the fact that her flight was leaving in forty-five minutes.

"You okay?"

Emma sighed. Wiping the tears away and working up a smile, she said, "I haven't even seen where you live." The statement made her laugh. "And I didn't even think to say good-bye to some of the folks—Connie, Quentin, or Richard at drug store." She sighed as her resolve returned. "Next time, maybe. A girl can only hope there's a next time. Okay," she said, taking a deep breath.

Topher pulled her close and gave her a long kiss. "Next time for me won't come soon enough, Emma Rose. But I will try to take it one day at a time. I'll see you in a week—five days."

...

EMMA BOARDED THE PLANE for Salt Lake City and settled into her seat. After takeoff, she reached for Richard's books and was surprised when she pulled out *A Tale of Two Cities* instead. She whispered aloud, "I haven't seen you for a long time" and flipped through for other highlights or notes from her father, almost immediately finding a page near the end with an underlined section she hadn't previously seen.

There is a great crowd coming one day into our lives.

Her father's margin scribble looked like something else had been erased. She turned the book sideways and could barely make out what he had originally written. It read something like, "Hope to meet them."

The words brought tears to her eyes as she reflected on how many people she had met on her time in Willow Creek, all the names she had discovered at the cemetery, and how many more she had learned about but not met yet. Bonnie's invitation to dinner and the family reunion was the tip of what had sounded like a very large family iceberg. She wondered if she would ever meet them all and then pondered just how much her father must have wanted this as well. Why he hadn't still puzzled her. She knew her father would have been so happy.

As the cabin pressurized, Emma let the book slip into her lap and dozed off for a few minutes before being interrupted with an announcement that it was okay to use laptops and other computing devices. She retrieved the two books Richard had given her and found the black, legal looking book was filled with women's names, names of the fathers, and details for each of the babies she had delivered—along with length, weight, gender, and overall health. Emma intended to comb through that later for clues.

Inside the manila envelope, Emma found a thick notebook. She felt a tingle from the tip of her head to her toes as she opened to the cover sheet and read the first words written on the liner page.

My name is Catherine Esther Rapp Walker, but everyone calls me Cassie. My story is one of blessings that have come through trial and tribulation…

Emma sensed what she was about to read would change her life. She remembered Catherine's grave at the cemetery—delighted to discover that Catherine had gone by such a cute name as Cassie. She read for the next thirty minutes before the pilot announced they would be landing soon in Salt Lake City.

While waiting in Salt Lake for her connection, Emma went immediately to the gate and found an open seat so she could keep reading. She became so absorbed that she jumped when she heard "final boarding call" for her flight to New York. She reluctantly put the journal away until she was seated again on the plane.

Somewhere over the Great Lakes, Emma reached the final pages of Cassie's journal. As she read about fifteen-year-old Iris getting pregnant and that she had given birth to twins, she began to cry. She was overjoyed when she read about her Rose family—her own grandparents—willing to adopt the twins but learning that the baby girl, little Sunflower, had passed. When she read, "The Roses will be blessed with a baby boy in the morning," she blurted out, "My father!" and caught odd looks from the passengers around her. Whispering, she added, "That makes Iris my grandmother!"

She had discovered her family connection at last—a grandmother and great-grandmother she had previously never know. And that her father was a twin after all—Richard was right! She concluded that the baby bones in the cemetery must have been Sunflower's.

From what she had read, Emma began to imagine Iris, a young unmarried mother giving birth to twins. What would have motivated her to leave with them in a May storm in what sounded like the middle of the night? How had she felt losing her baby girl? How did she feel giving her baby boy up to the Roses? What happened to her from there?

She read on, confirming some of what she now knew. From what Cassie had written, Emma gathered there was no proper funeral, which explained the absence of a casket and answered the mystery that had begun her search months before. She once more heard Quentin saying over the phone on that fateful day the winter before, "There's been a discovery…an issue…with the burial." Which was responsible for her meeting Topher that same day at the funeral home. Had Topher not noticed her playing with the pendant her father had given her, nothing more may have ever been said. And the journal? Where would she be without it?

And how Iris had the strength to bury her own newborn was beyond Emma. She began to cry at the thought, unable to imagine the pain, no matter the circumstances. Emma took the necklace from around her neck and held the pendant. "Iris," she whispered. "You're the missing link.
I wish I had known you."

She had so much to tell Topher. She quickly wrote him an email. "Iris is my grandmother, my father's mother. There's so much more to their story."

...

ON TOPHER'S FIRST VISIT TO MANHATTAN the next week, they spent all of Saturday exploring the city hand-in-hand. Emma loved holding Topher's hand. She laughed that he was so drawn to the street vendors, stopping at most at first to see what they were selling.

"You clearly haven't been here before," Emma said, reminding him that most of the merchandise was fake, but he still bought a "Rolex" that stopped working the minute they got back to Emma's apartment. While Emma worked, Topher hunted for the same street vendor for three days straight, to "return it," he said.

Over lunch at a bagel shop, they discussed the police DNA report Topher had emailed her a few days earlier. It confirmed Sunflower was likely Emma's aunt based on their percentage of matching DNA.

"It's surreal to think you're one person and then find out you might be different than you think," Emma kept saying.

"Well, you're still really who you were but now just have more information to work with about your ancestors," Topher asserted. "And because of you, not your DNA, you have a lot of people back home asking about you. Come back, and I'm sure you will have plenty of invitations to Sunday dinner!"

Fidgeting with her heart pendant, Emma smiled and asked, "Do you think we will ever find what happened to Iris? I mean, no grave or death record."

Topher shrugged and reached for Emma's hand. "Well, I am a part-time detective after all, you know. There have to be more clues out there somewhere. People don't just disappear. I'll keep looking."

After Topher returned to Willow Creek, Emma talked with him every evening and texted throughout the day. Early one evening in mid-August, he called.

"I'm on my way to see the Great Feeder. I loved our first visit there. I miss you so much."

Emma reflected on that day, sort of the beginning of their relationship, when he had pulled her over in his squad car. "I wish I could be there with you," she said.

The connection got bad, and Topher said, "Sorry…too far from town…" before the line went dead.

Emma was disappointed, looking down at her phone before being startled by a knock at her door. She looked through the peephole and saw an eye looking back at her and swung the door open to find Topher standing there. Pulling him in, she covered his face with kisses, "You are such a tricky one!"

"The phone thing wasn't really cutting it for me. I had to see you again." He held her until it was time for dinner.

Walking in Central Park later that evening, Emma shared how excited her publisher's team was about her book and that "no," she had not handed them a printed manuscript wrapped with a bow after all. "I simply attached it to an email and hit send," she said. "No pomp. No meeting in the lobby. No meeting at all." Laughing, she added, "Edits are now nearly completed, and the book should go to press before the end of the year."

When they returned to her apartment, Emma showed Topher her three favorite book cover designs—one of a man staring with his nose against a blank wall, one with a school of blue fish with one orange one in the middle, and one that looked a lot like the picture he had seen hanging on Emma's office wall of a lone goldfish in a pool of blue water.

Emma asked, "Which would you pick?" They discussed the pros and cons of each. She said that Lacy had picked the person staring and her two interns wanted the school of fish.

"Easy. The single goldfish," Topher said. "It's your trademark. Your title isn't about being confused about culture or lost in a crowd. It's that there's so much you don't know about—breathing without knowing there's air, swimming without knowing there's water, and living without knowing much about what makes us who we are. I like how this fish almost looks excited about discovering all of that!"

Emma hugged him and said, "Wow, you really did read the draft! That's all I needed." She opened her laptop and quickly composed an email telling her publisher which cover she had selected. "Done. Now onto better things!"

…

THE NEXT DAY, TOPHER TOLD EMMA he had made reservations for two at Maison Pickle, her favorite. "You have talked about the energy in that place," Topher said, "so I figure it's time we try it out."

It was exactly as Emma had described. Moving through the crowded restaurant, Emma recognized a few friends and introduced Topher as her "friend from Idaho," catching a few surprised looks and comments like "Idaho?" and "Howdy, stranger!" One person even said, "Love those spuds!" Emma felt like an insider.

After dinner, Topher casually suggested they walk the three blocks to Central Park before taking the subway back to her apartment. Along the way, he confessed, "I have a surprise."

Emma smiled. "You're full of surprises. I wouldn't expect anything less from you."

Topher feigned shock. "Me? Oh, yes." He began making a list. "First there was the bones and the box…then the invitation to come to Willow Creek…"

"—Invitation to come to Willow Creek? Is that what that was? I thought it was just a creepy text from…a handsome police officer." Emma elbowed him.

"I had to get you there somehow. I figured if you fell in love with the place, you would be more likely to fall in love with me."

Emma pulled up close and said, "You got that right."

"Oh, and the cowgirl boots…showing up here the other night. Should I go on?"

Kissing him, Emma whispered, "You forgot the siren while I was running and climbing a water tower after the rodeo. Too many, I guess."

Topher smiled. "But wait. There's more."

They walked quietly hand in hand toward the park. As they entered, Emma pulled him toward the Romeo and Juliet statue by the Delacorte Theater. "They do a lot of Shakespeare here," she explained.

"I think we can do better," Topher said, pulling her close and looking at the statue to imitate the lovers' pose.

Emma said, "Oh, I love it here."

Topher said, "I know."

Emma gave him a puzzled looked. He clearly had something on his mind. He pulled her down a path into the trees and toward a small grassy area. In the middle, a blanket was spread out with a basket sitting on it. Topher walked directly toward the blanket, and she pulled at his arm saying, "Don't you see the blanket? It's probably someone else's. We shouldn't—"

"—I see it," Topher said, taking her hand and pulling her along.

When they neared the blanket, a series of tiny lights turned on, illuminating the blanket. The lights were wound around the basket, from which an instrumental version of 'Take Me On' could be heard. Emma squealed, looking around and wondering how this was all happening.

With a calm and satisfied look, Topher took her hand and guided her to one side of the blanket. "This is all for you," Topher said, sitting down and opening the basket. After poking around for a minute, Topher retrieved a small box and got on one knee. He leaned toward Emma and said, "Emma Rose, I have something I've been dying to ask you."

Emma teared up and began shaking. She started to say something, and Topher said, "Shhh. I have a few things I need to say first. You okay with that?"

Emma nodded excitedly, wiping at her eyes.

Topher continued. "I need you to know that I will do whatever it takes to make you happy. I'm willing to move here, there, or anywhere. I probably can't get much better at bowling, but I would take on a coach if that meant anything to you."

Emma laughed.

"I want to have little Emmas and Tophers with you, and I promise to always provide—even though you're doing a bang up job of that yourself. I'd even go back to practicing law if needed." He paused and then added, "I'm all in."

Emma began crying. She couldn't believe what was happening. She only wanted to hold him, kiss him.

Topher took a deep breath and opened the box, revealing a ring. "Emma Rose, will you marry me?"

Emma whispered, "Yes."

As Topher slipped the ring on her finger, Emma grabbed his hand and pulled him off balance. They laughed as they fell awkwardly onto the blanket.

...

THE NEXT DAY, EMMA'S ENTIRE STAFF surprised her when she walked into her office.

"Congratulations!" they cheered, each eventually confessing their role in what had happened the night before. Lacy showed the remote control she had used to turn on the fairy lights. And the two interns joked about how hard it was to keep curious people off the grass and away from "that basket on the blanket over there." They had worried whether Bluetooth would really reach the speaker hidden in the basket from their hideout in the trees. Emma's intern held his smartphone and said, "While we were waiting, I was listening to 80s rock and stressed I'd play the wrong song!"

Slightly embarrassed, Emma asked, "You watched it all?"

"Every bit of it," Lacy said.

After the questions of "when" and "where" were answered with, "I don't know," Emma encouraged everyone to get back to work and asked to meet with Lacy.

Once they were in Emma's office and with the door closed, Emma said, "I don't know how this is going to work out, but I've never been so committed to anything in my life. We barely know each other on one hand, but on the other hand, I feel like I've never known anyone better."

Lacy said, "I'm so happy for you, Em. We will make things work—we always have. When Topher came to town on Wednesday to put all this together, I became a Topher convert."

Surprised, Emma asked, "You mean he was here an entire day before I knew it?"

Lacy sighed and said, "I guess he needed to plan everything. The guy is amazingly resourceful. He even explored using a drone to bring the ring box over but then found out those can create hassles with the police—and you know where he stands on that! I helped him scout the place in the park yesterday at lunch—he wanted somewhere quiet in a city of eight million."

Emma said, "So that's where you went yesterday. Aha! Well, he couldn't have done this without you. And I can't do whatever comes next without you. Can you handle *that* from now until who knows when?"

Lacy nodded. "Of course."

Emma went to work. She had a conference call with her agent, Amelia Whitehouse, and the publisher's team about the manuscript and publication timing. Everyone approved of the cover choice. Advanced reader copies would be available within a week, which would be used to secure endorsements from business leaders, authors, and other notables. The book launch was slated for mid-October. Marketing efforts were underway—there were already over a thousand pre-orders for *Staring Down Culture* on Amazon.

When Emma hung up, she briefed Lacy about the plan and made a few assignments. As they wrapped up their huddle, Emma told Lacy she was meeting Topher for lunch and may not make it back to the office, "so that leaves twenty minutes to cover anything you might need," Emma said.

Lacy looked up at her slyly and said, "What do you mean, 'may not make it back to the office'?"

Emma blushed and said coyly, "We have lots to go over."

Her chat with Lacy took only five minutes, which gave Emma time to go through some emails. After hitting delete on several, she found herself practicing signing 'Emma Jones' on a scratch pad before wondering how someone her age could still get caught up in that. She got a call from an unknown New York number and decided to take it.

A few minutes later, Lacy barged into Emma's office, not realizing Emma was on a call. "I found the missing link!" Lacy exclaimed before seeing Emma point to her tiny earpiece. She whispered it again. "I found the missing link!"

Glancing at her ring, Emma smiled and said to the person on the phone, "Great! Is there any way we can revisit this in the morning?" She listened for a moment and then said, "Ten o'clock? Perfect," before hanging up. "That was *Forbes* magazine. They want to review the book. This is getting good already!"

Equally excited, Lacy looked like she had better news.

Emma took a breath and said, "Did you say missing link?"

"I found Iris!" Almost breathlessly, she went on. "You know how Cassie's journal talked about Iris having babies but then nothing more? Well, I talked with Topher about that on Wednesday and along with everything else, he made a call to the Willow Creek sheriff's office on anything that would have happened around that time with someone named Iris Walker. His assistant called me just now and said they found an old report they hadn't previously seen but that it was complicated. She promised to email me the detail as soon as she gets it cleared."

Grabbing her bag to leave, Emma said, "Amazing! Forward it to me when you get it."

...

EARLY THE NEXT MORNING, Emma looked out her office window over the Hudson. She knew Willow Creek had touched her—already more than she could possibly describe. Because of one small town, she had discovered new friends and new family. And if it hadn't been for her father's out-of-the-blue request to be buried there, she would never have met Topher. Feeling a bit swept along by new currents in her life, she was eager to discover and embrace whatever came next.

Briefly wondering about the police report that should be coming at any moment, Emma watched boats passing, startled as arms slid around her from behind.

"Good morning," Topher whispered, kissing her neck.

"What a nice surprise!"

Epilogue

Chapter 41

Walking with Angels

S*taring Down Culture* became a *New York Times* bestseller in its second week and garnered accolades from business writers and executives for months thereafter. By the following spring, Emma's book was responsible for a wildfire of dramatic conversations across social media and in company meetings everywhere. That year, Emma's speaking fees more than doubled, and within the first year of publication, her articles had shown up in *Forbes, Fortune, Inc,* and the *Wall Street Journal.*

Her publicist was working on interviews with bunches of podcasters and possibly even Oprah. Even another TEDx speech was in the works. All was going better than she could have imagined.

Emma and Topher were able to block out a week in late April to get married. They honeymooned in Cabo San Lucas at the Sandos Finisterra, enjoying the tiny shops of Los Cabos and beachcombing at Lover's Beach every morning. In early May, Emma relocated to Willow Creek—"for the summer," she said, eager to give the idea of a virtual office a try, agreeing to move into Topher's tiny home out near the golf course. Working remotely worked out so well that by July, she and Lacy decided to not renew their Manhattan office lease.

In early September of the next year and while taking a much-needed break at the Jones family cabin in Island Park, Emma bought a pregnancy test at a gas station convenience store and confirmed she was pregnant—not exactly a surprise but a new consideration against the backdrop of her busy schedule. While she and Topher had talked a few times about how they might pull off having a family, the conversation instantly became more urgent.

Topher confirmed his support. "Work as long as you want to, Emma. As long as you're healthy and it's working for you, I can fill in around the edges."

Two years almost to the day of her first visit to Willow Creek, Emma delivered a healthy baby girl, one with blonde hair and the slightest dimple on her chin.

They named her Iris Rose Jones.

…

FINALLY MAKING HER FIRST VISIT to Willow Creek that summer, Lacy drove the dirt lane that passed under an arch with "Meadowlark Ranch" written in bold letters across it. As she pulled into the circle in front of a large ranch house under construction, she spotted Emma and Topher walking around the property. Topher held a bundle in one arm and was leaning down to pick wildflowers. Emma waved and ran toward Lacy's car.

"You came!" Emma hugged Lacy.

Topher came over with the baby, and Lacy reached for the tiny bundle. "She's sleeping… gently now," he said, carefully handing her over.

Lacy peaked under the blanket covering little Iris's eyes. "Oh, my gosh, she's even cuter in real life." Lacy oohed and awed.

Topher said, "Glad you're here, Lacy. And thanks for making things work when the baby came—for everything. It's been a bit of a madhouse around here."

Lacy affirmed, "It's actually not been that hard. The whole world seems to understand that babies change everything—event organizers understand that a new momma is probably not going to be there. We offered one a video chat from the maternity ward, but she politely declined."

Emma laughed at the thought and looked up at Topher. "We're easing back into things, right Toph?"

He nodded.

"Even though I felt a bit rusty day-tripping to that marketing summit in Seattle last week, it worked out about pretty well," Emma said. "It's been a big help to have Topher's mom nearby—he's a pretty good stand-in for a mother, but she has the real touch—with five children of her own."

Lacy looked up amazed and said jealously, "You have four siblings! I wish I had even one brother or sister. It's so hard to have a party by yourself."

Emma looked at Topher and smiled. "Don't we both know that! In Topher's family, the party never ends."

Iris began to stir and one arm poked out from the swaddle as she stretched. Lacy's excitement grew as the baby took her finger. "Oh my, you are the cutest, blondest little girl I ever saw."

Baby Iris stretched lazily and opened her eyes.

"She looks just like you," Lacy said to Emma.

Topher silently protested.

"Fortunately," Lacy joked. Turning toward the house, she said, "Show me what you're doing here." They walked toward the building under construction. A few workers were busy framing up walls. Another drove a small loader that was putting dirt and rock around the concrete foundation. Lacy looked around and commented, "I love what you've done with the place! This house is immense! I could probably fit five studio apartments like mine in it. It's amazing how the water company…"

"…canal company," Emma corrected.

"Okay, how exactly did that 'canal company' thing work out?"

"You remember the part in my great-grandmother Cassie's journal about the Snake River Canal Company, right?"

Lacy nodded.

Emma continued, "Well, apparently, the way she wrapped up business with her partner that gave her controlling interest in the company was true."

Lacy looked around expectantly. "Okay…and how is that related to this?" she said, sweeping her hand in front of her across the landscape.

Emma said with a wink, "I had my incredible attorney—Topher Jones—check into it. Apparently, everyone thought Great-grandma Cassie had no heir, that is until we discovered Iris's name in the journal and connected the dots between her and my dad. Back in the day, even though someone must have known what happened to Iris, it never got recorded—at least by the canal company. That Cassie passed away unexpectedly with no further mention of Iris left them holding Cassie's shares, concluding that she was the end of the line. Nothing more was ever really explored. And until Topher contacted them, nothing had ever been done with Cassie's shares."

Topher interrupted with, "Well, except that since water is a use-it-or-lose-it kind of thing, unused water just flows on downstream if you don't open your flood gate at the right time."

Emma looked at Topher adoringly before turning back to Lacy. "Too much detail, Lacy?"

Lacy shook her head. "Keep talking."

"Topher?" Emma said, inviting him to continue.

"Well, you could argue that there wasn't really a loss or any damages. The shares simply sat idle for a few decades before being sort of absorbed into the company—which was all very clearly documented. When I informed them how the Walker line continued in my wife, Emma Rose slash Walker Jones, the board of directors reacted in a way none of us even remotely expected."

Baby Iris began to fuss so Topher reached to take her from Lacy. Watching Topher rock her baby in his arms, Emma spoke up, saying, "They immediately wanted to set things right with me—since I am my great-grandmother's only descendent. They kept referring to this as 'the way we do things around here' and 'the code of the West'—I honestly didn't expect anything from this after eighty years of people coming and going. I was happy enough just to find my family."

Lacy asked, "And?"

Emma looked around. "We ended up with hundreds of water shares but no land to irrigate. That inspired us to find some land, and we found this lot right here along the Dry Bed. Seemed like the right place for so many reasons. We still have way too many water shares—enough for a five acre swimming pool, but we're leasing those back to the canal company for now. " She drew near Topher. "I owe it all to this man—the most amazing lawyer I know. He's still checking into other things that got tied up in probate or whatever they call it—Catherine...err...Cassie Walker's land holdings and apparently her interest in an auto dealership—that I'd be willing to share," she said winking since Topher's family owned the dealership in town. "When there are no heirs left, we now know that stuff back then could just get absorbed into the system."

...

THAT AFTERNOON AT TOPHER AND EMMA'S RENTAL HOUSE, Lacy said, "Oh, I have an email to show you. You know I've been corresponding with the people at the Idaho State Hospital, and they finally came through. Getting them that next of kin proof finally opened the door to sealed records. Thank heavens for DNA tests! I'm excited to show you what they sent!"

"One second," Emma beckoned as she walked into another room to check on her baby. Coming back, she sat next to Topher on the couch and said, "She's sound asleep."

Pointing to her laptop screen, Lacy said, "Okay, here's what the hospital sent me. I've been holding on to this till I got here." She looked at Emma, reassuringly. "I wanted to be here with you when you heard it. It's kind of heavy." She began reading.

Dear Lacy,

Your request on behalf of Ms. Emma Rose for records regarding Iris Walker has been approved. In summary, our records show Iris was involuntarily committed to what was then called the Idaho State Hospital East in Blackfoot, Idaho on August 15, 1936. "Involuntarily" would most likely signify a court order.

Lacy looked up to confirming something. "The original police report hinted at that, right?"

Topher replied. "We knew from the bones and Emma's DNA test that the baby was Steven's twin," referring to Emma's father. "Cassie's journal confirmed that. But finding that box of records from 1936 in storage put us back on Iris's trail. It said something about 'committed' but little else."

Emma listened, curious about what would come next.

"Okay, if I keep reading?" Lacy continued.

Our records show that Iris lived here for nearly three years before passing away from what looks like tuberculosis on June 21, 1939. As was the unfortunate case with nearly all patients who died in the care of the hospital at the time, she was buried in an unmarked grave on the hospital grounds.

Emma gasped. "An unmarked grave? But how…?" Topher put his arm around her and pulled her close.

Lacy urged, "There's more." She continued reading.

Please find attached two items, one being a summary kept during Iris's time at the hospital.

Also, you may want to be aware of a project carried out by our local community leaders and the current hospital administrator. It was recently determined that 921 people died at the hospital between its opening in 1886 and 1960. All were buried in unmarked graves, an unfortunately common practice for state hospitals like ours across the country at the time. A community group raised money for a project last year to erect a bronze plaque with all 921 names.

Here's a link you should reference for information on the recent memorial service at the Blackfoot City Cemetery where those patients were properly remembered. A plaque was erected there, and I have confirmed Iris's name appears on said plaque.

I am confident that what I am sending you is all that we have on this patient. You see, our hospital has gone through several renovations over the years, and most recently, our records facility was condemned, and all files were moved to storage. We took the opportunity then to scan all materials and can now easily search what we have in storage.

Lacy said, "And on and on with a few more disclaimers, then signed 'Sylvia Lopez, Archivist.'" She followed with, "I've spoken with Sylvia several times over the past year, and she has actually been very helpful."

Lost in thought, Emma looked up with a discovery. "—on the summer solstice and only a few weeks after her nineteenth birthday. That's when Iris passed, isn't it?"

Lacy looked at Topher with a wink that Emma missed. "Wow, that's like tomorrow," Topher said.

"Oh, we should do something to…" Emma was growing excited.

"…we really should look at the attachments," Lacy said kindly, redirecting the conversation. She opened the first one. "Oh, it's on a very official looking hospital form with 'Patient Record' written across the top. In addition to Iris's full name, it lists her as patient number 836." Lacy began to read aloud again.

August 15. New patient orientation. Patient will be stationed in the women's sleeping quarters, bringing the number there to 15. She arrived with bandaged hands from some type of injury and brought only a small bag of items which can be accommodated in her locker. Talks almost non-stop about Steven and Sunflower. Otherwise pleasant disposition. Hospital policy supports that.

The Meadowlark

Aug 16. We met together with a doctor. Discussed keeping her safe. Replaced bandages on hands. Healing nearly complete. Note: Doctor indicated to me (Nurse Smith) to expect sudden changes in behavior with Iris and that her safety despite possible confusion is critical to all. Instructed me to have someone with her for at least 14 days to observe as Iris gets oriented. She has asked for paints and canvases. Purchase of materials approved.

Sept. 15. Phone call from a Ruby Walker asking to arrange a visit with Iris. Visitor policy described. Confirmed with doctor that Iris is too unstable and that visitors could trigger negative behaviors.

Oct. 20. Update (by Nurse Smith). Iris keeps to herself and says little when asked. She seems to enjoy the hospital grounds. Quite curious and very intelligent at the same time.

Jan 15, 1937. Update (by Nurse Cook). Now confined indoors, Iris seems morose and mainly draws and paints in the common hall. Doctor wants to test new treatment for melancholy. Begins tomorrow.

Jan 20. Iris seems more responsive.

Lacy said, "The notes from here on appear to be mostly clinical and cover her regular checkups. Nothing until the note on her sickness and passing."

Emma said, "Sylvia's email said there were two attachments. And?"

"Oh, yes," Lacy said, scrolling back to the top of the email. "You're going to love this one!" She opened a black and white photo of a large open hall. A woman standing in the middle of the hall near an easel was holding what appeared to be a painter's palette in one hand and a long paintbrush in the other. She was looking directly at the camera.

Emma leaned toward the laptop monitor and whispered, "Is that Iris?"

Lacy panned the picture and pointed to handwriting along the bottom. She read aloud, "'Iris Walker and her paintings in the common hall.'"

Emma asked, "Paintings?"

Lacy zoomed out. "Look," she said knowingly, and pointed to the easel near Iris and paintings of matching sizes on the walls around the hall. "There are twelve in all."

Emma counted to confirm and said, "The writing makes it sound like they were all hers, doesn't it? What did she paint?" She noticed those along the walls were slightly out of focus and hard to make out, but the one on the easel was clear. "It has wings. It looks like an angel."

While baby Iris slept, Emma sat with Lacy sat on the front porch. Emma said, "Topher and I have been talking about starting a foundation—a non-profit. What do you think?"

Lacy asked, "What would it do?"

"That's the only thing we can't resolve. It's not like we have all the money in the world, but we want to help others. We've talked about focusing on teenage mothers in some way—helping with college degrees or virtual jobs or something. Still working on it. Got any ideas?"

Lacy looked around before saying, "I don't know why, but this idea gives me the chills. Why not work with state hospitals across the country to reconnect forgotten loved ones with their families—help other people with the journey like the one you've been on. What do you think?"

Emma was touched and began to cry. "That's the best idea yet."

...

THAT EVENING, THEY PICKED EMMA'S MOTHER UP at the hotel for dinner at Carter's. Emma had persuaded her to come to town for Willow Creek Days. Connie delivered the basket of scones like clockwork.

"It's delightful to have you back in Willow Creek, Mrs. Rose. And so good to meet you." Turning to meet Lacy, Connie said, "And who's this pretty young thing?"

After introductions, Lacy bit into her first scone. "Oh my…this is so different—and amazing," she said, licking at the honey butter dripping down her fingers.

Emma turned to Lacy, "Tell my mom what you found out about Iris."

Lacy took another bite and then said, "From everything—the DNA from the box and Emma's DNA test results, the midwife's ledger, and the records of the state hospital, we're ninety-nine point nine-nine percent confident that this Iris was your husband's birthmother." She added, "And the bones they found way-back-when were from what would have been his twin. A little girl named Sunflower."

"Doesn't that give your chills," Emma asked, turning to her mother.

Her mother smiled and said, "And that would make her my mother-in-law…I guess. As your father's parents said…well, his adopted parents…"

"It's hard to keep straight," Emma said, "Anyway, as Granny Rose always said, 'You just can't have too many people who love you—or too many people to love.'" Emma looked satisfied that she had simplified things.

Her mother smiled and said, "And so many good people around you now."

"I love it!" Emma added, "Clearly, more is better when it comes to family." Looking around the table, she exclaimed, "I feel more blessed every day!"

Lacy said, "I wasn't going say anything, but I've been…well, we've been…working with Quentin at the mortuary for weeks on a surprise. I know how you feel about surprises. I guarantee you'll like this one."

Emma scowled before catching Topher smiling. "Are you in on this too?"

Topher shrugged before saying, "Of course! We have planned a sunrise service for tomorrow morning at the cemetery. That'll give us time to get back for the parade at ten o'clock. I guarantee you're going to love this."

…

EARLY THE NEXT MORNING, Topher pulled a new suit from the closet.

Emma asked, "New suit? When did you buy a suit?"

"Two days ago. And just for the occasion!"

"Wow, this surprise has lots of moving parts!"

Topher said, "It sure does." He pulled another item in a long bag from the closet and handed it to her, saying, "And here's something for you."

Emma removed the bag to reveal a dark dress. "Oh, it's beautiful." Emma checked the size and said, "Good to see you've got my size finally figured out." They laughed together.

The sun began breaking across the valley's green fields as Topher drove Emma and Iris to the Willow Creek cemetery. On their way, he revealed a little more of what was planned. "Just to take the edge off the surprise, you have to know that there may be more than a few other people there," he said. "Well, a lot more than a few."

As they pulled into the cemetery, Emma could see a large group already gathered around the family section where her father was buried. Three police cars were parked in a line behind the long white hearse she recognized from

Waldrup's. As they pulled closer, Emma could see Quentin in his trademark fedora and bowtie, and behind him, a line of police officers.

Emma pointed at the police officers and smiled. "What's Quentin done now?"

Topher laughed. Joking, he added, "It's the bowtie. They're taking him to jail right after." As they got out of the car, Topher signaled for Emma to wait a moment before walking over to greet the officers, all coworkers. As Topher embraced each of them, the sounds of backslaps echoed in the early morning air.

Looking around, Emma spotted Connie from Carter's at the edge of the group and walked over to greet her. "I'm so glad you came!"

Connie wiped at her eyes. "We wouldn't have missed this, dear. We lost a son years ago. Losing a child is so very hard."

Emma squeezed Connie's hand before spotting Richard and Bonnie nearby and Topher's entire family behind them. Emma greeted them all. When Topher rejoined her, she nudged him and said, "How nice your family came! We have to introduce Lacy to Blade! Where is he?"

Topher pointed toward Blade, who stood under a tree away from the group moving his hands in an animated fashion, clearly on a phone call.

"If we can get him off his phone," Topher said. "He's probably working on some sponsorship or appearance fee."

Emma recognized the couple getting out of another car as her Rose cousins. She hurried over to greet them. "Jennifer and John, thanks so much for coming all this way. I haven't seen you in forever—since the funeral!" Emma waved Topher over.

"So nice to meet you!" Topher said. "And thanks for coming."

"We wouldn't have missed this," Jennifer said. "You can never have too much family!"

More cars pulled in. Eventually, even the entire canal company board came—with their spouses. Bishop Thompson was the next to arrive and greeted Emma's mother, remembering her from when Emma's father was buried. A reporter from *The Willow Creek Sentinel* stood to the side snapping pictures.

Topher swept his hand in front of him and said to Emma, "These are your people. So much love!"

"It's positively overwhelming!" Emma said.

...

BISHOP THOMPSON WELCOMED THE GROUP and then Topher's father, Jim, offered a prayer. Topher stepped forward to make a presentation, looking so handsome in his new suit. When he asked Emma to join him, she noticed the tall object next to her father's headstone for the first time, one covered by a gray tarp. A fresh hole had been dug off to the side that she also hadn't noticed earlier either.

Topher addressed the group, "We all know what goes on among the living, but many of us barely know or will ever fully understand the journey those before us endured to make our lives possible. Today, we want to honor a few women that have made this gathering here today possible."

"First, Emma, who followed her father here to Willow Creek and then began asking questions—good questions. And her mother, Cheryl Rose, too, of course. It seems that Steven Rose never got the chance while he was alive to bring the two of them here. But bring them here, he did—only after his passing."

Emma smiled at her mother who was dabbing at her eyes. The sun broke through the evergreens throughout the cemetery, streaming brightly and causing people to shield their eyes from the glow.

Topher cleared his throat and continued, "Then we discovered Catherine Esther Rapp Walker, who we are so glad we now know as Cassie." He pointed toward her grave. "What a life! What a legacy you left us! We are so glad we know you and better understand your hard, hard life. And with that, we discovered Emma's great-grandmother."

He paused and took a breath, looking as though whatever he was about to say would be difficult. "And…," he began before being overcome with emotion. After a moment, he continued, "…Cassie's daughter, someone we also only recently discovered and who is also my wife's grandmother, deserves our recognition as well."

On Topher's signal, Quentin pulled away the gray tarp revealing a monument of a young woman with angel wings looking up to the sky. Topher bent to read the inscription. "'Iris Ray Walker – our angel – April 23, 1920-June 21, 1939.' Her children were 'Steven and Sunflower,' also inscribed here along its base." Topher breathed in before saying, "Iris Ray Walker, we are gathered here today on the anniversary of your death—and summer solstice—to pay tribute to you. We now know you became a mother of twins at fifteen. Because of the clues you left, and thanks to your own mother Cassie's amazing journal, we found you—and in our search for you, we found a bit more about ourselves as well."

Emma reached for the heart pendant hanging around her neck.

Topher pointed toward the sky. "Today and always, we see you for who you are. And we will never forget you again." He choked up as he said, "Our hearts are finally whole. Iris, you are an angel. Welcome home!"

The crowd remained reverent, most wiping at their eyes and a few talking quietly.

Emma drew close to Topher and whispered, "It's beautiful."

Addressing the gathering, Topher said, "Folks, we have one more thing to do here today. One thing started all of this. It wasn't until yesterday that we remembered something that was forgotten far too long ago." His voice trailed off. He kicked at the ground with his toe before recovering his composure. Looking up, he said, "Or someone, I should say. We can't forget her any longer."

Emma was puzzled. She looked over at Lacy, who shrugged, unaware herself of what was happening next. Both were overcome with emotion when they heard Topher say, "It's time to properly bury a little girl who never had much of a chance."

On signal, Quentin walked to the hearse. Retrieving a small coffin, he passed it with both arms to the police officer at the front of the line, who carried it past the other officers looking on.

"Sunflower!" Emma whispered.

Topher hugged Emma tightly and then said with a shaky voice, "Until recently, the only official record of Sunflower Walker was in the ledger of the midwife that delivered her, Emma's great aunt Sarah. Because of that ledger and Cassie's journal, we have now properly recorded Sunflower's birth on the twenty-first of May 1936 and death two days later. She was Steven's twin." Topher held a certificate for all to see. "Until this week, her bones were stored as evidence in police custody, bones originally found a few winters ago in this very location. We have now been authorized to re-inter them exactly where she was first buried in 1936." The officer handed the small casket to Topher. Topher turned to Emma and asked, "Will you help me?"

Overcome with emotion, Emma handed baby Iris to her mother and carried one end of the casket the final few feet to the open grave. Quentin motioned for them to place it on a small platform at the foot of the statue.

After the crowd dispersed, Emma walked to Cassie's headstone and then her father's, pausing briefly at each and whispering, "Thank you." She then approached the angel statue and knelt.

With tears flowing freely, she reached with one hand to touch the angel's hands, placing the other on the tiny casket. "Oh, Iris. Oh, Sunflower. I'm so glad we found you."

In building the Great Feeder, buck scrapers like those shown above were used to load wagons with soil so it could be transported elsewhere. (photo credit: Farnsworth TV & Pioneer Museum)

Great Feeder Day, June 22, 1895 (looking upstream toward the original Great Feeder dam with the Snake River on the other side of the dam). (photo credit: Farnsworth TV & Pioneer Museum)

Canal leadership at a new headgate somewhere in
the Upper Snake River Valley. (photo credit: B.C. Walker)

Upgraded in 2015, the Great Feeder is shown
with the Snake River flowing to the right. (photo credit: B.C. Walker)

The Meadowlark

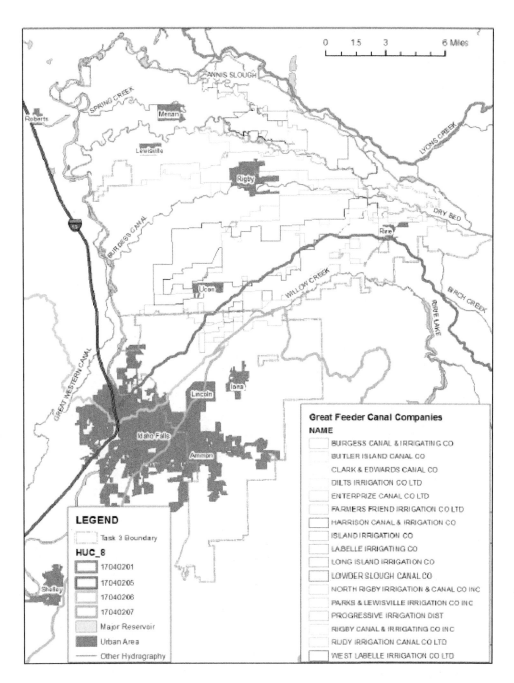

Detailed in the legend on the lower right, each line coming off the Dry Bed (middle right) represents a canal system enabled by the Great Feeder. (idwr.idaho.gov)

Acknowledgments

They say when you shake the family tree, you may be surprised at what falls out. True. Climbing mine has revealed views I never knew existed—of the bold, brave, amazing, and often stunning lives of those who went before.

First, let me say that I'm grateful for cemeteries. For decades, I felt an "Idaho" story rumbling around my mind, one without any organizing force that finally came crashing together after visiting several Idaho cemeteries over one Memorial Day weekend. Individual stories began combining in my mind—words from headstones and linking to rich histories at familysearch.org that had been uploaded by caring family historians.

Connecting people, place, and time produced a creative surge that was compounded by driving around. There, we drove over so many canals, all with names, that provoked another question: "how and why so many canals." In dozens of similar trips, I had never once tried to answer that question. They were just there, everywhere.

Back home, we visited one final cemetery and came across a wall of plaques organized by Janina Chilton with the State of Utah honoring over 400 souls buried over decades in unmarked graves at the Utah State Mental Hospital.

So, in many regards, this book began where it ends—on a late spring day at a cemetery. My wife Kristin may be the only person who could describe the zigzag thought process from there. When I discovered the 1885 map of Idaho in an antique book her late-mother Barbara gave us years ago, I felt an angel looking down on me. Kristin has been as much story advisor as consultant, wading through the intricacies of this story and listening to my constant recounting of droll documentaries about homesteading and irrigation. She watched me dance in the cold on a miraculous cold and snowy day at the Great Feeder and again when we visited the Idaho State Hospital in Blackfoot and learned that 900 unknown patients had recently been honored there just as those in Utah had. Kristin is the most amazing, supportive person I have known. Ever.

That she read every draft says so much—especially if you knew the count. And in so many ways, she's my Cassie and Emma combined.

My mother, Alice Jensen Walker, pursued her ancestors her entire life—they weren't going anywhere but she went to great lengths to locate histories, piece together collages of family photos and pedigrees, reproduce those in binders for family reunions, and assemble file cabinets full of the past. She instilled in me a love for those she loved. Fortunately, when we lost her in the summer of 2022, she left a rich, multi-generational compilation behind.

Thanks to my son Jesse and his wife Jessica for painstaking readings and feedback, Kassidy my daughter who cried with me over burgers one night as I introduced her to Iris, Brittany Beahm for deep edits of early drafts, my sister Ronda who provided abundant insights around voice and color (along with pioneer stories from her own research), and my son Dakota and his wife Alex for their supportive lift. Thanks to Joanna and Drew Johnson, Steve Coffin, Scott Weaver, the Riverside Ladies Book Club, and so many other early readers for their critical insights and tremendous input on my first drafts.

A big thanks to the unnamed former secretary of the Farmer's Friend Company who tipped me off to the book *Pioneer Irrigation: Upper Snake River Valley* (1955), a book that inspired me beyond measure and told me more about Water District No. 36 than most around me wanted to hear. Thanks to Kate B. Carter and her team from the Daughters of the Utah Pioneers for compiling that book—a treasure trove of pioneer interviews and canal company records.

And to the small towns of Southeastern Idaho that shaped my boyhood and continue to tug at my heart. They're all a part of Willow Creek—somewhere special.

Printed in Great Britain
by Amazon